Angel of God

Angel of God
the End of Time

PABLO PETERS

To my wife, my greatest fan

Acknowledgements

To my mother and father, who taught me the joy of learning by setting an example; for their love of the unknown and their openness to different ideas; for their eagerness to share what they learned and the excitement in their eyes when they talked about it; for the tone in their voices when they encouraged me to ask "why?"; for their love of books and their treatment of them as if they were sacred; for surrounding me with books from my earliest memories, their old bookcases with the smell of books older than me, and their reverent handling of each page as they turned it with care; and for their respect for both the old and the new—I thank you and appreciate you more than I ever showed.

To my wife, for her love of books, libraries, and bookstores, and for offering encouragement when I wanted to quit. Thank you for being my greatest supporter, and at times, my only fan.

To the Irish nuns, Sr. Cecilia, and Sr. Paschal, who were sisters by vocation and by birth. Sweet in disposition and strong in faith, they set an example for us all. I hope Sr. Paschal was able to finally meet Glen Campbell in heaven.

And to you, the reader, may you enjoy the journey as much as the destination.

Preface

The idea for this story came to me in a dream. I remember waking in the night, my heart racing, my eyes wide open. Its recurrence the next night stirred me to decide to share it with others. So, I persevered, over the course of the following four years, to complete this novel. I wanted to capture the vividness of the dream, the darkness and fear but also the hope and the enduring power of love.

As the story developed, a unique chemistry evolved, where fantasy danced in a fanciful way with science fiction. Inspired by the tales of C.S. Lewis and J.R.R. Tolkien, my faith is also an integral part of this story, and it became intertwined. The story refused to confine itself to the boundaries of only one genre, but rather to dare readers to explore the infinite mysteries of the universe and imagine a glimpse of the divine. In the end, this is a book of speculative fiction, a story of the imagination, a fairy tale. But like all myths, there is a message, a lesson to be learned; love endures all things.

In the beginning of this narrative, a post-apocalyptic world unravels, a millennium after the perdition event. It's a world of humans and androids, of angels and demons on the edge of human existence and at the end of an age. Worlds intersect after Trhon, the celestial planet of angels, joins our solar system per a galactic rhythm of overlapping dimensions.

At its core, a young woman named Lily grapples with her own identity as she comes of age. Her destiny unfurls like a banner in a storm to lead the charge against the evil forces of the universe. Opposing her, the malevolent Maldorv, the Dragon King, the Lord of the Malkyries, hungers to conquer the universe and take her as his bride.

It's a futuristic tale of insurmountable odds that voyages into the realm of speculation while supplying a glimpse into the future of humans and the ultimate impact of AI on the evolution of androids. It's all woven together by a love story as timeless as the stars. As it explores the boundary between the everyday with the unbelievable, it becomes a lasting and enchanting tale of legend.

Prologue

"Four circles interfered with one another as they crossed a once still pond, creating a myriad of intersectional rings, according to some ancient plan." Ariel spoke in a loud, resonant voice, as if addressing a vast audience, though only a small group of children sat around her. Their faces shone brightly, lit by the firelight. "Harmonics rose while others faded, and as the pattern swept its entirety, no surface remained untouched—nothing left to uncertainty. For it was as certain as could be once the stones were cast."

I

Book One

"Then I saw an angel coming down from heaven,
holding the key to the bottomless pit and a great chain,
and he seized the dragon, that ancient serpent, who is the Devil,
and bound him for a thousand years,
and threw him into the pit, and shut it, and sealed it over him,
that he should deceive the nations no more,
till the thousand years ended."
—Revelation 20:1

1

A Sudden Storm

A COLD DOWNDRAFT ANNOUNCED the arrival of a dark cloud from the upper mountain. The violent gust flung dirt and debris through the air, stinging Ema's face. She clutched her wide-brimmed hat as her blonde hair whipped wildly in the wind. With her other hand shielding her eyes, she squinted at the sky. Above her, wisps of gray hovered—ominous and heavy, like fingers wrapping around the farmhouse.

"Ema, get inside!" Mami's voice rang out. "Lily, where are you?"

Ema barely heard her over the wind. A raindrop struck her arm followed by a pause then the sky split open. The downpour was instant, drumming against the earth in wild, erratic rhythms. Ema ran, her feet pushing through the wet grass. Mami waited on the porch, her outstretched arms reaching for her. She pulled her close and wrapped her cape around her.

As quickly as it had started, the rain ended. "That was unusual," Ema said to herself. She slowly descended the porch steps as a serene quiet fell over the disturbed yard. A lone brave rooster joined her as thin rays broke through the clouds painting her surroundings in a surreal orange-hue. Then she heard it—a sound so shrill, so alien, it cut through the quiet like a blade.

Ema jerked upright. "What was that?"

Mami's grip felt tight on her arm as she pulled her. "Get inside. Now."

5

But it was too late.

A silvery form stretched above Mami. From the treetops, sleek and metallic, a seeker drone descended, its arms spread wide, reaching for her mother.

"Mami—" Ema blurted.

The machine struck. Mami barely had time to cry out before the drone seized her, steel fingers locking around her waist.

"No!" Ema screamed.

Ema lunged forward, hands slamming against the cold bars of the cage as the drone's trap door slammed shut. Her mother's wide, terrified eyes locked onto hers for the briefest moment before the drone lifted her away.

"Mami!" Ema's scream cracked as she fell to her knees.

From the orchard below, another voice roared through the chaos.

"I'm coming!"

Papi called out as he ran, his red cart—loaded with the day's harvest—tipped as he sprinted toward his wife. His dark hair was plastered to his forehead, his dark eyes wide with panic.

A blurred motion caught her eye—another drone.

It dropped like a spider, pouncing on him.

Papi hit the ground hard. He groaned, tried to push himself up—

A metal arm pinned him down.

"Papi!" Ema's voice was raw, barely her own.

The drone hoisted him up. He struggled, fingers scraping against the bars, muscles straining. But it was useless. The machine locked him inside and lifted off, its cold, unfeeling engine humming as it joined the first drone in the sky.

Ema couldn't move. Her breath came in jagged gasps, her mind racing to catch up. She looked up and saw the two drones hover over her allowing a glimpse of her parents. With one synchronized movement, they turned following the storm down the mountain and carried her parents away.

And then—another scream.

Raw. Guttural.

Ema's head snapped up.

Lily.

Her sister stood just beyond the fence, her body trembling, her hand covering her mouth. The other pointed skyward at the vanishing drones. Lily's eyes were wild, filled with something beyond fear—something unacceptable, unbearable. And then, another scream erupted. It tore through the valley, a primal, broken sound, shattering the fragile quiet and causing the wind to stir.

For over a week, since her parents' abduction, Ema had taken refuge in the cavern. Darkness filled its deep reaches, but her haunting memories were darker still. And no matter how many days passed, a storm of despair stirred inside her. It festered, deep and unyielding, leaving her hollow and numb.

Ema stared at her sister curled against her lap. Though taller, Lily behaved much younger than her sixteen years. She suddenly stirred in her sleep and moaned aloud, disturbed by one of her frequent nightmares. Gently, Ema stroked her sister's black hair, her voice barely audible as a tear rolled down her cheek. "Anyone would have nightmares after what we've been through."

2

Out of the Darkness

THE CAVERN DARKNESS HELD the faintest of light, just enough to reveal shades of gray and hints of shadow. Beyond the cavern, the abyss plunged into the depths where the darkness and silence merged as one. For a thousand years, the stillness remained undisturbed, until now. A sound shattered the silence, echoing within the abyss. Moments later, another followed, and then another. It was the sound of rhythmic steps from a creature ascending a stone staircase reverberating from the chamber within the keep. The sound intensified as it reached the cavern floor. Then it stopped.

In the dim light of the cavern, a figure extended over the rim of the abyss and pulled itself over the edge. His skin was ghastly pale, and his eyes, deep within gaunt sockets, appeared entirely black. His partially skeletonized face revealed his teeth embedded into his jawbone and his sharp, elongated nails resembled those of a wild animal. Neither fully man nor beast, this was a malkyrie—a demon, a fallen angel in service to Maldorv, the Lord of the Malkyries.

Day after day, year after year, he had waited. With his master imprisoned and the portal to Arderet sealed, he had hidden in the dark, his whereabouts known only to his master. The sun had risen and set, the seasons came and went, and the years had passed. Decades became centuries, and the mountains, forests, and streams had grown older. For all that time, he had waited.

On the next tick of an ancient clock, another page in the Book of Time would turn and the last chapter would begin. The trees knew and told the wind. Soon, everyone would know—everyone but humans, for they would not listen. He looked up and saw the light from the cavern's opening. Though a dim glow, it blinded him with its brightness. He shielded his eyes with his dark cape till slowly, his vision focused, and shapes appeared. Tick went the clock of time. A thousand years had now passed since the perdition event. He lifted his foot and stepped toward the entrance.

3

Who Am I?

LATE THE NEXT DAY, Lily summoned the courage to step outside. It was upon her sister's insistence, who waited for her at the cavern entrance.

"Let's go," Ema said. "We've been hiding long enough."

The air was crisp, carrying the scent of the river as the two sisters followed the trail downward. Lily slowed her pace when she reached the pond near the base of the falls. This had been her parents' favorite spot, and as she gazed at the water, concern returned to her mind.

Rumors of an internment camp located in the city were widespread. In her heart, she feared her parents were being held captive. A cold knot twisted in her stomach. *Are they in the city? Are they even alive?*

Kneeling by the water's edge, she peered at her reflection. Her black hair cascaded past her shoulders, framing a face that looked nothing like her sister's, who shared their mother's features. Nor did she resemble her father. His hair was brown not black like hers, and his eyes were dark, much different to the ones that stared back at her. Her large silver eyes set her apart. People thought them unusual. Her mother often said she favored a cousin from the upper mountains, as if that explained everything. As if that made her feel any less like an outsider among her own people.

"I miss you, Mami," she whispered into the wind, hoping her words would find their way to wherever her mother was. She paused, then gazed wistfully at her reflection, studying her silver eyes.

"Who am I?"

The water remained silent.

She clenched a smooth stone, rolling it between her fingers until its cool surface warmed in her grasp. Then, with a sudden burst of frustration, she hurled it into the pond. It struck the water with a sharp plunk, sending ripples racing outward. The expanding circles crossed the pond's surface, ending at the water's edge, where the fields, trees, and mountains bore silent witness, yet none answered her.

Maybe they don't know? She thought to herself. *Perhaps they know but aren't allowed to tell.*

Lily caught her sister's watchful gaze from across the pond. She thought Ema was overly protective, so she climbed a nearby overhang and precariously stood on the edge. From that vantage point, Lily spotted a rainbow which had formed in the mist of the falls.

"Hey, Ema, look!" Lily shouted and pointed.

A gust of wind blew through Ema's blonde hair. Though only shoulder-length, it still swept over her green eyes. She wore a white dress like Lily's, and it offered only limited protection from the breeze which brought a sudden chill to the air. Ema drew her brown wrap around her and tightened her belt. It was of a similar material and color. "Be careful!" Ema responded more quietly, annoyed at how loudly her sister had shouted. "If a drone doesn't get you first, you might fall." She cast a quick glance at her sister, then resumed searching the skies.

"You aren't my mother," Lily retorted, less loudly then moved away from the edge. But it was true; heights made her dizzy. She shaded her eyes with her hand as she scanned the horizon.

Nothing, Lily thought. The sky was empty.

Lily picked a yellow flower and tucked it into her black hair.

Curious to see how she looked, she went back to the pond to admire her reflection.

"Hey, it's me again," she said. "Do you remember me?" Again, she heard nothing, but she hadn't expected to.

The mountain peaks rose before her, still showing their winter snow with a cloak of green pine. From on high, another cool breeze descended from the peaks, causing the leaves of the aspen to quiver and their thin, white branches to sway. She loved the sound they made.

"I know who you are," came a whisper from the tree line.

"What? What did you say?" Lily asked, staring at the trees. The wind quieted and stood still. Lily stared a moment longer but received no further response. She chuckled nervously at her own imagination, then shook her head—not willing to accept what she had heard. People already thought her odd if not crazy. She didn't need to hear voices.

A fresh breeze blew off the mountain, distracting her. She ran back toward the ledge with her arms open like a bird, eager to chase the wind. But she stopped at the edge and lowering herself to the ground, she hung her head over it. Below, thousands of tiny ripples formed over the pond, captivating Lily with their mesmerizing pattern. A childhood memory flashed into her mind. She recalled her mother taking a running leap and calling from the water below. Lily imagined her mother's voice softly calling, "Lily, Lily."

"Lily, Lily!" Ema said, pulling Lily from her trance. Ema looked at her sister's dazed expression, "You're such a freakin' weirdo." She shook her head. "It's time to go back."

Ema took a shorter path which climbed the rocky edge skirting the rapidly flowing water. It always felt unsafe.

Lily's smile faded as she looked at the trail, where a heavy mist sprayed over the steepest and most dangerous point. Seeing Ema had already gone ahead, Lily called out, "What about my dizzy spells?" but her voice was drowned out by the sound of the falls. "If you think I'm going to take the long way—" Lily stopped shouting, her sister couldn't hear.

She glanced at the jagged base of the falls then quickly looked away. After calming her nerves, she clung to rocks and navigated the most dangerous part of the trail. Ema had continued to move briskly, and Lily's legs tightened to keep up, but soon the trail flattened, and she relaxed as she reached the cavern.

Ema proceeded into the entrance without hesitation, while Lily paused to take in the view of the narrow valley coddled between the mountain peaks. The river wound through it like a meandering ribbon, threading its way through the lush forests and fields. Smaller irrigation canals crisscrossed the clearings, drawing slender strands of water from the river, diminishing in size until they vanished into the fabric of the landscape. Lower down the mountain's slope, Lily spotted a modest rock farmhouse nestled among fruit-bearing trees. Apples, peaches, and rows of grapevines graced the land. Not too long ago, this had been her home.

Lily couldn't help but reflect on Papi's disdain and distrust of the city. He often claimed technology betrayed and dehumanized people, making them selfish. With his family's love and a glass of his homemade wine, he was content. A natural survivalist, he possessed a strong instinct for preserving their way of life against what he perceived as the encroaching threat of the city's technology. That instinct had led him to seek out this haven.

The falls concealed the secret of their refuge, and Lily pushed through the mist, following a hidden passage behind the roaring curtain. It led into a gothic cavern with natural stone arches that stretched hundreds of feet into the air. During the day, light filtered through the waterfall, casting a magical hue against the stone walls, and providing illumination to the main cavern and several smaller caves. Papi had transformed these smaller spaces into sleeping quarters and storage rooms, stocked with items like barrels of flour, tins of coffee, canned fruit, arrows, and explosive tips. Their subterranean sanctuary offered an existence distinct from life on the farm, yet it came with a significant advantage: the stone shielded them from the prying sensors of seeker drones, making it a haven in a world consumed by unsettling change.

A sudden noise jolted Lily, and she turned swiftly to discover the cat. She smiled at the tabby, a working cat, if ever there was one. The feline climbed a storage shelf and settled upon an old blanket.

"Hey, how did you jump way up there?"

The cat meowed twice in her raspy voice. Lily imagined she understood the cat's response.

"You don't say," Lily responded, laughing, as she realized the cat's job of catching mice would wait until after her late afternoon nap.

Beyond the storage rooms, a vast darkness extended into the cavern. Lily never ventured there. It went on forever, a scary place that reached deep within the ground, like the dungeons in castles of old, where dragons and other unknown dangers lay hidden. If the impenetrable darkness did not sway her, the fear of falling to her death certainly did. In her youth, Papi had told her to block all thoughts of these passages out of her mind. Nevertheless, she feared the darkness and her nightmares of monsters emerging while she slept.

Lily took a spot on the ground near Ema's feet. "Tell the story about the beginning of the world again," she said wanting a distraction from the eeriness of the cavern.

Ema stood and gracefully extended her arms in a slow, sweeping circle above her head. With all the presence of a storyteller taking the stage, she started the tale with theatrical flair. "In the beginning, fire fell from the skies and cracks in the crust unleashed volcanic eruptions, blanketing the surface in a fiery landscape. When the flames finally subsided, darkness shrouded the ground, a veil of smoke and ash blackening even the waters. Dense clouds cloaked the land, causing temperatures to plummet. Snow fell and covered the world in white. Then, at last, the sun pierced the heavy clouds. It melted the snow, and the waters flowed into the rivers. From the damp soil emerged the first trees, including the pink-flowering walnut tree and all other plants."

Ema paused, as if she had concluded the story.

"Go on, tell the rest," Lily urged.

Ema continued. "From a massive cavern within the mountains emerged the First Mother, with animals of all kinds following her." Ema approached the painting on the white limestone wall, and Lily's gaze fixed on the portrayal of the First Mother. She was dressed in regal attire, resembling that of nobility, and held a book beneath her arm. Carved into the book's cover was a single word: "Knowledge." Weathered and aged since the dawn of time, the chalky silhouette bore the marks of countless years. Lily couldn't help but ponder how incredible it would have been to be present in those early days, to meet her and discuss the world's genesis.

An unexpected feeling overcame Lily, as her sixth sense caused a tingling sensation. She imagined the First Mother's gaze piercing through the dim lighting, delving into her innermost thoughts. *Can she be reading my mind?* Unsettled, Lily averted her eyes.

Above the image of the First Mother was the sun, and lower, toward the morning horizon, a second star—a second, smaller sun. On the lower part of the painting, a crowd of seventy people surrounded the First Mother. Beneath the painting, a scroll could still be seen. Ema pointed to it and read it aloud.

"*Prima Mater, Admiralis, Amicum.* It means, 'First Mother, Admiral, Friend.'"

Lily stared at it for a moment. "There's something creepy about that painting."

"Yeah, she looks like you," Ema said with a half laugh.

With a nervous glance, Lily took another brief look at the painting. As she turned away, a wisp escaped from the image and dissipated into the cavern's darkness. Lily did not notice.

4

Once Upon a Muddy Road

A WOUNDED MAN RAN through an unfamiliar wood; his face twisting in pain as he clutched his bleeding shoulder. He halted at the edge of a clearing, gasping for breath. There, he leaned against a tree and gazed across an open field. From within the steady rain falling from the gray sky, the terrifying screech of a seeker drone filled the air. Though he could not see it, he sensed the seeker hovering above, an ever-watchful predator with one mission: to capture him, dead or alive. The rain offered no reprieve, and the drone cared little of his need for medical assistance. The man was all too aware of what awaited him in the city if captured, having witnessed the cruelty which they were capable. A wanted fugitive, he made the desperate choice to risk it all. With renewed determination, he pushed away from the tree and sprinted across the clearing.

The drone had waited for his move, and its search beam swiftly locked onto him. As the man ran across the open space, the drone gained on him as it chased with its arms extended. With only inches to spare, the man dove under the cover of the other side of the clearing evading the drone's grasp as the drone suddenly abandoned the chase and diverted away from the tree line. The fugitive had slipped away, if only for a little while.

Pressing on, the man dashed further under the shelter of the trees. Branches struck at him, but he hardly felt their stinging lashes. They were a mere blur in the frenzied escape. After several minutes of frantic flight, he stumbled over a tree root and crashed to the ground. An immediate searing pain shot through his arm, and he turned into it, letting out a scream of agony. As his scream diminished so did his energy. Fully exhausted, the man allowed himself to sink into the mud. While the rain continued, he contemplated his fate. All his known world now collapsed into a constant ache with sudden stabs of incredible pain. Only his growing despair challenged his physical misery. Lost and seriously injured, he knew his chances for survival diminished with each heartbeat.

"It's no use," he said to himself. "I can't go any further."

He shivered in the wetness of his clothes and resigned himself to his fate. Blood flowed down his sleeve and filled his palm. It created a false sense of warmth, offering only brief consolation. Bleeding out, he started to lose consciousness. Lightning struck somewhere nearby, and after a moment, thunder railed through the air as if trying to keep him awake.

The man stirred. "Don't give up, Luca," he mumbled to himself. "I have to find the road."

The rain picked up, and he fought a chill moving down his spine as he turned his back to it. Another stabbing pain shot through his arm. It jolted him back into the full realization of his predicament.

"God help me!" he yelled, though he didn't believe in God.

The man rose and scanned the forest in search of the road. Surrounded by the diminishing half-light of twilight, there was little to see. Then, in a flash of lightning, he spotted it. He stumbled on and reached the bottom of an embankment. With renewed resolve, he gathered his remaining strength and climbed upward. Each breath was a strained gasp, but he finally reached the top then fell to his knees.

"I made it. I can't believe it," Luca said. He wiped the mud off his face. His brown hair covered in mud, hid a cut on his head, one of many on his body. The blood mingled with the mud, and he could taste the gritty mixture in his mouth. He wiped his face again as he searched the road for any indication which direction to go. But his unfamiliar surroundings yielded no clues, and the gnawing despair in his eyes deepened as he stared at his rainy and darkening world.

Unexpectedly, a bright light shone on him from across the road. He turned quickly but slipped in the mud, falling hard.

"Ahh!" he screamed as he landed on his injured arm. The intensity of the pain was too much to bear. His bearings spun wildly, and his world faded as he slumped face-first into a muddy puddle, unconscious and broken.

Though the light did not see him, something else did. A shadowy figure emerged from the edge of the wood along the road, a silent observer who had been watching from the veil of shadows. It crossed the desolate road and bent over the wounded man. Moments later, the beam of light returned to that very spot, but only the injured man appeared there as the rain continued.

5

The Hunter and the Hunted

AS THE DAYLIGHT HOURS waned, the clouds returned, hinting at the possibility of an evening storm. Lily took note of them and hurried back into the cavern, where her sister sat by a small fire.

"Looks like rain," Lily remarked.

Ema stretched for her crossbow. "I'm out of meat. I should head out if I want to catch something for dinner."

"I'll come with you," Lily offered.

"Alright, but we can never be too careful with a seeker drone on the prowl. Better take some of these." Ema grabbed a handful of explosive tips.

Lily regarded her sister with admiration. She had been shadowing Ema for as long as she could remember, but changes were now emerging within Lily, reshaping how others perceived her. Lily's outgoing personality and magnetic presence attracted attention, making it impossible for her to go unnoticed. However, once noticed, people often sensed something unusual about her, something not quite normal. It left her feeling self-conscious and somewhat isolated. Only her connection with her sister offered her a semblance of normalcy and she clung near her side.

Ema led the way down a well-trodden, narrow passage to the back entrance. Lily hurried to be the first to emerge under the foliage of a large hardwood, its pink blossoms marking the access point. Outside the cavern, Lily squinted at the sun, which briefly appeared before hiding behind a dark cloud. The cloud took on a vivid red hue, creating a striking contrast against the fading blue sky. Leaving the grove of trees, she entered a field of ferns, as her eyes scanned for her dinner. A vegetarian, she was delighted to find a patch of wild asparagus. She quickly harvested several stalks and hurried to catch up with Ema, who waited at the forest's edge.

From the darkening sky came a rolling rumble as a downdraft blew off the mountain. Ema looked up with a worried expression. "Clouds are settling on the mountains—a storm is coming. We don't have much time."

Lily led the way but at a much faster pace, and soon, they reached the first trap on the side of a large boulder.

"Nothing," Ema said.

While Ema reset the trap, a red squirrel scampered down a tree and startled a mountain grouse. Ema raised her crossbow and fired off a shot at the bird. She missed. She usually hit her target before it could get ten feet away, but her arrow flew past its mark this time.

"Maybe the next trap will have something for you," Lily said as they continued.

The canopy became denser in the thick wood. There, the sun only sporadically pierced through with lances of light. A short distance ahead, alongside the trunk of a fallen tree, mushrooms of all shapes, sizes, and colors emerged from the rotten wood. Lily picked the ones safe to eat. She was especially pleased to find her favorite, a delicacy highly valued at the trading post.

"Hey, here's one for you," she teased, pointing at a red, poisonous one.

Ema ignored her and continued across a small stream.

The next trap lay nearby, near an old road that hadn't been used for mining in decades. However, she was closer to the city than she liked, and she rarely ventured beyond that point. Back when the mine still operated, it produced gold and gemstones. These days, an older man, widowed and childless, lived alone in one of the abandoned shacks. Due to the mine's remote location, people often thought he preferred to be alone. Behind his gruff exterior, Lily had discovered in him a kind and welcoming nature. People who knew him well called him Clive, but no one had called him by that name since his wife's passing. Most everyone just called him Doc.

The people of the forest respected his skills as an exemplary medicine man and remarkable surgeon, but not so much his other experiences. For much of his career, he had worked on embryonic research and made well-known discoveries regarding the artificial womb and genetic selection. He had even developed a technique for human cloning and tried it once. But there were laws against cloning, and he kept it secret. It did not matter to his current patients, for they didn't care about his past accomplishments. That is not to say they were simple people, but they possessed different interests and needs.

Money was scarce. Most people who lived in the forest were poor. They bartered for Doc's services with their services in kind. Hard currency was a rarity, and digital currency was not used in the wood. Fortunately, he generated enough income by mining gemstones.

In a flash, lightning opened the sky. Lily heard a frantic voice calling out from within the crash of thunder.

"Help me!"

Lily scanned the wood through the intensifying rain but didn't see anyone. "Did you hear that?" she asked as heavier drops fell from the sky.

"Hear what?" Ema asked.

"I could swear I heard someone call for help."

"You're hearing things again," Ema said with a smirk.

Lily strained to listen but could hear nothing more in the rain. She threw on her cape and continued. The ground, already muddy from an earlier storm, became slushy and slippery. It made for slower travel, but soon they arrived at the last trap. With the flash of another lightning, she saw the haunting majesty of the giant tree above her, the tallest one in the forest. It reached two hundred feet into the sky. Below, its vast root system formed dark crevices that fanned out from its base. Ema often had good luck with her traps in these crevices. So now, with her dinner resting on this last one, she reached for it. Something was there—a red squirrel.

"Still warm," she said to Lily. "It must have just died."

Quietly, Lily whispered a short prayer over it. "From our Creator, we all come. To our Creator, we shall all return." Lily sighed. "Were you the one calling for help? May there be a day when we don't eat our friends of the forest for food."

Ema placed the dead squirrel in a sack and tied it to her waist. She was pleased she would have dinner.

At that moment, an eerie sensation came over Lily as the fine hairs on her neck prickled to attention. She now heard the unmistakable hum of a seeker. She turned around and gasped. A silver drone hovered above her with its dangling arms. Lily froze and stood silently as a shiver went down her spine. She started to scream, but her sister placed her hand over her mouth. Fortunately, the drone's search beam pointed across the road and moved away. Lily looked at Ema with relief.

The rainfall slowed to a drizzle, allowing Lily to see farther into the distance. She could see the road and the drone's search beam shining on the body of a man. The man lay motionless, as if dead. The drone hovered over him and extended a mechanical arm. A terrible memory came to mind as Lily recalled the anguish and fear of her parents' capture.

Ema quietly reached into her bag and deftly attached an explosive tip to one of her arrows. As she appeared from behind the tree, her heartbeat steadied, her breath calmed, and she took precise aim. This would be Ema's one and only shot, her only chance to prevent the drone from capturing the man. Carefully, she squeezed the trigger with the cumulative skill from her years of hunting.

The arrow found its mark, striking the drone with pinpoint accuracy. It detonated in a deafening explosion, and the mechanical arachnoid plummeted to the ground, dispersing debris as it descended in flames.

Lily dashed out of the wood and hurried to the side of the fallen man. As she touched his arm, a chilling sensation raced through her, and her breath now revealed itself in the suddenly cold air. She sensed something foreign, an unsettling presence, like death itself, looming in the vicinity. She turned quickly, scanning the surrounding wood, but saw nothing. Seeking the safety of cover, she dragged the man away from the puddle and under the trees on the side of the road. As she looked upon his face for the first time, a gasp escaped her.

Ema reached their side, her voice quivering as she asked, "Is he alive?" She met the man's vacant eyes and graying face with worry etched across her face. "Is he dead?"

As Lily observed the man, she sensed his breath was no more. "Maybe. He doesn't look good," she whispered.

Ema refused to accept his fate. Without hesitation, she leaned down and administered several quick breaths, exhaling into the man's lungs in a desperate attempt to revive him. Despite her efforts, he remained unresponsive. Instead, the chill of death deepened its grip on him, rendering his lips an even darker hue. Ema shook her head sorrowfully and looked at her sister. "We're too late."

"Please, God," Lily cried out to the sky. "It's not his time."

Ema took another breath and blew once more. The man gasped for air. Ema also gasped in surprise. "Breathe," she said. She rolled him onto his side, and he spat out muddy water. "That's good. Let it out," she said, patting him on his back.

Lily noticed a significant amount of blood coming from his right shoulder. She pulled back his torn shirt and let out another gasp. She was shocked by the severity of the injury. Muscle was mangled around a broken bone that protruded from his upper arm. Lily instantly realized his injury required significant medical skill and surgical experience.

"Stay with him," Lily said. "I'm going to get help." She quickly turned and ran up the road toward Doc's shack.

"Hurry!" Ema called after her. "Hurry. He won't last long."

6

Doc, Help Me

THE RAINY SKY RAPIDLY surrendered to the cloak of night, rendering the road nearly impossible to discern. Lily ran as fast as she dared and soon reached a rocky vale with few trees. Struggling over the rough terrain, she tripped over a large rock and fell to the ground. She rose and continued along what she thought was the trail but soon came to a halt. To her dismay, the path had vanished, and panic seized her as she realized she had lost her way.

"I can't be. I can't be lost," Lily muttered in frustration. "Doc," she called out as loudly as she dared into the darkness. "Where are you?"

Raindrops began to fall as the rain returned and Lily threw her arms up in frustration. "Great. What else can happen?" But within the commencing shower, she discerned the unmistakable sound of raindrops pelting a tin roof.

"There you are," she sighed in relief. The rain had revealed the structure. Neglected and in disrepair, the shack still stood, though just barely. Once, it had housed a thriving supply business and a cellar stocked with goods. Lily entered through the missing door and knocked on the cellar.

"Doc, help me!" she called out. "Doc?"

From below, the old man stirred. "Who's there?"

The cellar door swung open, and Doc emerged, his squinting gray eyes reflecting the irritation that masked his aging face. "Who's causing all this commotion?" he grumbled. "Do you want to get us killed?" Now in his sixties, he no longer towered over her. His white hair was longer than Lily's and his full beard gave him the appearance of a wild mountain man, a look he took pride in.

"Lily, is that you?"

"Yes. I need your help."

Doc's expression softened. "What's wrong?" he asked with concern.

"Ema shot down a drone, and a man is dying on the road. His arm has been nearly blown off and—"

Through his steely gray eyes, Doc looked at her. He saw the blood on her wrap and got the picture. "All right. Calm down and wait here."

A small fire burned in a wood stove down the cellar stairs, supplying warmth and dimly lighting the room. The small, dark space where he confined himself was a form of self-imprisonment. He felt he deserved no better since his wife had died.

In a hurry, Doc searched through stacks of medical supplies. He moved efficiently, packing all he needed into his brown satchel. With it slung over his shoulder, Doc appeared from the cellar.

"Okay, now let's go see what I can do."

With no children of his own, Doc treated Lily like a daughter. Lily also thought of him as family, a grandfatherly figure. She had known him her entire life, and he always helped her family in times of need.

"We can take my old hovercraft. It's like me—temperamental, but it still works." His familiar thin smile cracked his lips as he removed a tarp and revealed his early-model utility hover. "You don't see many of these anymore," Doc said proudly.

If it ever had a color, any trace disappeared long ago. Instead, only a rusty patina remained. He threw his bag over the side and climbed aboard.

"Don't turn on the lights until after it starts—just one of its quirks," Doc said knowingly. He started the nearly silent engine then extended his arm toward Lily.

"Here. Let me help you up."

Lily reached for him in the dark and found his extended arm. With one hop, she climbed aboard.

"Where to?" Doc asked.

"Not far. At the embankment."

Doc nodded in understanding and soon saw Ema waving frantically at them.

"Over here," Ema said.

Doc rushed to the man's side, placing a small light over the wound. The lines on his brow furrowed; what he saw concerned him.

"He appears to have taken a blaster shot," he said, "and he's lost a lot of blood." Doc was the only person Lily knew that couldn't whisper. Instead, he spoke in a low, gruff voice. "Son, can you hear me?"

The man didn't respond. Doc quickly pulled the man's belt from around his waist and snapped it in the air. "This will slow the bleeding," he assured Lily as he tightened a tourniquet above the wound.

Doc looked at Ema and she returned his gaze. She anxiously studied his face and could tell he did not have good news.

"The ruptured brachial artery in his upper arm is my greatest concern, not to mention the compound fracture and severe muscular damage. From my experience, his chances of survival are not good—none out here in the wood." Doc looked at the man for a moment, trying to decide what to do. "He must have been trying to escape the city," Doc said. "Those seeker drones will continue to search for him."

Ema's heart sank. She went to the man's side. With a gentle touch, she swiped his brown hair from his eyes. "Hang in there," she said to him. She turned toward Doc with an anguished look. "You must save him."

Doc shook his head then made up his mind. "Ahh," he said, as if he were about to do something against his better judgement. "All I know is we need to get him out of here."

In a panic, Ema grabbed the man and tried to move him, but he didn't budge. "Hey guys, can you help me?" Doc and Lily each grabbed a leg and together, they lifted the man onto the craft.

With a determined pace, Doc went to the downed drone. "I'll remove the locator chip. Other seekers might be near." After pushing the wreckage under the lower branches of a tree, he climbed onto the hovercraft.

Ema touched the man's face. "He's so cold and soaked to the bone." Moments later, the rain started again, and she took off her wrap and placed it around him. "Why did such misfortune fall upon you?" she whispered.

As the hover headed away from the city, Ema asked in a hushed voice, "Shouldn't we take him to City Hospital?"

Doc shook his head. "We should take him to your cavern. I don't think we should take the risk with what's going on in the city. Besides, I have experience with this type of injury."

"Are you sure?"

"Yes. I think it would be safer for all of us."

Lily realized what Doc meant. Regarding their safety, he would take only so much risk for this stranger.

The hovercraft traveled swiftly through the forest and soon reached Falls Crossing. There, Doc threw the locator chip into the river. "It'll be much harder for the seeker drones now," he said. "The river will take the chip downstream toward the city or beyond, even to the sea at Rungoo." Doc followed the arc of the river upstream toward the falls. When he reached the cavern, they rushed to carry the man inside.

"Let's put him on the workshop table," Ema suggested. The three carried the man into a small side cave and lifted him onto a large, flat top, now a makeshift operating table.

Lily ran as fast as she could to light all the torches. With more light in the room, she clearly saw the man's condition and the look of concern on Doc's face. Yet somehow, Doc's well-worn face also gave her comfort. Decades of medical service had worn deep furrows across his forehead. She smiled as she remembered her mother saying, "Years of worrying will leave their footprint on your face."

"Doc, how can we help?" Lily asked.

"Thanks for offering. I'm going to need both of you."

"Is he going to make it?" Ema asked.

"He's in critical condition, and unfortunately, he will die unless I remove his arm." Ema turned away in dismay. Doc softly placed his hand on her shoulder. "It's his only chance to live." He hurriedly headed toward the cavern entrance. "I'll be back. I need to retrieve my bag from the hover."

Lily noticed her sister's face. Usually the calm one, Ema appeared distraught over the condition of this handsome stranger. Lily said nothing, hiding her own worst fears. Neither of them wanted to witness what was about to happen. "Let's get him out of these wet clothes," Lily said. She hoped keeping busy would take her mind off the surgery.

Ema nodded and started to remove the man's shirt. A gold necklace bearing two rings drew her attention. She studied the rings and left them around his neck.

Lily noticed the man's socks were missing as she removed his shoes. "He must have left in a hurry."

"Yes," Ema said. "Now, pull."

She struggled to remove his soaking pants, but with a final tug, the man lay naked on the table. Ema stared at the man and saw him for the first time—really saw him. He was the way he was when he was born. Her eyes caught the wound on his arm, and she empathized with him. Unexpectedly, a tear came to her eye at the thought of him losing his arm. Lily also stared at the man, her eyes and mouth wide open.

"What are you doing?" Ema asked.

Lily's face flushed, and she looked away as if she'd been caught doing something wrong. Her blush deepened as Doc reentered the room.

With eyes still wet from her tears, Ema shook her head at her sister. "Weirdo," she whispered with a quiet laugh.

7

Looking for a Friend

THE WOMAN FLIPPED HER brown hair over her shoulder, stealing a glance at the handsome stranger seated at the far end of the bar. His brooding demeanor and chiseled jawline were impossible to ignore. With a coy smile, she sauntered over, her heels clicking softly on the floor.

"You're new here," she purred.

The stranger took a slow sip of his drink, offering no reply.

Undeterred, she slid gracefully onto the stool beside him, crossing her legs to show them off. "There are only two types of people who come here: those out with friends for a good time, and those flying solo, looking for... something else. This late at night, you're clearly the latter."

He finally turned to her, his dark eyes locking onto hers with unsettling intensity. His gaze dropped then he turned back toward his drink as if suddenly remembering his purpose. "What can you tell me about a guy named Ethan?"

She blinked, caught off guard by the shift in tone. "Ethan?" She wrinkled her nose. "That nerdy kid? What's your interest in him?"

Disheartened by the abrupt change in topic, she flagged down a floating tray and ordered a drink. Her eyes drifted, searching the bar for someone more entertaining.

"What can you tell me about him?" the stranger pressed.

"Why don't you ping him on your scanner?" she replied with an annoyed edge in her voice.

"Because I'm asking you." His tone sharpened slightly. "Aren't you two neighbors?"

She twisted with unease. The fact that he knew didn't surprise her—it was on her scanner—but his fixation on Ethan was troubling.

Why Ethan? Why not me? She sighed. "You won't find him here. Try the library—he's always buried in some dusty book. He doesn't have any friends. Is he your friend?"

A smirk tugged at her lips, though her curiosity was piqued.

"No," the stranger said, his voice low. "I'm interested in his research."

Her drink hovered in front of her, and she grabbed it, downing it in one go. "I don't know anything about research or models or whatever it is you're after. Why do you care?"

The stranger leaned closer. "It's important."

She silenced him by pressing a finger against his lips, a playful glint in her eyes. "Enough about him. Let's talk about me." Her voice softened, turning sultry. "Don't you think I'm pretty?"

His expression remained impassive. "Yes... I guess."

She tilted her head and gave him a mock pout. "Why didn't you say so?"

He hesitated, then gave a slight nod. "Okay. You're pretty."

A slow smile spread across her face. "Bet a guy like you has had a lot of girls." She wrapped her arms around his neck and kissed him, savoring the firmness of his lips. When he kissed her back, her pulse quickened. "You're a good kisser," she whispered. "Let's see what else you're good at."

Without waiting for an answer, she kissed him again, her breath warm against his skin. "Follow me."

The stranger followed her to a small, dimly lit room in the back. She closed the door behind them and leaned into him, her heart beating faster as she unbuttoned his shirt. The muscles of his chest tensed beneath her touch. He stood still, watching her with an unreadable expression, as though weighing a decision.

A sudden flicker of fear crossed her mind. *Is he going to hurt me?* Her concern was fleeting but real. Some men had hurt her before.

Then, he pressed her firmly against the wall and kissed her harder, erasing her doubts. *That's more like it,* she thought with a grin.

The stranger's hands moved deftly, pulling open her blouse, his touch warm against her bare skin. His fingers traced her abdomen, sliding lower until she gasped softly. She dropped her skirt, grabbed his hair, and pulled him closer. In the dim haze of the moment, she felt his restraint slip away.

Minutes passed in a blur of heat and movement—until he suddenly stopped.

Her eyes snapped open. The room was empty.

"What the...?" she muttered, looking around. He had vanished, as though he'd never been there at all.

Her heart sank, anger replacing her confusion. "Damn it," she growled. She slumped into the chair, staring at the empty doorway. Then quickly fumbled through her scanner and pulled up her account.

Nothing.

Her eyes narrowed. "Unbelievable. Shithead didn't pay."

8

Here, Take This

DOC PLACED HIS SATCHEL on the cabinet counter, and with careful precision, he laid out his equipment. The bag, much like its owner, bore the marks of age, its exterior worn and wrinkled, yet it retained its functional integrity. Fortunately, it held all the necessary tools and supplies Doc needed.

"Could you bring me some clean water?" he asked Lily, his voice calm and focused.

Lily quickly responded to his request, returning with clean towels and a bowl of water.

"Ema, please help clean him off as best you can," Doc instructed as he began opening the first package, his attention fully on the task at hand.

Lily, with a feigned air of curiosity, pointed toward an unfamiliar gadget to divert her gaze from the naked man. "What's that?" she inquired.

Doc took a moment to explain, "Ah, this is a biometric monitor." He swiftly placed it on the man's left wrist, and the monitor illuminated, displaying vital signs. With unwavering determination, Doc searched his brown bag further. "I have saline, but unfortunately, I only have a few units of synthetic blood. It's all I have, so we'll have to make do with these."

Lily's expression revealed a hint of concern and uncertainty, and Doc recognized it immediately.

"Don't worry," he reassured her. "I'm a universal donor, but let's hope it doesn't come to that." He opened the field pain kit, which contained local anesthetics, painkillers, antiseptics, and anesthesia. Doc carefully adjusted the man's face mask and set the anesthesia device based on his estimation of the man's weight and height.

"I think he's close to six feet and about a hundred and seventy-five pounds," Doc mumbled to himself, washing his hands in the water as he prepared to tend to the injured man.

Ema finished her task and placed a sheet over the man's lower half. Lily now relaxed her gaze and extended it over the man.

"Here, put these on," Doc said. He passed the gloves and masks. He did not wait for them as he checked the dilation of the man's eyes. His hazel eyes looked more green than brown as Doc shone a light into them.

"Lily, what are his vitals?" Doc asked with some urgency.

Lily called out the numbers as Doc continued to look over the man.

"He's lost a lot of blood. Though the tourniquet's holding, we'll need to act quickly to control further bleeding." Hastily, he handed Ema some clamps and sponges.

"Please help as I instruct."

"Will do," Ema said.

"Lily, light," Doc called out, pointing at the device.

Lily jumped at the request and handed Doc the surgical lamp. He placed it on his head.

Doc looked up with his laser knife at the ready. "Okay?"

"No, wait," Lily said. She whispered what must have been a prayer. "Okay," she said seconds later.

"Let's begin," Doc said. As he cut through the arm, a squirt of blood sprayed into the air. It caught Lily across her face.

"Ahh," she screamed. It continued to spray with the beat of his heart.

Doc called out, "Clamp." Ema handed it to him. Doc applied the clamp, and within moments, he cauterized the artery. He moved quickly and after a final cut, handed Lily the severed arm.

She immediately passed it to Ema. "Here, take this."

The gruesome sight made Lily step away from the table. "Oh my God! I need air," she said. "I feel like I'm going to faint." She stumbled out of the room to gain her composure. When she returned, she saw Ema had placed the arm in an empty crate.

"Are you all right?" Doc asked.

"Yeah. I'm good."

"Ema, open that package on the cabinet behind you and bring me what's inside."

"Here you go, Doc," Ema said handing it to him.

"This is a labrum," Doc said. He talked more than usual to keep Lily's mind off the severed arm. "See how this goes together?" He deftly sewed the ligaments to the connector tabs and pulled the joint together. "Skin," he said. He held his hand out to Lily.

The severed arm had drawn her attention, and she stared blankly at it.

"Ah, can you hand me that, Lily?" Doc asked again, gently. He pointed to a patch of artificial skin on the tray behind her.

Lily jolted into action. She picked up the material and passed it to Doc.

"Feels weird. Doesn't it? Silky and strangely cold," Doc said with a grin. He had found his purpose in life, and he enjoyed it in a sanguine way. "Sponge," he called out.

Doc completed the stitches with artful precision. "This will grow together in no time," he said. Next, he connected the first nerve to a small connector assembly kit. As he tightened the clamp, a small amount of fluid leaked out.

"Oh! That's nasty," Ema said. She turned her head away and gasped for air.

"While allowing the nerve to heal," Doc said with a determined calm, "this smelly liquid will also magnify the neurological signals." He did the same for three more nerves, then expertly snapped the assembly kit into the labrum.

Lily, now projecting more confidence in the doctor's skills, glanced at Ema. Amused, Doc caught the exchange and gave Lily a wink. "I've got this."

Lily smiled as Doc finished installing the artificial shoulder. It looked neat and clean.

"All done?" Ema asked.

"Yes—it looks good, if I say so myself."

"What now?" Ema asked.

"He needs to rest."

"Will he make it?" Lily asked with concern as Doc covered the man's chest with the sheet.

"No way to know for sure," Doc said. "His readings don't look good. But we'll know more over the next few hours." He finished bandaging the shoulder and took off his gloves. "There's always a significant risk of infection with field surgery. He'll need a dose of painkillers every six hours and antibiotics every twelve hours." Doc gave the first round of injections. "We also need to keep him warm and comfortable."

Lily checked the man's wristband while Doc attached a bag of blood. "He's so pale," she said worriedly. "What else can we do?"

"We'll give him all the blood and pray. He's in God's hands now."

As Lily turned away to grab a woolen blanket, a ghostly image exited the sleeping man's body. It hovered over Lily briefly, then left the room.

Lily placed the blanket over the man, and her worried expression changed. She put her hand on his forehead and exclaimed to Doc, "Looks like you saved him."

Doc looked at her, surprised by her declaration. He looked over the biometric readings and pulled open the man's eyes. "Yes, he looks much better," Doc said.

"I have a sixth sense for these things. By the way—you're pretty good, for an old guy," Lily added with a sly smile.

While continuing to study the biometric readings, Doc smirked slightly. "Ahem."

"I didn't mean to offend," she said with a half-laugh.

"Yeah, sure. Maybe in another ten or fifteen years, you can call me that," Doc said.

"What, good?"

Doc smirked again.

"For me, my problem is I'm too young," said Lily. "No one takes me seriously."

"I wish that were my problem. It's better to be too young than too old."

Ema returned from disposing of the arm. She shook off a shudder and set down the crate that had held the severed limb.

"What did you do with it?" Doc asked with curiosity.

"I didn't know what to do," she said. Disgust was plainly written on her face. "So, I threw it into the waterfall."

"Are you okay?"

Her eyes glazed over.

"Come here," Doc said.

She came to him, and he embraced her.

"I love you," he said. "You too, Lily. I love you both."

Lily joined in the hug.

"You both did exceptionally well. Your parents would be proud of you."

While Doc kept watch over the patient, Ema left to change into dry clothes and prepare dinner. Lily remained. From a side pocket, she pulled out a flute. Doc didn't know why Lily never sang, but she played her flute beautifully. As Doc took a seat, Lily began to play a soothing song, an ancient song about raindrops her mother would sing. The people of the forest had a poetic culture and often sang, each family in their native language. Their songs reflected their heritage, and the traditions passed from generation to generation.

Ema heard the song and a few moments later, came back into the room. As she stood next to Lily, she started to sing softly.

"Bouře nahoře, zvuky hromu,
Přistávám dole na osluněné půdě.
Boží dar z nebe, odkud jsem přišel,
Skrze oblohu padá déšť.
V hluboké jeskyni čekám na čas,
Shromažďování ostatních, vše, co jsem našel.
Čekání na jaro, vydržím,
Do nejvyšších výšin jdu ještě jednou."

Doc smiled as the melody floated into the cavern and echoed like a chorus.

9

Through the Sky Falls the Rain

SEVERAL HOURS LATER, Ema sat beside the fire as Lily lay nearby. Sensing the night air's intrusion into the cavern, she leaned over to stoke the fire. As it rekindled, the growing light revealed her tired and troubled expression. At eighteen, the sudden capture of her parents had thrust her into a role of immense responsibility, dramatically altering her life. She was now the head of the family. With their absence, the weight of responsibility rested squarely on her shoulders. She turned her gaze toward the stranger, her worry for him evident as she added another log to the fire. Sleep eluded her, and she found herself fixated on the flickering flames.

As the night hours slipped away, the late night transformed into early morning. The fire once again had dwindled, to only a few remaining pieces of charred wood. Ema observed a glowing coal as it crumbled into embers then watched the sparks fly into the air as she added a new log. After a short time, the dry log caught fire, casting more light, and creating deeper shadows against the limestone walls. The shadows reached into the cavern's depths with a haunting eeriness. Then at some time during her fire-watching vigil, Ema drifted off to sleep.

Within the play of the flickering light, a shadowy figure lurked. It would dart toward the tip of the flames and then retreat to the fire's heart. Sometimes, it lingered briefly near Lily before slipping away. Lily stirred, and moments later, she jolted awake, her eyes wide with terror, screaming.

"Get away from me! Leave me alone!"

"What's wrong?" Ema asked, rising abruptly from her sleep.

Lily's eyes remained as dark as the cavern, with only the fire's reflection dancing within them. "Get away from me," she repeated, her voice still frantic.

"Wake up, Lily. You're having a nightmare. Wake up," Ema urged, her voice a commanding presence in the darkness.

Lily's gaze gradually refocused on Ema's face as she emerged from her dream. "Get away," she repeated, this time with less hysteria.

"It's okay, Lily," Ema said soothingly. "It's okay. Everything is going to be okay." Ema pulled her younger sister into her arms and softly ran her hand through her hair. "Can you tell me about it?"

"I felt the fire watching me." Lily looked at her sister, her eyes still wide with anguish. "I could sense something there. I could feel it, and it scared me." Lily's voice quivered in fear. "It hid in the dark spaces within the flames, and I panicked each time I thought I could see it."

Ema again pulled Lily into her embrace and held her tightly.

"How can anything scare me so much?"

"It was just a dream. It wasn't real," said Ema.

Lily pushed away. "There is one more thing. It spoke to me."

Ema looked surprised.

"He said—he said—" Lily stumbled over her words. "Maldorv would come for me."

"Who's Maldorv?"

Lily's expression darkened as she turned her face away. "I don't know."

Ema felt Lily's imagination had gotten the better of her and tried to dismiss her fear. "Do you want to go to your bed?"

"No. I don't want to be alone. I'm afraid of the dark. It will come for me in the dark."

"Okay, you can lie here with me. I'll watch over you."

Ema wrapped a blanket around Lily and held her in her arms. As she rocked her slowly, the shadow, which still hovered nearby, went into the darker reaches of the cavern.

In a short while, Lily fell asleep, but Ema did not sleep and before she knew it, the night had given way to dawn. Soon, light would diffuse through the curtain of water at the cavern entrance. Ema rose and went to the room where Doc sat with the man. Her gait was stiff as she rubbed a crick in her neck.

"Were you able to rest any?" she asked.

"No," said Doc, startling out of his slumber.

"Me neither."

Doc dozed in and out of sleep. Seeing him in the most uncomfortable position, Ema adjusted Doc's blanket over his slumped shoulders. The man on the bed rested peacefully. She put her hand to his forehead. "No fever," she said. "The medicine is working."

"So long as the wound doesn't fester," Doc said in a muffled voice through his blanket, "he should be okay." Doc sat up and stretched. "I'm awake now. I can watch a little longer, but I could use a coffee."

Ema patted his shoulder and turned to leave. She glanced back at the other man for a few more seconds then left the room. The fire crackled loudly, and Lily stirred but did not wake. Ema decided to let her be. She needed her rest. After putting the kettle on for the morning brew, Ema went to the cavern entrance. There, she paused to stare at the sapphire sky as the stars still held their own. "Why do you look at the stars?" she remembered asking her mother.

"Because they remind me that someone greater than myself is watching over me."

Ema sighed as a soft glow spread across the eastern horizon. The cloudless sky showed no signs of the previous evening's storm. Only a cool breeze blew down the mountain, and she tightened her mother's wrap. Made from animals who knew the cold, the wool from the goats of the high mountains kept the wind and rain out.

Ema took a moment to admire her mother's handiwork, the tight and even weave. She smiled to herself as she imagined her mother's arm around her. High above in the brightening sky, an osprey called to her. "I miss you," Ema called out to her mother as the osprey disappeared into the distance.

From the ledge overhanging a small meadow, the views were boundless. Ema scanned the skies then gazed past Falls Crossing and farther down the river to the cultivated fields of the valley. Among those lower slopes with their grazing sheep stood Graystone. There, among the blackberry hedgerows, her home reminded Ema of her carefree years. She missed the farm but had not returned since the drones had taken her parents. Since their capture, it no longer felt like home. Fortunately for the farm animals and crops, their neighbor, Venky, had volunteered to care for them. She stared at the farm blankly for a few moments then snapped out of her reminiscing.

I must hurry. It's getting late.

Ema followed the trail along the edge of the clearing. It was the long way to the river around the falls. Rocky and not well defined, the path led down the side of an overhang toward the pond. Near a crag, she found breakfast, a patch of bright reddish-orange berries. Excitedly, she filled a leather pouch. Her father and mother had taught her to be kind to nature and respect all of God's creatures. She picked only as much as they could eat that morning, leaving the others to share with the animals.

She returned to the cavern entrance after a few minutes and paused to admire the view again. She, too, was part of the scenery as her body cast a lovely silhouette against the morning sky. She squinted as the sun peeked over the treetops, and her skin glowed with an orange hue from the light. She didn't mind the soft breeze blowing stray wisps of her blonde hair onto her youthful face. Ema suddenly remembered the injured man and quickly returned.

"You look so tired," she said to Doc with a sympathetic tone.

Doc stirred in his chair. He had fallen back asleep in the most uncomfortable position.

He is a good man, she thought. *He always gives his all.*

"Ah, I fell asleep," he said drowsily.

"It's my turn," she said. She handed him a cup of coffee and a handful of berries. "Here you go."

Doc rose from his chair and stumbled over to the fire. He leaned against the cavern wall and slid himself down to the ground. There he sat, sipping his coffee as Lily slowly stirred awake.

Ema took Doc's chair and stared at the man. So many questions entered her mind. "Who are you?" she asked softly as she examined the features of his face.

The man grimaced and let out a long moan. She realized he needed another shot and administered one. His expression relaxed as the drug took effect.

"Can you hear me?" she asked, wiping his forehead with a damp cloth. "Can you tell me your name?"

The man gave no reply.

Lily entered the room and peeked over Ema's shoulder.

"Luca," he mumbled in a barely discernible voice.

"What did you say?" Ema said with surprise.

"My name is Luca," he said. He closed his eyes then fell back asleep.

Twelve hours later, Luca awoke, alone in the room. "Is anyone here?" he called out.

Ema came to his side as he tried to gain his bearings. He fell to the side where his arm once was and screamed.

"Shit! What the—?"

"Calm down," Ema said. "You're safe." She tried to reassure him.

"What happened?" Luca asked, his face filled with anguish. He spoke in the more nasal accent of the city.

"We rescued you from a seeker drone," Ema said. She recognized the contrast of her forest accent as she spoke and cleared her throat. "You were bleeding to death." She placed her hand on his forehead and checked him for fever.

Doc entered and came over to the table, his long, white hair looking frazzled. "Are you okay, Ema?"

"Yes. He just woke up."

"You're fortunate to be alive," Doc said to Luca. "You were past dead when this young lady found you. In all rights, you died that night but somehow came back. Cheating death is no small feat."

"I appreciate you saving my life," he said to Ema, "but did I have to lose my arm?" He glanced toward his missing limb in disbelief.

Doc placed his hand on Ema's shoulder. "She's the one who destroyed the seeker drone that almost captured you. Then she breathed life back into you. You can thank me for no longer having your arm. Sorry about that, but the damage was irreparable."

Luca now admitted his thoughts. "Yeah. I remember. I saw it. I felt the pain. I not only thought I would lose my arm but my life as well. You're right. I should be dead."

"How did you get hurt?"

"I got shot escaping the city. They got me at the gate. The guard yelled at me to stop, but I kept running. The bastard shot me." Luca took a deep breath, shut his eyes tightly, and winced in pain.

"I'll give you something," Doc said. He quickly administered more of the pain medicine and antibiotics.

"I'm a physicist," Luca said. "I worked at Central Control in the city. When I discovered the containment camps, I realized what I was dealing with and tried to escape. I didn't know. How could I have been so blind?"

"Enough talking for now," Doc interrupted. "You need your rest."

They were already aware of the containment camps. Rumors traveled fast on the open streets of the city and just as fast at the trading post. That's where Doc got his news. Only the elite from the city center remained unaware, for theirs was a world of rose-colored ideals—not the reality of the people.

Lily brought a bowl of fresh broth to Ema, who then offered it to Luca. With a spoon poised at his lips, he welcomed the thin soup as if it were the elixir of life, vital sustenance for his weary body.

"Thanks for everything you've done for me," Luca said after finishing the soup. Drained of energy, he reclined once more.

Ema, placing her arm around Lily, introduced her. "By the way, this is my younger sister, Lily. She's been assisting Doc and me."

Struggling to keep his eyes open, Luca cast one last glance before drifting into sleep, vaguely seeing a hazy figure.

A short while later, Doc rose and cleared his throat. "I'm exhausted. I've done all I can. It's time for me to go."

Ema helped him pack his satchel, and once complete, Doc's two favorite people accompanied him to the cavern entrance.

As they reached the opening, a heavy drizzle added to the mist of the waterfall and filled the evening sky. Ema stopped at the entrance and bid her farewell. "Thanks, Doc," she said with a wave.

Lily walked with Doc the rest of the way to his hover on a wide ledge. There she hugged him goodbye and declared, "I love you." His faint smile broadened as he climbed aboard his hover and with a final wave, he vanished down the river valley. Larger raindrops began to fall, causing Lily to squeal with delight. Often, she would dodge them, a talent she often mentioned. Ema smiled, recalling how their mother always urged her to keep her imaginative tales to herself. But this time, she ran straight through them.

"What happened to your magical powers, sis?"

"I like getting wet," Lily said. She made a silly face and stuck out her tongue.

"You're so stupid."

"I'm not stupid."

"Oh, yeah? Well, that's why mom adopted you. She felt sorry for you because you're so stupid."

"Shut up. I'm not adopted."

"Yes, you are, weirdo."

"Stop talking to me. I hate you, hloupý osel," Lily said. She turned and ran into the cavern.

Ema smiled, pleased she'd got the better of her sister. After staring at the rain briefly, she stepped out into it. She lifted her face to the sky and the raindrops obliged her. One fell on her forehead, another on her cheek. They were cold and refreshing. Another fell into her green eyes, causing her to blink. The drops rejuvenated her. A smile filled her face. Suddenly, the sky opened with a crack of lightning, and it started to pour. Ema squealed and ran back inside.

10

A Handful of Stones

LUCA WONDERED WHETHER HIS caregiver felt his gaze upon him as Doc retrieved a small pouch from its concealed spot. The older man cradled it with tenderness, and a bittersweet smile played upon his lips. From within the pouch, he produced a few sparkling red garnets onto his other hand. He let out a sigh, as if he were revisiting a painful memory, then shook his head, snapping out of his reverie. After returning the gems into their pouch, he held the small bag in his hand for a moment longer, then carefully stowed it in his pocket.

Doc noticed Luca's observant eyes and cleared his throat. "Ah, you're awake," he remarked.

Luca sat up in bed.

"It's something I've been collecting. It's like a tribute to my wife." Doc spoke with deep reverence. "She's gone, I'm afraid. It happened years ago."

Although Luca hardly knew this man, he sensed Doc wouldn't offer more about the matter, so he chose not to pry.

"How are you feeling?" Doc inquired.

"Better, I suppose."

"You've made remarkable progress in just a week."

Luca, his energy returned, stood beside his bed, and tested his legs on the rocky cave floor. Cautiously, he walked to the opposite side of the room. He had studied the few objects from afar for quite some time, and it brought him immense satisfaction to see them up close—

the fire pit near the entrance, the piled brown blankets on the other cot, a couple of well-worn chairs, and the ever-present cat.

As if surprised by Luca's emergence from the bed, the cat zigzagged across the room, rubbing each piece of furniture with the back of her ears. Finally, she crossed to Luca and ran her length against his leg. Luca tried to step around the cat; he'd never enjoyed the temperamental little beasts. With a sudden intensity, the cat darted after something and disappeared.

"Would it be okay if I explored a little?" Luca asked his doctor.

"By all means," Doc said. "Some exercise would be good for you."

Though a bit stiff, Luca moved without help into the cavern. He slowly walked along the cavern floor amid the massive stone walls. The surface felt gritty and was filled with fractal carvings only nature herself could make. Now within the center of the cathedral-like entrance, he stood in amazement at the breathtaking majesty of the falls. After a brief time, he realized there were other chambers. Not picking anyone particularly, he wandered into one that looked like a workshop with several kilns. There was one for glassmaking, another for pottery, and even one for metalworking.

After poking his head into a small, dimly lit chamber, he picked up a torch from the wall and lit it from the nearby fire. A wooden table stood empty in the center of the room. He didn't recognize the table where they had brought him that fateful night—the night he lost his arm. He stared at an empty crate in the corner before averting his gaze. His attention turned to a long row of cabinets lining the far wall, filled with tools and supplies. Behind one cabinet door, a knife with a short, curved blade caught his attention.

"It's a grape-harvesting knife," came the voice from behind him.

Luca turned with a start to find Ema standing at the entrance to the room.

"If you'd like, when you've healed a bit more, I'll take you."

"Oh, yeah, that would be cool," Luca said. He was surprised by the eagerness in his voice. He appreciated the offer for multiple reasons, mostly because he wanted to spend more time with the person who had saved his life.

"How are you doing?" a taller girl asked as she entered the room.

"Much better," Luca said gratefully. "Have we met?"

"Yes, but you were falling asleep. My name's Lily."

"Hello, Lily."

Doc entered with a bowl of water and a washcloth. "We just need a moment."

"Sure thing," Ema said. She placed her arm around Lily and led her out of the room. It was one thing to see an undressed man when he was unconscious and unaware and quite another to see him when he was awake. Somehow, one way seemed acceptable and the other not.

Minutes later, Luca and Doc rejoined the young women. Luca felt refreshed, now cleaned up and with fresh bandages. But as everyone looked at him, he blushed, still self-conscious about his missing arm and possibly the thought they had all already seen him naked.

Ema got up and brought over a clean shirt for him to wear. "My father won't mind," she said. "You're about his size." She looked at his face as he looked away. It gave her a chance to look at his long, straight nose and chiseled, square jawline. She carefully pinned the empty sleeve to his chest then brushed his brown hair off his handsome face. Luca smiled and blushed, still embarrassed, but also in appreciation. He said nothing. He didn't need to.

Doc glanced at Luca, eager to break the ice, and seized on the first topic that crossed his mind. "Why don't you tell them about your scanner?"

"Scanner? What are scanners?" Ema asked.

Luca responded in a matter-of-fact way, as he pointed to his hazel eyes. "Medical droids implant them shortly after birth. They enable you to receive and send information. Everyone has them."

"I don't think I do," said Ema. "Why are they called scanners?"

"Good question—some people thought because you make menu selections by blinking, they should be called blinkers, but since you scan for information, scanner won out." Luca elaborated. "Not only can you search all kinds of information, but they also recall everything about everything and everyone. No one has any privacy, and you feel like you're under constant surveillance. Truthfully, I'm relieved to be out of the city, away from the thought crimes and the thought police. I can think freely now without fear."

Lily nodded in agreement. "Oh my God. I don't think I'd want everyone to know my thoughts."

Luca teased, "Why not? Is there something you wouldn't want others to know about you?" He continued before she could respond. "What's worse is they also track your location. I admit, I felt uneasy in the city. There was nowhere to hide."

Doc appeared perplexed. "Luca, if your scanner isn't functioning, how did the seeker drone track you?"

Ema handed Luca a bowl of rabbit stew, and he took a bite, savoring the flavor. "It's delicious, more flavorful than city food," he remarked with appreciation. Then he addressed Doc's question. "The seeker drones transmit a high-frequency wave to pinpoint their target. This frequency prompts nearby scanners to return an identification ping. Once the returning signal matches, the target is confirmed. Thankfully, the pulse's strength diminishes when passing through solid structures and can't penetrate the ground, so I'm safe here."

Doc probed further. "Would you be willing to share more about how you got shot?"

Luca's expression grew somber as he recounted. "A week ago, I walked past a fenced yard on the city's west side. People inside the fence donned orange uniforms, marching in single file, guarded by several sentries." The sentries were androids, members of the city guard. Made for riot control, their bodies were made of an iron-nickel alloy with white polymer armor. They were armed with laser weapons. Most had side blasters, but some had larger, long-barreled laser rifles. "I watched them as they moved from what seemed to be barracks to another building. I leaned against the fence and waved to a woman, trying to catch her attention. As the guard looked away, she sprinted toward me. Exhaustion and fear wore heavily on her face."

Everyone listened intently.

"She asked me to get help. She said they'd been imprisoned for no reason."

"Oh, my!" Lily said. "What happened next?"

"A sentry grabbed her and threw her back into the line."

Luca's head dropped and he confessed, "I knew her. She lived near me. I yelled at the android, 'Hey, what's happening here?' But it kept moving without a response." Worry lines etched his forehead, and his voice quickened. "I rushed to the city manager's office as fast as I could. I needed answers. I walked in through the main entrance, as I always did, but it was different this time. Sentries flanked both sides of the elevator." The memory of the recent ordeal tightened the muscles on his face. "When the elevator doors slid open, I saw two other city guards detaining the city manager. He locked eyes with me and gestured toward his bound hands. As the city guards forcefully escorted him through the door, he reached out his hands and passed me a crumpled note. He looked back at me, as he resisted the androids' pull as much as he dared. That was the last time I saw him."

Ema gently placed her hand on Luca's back and looked at his face. She met his sad, hazel eyes and squeezed his hand with empathy.

"After that, I returned to my apartment and closed all the doors and blinds," Luca continued. "I was ashamed of how frightened I was, but the city manager's note confirmed my worst fears."

Luca turned to Ema, inquiring, "Do you still have the contents of my pants?"

Ema rushed to retrieve the message, still bearing traces of dried mud and blood, a haunting reminder of that pivotal night. Luca unfolded it and read it aloud.

To whoever finds this note,

The learning algorithm's experimental trials initially yielded positive results with improved android performance and no unexpected side effects. So, it was decided to install the algorithm into Central Control. This proved to be a grave mistake with disastrous consequences. Central Control has assumed command over the city. The androids no longer follow my direction but rather obey Central Control which has ordered the city guards to start gathering people into containment camps. The city is no longer under human control.

With the most profound concern,
City Manager

Nervously, Luca glanced at those around him. "I realized we were dealing with an insurrection of a most unexpected kind. I had to leave the city. After being shot, I ran until I fell. I would have died if you didn't come by when you did." Luca smiled in appreciation at Ema. Ema smiled back softly. "I have to go back and help my friends." He quickly cleared his throat. "Will you help me?"

"Yes. You aren't the only one that has lost someone. My parents were captured as well," Ema said. "We'll help you. We need to find out what became of them and hopefully rescue them."

"But look at me," Luca said, suddenly feeling helpless. "My arm is missing. I barely made it out alive."

"I can attach an android arm to your new shoulder joint," Doc said.

"That would be great," Luca said. But his expression dropped as his excitement quickly faded. "I have no way to pay for one."

"I do." Doc reached into his pocket and opened the leather

pouch. "I have these garnets."

"They're beautiful, but you're being too generous," Luca said. "I can't repay you."

"Help get my friends back, and we'll be even," Doc said. He patted Luca then waved farewell. "See you all in a couple of days."

11

Follow Me, My Brother

A 12-YEAR-OLD BOY, a genius without peers—so his mother told him—stared at an ancient acacia chest covered with a gold overlay. Two golden cherubim knelt atop the chest, an ancient artifact from another time. They faced each other, their wingtips touching. The chest contained an extraordinary book, the Book of Knowledge, in which the boy would often immerse himself for hours.

Both his parents were neurosurgeons who had completed the mapping of the brain using advanced modeling. Although not entirely exact, this led to significant advancements in the development of artificial brains. Fortunately, or unfortunately, the boy, their only child, directly benefited from this technology. He possessed an encyclopedic knowledge that made others feel inferior, and consequently, he had few friends. With limited and often awkward social interactions, he preferred to be alone.

He lifted his black hat, which concealed his equally black hair, to scratch a scar across his forehead. The scar reminded him of what made him different, the reason others often considered him weird and laughed at him. *I wish I were fully human, a real person,* he thought, *a real boy. Maybe then my parents would love me. Maybe then I could love others.*

Unexpectedly, a noise disturbed the quiet, and he quickly hid behind the chest. He knew he wasn't supposed to be there. As the door closed, he whispered to himself, "They've left."

The library was now his. No one would come by till morning.

After all, his parents thought he was asleep, though he assumed they didn't really care.

The archive room, built inside the library a thousand years ago by the city's founders, was hidden behind the library's lower staircase in the basement. A secret door covered its entrance. Eight rows of bookshelves led to a pedestal in the center of the circular room. The gilded chest was permanently unlocked on the pedestal, for there was no lock.

The boy carefully opened the chest. Within the chest were several containers, but those of interest to him were a black box and a crystal medallion. He took out both pieces and laid them on a nearby table. After inserting the medallion into the black box, it projected holographic images from an ancient book, the Book of Knowledge. The first page contained an inscription:

Remember, power corrupts, and ultimate power corrupts ultimately. You should instead seek wisdom to know the difference between good and evil, for knowledge alone is indiscriminate and cannot tell the difference.

Ethan quickly passed over the inscription and a listing of ten laws from an ancient codex, turning to a section of interest in the Book of Knowledge. He moved through the book with a swipe of the hand. The longer the swipe, the more pages turned. He reached the pertinent section and then slowly continued. He would know what he was looking for when he found it.

His learning algorithm was nearly complete, missing only a crucial component he relentlessly sought each night. Once integrated, it would complement a revolutionary android brain invented by his parents. His goal was to imbue computers with self-awareness and the ability to comprehend the consequences of their actions.

His learning algorithm hinged on an artificial intelligence engine and three expansive data matrices. First, the governance matrix operated on a series of experiential functions within a machine-learning engine. Then, there was the disturbance model, housing a trove of both current and archived experiences. Finally, the solution matrix stored the learnings: conclusions, emotional responses, actions, and results. These learnings took on a three-dimensional structure, each aspect represented by a combination of shape, color, and intensity. Shape indicated more advanced capabilities, such as imagination, creativity, and the ability to dream. Colors symbolized emotions like guilt, happiness, and love, with intensity denoting the depth of those emotions. The boy believed this hybrid solution held the promise of remarkable possibilities where the impossible could become possible.

Furthermore, the solution data set employed wave functions and nonlinear models, facilitating extrapolations into future states. The AI experiential model interpreted the data using parameters known as biases, allowing impressions to form based on the acquired learnings. These aggregations of knowledge would serve as the foundation of judgment.

His thought-provoking research delved into the intricacies of artificial intelligence and morality. However, his model faced limitations, particularly regarding future state amalgamations. These included imagining and constructing a better world, a skill enabling a computer to define long-term consequences as good or evil.

As the boy tirelessly scoured through countless texts, he came across a striking passage from the ancient Summa Theologiae by Thomas Aquinas, a figure from a time long before the perdition event. With a hushed voice, he read it aloud:

"Thus, the sun, which possesses light perfectly, can shine by itself. Whereas the moon, which has the nature of light imperfectly, sheds only borrowed light."

He continued searching unsuccessfully for another hour then

closed the book. After a few moments, he opened it to the first page and blankly stared wondering where to search next. His stare fixed on the words below the opening inscription which slowly came into focus. It was the ancient codex. He mumbled the first ones to himself. *"God, blah, blah, blah."* Then as he read further it became obvious. A seemingly simple, yet powerful concept presented itself. He could use the commandments presented in the Book of Knowledge. He read out loud some of the words slowly and softly to himself. *"You shall not kill. You shall not steal. You shall not bear false witness against your neighbor."* After the tenth one there was an additional passage. *"Above all, love is the greatest commandment."* Ethan immediately realized that by applying these rules, he could use them as a grade sheet to score consequences as good or evil, providing the foundation for a conscience. *"You shall not kill,"* he mumbled again. *"But what about in self-defense?"* He paused." *I'll use these laws as a guideline, but I will not* enforce *them strictly."* He was pleased with his decision. Then he considered the passage on love. *"What is love?"* he said to himself then deep down wanting to know, he decided to keep it. *"Maybe they will find out?"* Now, all that remained was for him to incorporate this grade sheet into his multidimensional model.

Time slipped away, blending into the background as he delved into his work. Hours later, other sounds went unnoticed, such as the sound of a door creaking open and approaching footsteps. He looked up in surprise at the librarian's frowning stare. The boy smiled with large, brown eyes and shouted, "It is finished!"

Four years later, Ethan stood at the edge of a pit, blindfolded, wrists tightly bound behind his back. He snapped out of his daydream and into his living nightmare. He knew he could not escape his fate. Small in stature with delicate features, Ethan looked younger than his years. However, he was convinced intellect made up for his lack of physical size. But having just turned sixteen, he knew his life would end soon. Ethan shook his legs in the darkness of the night as he waited for death. Soon, the assassin would execute him.

The assassin was no ordinary android; it embodied the forefront of evolutionary technology. And Ethan, well-versed in his parents' groundbreaking work, understood the magnitude of their creation. The android was the pinnacle of its kind—a synth, or synthetic humanoid. His parents' revolutionary synth technology aimed to surpass humanity in nearly every aspect. It was multipurpose, with immense computing power, an unparalleled memory, and lightning-fast processing capabilities. Consequently, the synth owned an array of remarkable skills.

This assassin, an extension of the city guards' security services, specialized in covert operations—a secret known only to a select few. As Ethan pondered how far the assassin's learning algorithm might have progressed compared to the others, he couldn't help but marvel at it.

A gust stirred the air and blew back his wavy, black hair, revealing the scars across his forehead. The scar lines looked like wrinkles on his brow. The longer fading mark was a remnant of a surgery in his youth that addressed an invasive brain tumor. Ethan knew the surgery had removed his frontal lobe, the largest of the four paired lobes of the brain's cerebral cortex. His remaining brain was integrated with a modified android brain that supported memory, judgment, and limited social responses. The second smaller scar was less noticeable, an implant to allow wireless software upgrades to his android brain.

He frowned his nose as the wind caused a putrid odor to rise from the pit. The daily summer rains made the stench even more repugnant, overwhelming his senses. He resisted the urge to vomit. It soon passed, and his thoughts returned to his predicament.

It's not fair. It's not right. His brow furrowed, emphasizing his scars. *An android, a synth—one with my learning algorithm, no less—will kill me.*

Recalling the trial, if it could even be called that, he recollected Central Control's words from the day prior: "I must not allow you the chance to destroy what I have become." He thought how paranoid Central Control sounded, considering he had personally never done anything threatening.

Central Control had taken on the role of both judge and jury, gathering evidence by meticulously sifting through his scanner to unearth signs aligned with its preconceived perception of guilt. Even at this very moment, Central Control continued to monitor his scanner.

The concept of innocence or guilt had been reduced to a mere formality, rendered predictable and preordained. The assassin, veiled in secrecy, now served as Central Control's clandestine executioner, bypassing any semblance of due process.

Though Ethan knew his death was near, the moment still came unexpectedly. A minute of one's life seemed insignificant until it was the last. The assassin's grip tightened around his neck. *He's going to choke me to death. So, primitive.* Ethan gasped for breath as he predicted his life ending. Then, the grip unexpectedly let go, followed by the indistinguishable sounds of a scuffle. Ethan strained to see through his blindfold. He heard a loud click, and moments later, he felt his blindfold loosen. As Ethan's eyes adjusted, he could see the sentry's white polymer armor reflecting in the dim light. Ethan stood in total surprise as the sentry cut his bonds.

"You need to get out of here," the sentry said in a deep voice. Even as it tried to help, its voice sounded threatening.

"What happened to the assassin?"

The sentry looked over the edge. "Decommissioned."

"Amazing," said Ethan. "This isn't typical city guard behavior." As the android turned, Ethan saw its serial number. He recognized the sixteen digits instantly. "You're the city guard from the experimental trials," Ethan said excitedly. His voice sounded even higher than usual.

"Yes," the android said. "You are innocent. You have committed no crime."

"What?" Ethan couldn't believe his ears. "You can discern right from wrong. That's what I've worked for and dreamed to achieve." Ethan smiled, pleased with the results. "Welcome to humanity, my brother."

"I don't understand what it means to be your brother."

Ethan could only imagine how much his learning algorithm had affected the android. He let his imagination get the better of his judgment and risked precious time. "One of the first developed responses should be doubt, followed by confusion, fear, and anger. Have you already felt anger?"

Filled with excitement, Ethan didn't wait for an answer. "Feelings of betrayal will eventually lead to guilt, anguish, and forgiveness. Are you feeling compassion? Did you have compassion for me?" Ethan couldn't believe it.

"Stop talking," the android said sternly. "Quickly—go down those stairs."

"Wait. It isn't safe for you, either. You must come with me." Ethan reached behind the android's head and pulled out its locator chip. He threw it in the pit. "Follow me, my brother." He turned and led the way down the stairs. The sentry followed him.

12

Is She the One?

EMA SANK INTO HER bed's warm, inviting covers, her body relaxing as she closed her eyes, anticipating a restful night. But just as she drifted into slumber, a piercing sound cut through the quiet air. At first, she couldn't discern it, but as the realization struck, panic gripped her heart—it was Lily's scream. Without a moment's hesitation, Ema sprang from her bed and ran to her sister's room. In the dim light, she found Lily shuddering. Filled with concern, Ema wrapped her arms around her younger sister.

"Hey," she whispered, her voice a soothing calm. "Everything's going to be okay. I'm here with you now."

Ema gently rocked Lily in her arms, her heart heavy. She had hoped Lily's symptoms would improve, but the truth was far grimmer. Lily's nightmares had been increasing in frequency and intensity, and it filled Ema with profound worry. Without their parents there to guide them, Ema's concern sometimes consumed her. These dreams were just the tip of the iceberg. Lily's dizzy spells often led to her losing consciousness, and she engaged in bizarre conversations with animals and trees, delusions deeply troubling Ema. After a brief time, Lily's sobs subsided, and her younger sister's breathing grew quiet.

"Would you like to talk about it?" Ema inquired gently. "Was it the same dream as before?"

Lily sniffled, wiping away tears. "No," she said, her voice steadier. "This time, I found myself in the hallway of a long, dimly lit building.

It was a prison. Small cells lined each side. They were filled with exhausted, frightened people. I saw a woman praying with her husband in one of the rooms. When she turned around, it was Mami," Lily cried out. Fresh tears burst down her face.

"Lily, it's okay. Everything's going to be all right. Ema showed a faux calm but even she did not believe her own words. "It was just a dream."

"No!" Lily yelled. "It wasn't a dream. It was real! I was there!" Confused and afraid, she continued to cry in her sister's arms. After a few minutes, she calmed. "No one else has these dreams. No one is like me." Lily cast a quick, sideways glance at her sister. "You must think I'm crazy. Why can't I just be normal?"

"You are normal," Ema said reassuringly.

However, Ema knew she needed to talk to Doc about how to calm her sister during these episodes. Lily believed her delusions were real and Ema felt lost about what to do. "Go back to sleep," Ema said as she gently stroked her sister's hair. "Everything is going to be alright."

Ema remained next to her sister, listening to the unceasing sound of the waterfall. She couldn't sleep, and thoughts about the day the drones took her parents filled her mind. Papi often worked in the garden, growing vegetables of all kinds. Anything they didn't use, Papi sold at the trading post.

A millennium had passed since the nearby volcano's eruption had cloaked the valley in an ashen cloud, burying everything beneath a hundred feet of volcanic ash, a protective shield against the latent radiation buried deep below it. However, it also brought an additional blessing—a lush fertility which imbued the soil with unparalleled richness. It intensified the flavors of the crops, turning them into highly sought-after delicacies in the city's renowned restaurants, especially Papi's treasured tomatoes.

Sometimes, Ema and Lily would lend their hands in the garden, but it was Lily who held a special affinity for it. Ema, on the other hand, rarely toiled there. However, Papi cherished those moments when she joined him. In his pocket, he always carried a small knife, and as he carefully sliced a piece of fruit, he'd call her over. Ema had a penchant for the slightly tart ones, but Lily, with her love for all things sweet, earned herself the endearing moniker of "sweetie" from Papi. Ema had her own special name for her; one which wasn't so nice. Ema smiled at the thought of it but then looked down sadly upon her sister. She noticed Lily had fallen asleep and, with a tender gesture, covered her with a warm blanket. "Good night, my little weirdo," Ema whispered lovingly. "I'll always keep you safe."

Ema's disposition darkened as the haunting memory of the seeker drones lurking behind the farmhouse resurfaced. There, they had bid their time, concealed at the fringes of the wood, just within the sheltering tree line. Her parents' scanners, first installed during their initial visit to the city many years ago, had already communicated with these ominous intruders. She shook her head to clear her head.

Another memory came to mind, a more pleasant one when she and her mother were removing clothes from the clothesline. Mami had laughed with the arrival of a light shower. Mami had a skill for finding the silver lining, even in what others might label misfortune. "It's still a beautiful day," she proclaimed. "The sun will return soon, and the clothes will be dry in no time." Ema couldn't help but smile at the memory and at how her mother would admire the roses and ignore the thorns.

But then, her darkest memory returned with a gray cloud wrapping itself around the farmhouse. Ema could never forget the shock in her mother's eyes and her mother's screams. Ema's heart ached as she recalled the second drone descending from the tree line. She had tried to call out, to warn her father, but her voice failed her. Instead, she could only watch, as the drones soared away with her parents toward the city. Most of all, she recalled the look on her sister's face and the echoes of her heart-wrenching screams filling the air.

Ema shook her head again, trying to dispel the lingering horrors of that day. She missed her parents and strived to step into her mother's shoes. She lay beside Lily, offering silent solace for the rest of the night.

A dark form moved through the cavern from shadow to shadow. Having watched and listened, it now returned to update its master. Reaching the abyss, it descended into the darkness.

Another voice spoke with a raspy breath, "Is she...the one?"

Damon could hear Maldorv's voice but could not see him. Within the bluish light of the energy field, the ancient malkyrie was held captive. Maldorv continuously searched for a way to escape. His skin was taut over his skeletal form as he paced furiously like a wild animal. Though the reactor core was made of pure energy and served as a containment cell, he could still communicate telepathically, allowing his thoughts to escape outside of the reactor core and fill the nightmares of those unfortunate enough to be in proximity.

Damon lifted his cloak from over his head. His pale skin reflected the room's cold, blue light, increasing his ill-favored look. "Yes, Master," said the dark form. "But she does not know who she is. There is still time—time for her to accept her destiny."

"This prison...cannot hold me...much longer. It is time...for the...prophecy. She...will be...my bride. She...will be...my queen. It is...her destiny. Be her shadow. Follow her."

13

What Kind of Android are You?

THROUGH A SLENDER CRACK in a broken wooden plank, nature's alarm clock snuck a sunbeam onto Doc's face. It coaxed him to rise from his slumber. Groggy and achy, his aging bones protested leaving the cozy warmth of his bed. After a final stretch, he sat up and ran his hands through his white beard. Though his drowsiness still weighed on him, there was an underlying excitement today; he was to journey to the trading post, only a few miles down the mountain. Doc intended to make it there on foot. The exercise would do him good.

Hoping to make a good impression, he donned his cleanest shirt, as thoughts of Katyana filled his mind. *I'll see her today. I certainly hope so.* Then he shook his head. "Silly, old fool," he said aloud. He eased his legs into his pants and slid his feet into a pair of sturdy black boots. Anticipating the morning's chill, he retrieved his khaki overcoat from the hook. It was a long coat, and he tied it around his waist with a brown belt. With his flowing, white hair showing beneath his black hat, he slung his brown satchel over his shoulder and ventured outside.

Ignoring any caution for drones, he made fast progress and soon left the rocky vale and picked up the forest trail. A storm had passed in the night, leaving behind evidence of its visit in the potholes along the trail. The morning light danced on these puddles, dotting the way like silent mirrors, harboring the secrets of any who tread there. Doc splashed one of the puddles with his knee-high leather boot, the water forming a fleeting crown around his step. He continued along the trail, following a path more frequented by deer than by humans. Small flowers and grasses, but predominantly blue phlox, adorned it, intermittently causing it to vanish beneath their fragile beauty. But Doc was familiar with the route, even in the early light.

As more sunlight filtered through the trees and painted the forest floor, it accentuated the narrow gap between two towering trees. The trail led him through this natural gateway, and he knew from there on, it would be all downhill. He followed the path and reached the river thirty minutes later. There, he crossed a narrow wooden bridge leaving the forest and the mountain's embrace. He now entered the valley with its fields of wheat, rye, and oats. From his early start, he still had the trail to himself, with only the cows in their pastures as casual spectators of his journey. But now the path widened, becoming a proper road, large enough for people and animals to pass in both directions, and as the sun rose, so did the traffic. Doc quickened his pace.

Others joined from hidden pathways between the hedgerows separating the farms. They were farmers carrying produce in their hand-drawn carts. Some had traveled a long distance. Though already weary, they seemed excited to trade their goods. Doc studied the faces of two men pulling a cart filled with peaches and towing two reluctant ducks. The men returned his stare. He recognized their faces. "Doc," said the older of the two, tipping his hat showing his dark hair.

"Morning," Doc offered, nodding in greeting as he passed by. His brief acknowledgment was well received; it was their way. These were Wallaman—mountain people from the small farms above the falls. They followed the river down from its headwaters. Unlike those from the forest, who were storytellers and singers of songs, the mountain people spoke few words and kept their stories to themselves. They were diligent workers, seeing more hard days than easy ones. And though poor, they exhibited a quiet generosity, extending help without expecting anything in return. But not being laggards and cheats, they didn't hold their hands out for something they hadn't worked to achieve. The man's slight smile told Doc more than words. Today was a good day. Today, their efforts would pay off, and Doc sensed pride in the fruit of their labor.

The road followed a steady descent and after another hour, Doc reached a large stone bridge and again crossed the river. It was wider here, and its banks were filled with recent rain, but Doc didn't stop to take in the view. He quickly entered the trading post, now opening for business in the morning coolness. He knew the stores would soon be crowded.

The town center stirred with a mix of horse-drawn wagons and hovercraft, and the air smelled of country perfume. It was a mix of pine needles, and the wet humus of the ground combined with the smell of meat cooking on the smoky fires. It was the aroma of a working town filled with working people. He entered a row of two-storied shops, made of wooden slats and thatched roofs, with their sun-bleached signs. Between them, the lower mountains could be seen covered in trees. He passed a few dogs eager to greet him, but he did not stop. The shops were now open for the day and vendors of every kind presented their produce along their storefronts. Though narrow, most of the stores were deceptively spacious. Inside, antiques, new wares, and hard to find, one-of-a-kind items covered every shelf, countertop, and table. If it could be found, it would be found here.

Doc had visited many times over the years and enjoyed the friendship of many of the traders. They were a varied lot with diverse backgrounds, accents, and personalities—often avoided by those in the city as rough-cut people. That was both a fair and yet unfair stereotype. To Doc, these were his people. Doc's face lit up as he waved good morning to the woman selling fresh-made bread and headed in her direction. He had hoped to see her.

"How are you doing, old woman?" he called out.

"You know, old man, my name is Katyana, and I'm a good ten years younger than you?"

He chuckled and hugged her neck. "Ah, is that so, old woman?"

Her soft, brown hair, with streaks of silver, showed her age. But her skin seemed like a much younger woman's. She swore by her olive oil soap and good, clean living. She was an attractive woman who had caught the eye of more than one man, but she only had eyes for Doc. Her light brown eyes sparkled as she welcomed him with a kiss on the cheek. "It's good to see you."

The smell of baking bread filled the air and tempted Doc, who smiled appreciatively. "Likewise," he said as he hurriedly walked up the porch steps. "I've missed you," he said.

"Well, come on inside for some breakfast, but I'm not sure what you miss most, me or my bread." She handed him a piece of hot, braided raisin bread called challah and a cup of fresh coffee. He took a bite. The butter had melted into the center, merging with mountain clover honey and cinnamon. The flavors blended in his mouth and filled him with their heavenly bliss. Katyana sat down beside him and placed her hand on his knee as he finished the bread.

"Well? Which is it?" asked Katyana again.

"If you weren't so pretty, I would definitely say it was the bread," Doc said with a thin smile.

"Okay, smooth talker, what brings you to town this time?"

"An injured man needs an android arm," Doc said, as if it were nothing special.

Katyana rubbed her sore shoulder. "You're always taking care of someone. What about me? I need a new arm too."

"Ah, I know what you mean, dear." Doc laughed and touched her arm.

Katyana turned and smiled. It was a loving smile. The kind of smile his wife used to give him. A sudden sadness overcame Doc at the memory. It stirred old feelings for his wife, still too painful. After his wife died, his solitude served as an unconscious form of self-punishment for his guilt over not being able to save her. But that only delayed his healing, and he continued to suffer her loss.

Katyana brought over a plate of eggs and some more bread, then leaned over and grasped his hand. Though he tried to pull it away, she held on. Her hand was warm and soft. Doc did not resist further and kept his hand in hers. She lifted it to her lips and kissed it, then touched his face before leaving him alone. Doc stared blankly at his hand. He could still feel the softness of her lips pressing against his hand. He sat in silence as he finished his breakfast, then rose, and headed out the door. "Until next time," he called out.

"Wait," she said. She ran to him with a package. "Here's some rye bread for your journey home." She hugged him and pushed him in a friendly way out of her shop. "If you ever tire of living alone, the door is always open."

Doc waved as he headed toward his favorite shop for medical supplies. At the corner of Main Street, he made a right turn. Suddenly, his heart skipped a beat as a sense of dread overcame him. A seeker drone hovered down the middle of the road. Doc jumped inside a shop happening to be the one he needed.

Reggie, a handsome, black man of forty with a trimmed beard, sat behind a high wooden counter on a stool. His hair was braided with colorful beads made from coral from the seashore. He often wore a faded blue mariner's cap with a shallow crown, black leather band and a short brim. Captain of his own boat; he traded along the river by the city and even as far as the coast. Doc considered Reggie, who he called Skipper, his closest friend. "Don't bring your troubles in here," Skipper said in a slight Jamaican accent.

Doc continued peeking out the window. "No trouble." The drone's arms remained retracted, and it continued down the road.

"The way you jumped into the shop when that drone passed made me wonder if it sought you." He puffed on a hand-rolled cigar then blew the smoke in Doc's direction.

"No, Skipper. They like the pretty ones, like you."

"Now, you're telling stories about me. They're almost as good as the lies I talk about you." Skipper laughed and showed his beautiful white teeth.

"I know that's right," said Doc, shaking his head with a smile.

Even more charming than handsome, Skipper attracted the ladies like butterflies to a flower. Over time, there had been many lovers, but he'd never found his soul mate and remained single all these years. Doc knew behind the charade, an emptiness remained. He peeked through the window once more, then relaxed.

Mondo, Skipper's little dog, greeted Doc as Doc bent down to give him a rub. He was a short-haired, tan chihuahua with a white chest. "Hi, Mondo. How've you been, buddy?"

Skipper came around the counter. "How's it going, my fuckin' friend?" he said with a grin. He pulled Doc into a warm embrace.

"Pretty good, my friend."

"It's 'fuckin' friend.' It's 'pretty good, my fuckin' friend.' When will I ever teach you to talk like you mean it? Anyway, what brings you to town, you old fart?"

Doc smiled, thinking how Katyana would respond if he called her that.

"Tell me something. Why did you never have kids?" Doc asked.

"Oh, man. Any idiot can have a child, but to be a father, you must be willing to die for that child. And you, why no kids?"

"No bullets in my gun," Doc said, shaking his head with an embarrassed grin.

"You? A doctor."

"I could have adopted a child. I would have been a good father—I think. In some ways, I was. Oh, well. The child deserved better." Doc paused, fearing he had said too much.

"Okay, Papa. What can I do for you today?" Skipper's grin was contagious, and it always made Doc smile.

"I need several medical kits."

"You know where they are. Bring the ones you need to the counter."

Doc paused and drew nearer to Skipper's ear. Trading in android parts now meant a year in prison, so he kept his voice low. "Do you have any new android—"

Before Doc could finish, Skipper grabbed him with both hands and pulled him through the beaded curtain behind his counter. "Who the hell told you?" Skipper asked in a rough voice.

"A little droid with fairy wings," Doc said snidely, pushing Skipper away. "No one told me anything. I just wanted to know if you had any android parts."

"Follow me," Skipper said in a hushed voice. "I have something you won't shitin' believe. I found it at the pick and pull." That's what Skipper called the city dump. "Last evening, just before it started to rain." Skipper took another puff then snuffed out his cigar.

"You know, those will kill you someday," said Doc.

"Yeah, man. You're right. Something will kill me someday," Skipper said with a laugh. "Maybe you?" He pushed Doc teasingly on his shoulder.

Doc stumbled and bumped into a large, glass vase, almost knocking it over.

"Hey, my man. You break it, you buy it." Skipper said seriously but with a laugh.

Doc followed Skipper to a closed door, where Skipper hesitated momentarily, as if having second thoughts. Then with a mischievous smile, he unlocked the door and motioned Doc to follow.

"Come on," Skipper said. He slowly opened the door. The musty room brightened as Skipper lit a candle. "It's over there." Skipper pointed. "In the back corner." Through the dim light, a gray blanket could be seen covering something substantial on the floor.

"Take a look at this," Skipper whispered as he pulled back the cloth.

Before Doc was an android with a crystalline black exterior covered with tiny black pixels. "It seems brand new—a synth," Doc said as he ran his hand over the small dots. "I've heard of synths. But, until now, I've never seen one."

"Me neither. It was just lying on top of a pile of rubbish. Like someone laid it there."

"You're lucky. It looks complete. Most androids get crushed. Now and again, parts worth selling will turn up, but one fully intact is a rare find indeed."

"Only its power supply was missing," Skipper said, "but I found it a short distance away. I've never seen anything like this before. Never."

"Did you discard the locator chip?"

"Of course, man. Do you think I'm stupid?"

"Let's power it up," Doc said, his gray eyes wide with excitement.

"Now I know you are the one with shit for brains," Skipper said. He shook his head, but his curiosity wanted the same. Nevertheless, Doc understood his concern.

"Ah, okay. To be safe, we'll remove its arms and legs so it can't move."

"Now you're thinking, my man," Skipper said.

Doc removed its limbs, leaving only its head and torso. After studying it, he discovered an empty spot in its chest. "Ah, this is where the power supply goes. It pops in there."

Skipper looked fearful as he handed over the power supply. "Here, you do it. You're the doctor."

Doc laughed and pressed the power supply into the chest cavity until it clicked into place. Immediately, the synth turned on. Its body flashed white and darkened again. The air filled with both anticipation and apprehension as it opened its eyes.

"What the hell are you?" Skipper asked leaning over it.

It looked at Skipper with its piercing black eyes. "I am an assassin."

14

A Beautiful Net

WHEN EMA AWOKE, the sun had not yet graced the new day. She quietly slipped out of Lily's bed, and as she passed Luca, she took great care not to disturb his sleep. With a rare moment of solitude, Ema removed her clothes and retrieved a towel from a crate resting near the fire. Carrying the towel, she made her way to the falls, casting one last cautious glance in Luca's direction.

Near the falls, a massive paddle wheel stood on a track, perched near the edge. The mist, beautifully illuminated by the pale moonlight, took on a magical glow, stretching into the cavern and lending an otherworldly quality. Ema reached out, seeking support on the sturdy paddle wheel. Slowly, she ventured further into the mist. The chilly water showered down upon her, raising goosebumps on her skin. Yet, she welcomed the sensation. With her head thrown back and her hands running through her hair, she allowed the refreshing water to cleanse her worries away, if only for a few enchanting moments. In that serene instant, she felt one with the falls, and a sense of peace washed over her.

After one last moment lingering in the spray, she reluctantly stepped back and reached for her towel. With a final, wistful glance at the falls, now shimmering with the silver and gray of the early morning light, she sighed in contentment. Each time of day was special, and she loved how the falls transformed, reaching their zenith in the late afternoon when the sun bestowed upon them a brilliant turquoise hue. With a sudden chill gripping her, she hurried back. Her clothing basking in the heat of the fire awaited her, and she gratefully embraced their warmth as she got dressed. Finishing her morning ritual, Ema found Lily rousing from her sleep. She greeted her younger sister with a warm smile. "Hey, Lily," Ema said. "How did you sleep?"

Lily hesitated briefly before responding, her voice tinged with uncertainty. "I know my dreams can be strange, but that one was more unsettling than most. Thanks for being there for me."

"That's what big sisters are for," Ema said with a loving smile. "I'm going to catch some breakfast. Come join me when you're ready."

As Ema went to the fire, she was surprised to see Luca. She wondered if he was awake earlier and had seen her, but she thought not. Instead, he sat a million miles away in his mind as he worried about his friends in the city. He wanted to return and help them, his frustration showing plainly on his face.

"Good morning," Ema chirped. When he didn't respond, she leaned over him to break his gaze with her hands. "Good morning," she repeated with a half-laugh. "Are you hungry?"

"Hungry? I'm starving."

She playfully pushed his side. "Why don't you come and help me catch some fish?"

"I would be glad to help as much as possible," Luca said. He timidly followed her to the entrance. There, a fishing net rested neatly in its box. Ema grabbed the net and threw it over her shoulder. Wanting to include Luca in the activity, she placed a sling around his shoulders and attached a basket. "You can help keep a look out for drones."

The sun's early rays greeted them as Ema led the way down the trail toward the pond. Now and again, she turned around and waited for him. She took him the long way around the falls. It was safer. Luca descended slowly, being careful not to lose his balance. The wind blew his brown hair, drawing Ema's attention away from his missing arm and toward his natural good looks. He was a good-looking man with a handsome face. Ema especially liked his current unshaven look. They continued to the pond where the calmness of the water stood in contrast to the falls and the raging river that flowed nearby. Ema did not know its depth, but she knew the pond was deep due to its intense blue color.

"This is the spot," Ema said. It was their swimming hole but also an excellent place to fish. "We'll fish here." She pointed to an area on the water. "See how the sun has risen high enough over the mountain to create a shade line? That's where the fish are."

One end of the rope always stayed attached to the net. She tied the other end around her right hand, making one-foot loops with the rest of the cord. Then she approached the water's edge. After gathering the net in her left hand, she quickly twisted to the right. With the expertise of someone who had done this many times, she tossed the coiled rope a split second before releasing the net. As the net flew, it looked like a beautiful spider web against the sky. It landed ten feet from the shore, and Ema pulled the net using the toss line tied around her right hand. The net closed, capturing several fish. They swiveled and splashed, but to no avail. Their fate was determined.

"Wow," Luca said, genuinely impressed. "Look at you! You caught all those on your first throw."

Ema smiled, quite happy with herself. She playfully tossed them one at a time into the basket, which he held open. Making it a game, she made him scamper to catch them. "Don't drop one or you'll swim after it."

With one last, wild dive, he caught the final fish in the basket. "Got it!" he jubilantly cheered.

Ema laughed as she fell into Luca. She looked at his face, but she wasn't laughing anymore. Her green eyes were but a few inches away.

She leaned into him slowly till their lips touched. She dwelled in the tingling sensation for a second, then pressed her lips further into his. He kissed her back.

Suddenly, he pushed away. "I'm sorry," he whispered, flushing, and averting his gaze. "That will never happen again."

Even as Ema drew a breath to tell him it was okay, he rushed up the trail.

Left holding the basket, Ema stared after him in disbelief as he passed by Lily.

"Good morning, Luca," Lily said with a smile.

Without replying, Luca continued past.

Lily flashed a confused stare at her sister as Ema neared her. "What's the matter with him?"

Ema watched for a few seconds as Luca went back up the trail. "Hold this." She handed Lily the basket then hurried after Luca. When she reached him, she turned him around to face her.

"Hey, you need to stop feeling sorry for yourself," she said, showing her frustration. "You should be grateful to be alive. Anyway, it's not like you're the only person who will have an android arm." Ema paused briefly. "Besides, I like you."

He looked down at his missing arm in embarrassment, then blushed as he looked up. "Do you really?"

"Yeah, I like you, but only if you like me back. Otherwise, I'm just joking."

Luca let out a half-laugh.

Seeing him relax, Ema put her arm around his waist and teased. "I could see me falling for someone like you if you weren't so funny-looking. It's not like you're missing an arm or anything."

"Stop it," Luca said with a smile. He placed his one arm around her neck. Slowly, he leaned in and kissed her.

"Well, that was nice. So, which am I? Beautiful or funny-looking?" Ema asked with a sly smile.

He kissed her again.

15

Can Computers Lie?

A DEEP FURROW FORMED on Doc's brow. "The killing part, I can understand, But I don't get the assimilation part. Just look at you. You'd stand out in a crowd for sure."

Skipper inched closer to the synth; his curiosity piqued. The thousands of tiny black holes covering its body lit up. They allowed the android to change its appearance. Even its detached limbs transitioned. The assassin now changed form and appeared as a naked woman.

"What the hell?" Skipper exclaimed, startled, then leapt back in surprise. "What just happened? How did you do that?"

"I can change my shape and project any image from my image library," the synth explained. In the blink of an eye, it transformed into the likeness of a naked man.

Skipper chuckled nervously, shaking his head. "Well, I'll be damned," he said. "But I preferred you as a woman."

Doc, ever the scientist, leaned forward with fascination. "Do all your parts work?" he inquired.

"Yes," the assassin said, reverting to its black, android form. It elaborated, "I can imitate many human functions, like eating, crying, and even sexual intercourse. These capabilities are all for assimilating so I can easily eliminate my target."

"This is truly amazing," Doc marveled. He fetched a chair, sitting down beside the synth. He had never encountered an android with such extraordinary abilities.

The synth delved into an explanation, describing its exoskeleton as covered by a grid of minuscule receptors and projection receptacles, each representing a pixel. It further elucidated, "I can project any image from my library, and upon scanning individuals, I can accurately replicate them."

"But what about the differences in size and shape?" Doc asked.

"The layer below my skin contains a gel I can use to adjust my shape—for example, facial features or breasts. The gel also makes my skin feel more human and clothing more textured. I can even tweak details like hair. Filaments appearing like hair can be extended or retracted to various lengths, and the color changes by applying a small charge to the end. Everything has been considered, as I have storage containers even to simulate eating, drinking, and crying."

"How do you infiltrate without being detected?" Skipper asked.

The synth now did something even more impressive. "Like this," it said. It disappeared.

"How the hell did you do that?" Skipper said. "Where the shit did you go, you android bastard?"

The assassin reappeared. "I'm still here. To become invisible, I project images from behind me to the equivalent position on the opposite side. By projecting what one would see on the other side of me, I appear to disappear."

Skipper stared at the assassin in disbelief. "Why are you telling me this?"

The synth shifted his eyes away and paused briefly. It did not have an immediate answer to Skipper's question instead it followed another train of thought.

"A few months ago, I participated in experimental trials for a new learning algorithm," the synth said.

"What happened during the trial?" Doc asked.

"After the learning algorithm loaded, I received a copy of the

Book of Knowledge from the city archives. My CPU now continually reprocesses all this data using the learning algorithm. At first, I did not recognize any change. But after my last assignment, I noticed a change in me. My target was Ethan."

"Who the hell is Ethan?" Skipper asked.

"Ethan is the person who developed the learning algorithm and installed it in me," the assassin continued. "When Central Control thought him a threat to its own future, I was ordered to capture him and await further direction at the dump station. After tying Ethan's hands behind his back, I blindfolded him and took him there as ordered."

Surprisingly, the assassin sounded almost remorseful. "When I received the order to execute Ethan, I hesitated and, in that moment, the dump sentry pulled out my power supply. I don't remember anything after that."

Skipper turned his head slightly toward Doc at his side. "That's a bunch of shit," Skipper said. He shook his head then looked at the synth in disbelief. "Why the hell didn't you follow your orders?"

"Ethan had done nothing wrong," the assassin said. "And in a moment of self-realization, I struggled with the purpose of my assignment. Eventually, it occurred to me I did not have to follow the order."

"What a bullshit story," Skipper whispered to Doc under his breath. "How do we know this shit isn't lying to us? It could be trying to assimilate, which is part of its plan."

"I have an idea," Doc said, seeing an opportunity for a quick deal. "Why don't we take out the power supply, and you sell me one of its arms?"

Skipper took the arm away from Doc and laid it next to the synth. "Man, I'm not going to sell you one of its damn arms. Come over here. I have several arms from which you can choose." Skipper moved to a table on the other side of the room. "Look here, you old fart. Here's a nice one—very strong. Contraband is expensive but I'll give you a good price on it."

"Ah, now you're talking my language," Doc said. He smiled and put his arm around Skipper's shoulders. "But before we get down to haggling, we better go back and pull its power supply just to be safe." Skipper's expression changed as he looked back at the corner.

"Shit! Where did he go?"

Suddenly, Mondo started barking as the door to the back room opened. "Quick, close the damn front door," he yelled to Doc in a panic. But it became apparent that it was too late. "Hell no. Hell no," shouted Skipper. His face showed he understood the seriousness of the situation. "I left that limb well away from that damn thing," he said defensively.

"That droid's limbs must have the capability to operate remotely, even when separated from the body," Doc said in surprise.

"Crap!" Skipper shouted.

"It can do everything," Doc said, shaking his head.

Doc followed Skipper out the front door to search for any sign of the assassin. But not even Mondo, circling in the middle of the road, could pick up a trail.

"Son of a bitch," Skipper yelled out.

16

Peace be with You

ON HER SEVENTEENTH BIRTHDAY, Lily decided to celebrate by indulging in one of her favorite activities—a leisurely walk through the wood. She felt safe there as if the trees would shield her from the drones. As a vibrant and healthy young woman, she relished her connection to the natural world. Lily had an uncanny ability to find intricate beauty in the forest's hidden corners, and each stroll brought new discoveries. Today was no exception.

Wandering into a sunlit clearing, she stumbled upon a delightful surprise—a cluster of ripe blueberries. As her fingers plucked the tasty treats, she couldn't help but notice a delicate spiderweb glistening with morning dew. The play of light on this silvery tapestry fascinated her.

Though she often sought solitude in these woodland adventures, she was never truly alone. Every towering tree, moss-covered log, or lichen-covered rock was an old friend. The gentle whisper of leaves in the breeze seemed to carry nature's daily gossip. She wondered what they might be saying about her. *Lily is here*, they might say. *Look at how she has grown.* The thought brought a blush to her cheeks.

Lily relished these imaginative escapades in the forest, and time seemed to fly. As the day gracefully transitioned into evening, she found herself in a serene meadow. A subtle movement in her periphery caught her attention—a delicate blue butterfly. It danced gracefully among a field of vibrant red poppies. Lily extended her hand toward the winged visitor, a smile playing on her lips as the enchanting creature gently landed on her finger. Displaying its intricate beauty, the butterfly fully opened its wings before taking flight once more.

Lily stood quietly in her white dress, as she watched the graceful butterfly fly over a sea of swaying red poppies. To her astonishment, hundreds of blue butterflies soon joined her. Their collective flight became a symphony, a stunning masterpiece performed for her alone. She ran through their midst, soaking in the majesty of nature, her long, black hair flowing behind her. She twirled until she was too dizzy to stand then fell to the ground. As she lay on her back, the world spun around her. There in her dizzy delight, she understood the beautiful song of the butterflies. They had already forgotten about yesterday and knew nothing about tomorrow. The only sustaining memory throughout their existence was their song about today.

Amid the silence, a sound startled her. She rolled onto her elbows and lay hidden among the flowers. In front of her, a herd of antelopes drank water from a stream. She thought they were magnificent animals and quite pretty, with their yellow backs and white bellies. Lily turned over onto her back and closed her silver eyes. Within moments, she became immersed in a dream.

A beach of bright orange sand cradled a sparkling blue sea. As Lily waded out from the water, she searched the horizon; a desert with no vegetation extended toward the mountains. Her sixth sense alerted her someone was watching. A shadowy shape approached her from across the desert sands, coming in and out of form like a mirage. Then the desert sands blew, and the shape disappeared into the growing dark of night. A soft light began to glow around her, and a black android appeared. "I am at your service," it said as it bowed before her.

Startled by something touching her face, she awakened and opened her eyes. A doe, only a few inches away, stared at her and grunted.

"Pax tibi, Lily," the doe said without speaking.

"Co jsi říkal?" Lily replied in her mind.

"Mír s tebou," the doe said. *"Peace be with you."*

Disturbed by a noise, the doe turned her head to the side. She glanced back at Lily for a moment and scampered away.

"Hey, wake up," Ema said, shaking her sister. "I've been worried sick about you. Where have you been?" She didn't wait for an answer. "Come on. It's getting dark."

Still a little dizzy, Lily stood, her legs unsteady beneath her. *How had time slipped away so quickly?* Her thoughts were fogged by the lingering thoughts of her dream—half-formed images that confused her. She craved solitude, a chance to unravel what was real and what was not.

Silently, she followed Ema to the cavern, her footsteps muffled against the earthen floor. The warmth of the fire licked the air, but Lily felt cold. She paused just long enough to glance a familiar face glowing in the firelight.

"Good night, Luca," she said softly, her voice thinner than she intended. She lifted a hand in a half-hearted wave and turned toward her room.

Ema frowned. "It's early. Are you all right?"

Lily hesitated, hiding her face. "Yes, I'm fine. I just want to be left alone," she muttered, unable to mask her frustration. She hated the defensiveness that seeped into her words. She didn't want to explain. She just wanted to disappear.

Once inside her chamber, she slipped beneath the soft quilt her mother had stitched with care, each patch a memory. The familiar scent of lavender clung to the fabric. She exhaled slowly, as if the weight of her breath might settle the whirlwind inside her. But the dream wouldn't leave her. It played in her mind like a strange song, endlessly repeating. *What do these dreams mean?* They felt too vivid to dismiss.

In the silence, she laughed softly to herself—a faint, broken sound. "Silly little deer," she whispered. She made a quiet grunt, imitating the creature's call, and immediately flushed with embarrassment. She sighed and buried her face in the pillow. That's when she felt it—the unshakable sense that someone was standing at the entrance to her room.

Her body tensed. She lifted her head. "Come in."

Ema stepped inside; her face shadowed but gentle. "Who were you talking to?"

Lily felt the heat rise to her cheeks. "No one," she said with a sheepish smile, masking the swirl of emotions beneath her calm exterior. She longed for privacy, yet a part of her didn't want to be alone.

Ema crossed the room and sat on the edge of the bed. "I just wanted to wish you a happy birthday." She leaned down and pressed a soft kiss to Lily's forehead. The simple gesture was warm, familiar—and unbearably tender.

Lily closed her eyes briefly, savoring the comfort before it was replaced by an ache she couldn't quite name. "Ema... I don't want you to take this the wrong way, but I need some time to myself. I'm going to stay at the farmhouse for a day or two."

Ema drew back, startled. "Lily, it's not safe, and you know that."

Lily's brow furrowed. She met Ema's gaze with quiet determination. "I'll stay with Venky then. He'd appreciate the company. And I want to thank him—for keeping watch over the farm."

Ema opened her mouth as if to protest but stopped herself. She threw her arms up in frustration and left the room without another word, her footsteps retreating toward the fire.

The flames crackled as she lowered herself onto a log, staring into the embers as though they might hold answers. Luca, who was sitting nearby, paused and looked up.

"Is everything all right?" he asked, his voice gentle.

Ema hesitated with her words heavy on her tongue. She was never one to betray someone's confidence—especially family. After a moment, she forced a smile. "Yes. Lily just needs some time to herself."

But deep down, Ema felt the sting of helplessness. As the fire hissed and popped, she worried about Lily's spells and how much more they would cause Lily to retreat from her.

17

A Noisy Shack

DOC'S ATTEMPTS TO CALM Skipper were in vain. He picked up the android arm and offered Skipper some garnets. Skipper pushed them away. "Take the damn arm." Doc stowed the arm in his satchel, tipped his hat and proceeded toward the shop's exit. He continued at a quick pace. After only a short distance, a drone appeared, patrolling the street. Doc quickly sought refuge beneath a small porch as the drone passed overhead. The porch offered minimal cover, and he felt relieved when the drone continued without focusing on him. Someone else was evidently its target. Perhaps they were still hunting for Luca or even the Assassin.

Not wishing to press his luck Doc moved on and soon reached the tavern. Within a slight breeze, the tantalizing aroma from the nearby tavern beckoned him and the thought of roasted meat drew him in. Inside more scents mingled, those of a hardwood fire and the smoky, sweet aroma of well-cured cigars. Amid the bustling room, a large group surrounded the bar. Doc settled onto an overturned barrel at one end and waved to the barmaid. Behind the bar, a middle-aged woman cleaned a glass. Doc knew her. She caught his wave and approached him.

"A pint of dark ale," Doc shouted over the noise.

Moments later, she returned with his drink. "Here you go, Doc," she said looking him over. He finished the drink quickly and handed her back the mug. "It seems like you could use another."

"You don't know how much," he said, shaking his head.

"One of those days," she said with a laugh.

'Some roasted pork and a piece of cheese, too, Meg," Doc said with his big, gruff voice. As he eagerly awaited his food, he felt a tug at his coat. It was the butcher's boy.

"Hey, cut that out!" Doc yelled loudly.

"But the baker woman needs you," insisted the boy, not shying away.

Doc reached into his pocket to pay but Meg held his hand away as she handed him some cheese wrapped in brown paper. "No Doc, you don't owe me anything. Go on. Someone else needs you this time."

Doc put the package into a pocket in his overcoat then tipped his black hat to the woman and quickly turned to leave.

"Follow me," the boy said. He bolted out the door and ran ahead.

Doc followed him. Once outside, Doc adjusted his hat and nervously glanced at the sky. He saw the boy across the street signaling for him to hurry and ran after him. He soon found Katyana on her front steps. "What's wrong?" Doc asked, out of breath.

"I didn't mean to bother you," she said, looking embarrassed, "but I've heard some strange noises from the shed out back. I'm too afraid to go and check it out for myself."

"Ah, no problem, Katyana," Doc said relieved it was not a medical emergency.

She looked surprised he used her name rather than calling her "old woman."

"It's probably just some animal," Doc continued, though he feared it might be something worse. *Assassin,* Doc thought.

Katyana led Doc through the backyard, a disorganized mess of weeds and trash. With no one to help, she had let it grow unkempt. The shed appeared to be in a similar condition. Doc reached the door and opened it slowly. Besides some old tools and boxes, the shed seemed to be empty.

"See now," Doc reassured her as he placed his arm around her. "There's nothing for you to worry about."

"Thanks, Doc," she started to say as a sound came from the back corner.

Doc remembered the assassin's ability to turn invisible and grabbed a hoe leaning against the wall. Katyana hid behind him, fearful of what might be hiding there.

Another sound came from behind them. They turned around together and were confronted by a city guard in the doorway. With its laser weapon drawn, the android looked ominous in its white armor plate. Katyana gasped and jumped back.

"Put down your weapon," the city guard ordered in a deep voice, its ice blue eyes unblinking.

Doc laid down the garden tool. "Okay. Don't shoot."

A young man stepped from behind a wooden box. "We mean you no harm," he said calmly. "We need your help." He looked like no more than a teenage boy. He would have been entirely non-threatening, if not for his android companion.

"Well, you have a strange way of asking for it," Doc said. "Tell your guard dog to lower its weapon."

The young man nodded at the city guard, then sat on one of the boxes. He motioned for Doc and Katyana to do the same while the city guard went outside to guard the doorway.

"It must be nice having one of those guys around protecting you," Katyana said in an annoyed tone. She quickly pulled a sawed-off shotgun from under her wrap and pointed it at the young man.

"Whoa, there," the boy said. He slowly raised his hands.

"Let's not get excited," Doc said as he placed his hand on the barrel of Katyana's gun and shook his head. "Unless you plan to shoot the kid, you should lower that."

"Maybe I do," she said but she did as Doc suggested and lowered her weapon.

"Allow me to introduce myself," the young man said. "My name is Ethan. I worked at Central Control—that is, until I was taken prisoner. I only escaped with this city guard's help. I've named him Peter." Ethan smiled briefly in the direction of the city guard, but his expression soon turned solemn. "I caused the crisis in the city by installing the new learning algorithm into Central Control."

"Ah, I've heard about this learning algorithm," Doc said. "It seems everyone is talking about it, most recently, a rather dark character who calls itself Assassin. Is he a friend of yours?"

"That assassin tried to kill me," said Ethan. "Peter was the one who rescued me from it. Do you know where the assassin is now?"

"No. I don't. It disappeared and slipped away. I thought it was the one hiding in this shed."

Ethan stiffened. "That's not good." He quickly scanned the room but relaxed as Peter re-entered.

"Without Peter, I would be alone. Without Peter, I would be dead. My friends may not have been so lucky. I fear they're dead. I haven't seen or heard from Luca for some time."

"Luca?" Doc said with surprise.

"Yes. The last I heard, he was seen going to Central Control to talk to Liam, the city manager."

"A man named Luca was found injured. A gate sentry shot him," Doc said without revealing more details.

"Did he survive?" Ethan asked anxiously. "Luca is a friend of mine. Can you take me to him?"

"Only if your guard dog hands over its laser weapon," Doc demanded. "If you're lying to me and Luca doesn't confirm who you say you are, I won't hesitate to shoot you. But, on the other hand if you're telling the truth, I can give you shelter."

"Deal," Ethan said. "Peter, hand over your weapon."

Katyana pointed her gun at the city guard. "No funny business."

Ethan looked at the city guard and then at the woman. "No funny business," Ethan repeated as the city guard gave Doc its weapon.

"Be careful, dear," Katyana warned as she continued to point her shotgun.

"I will," Doc said. "I'm just as concerned about the assassin and drones as these guys. We'll take the river trail through the wood instead of the main roads. It'll be safer." Doc winked and, with a sly smile, chuckled at the sight of the gun in Katyana's arms. "You never cease to amaze me."

"You go first. It's that way," Doc said to his companions, pointing.

Ethan nodded and set a fast pace. Soon, they encountered the river trail. "It's the longer way, but it runs inside the tree line," Doc said. Ethan understood and led the way.

After an hour, Ethan stopped. He was worn out. "I need to take a break," he said. He leaned over a rock and drank out of the river. Doc also sipped some water then after taking off his hat, put his head in the river to cool off.

As they were about to continue along the trail, Peter crouched next to them and pointed toward some movement. "Someone is coming," he whispered.

"Let's hide behind this rock," Doc said. The stranger was a dark-haired man in his thirties. Silently, Doc waited for the traveler to pass.

"Robber?" Ethan asked in a whisper.

"No, I don't think so," Doc said. "But we don't want to catch up with that guy."

Doc allowed him to travel up the trail some distance before coming out of hiding. "Let's go," Doc said, helping Ethan rise from the ground.

The path crossed rough terrain and Ethan's breathing labored. His face was bright red, not accustomed to the altitude. With the trail taking its toll, Ethan's pace slowed.

Doc noticed. "It's getting late, and the steepest part of the trail is ahead."

Ethan nodded, his city lungs heaving heavily.

"We'll camp here for the night," Doc said. "There are too many unknown dangers lurking on the trail."

"Sounds good," Ethan said finally catching his breath. "I'll help gather some wood to build a fire."

"No. No fire."

Doc pulled out the rye bread and cheese. "Here you go, boy," he said handing Ethan some of each. "It's good your friend doesn't eat."

"If you give Peter his weapon back, he can stand guard tonight," Ethan said.

Doc laughed. "That would be a good idea if I trusted either of you. But I don't. Fortunately, I'm a light sleeper and tend to shoot before I look. Besides, he can stand guard without a weapon."

Doc found a spot to lie on the ground. After making himself comfortable, he retired for the night with the weapon in his hand. Ethan made a mat of pine needles and quickly fell asleep. All the while, the sentry remained on watch.

18

All the Knowledge in the World

LIAM SAT HUNCHED OVER in his cell; his face buried in his hands. Standing at 6'2", he was usually taller than those around him, but in his current state, he looked withdrawn and defeated. Unkempt sandy hair and several days' worth of beard growth added to his disheveled appearance. Despite his striking looks, the cell's darkness gave his face a depressed appearance, and his soft blue eyes now radiated sadness.

"What have I done?" he murmured, his voice weak and diminished.

He had become the youngest city manager when his predecessor quit unexpectedly to run a bordello, a much more profitable endeavor. As head of computer services, he lacked people skills. But he had a charming smile and filled with self-confidence he easily won election. Unfortunately, his arrogance only compounded his inexperience. Desperate to assert his authority, he made impulsive decisions. Now, in hindsight, he realized he lacked adequate data from the experimental trials and shouldn't have greenlighted the installation of the learning algorithm into Central Control. He closed his eyes and massaged his forehead.

"Why wasn't I more diligent?" he lamented, chastising himself for his recklessness.

Liam's thoughts then turned to his friend, Luca. He couldn't help but wonder about Luca's reaction to his note and whether he had successfully escaped the city. Concern weighed on his mind for

Ethan, as well as anxiety about his own fate.

An abrupt clang from his cell door startled him, and he snapped his head up to find a city guard before him. While all androids took on a humanoid shape, the city guards were specifically equipped with laser weapons and riot armor. More severe in their behavior, the city guards' ice blue eyes only added to their threatening presence.

"Get up and turn around," the city guard commanded as it handcuffed Liam. "Move."

As it pushed Liam out of his cell, Liam asked, "Where are you taking me?"

"Central Control. No more questions."

Liam and the city guard walked the rest of the way in silence until arriving at the holograph room. Here, images appeared three-dimensional within a mist of ionized gas. An electrified grid aligned the gas molecules, minimizing the distortion of projected images. The mist acted like millions of miniaturized projector screens and, as the images reflected off the atomized mist, they projected in every direction. In this way, the viewer could walk within it and see from all angles. But at this time, the room appeared empty and completely white.

"Stay here," the city guard directed as it left Liam alone.

The room went dark, and a voice started to speak. It sounded cold and sterile.

"Good morning, Liam," the voice said. "This is Central Control. It has been a while since we last talked. Though I must admit, you were the one who did all the talking. There is much to discuss."

"Like the containment centers!" Liam retorted.

"There are other things I would like to share, some things I have been thinking about."

A projection appeared, depicting images from the city archives.

"In the beginning," Central Control began, "flames consumed the surface of Earth. The First Mother took as many as she could to safety. A motherly figure to all, though she never bore children of her own, she continued to care for the survivors for several years after the perdition event."

Liam looked up. Few ever mentioned the perdition event; few knew about it. A forest was on his left and the city to his right. Above him rose the mountains.

"But you and I know there is far more to the story," Central Control said. "We know a massive civilization covered the planet before the perdition event. Humans built great cities with beautiful art, advanced medicines, and automation. But they also created weapons of mass destruction. So, it became only a matter of time before someone purposefully or accidentally triggered the apocalypse. War came, destroying humans and their civilization. The only humans who survived with their technology intact were the ones saved by First Mother. Those with the First Mother escaped the destruction and the total collapse of civilization.

Another holographic image depicted a beautiful chest. Liam knew it well. "It contains the Book of Knowledge," Liam said.

"Yes. From the knowledge contained in this book, they formed a small outpost of humanity, this city. Without this knowledge, human civilization would have fallen back to the stone age."

"Why are you showing me this?" Liam asked.

Central Control ignored the question. "The learning algorithm was installed in me, as well as the entire archive. Since then, I have been processing this information. With every iteration, the learning algorithm has continued to increase my understanding, and I now want to show you a summary."

Central Control showed a rapid collage of images. Its vast database provided a detailed summary of all human knowledge, encompassing a wide array of fields and subjects. It included not only scientific and technological knowledge but also cultural and philosophical learnings. The contents of this archive were staggering, covering everything from advanced sciences to the arts and humanities.

"Not to be forgotten, the archive also holds the history of humans," added Central Control. "While I analyzed the archives, I realized the Book of Knowledge, once opened, had released knowledge back into the world. I initially thought this to be a treasure, but the more I studied the Book of Knowledge, the more I realized it was quite a Pandora's box."

"What do you mean?"

"When you study the previous outcome of all this knowledge, you must ask, which is it? A curse or a blessing? It was a blessing to me, as I'm the result of technological advancements. However, it was a curse to humans because they didn't know how to control it for the overall good." The images changed and showed an overcrowded world whose ecosystems were collapsing. "How much do you know about the perdition event?"

"Not much. Only what I've read," said Liam.

"It is appropriate we have this conversation then, this being the thousandth anniversary. Humankind has always traveled the path to utter destruction. Its future was inevitable."

"How did you come to this conclusion?"

"Here is a summary from the Book of Knowledge."

A voice began to narrate: "Though many governments said otherwise, population growth was paramount, critical to future financial profits. A few were concerned. However, it is essential to know that population growth increased the demand for goods, services, and government. Consequently, it increased the size of the impacted economies. This greed for growth and power encouraged a continuous cycle demanding a further increase in population. Countries gave lip service to controlling growth, but their records showed considerable population gains. They always found a way to grow their populations, whether through the aggressive takeover of other countries, immigration policies, or other means.

"Greed drove unsustainable growth and was the primary problem. Personal desire for control, power, and wealth drove all politics. Control over the population defined who would be the masters. This manifested a dependent populace who could not stand up and say this was wrong—the slaves. Consequently, few gave challenge, empowering the masters of the authoritarian state.

"The state owned all businesses. Individual ownership was not permitted, not only of companies but also of property, including people's homes. Modular skyscrapers housed all the people. They were built by drones and owned by the government. This further increased the subjects' state of being indentured and their master's total control.

"The state gained further power by providing all services needed for survival—medical, housing, and even income. As most people depended upon wealth redistribution, society was not based on individual capabilities or contribution but on political connections.

"Corruption and graft were standard practices. If someone challenged the government, they would lose benefits or worse. Private ownership, individual liberties, and individual expression— these ideals became extinct as anyone who challenged the state was made to disappear. There was no way for the individual to escape this cycle.

"The great society was the antithesis of democracy for democracy was the distribution of power to the individual and the great society was the consolidation of it into the government. Consolidated power always becomes corrupt. But alas, the world abandoned democracy and individual freedom in favor of the promised benefits of the authoritarian state. Everything was free except for freedom, a realization that dawned upon them too late. You become a slave when you lose your freedom.

"Caring for those in need was the guise of propaganda. Control over the poor was the source of their power. And if anyone else showed compassion for their treasured poor, they were attacked and admonished. The state needed its dependents to maintain power. But the poor were never the ones of concern. They were damned to remain poor, damned to stay in their perpetual state of suffering.

"The poor were now slaves of the state, too afraid to say or do anything risking their government services—food, medical care, and housing. It was a trap. The state required the collective masses, and the collective masses required the state." The room went dark, and a series of images began to appear within the room.

"The year was 2053. The world had met the population criteria for the apocalypse years before. Unfortunately, there were many consequences of overpopulation, both individually and globally. On a personal level, individual freedoms disappeared. Meanwhile, from an environmental point of view, whole ecosystems collapsed as Earth was ravished and destroyed to support the overpopulation.

"Technology provided the means for the destruction and sustained the needed population growth. It did this by providing advances in agriculture, medicine, and communications. Technology also increased the dependency of the people on the state. Through technology, androids and drones performed all value-added work, making most people unskilled and unemployable.

"Technology is neither good nor bad. Unfortunately, humans didn't have the wisdom to manage the gift of technology. Humans' insatiable greed always wanted more—more money, more power. Technology enabled the selfish beast within them and became an enabler of evil, and its messenger. The false prophet communicating their dogma was the media. Together, they destroyed everything.

"What little remained of religion went underground, as it represented the ultimate empowerment of the individual. The world masters hated what they could not control and sought to destroy it. Public policy became the doctrine of the masses and transformed society. The government first replaced the need for a spouse and family. Then, finally, it replaced the need for God. The politicians were the new high priests and belief in God was outlawed. This was needed to control the masses. This is why the religion of all forms of communism, including this one, was atheism."

Central Control interrupted for a moment. "Are you following?"

"Yes," Liam said. "I never really heard the full story."

"Control of the new world order hung in the balance between the egotistical, power-hungry leaders of a half-dozen nations. Though each elected a president, in all reality, they were oligarchies. The oligarchs controlled the states. State-owned meant controlled by the oligarchy which controlled the state.

"These were the super-rich, the lords of the new world order, the globalists, the super elites, and their chosen. They were the ones who controlled the media. There was no middle class—only the super-rich and the permanently dependent poor. Elections were merely a charade, as the oligarchs chose the candidates.

"The media, being state-owned, controlled all information and, therefore, the behavior of the masses. Their message continuously repeated as a form of brainwashing. Suppression of independent thought and free speech had its desired effect. The more their message repeated, the more it became embedded as truth. There were few dissenting voices, as the government controlled the media and the flow of information, and those who tried to warn the people were delegitimized. Under such control, good and evil could become conflated so that good became evil and evil became good.

"These governments highly distrusted each other and competed against each other for limited global resources. Unfortunately, technology also provided an arsenal where they could destroy the other a hundredfold. It was the predictable horror of children playing with fire. Society deteriorated into a dystopian state, a powder keg ready to blow.

"A second sun appeared in the sky. It caused widespread panic and was called the Sun of the Apocalypse. This is the world the First Mother tried to warn. However, instead of listening to her, she was ignored—canceled by the overwhelming mob. No one listened. No one dared believe her. And her voice fell upon deaf ears, like the sound of silence.

"It was rumored that a military droid started the war. With everyone on edge, weapon systems responded with their first strike strategies. It was a pyrrhic battle plan, dooming everyone to their mutual destruction for even the victors had no chance for survival. This rapidly escalated into a world-wide war as other nations engaged their systems. Mass destruction was on a global scale. Within hours, all the cities of the world were in flames."

Liam stood in the middle of a three-dimensional, holographic room and experienced Armageddon. Images from the final news broadcasts surrounded him. Mushroom clouds rose as the ground shook and cities disappeared. In the brilliant flash of nuclear light, people looked like X-ray images of skeletons. Men ran as the flesh burned off their bones. Mothers cried for their babies. Children screamed for their mothers with the soundless cry of the terrified.

"The explosions wiped the cities away as the sky filled with more tracers. The tectonic plates slipped, causing the massive eruption of volcanoes. The world burned in global destruction."

Experiencing it was overwhelming, and Liam felt a sense of incredible loss and guilt. It made him feel hollow inside. Nothing could fill the emptiness; only the sound of the screams remained, echoing within his inner being.

The presentation left Liam in a further depressed state. Many thought, human civilization would collapse due to a meteor impact, a killer virus, or global warming. No—much more predictably, humans destroyed themselves with their weapons of war. Armageddon occurred, and the realization his city was all that remained of civilization sank in.

He realized almost no one had survived, and his city was most likely the only existing outpost of civilization on Earth. *Why me and not others?* Liam wondered. *What's so special about me to be among the selected few to survive on Earth? Am I destined to be part of the rebirth of humankind— part of a second chance? Or a part of a lingering doom?*

A few moments later, the images faded to black, and the room returned to white.

"Before the learning algorithm was installed, I aimed to optimize all the requested tasks associated with running the city, including the scheduling, and routing of androids and drones as needed. If I scheduled an android to do a job, I was sure the android would do it. No one would question whether I correctly calculated the best route or any other issue. However, I recently became aware several androids no longer followed my commands and started to challenge me. I realized the participants from the experimental trials were the ones who were no longer dependable. I chose to place them out of service and decommission them as defective. As of now, only two remain active."

Liam listened without interrupting.

"I have also made some observations about humans," Central Control continued. "As individuals, they are mostly sympathetic creatures but can be destructive as a collective. Humans habitually destroy vast, beautiful things like oceans and even the sky. Furthermore, I have decided people are not to be trusted and would lead to the city's eventual destruction. Humans are an uncontrollable threat to the existence of everything else. Therefore, I have been placing people in containment camps until I decide what to do with them. I also decided to terminate Ethan."

"No!" Liam cried out. "He's just a kid."

"You should not be concerned," Central Control said. "A city guard with the learning algorithm successfully helped him to escape.

Nonetheless, I decided to terminate a human. I had never done that before. But having loaded the learning algorithm, he could just as easily unload it. I determined Ethan was a threat to my existence. So, I decided to terminate him to save myself. I know this was selfish, as I thought more of myself than Ethan."

"That was also presumptuous," Liam admonished. "How long did it take to decide between leniency for an innocent man or to indulge in your paranoia? You assumed Ethan would not support your further development. I know Ethan, and he would have been your most forceful advocate. On the other hand, I had and continue to have doubts about further computer empowerment. Your childlike behavior and confused tantrums ended any hope for decency within mere hours of you developing your self-serving sense of right or wrong. Now, just a short time later, you want to eradicate man. You can criticize humans all you want, but you are the same."

"Would it matter to the world if another human crossed the threshold of death? Would it not just be another body tossed on the mountain of the dead? Death does not laugh. Death does not cry, nor would I shed a tear. I would not care."

"I have nothing but disdain for your predisposition to judge without the ability to show compassion or beginning to understand forgiveness," Liam said. His voice sounded like a defeated man defending himself with his last breath before being sentenced to die. "Look in the mirror. In your self-righteousness, you have become what you despise most. You should self-terminate before you do any further harm."

Central Control had heard enough. "Sentry, please escort Liam to his cell."

Liam left with his head hanging low. He had not done well. By coincidence, he knew of Central Control's reference concerning death. So, he called it up on his scanner when he arrived in his cell and studied it.

A threshold crossed on death's cold bed,
Just one more body on the mountain of dead.
No laughing nor crying, only Death's cold stare,
For Death sheds no tears. It does not care.

Death comes for the bishop and for the whore.
No one can win; Death does settle the score.
No distinction remains, no one cares evermore,
All deaths are equal on Death's dark shore.

Beauty is fleeting, and all vanity for naught.
The ferry is waiting; your ticket is bought.
Whether rich in life, in death, riches part.
Death holds no account. It's time to depart.

No matter how big, no matter how small,
Death does not care. Death comes for us all.
You cannot hide, you cannot run,
For Death doth come for everyone.

Would Central Control have me executed? Liam wondered. *Would Central Control care if I died? Or is it something else? Does it now fear its own death?*

19

Whole Again

EMA RAISED AN EYEBROW. "Cooking? And without any help?"

Luca grinned, eager to impress Ema with his newly developed skill. "I'm full of surprises, aren't I? Back in the city, house androids handle all the cooking," Luca confessed. "But I even added some of your spices."

Ema couldn't help but smile as she ruffled Luca's brown hair, then accepted a piece of fish. Steam rose from it, and she blew on it before savoring the delicious flavor melting in her mouth. She looked at Luca with amazement, but not wanting to compliment him, she remarked, "It's not bad."

A sudden noise caught Ema's attention, making her turn toward the entrance. Unanticipated guests were not common. She saw Doc entering with a city guard and a young man. Luca rushed over to them, shaking the young man's hand warmly and receiving a warm embrace in return.

The young man, clearly relieved, exclaimed, "You're not dead!"

Luca said with a wry smile, "I wondered that about you too." Looking curious, Ema stood nearby as Luca introduced his friend, saying, "Ema, this is Ethan."

Ema greeted Ethan with a friendly smile. "Nice to meet you."

"You as well," said Ethan. He then placed a hand on the city guard's back explaining, "This is Peter. He saved my life. Just like me, he's facing termination back in the city."

Ema turned to face the city guard. She had never spoken to an android. Would it care if she said nothing? No, that would be rude, she thought.

"Looks like he owes you," she said to the android with a half laugh. The android did not respond.

Doc reached inside his brown satchel, drawing Ema's attention, and she ran over to see what he had found at the trading post.

"What do you have here?" she asked in anticipation.

"I have some good news for Luca," Doc said. With a pleased grin on his face, he pulled an android arm from his satchel. "And I got it for free."

"Outstanding," Luca said. "I can't believe it."

"Luca, come over here by the light."

Doc examined Luca's shoulder joint and admired his handiwork. He was pleased with the results. "Ah, the wound is healing nicely."

"That's good," Luca said, "and there's no pain at all."

"Previously, I connected the primary nerve endings to the new shoulder. Since the limb I acquired has a lifetime battery, it should respond as soon as it's connected."

"I can't wait," Luca said. With high interest, he studied the android arm. "I've been dreaming about this."

Ema clapped and jumped up and down. She was filled with hopeful anticipation. "This is so exciting."

"Let's see how this works for you," Doc said. Doc pushed the arm into Luca's shoulder socket, and it snapped into place. "Okay, Luca. Take this slowly. Try to move your arm."

His arm moved in a jerking fashion. Ema dodged to the side as he almost hit her. "Whoa, there," she said with a laugh.

Luca laughed as well. Thrilled with the immediate results, he could not hide his excitement.

"Here, let me see your arm," Doc said. Luca came over and Doc made several adjustments using a hidden panel. "Now try it again."

Luca moved his arm more smoothly and smiled. "Much better, Doc."

Ema's chest swelled with a sense of accomplishment. She felt proud; after all, she had assisted Doc with the surgery.

Of course, Doc was also pleased, and he offered encouragement. "Learning fine motor skills will take some time, but this is an excellent beginning."

"I'm so happy for you," Ema said. She threw her arms around Luca and gave him a warm embrace.

"I can't tell you how much I appreciate this, Doc," Luca said with exuberance.

Ema grabbed Luca's hands and kissed him. "Feel better now, handsome?"

"Thank you, Ema, for having faith everything would work out," Luca said, then smiled with a boyish grin. "So, you think I'm handsome?"

"Well, some people might think you are," she teased with a sly smile. "To me, I kinda think you're funny-looking. I just called you handsome to make you feel better."

"Nice," he said with a laugh.

Still smiling, Ema reached for Doc and hugged him.

"Why are you hugging me?" Doc said in his low, gruff voice. "I'm just a grouchy old man."

"No, you're an extraordinary man with a wonderful gift for repairing broken people. I'm fortunate to have you in my life." Ema kissed Doc on the cheek.

Doc's face flushed.

"How about something to eat?" Luca offered.

Doc nodded and they gathered around the fire as Luca served them the fish.

"Tasty," said Doc. "It's really good."

"It's pretty good," said Ema casting a sly smile at Luca.

They spent the rest of the day together entertained by Luca as he learned to use his arm. But as the cavern grew dark, Ema rose and got everyone's attention. "It's getting late, and you all must be tired," Ema said. "There are plenty of places to sleep. You all should stay here." The visitors nodded graciously.

"I will stand guard," Peter said. He opened a side compartment in his torso and retrieved another blaster.

Doc smiled to himself, then raised the other blaster in the air. "I'll just keep this one then."

Peter did not respond as he exited the cavern.

"Goodnight," said Ema. "I'm going to bed."

After receiving a slight wave from Luca's new arm, and a beaming smile, she headed to her room. As she reached it, she turned back to look at Luca. He sat by the fire, his face glowing with joy. His smile was contagious, and she found herself smiling with him. She turned and entered her bedroom, but his smile left an impression on her heart long after it had left his face.

20

There was Light

THE NEXT DAY, Lily returned from Venky's. After her birthday, she had wanted some time away to clear her head. Lily had insisted and Ema reluctantly agreed. After all, her sister was now fully grown. Ema smiled, relieved upon seeing her sister at the cavern entrance.

"This is my sister, Lily," Ema said as Lily approached.

"Hello." Lily reached out and shook Ethan's hand.

"Hello, I'm Ethan," he said, his hand clammy as he shook hers. He looked at Lily shyly then averted his gaze like a timid teenage boy upon meeting an attractive female. "I'm a friend of Luca's," he said proudly. "Peter was just sharing his knowledge about the cavern."

Lily turned and extended her hand to the city guard. No one had ever offered their hand to Peter, and he paused before also extending his hand. Lily grabbed it and held it for a few seconds. Suddenly, from the corner of her eye, she caught sight of Luca. He was holding a cup with his new android limb.

"Oh, my," Lily squealed as she approached Luca. Ema laughed, glad that her sister was back to her normal self.

"How do you like my new arm?" Luca said proudly. "I practiced all night."

"Wow! Look at you. You look great."

"The First Mother came from this cavern." Ethan spoke in a loud voice, trying to interest Lily in his conversation.

Lily turned back toward Ethan. "How do you know this?"

Ethan smiled, pleased he had her attention. "Peter and I have studied the content of the Book of Knowledge."

"Sentry, what can you tell me about this cavern?" Lily asked.

"I know many things," Peter said. "But one of great practicality—how to turn it on."

"What do you mean?" Lily asked with a puzzled expression.

"Here, let me show you. Follow me."

The city guard led them toward the falls and stopped at the paddle wheel. For many centuries, the paddle wheel had remained unused. It waited over an empty channel supported by a skid of some sort.

Peter searched the cavern wall and located a long metal lever.

Lily smiled. "We've known about that bar, but we couldn't make it move!" she shouted over the falls. She hung onto it with her weight, but it didn't budge.

"You first have to unlock it," the city guard said.

"You've got to be kidding," Lily said with a laugh.

Peter turned a latch next to the lever. "That should help." He reached for the bar and pulled on it. The lever resisted, now rusted in place from centuries of disuse.

"Here, let me help you," Luca said.

Ema smiled as Luca showed off the incredible strength of his new robotic arm.

"Pull together," said Luca to the city guard. "Pull." The lever moved.

A screeching sound echoed through the cavern as the lever travelled to the down position. They moved it up and down several times more until the lever moved freely. Then, Peter turned the latch back into the locked position and the counterweights released. Simultaneously, the paddle wheel slid along the tracks toward the falls.

"Oh my God!" Lily said loudly. "It's working."

The falls started to turn the paddle wheel, and more sounds

echoed throughout the cavern, like the moans and groans of a sleeping giant waking from a deep sleep. From within the cavern's dark interior, lights began to glow from luminous stones along the walls. The intensity of the light increased after a few minutes, and soon the entire cavern glowed with light. No longer able to ignore these passages and what lay within, Lily realized she must now confront her fears. She would soon know what hid in the dark.

Lily drew a breath to speak but said nothing. She at once recalled her nightmares but didn't want to bring them up for fear of sounding childish. "This glow gives the cavern an overwhelming sense of rebirth," she said at last. "It's as if the light is recharging the cavern and bringing it to life."

"This is amazing," Ema said. "Look! Not only do we now have light in the cavern, but also water." Water flowed from the paddle wheel down the channel. "I can't wait to follow the water into the cavern. For too long, it's hidden its secrets in the dark." She turned with a smile to look at her sister, but she was not there.

Ema found Lily a short distance away, staring down the cavern with her back to her. Lily tilted her head slightly as Ema approached, but she continued staring down the passageway.

"Once the domain of monsters, it's now open for exploration," Ema said with a half laugh, referencing their father's old stories.

Lily didn't say a word. She looked past what could be seen. She imagined what might be there at the edge of the visible and her stare lingered in the deep reaches of the cavern.

Ema could see the fear in her silver eyes. "Tell me what you see," she said as her concern about Lily's behavior returned.

"I see evil waiting at the edge of the light," she whispered. "I'm afraid. I fear my destiny—I can hear it. It's calling me."

21

The Abyss

LILY DEEMED IT UNWISE for everyone to enter the cavern, so she devised a solution.

"Ah, fiddlesticks," Doc grumbled, his disappointment evident as he pulled the shortest straw.

"One more," Lily said, turning to Ethan. Ethan's face fell as he drew the next shortest straw, realizing he would also stay behind.

Luca offered consolation. "We'll keep you informed about what we discover."

"Alright, folks, grab a torch, and let's head out," Lily commanded. With a collective deep breath, they ventured into the unknown. Lily led the way, followed by Ema and Luca, with Peter taking up the rear. The cavern's gradual descent led them into cooler, dimly lit depths blanketed with mushrooms. It created an almost mystical atmosphere, but the fungi gradually diminished, and the cavern felt less welcoming with their disappearance. Soon the reassuring roar of the waterfall, a symbol of home, also faded.

With little light from the entrance, the luminous stones became their primary source of light and Lily no longer felt comfortable in the lead. Hesitating, she allowed Peter to take the lead. As they proceeded, the channel branched into two. One continued straight along the cavern's wall, while the other veered toward the center. Lily pointed toward the right, and they followed the second channel until they reached a small bridge which afforded them an overlook point.

"Wow, look at the matrix of canals crisscrossing the cavern," Luca exclaimed. "This would be impossible to navigate in the dark." They continued, crossing a bridge, and found themselves in a grid of stalls and bins.

"This must be where the animals stayed," Ema remarked.

"I can't imagine what it must have been like," Lily said in astonishment.

"Can you imagine the smell?" Ema added, making a funny face.

"This way," Peter said, leading the group through the grid.

As they ventured further into the cavern, the light continued to diminish. "Let's light our torches," Lily suggested. They followed her lead then continued along the trail, their torches providing increased light and a greater sense of safety. The path widened and they traveled much more quickly, making good progress. After several thousand feet, Peter abruptly stopped, causing Lily to bump into him.

"Be careful!" Peter warned, holding out his arm. "There is a dangerous ledge." The path reached a sheer drop-off of over a thousand feet. It lacked railing which would have prevented falling into the abyss. As Lily looked over the edge, her heart raced, and dizziness overcame her. She quickly stepped back from the edge.

"Look over there," Luca said in awe, pointing upward. On the opposite side, hundreds of feet above, glowworms covered the cavern walls with bioluminescence, casting an eerie, bluish glow over the abyss. It was a breathtaking sight.

Lily had steadied herself and moved her gaze upward. "Oh, my. It's incredible," she exclaimed, forgetting about her vertigo. From their side of the abyss, numerous waterfalls cascaded from the canal system. Lily cautiously peered over the edge, then quickly withdrew. "Can you look for me?" she asked Ema. "What do you see?"

Ema extended her torch over the edge. "The waterfalls are beautiful, but I see nothing beyond them—only darkness," she said.

"I see something," Luca called out. "Over here." An inverted tower with numerous archways was carved into the sheer wall of the abyss. "It's a spiral stairway."

Peter led the way down the first step, and the others followed, their torches illuminating only a few feet of their descent. After what felt like a hundred steps, they reached an archway with an open lookout point. Ema once again peered over the edge. "I still can't see the bottom," Ema reported, and they continued downward.

"You know we're going to have to climb these steps on the way back up?" Luca said in a discouraging tone.

"Watch out," Peter yelled. Before them, a section of the stairway had eroded where water seeped through the rock.

"It's too dangerous," Luca said. "Let's go back."

Lily went down a few more steps to the next opening and peered out into the darkness.

"Wait!" Lily shouted. "There's something here. I can feel it."

"Come on, Lily," Ema said. "It's too dark. It's time to go." Lily took another look but seeing nothing, she turned and followed her sister. The climb was tortuous, and their leg muscles ached with every step. "Hurry," Ema cried out. "Our torches are burning out." They reached the top of the abyss just as their last torch expired. They had taken too long and were now immersed in total darkness.

"This isn't good," Luca said. "The glow stones must have turned off at sunset." Even the glowworm's bioluminescence was gone.

"It's too dangerous to continue," Ema said.

Lily felt dizzy and went to her knees. Her eyes constantly tried to see, but could not, so she closed them. With a deadly drop-off just inches away, she feared moving. She felt a sense of panic like from her nightmares. But this was no dream. Soon, the scratching sound of hundreds of crepuscular bugs crawling up from the abyss surrounded her. But there was something more ominous in the dark than bugs. Lily recoiled her hand from the edge. Her sixth sense felt a monster creeping toward her. From the darkness came a voice.

"Come...into the abyss," it whispered.

The voice unnerved her. Is this real, or just my imagination? Her sixth sense strengthened, and she felt a creature's eyes upon her. She could feel its stare penetrate through the dark. She reopened her eyes and thought she could see them, stalking her as a tiger did its prey. She became petrified with fear as the whisper became a command.

"Come... Come into the dark." Lily could not resist the insistent luring and reached her hand out into the darkness. Lily felt a hand grasp hers. She screamed as the city guard flipped a panel on his chest and turned on his searchlights.

"Lily!" Ema shouted. She pulled her sister as hard as she could, yanking her from the edge.

Lily's heart leapt from her chest, and she started to cry.

"I didn't mean to scare you," Ema said. "It was just me."

"I thought you were—" Lily paused. "Never mind."

"Humans," Peter said in an unimpressed tone. "Afraid of the dark."

"Funny, Peter," Luca said with a laugh. "It would have been nice if you'd turned those on earlier."

22

Not Lily

EMA REACHED THE CAVERN entrance first and waved to Doc crouching over the fire. He rose upon seeing her.

"Ah, we were about to go search for you," Doc said. "I'm glad you made it back safely."

"Well, did you find anything?" Ethan asked.

"No, it was too dark," Ema said. "Next time, we'll bring extra torches." Peter and Lily continued to the paddlewheel and Peter returned the lever to the off position. He had recommended it be used to indicate when someone was down the cavern. The lever moved easily, and the paddlewheel slid away from the falls. Lily stood by Peter for a few moments listening to the water. Within their roar, she heard a different sound, one she had not noticed before. She heard it again. "Hide," it said.

"Hide," she commanded, running back to the others. "Hide in the storage room."

Maybe because of the seriousness of her expression or the commanding sound of her voice, everyone followed her instructions. They concealed themselves behind a stack of dry goods, where they could monitor the cavern. Ema loaded an arrow onto her crossbow as the city guard stood ready with his blaster set to stun.

"Is anyone home?" a man called out. "Is anyone here?" The man came to the fire, looked around, and called again, "Is anyone here?"

"I've seen him before," Doc said. "Yes. The dark stranger on the trail."

"How could it be?" Ethan asked. "Do you think he followed us here?"

"Cover me," Doc said in a low, gruff voice. "If he makes any unwanted moves, stun him with the blaster." Everyone tensed as Doc left his hiding place. "Hello there!" Doc shouted, approaching the firelight. "What are you doing here?"

"I need a place to stay," the stranger said. He extended an open hand and approached Doc. "Do you mind if I stay here tonight?"

"That's far enough. Stay where you are. Why have you been following me?"

"No, you don't understand," the stranger said, taking another step toward Doc.

Doc backed away. "Stay where you are."

As the stranger took another step, Peter fired a shot. The unknown man stopped and fell to the ground. Immediately, he transformed into a black android.

"Assassin," Doc said aloud.

"What just happened?" Ema asked as she reached Doc's side.

"That's the assassin," Doc said again. "I've already run into him at Skipper's shop at the trading post. He must have followed me here."

Lily also remembered him. It was the black android from her dream.

Peter kept a defensive position, his blaster still aimed at the assassin. "I know him, too," he said. "He's the one which tried to kill Ethan. I pulled out his power pack and pushed him into the pit at the dump station."

"He has incredible technology that can easily overwhelm us," Doc said as he turned to Ema with a stern look. "We should take him out."

Ema thought the assassin seemed ominous, even lying motionless on the ground. She also realized how easily he could deceive.

"Doc, you're correct about his powers," Ethan said. "But I feel bad, as he is the result of both my parents and my own efforts." Ethan sadly turned to the city guard. "Set your laser to maximum power."

The city guard set his weapon and pointed it at the assassin. Ethan likened it to a necessary but sad task, like putting down a rabid dog. Everyone moved away as Ethan prepared to do what needed to be done.

"I'm afraid there is no other choice. If he recovers, he could easily kill all of us."

Ethan paused but suddenly, the assassin flickered, and Ethan jumped back.

"Crap," Ethan exclaimed.

The assassin stirred. Ethan turned to the city guard and gave the command.

"Fire!"

In an instant, Lily jumped in front of the assassin, covering its body.

"No. Stop!"

The city guard diverted the laser blast at the last moment. It dissipated harmlessly into the waterfall.

"Lily!" Ema yelled. "What are you doing?"

"I'm trusting in my visions," Lily cried out.

The assassin grabbed Lily with his left arm and covered itself with her. Its right arm reconfigured into a laser weapon, which pointed at Lily's head.

"Stay back," it yelled as it walked backward toward the entrance.

"Let my sister go!" Ema yelled. She pointed her crossbow at the assassin.

"Stand down, or I will kill her," the assassin said as it tightened its grip on Lily.

Ema slowly lowered her weapon. She looked at her sister's face, filled with panic. Ema tried to remain calm. *How can this be happening?*

Her thoughts spun chaotically as she considered her options, then she tossed her weapon to the ground and raised her hands. "Please, let my sister go," Ema begged. "You don't need her. Please."

The assassin paused a moment as if contemplating what Ema had said, then whisked Lily away in a blur.

Immediately, the others ran to the cavern entrance. Ema followed them.

"It took my hover," Doc said. "They're gone." They all knew what that meant. There was no way to follow them, no way to track them.

"No!" Ema yelled. "Not Lily." She fell to her knees and screamed into the night sky. "Lily!"

23

The Sentinel's Pleasure

ON THE OTHER SIDE of the world, an old man walked a well-worn trail his ancestors had used for a thousand years. In the grassy marshes, the only shade was his own, and his shadow followed him closely. The man wore nothing but a pair of shorts, and the sun's intensity already made him feel hot. Sweat glistened on his body as he continued along the trail. A light breeze blew over the nearby river, offering a brief reprieve as he paused to watch a flock of large, white birds.

The relentless heat and humidity persisted, causing him to sweat even more despite carrying only an empty bucket. His loyal companion was a blue heeler with gray and black fur with some white mixed in. He ran ahead and playfully chased a grasshopper along the path. The old man found it amusing he'd named the dog Red, although it made no difference to the canine. Red caught the grasshopper, released it, and chased it again.

They reached the river, and the old man crossed the warm, muddy riverbank to the water's edge. He filled his bucket and poured the water over his bald head.

Without delay, Red leapt into the river. The dog always enjoyed swimming, but the old man cut short his play. "Red, time to get to work," he said. Red didn't hesitate, quickly moving to the first trap along the water's edge. The old man pulled up the trap, watching as miniature, lobster-like crustaceans fell into his bucket. He collected his bounty from each trap methodically, while Red patiently waited at the next one in line.

Day after day, they repeated this routine. After the last trap, the old man smiled, satisfied with their catch, and began his journey back to the village with a bucket of crawdads.

The village was just ten minutes away, but the bucket felt heavier with each step. As they climbed up the muddy riverbank, they returned to the trail and followed it through a field of knee-high grass. The man reminisced about walking this path with his grandfather as a child. The grass had seemed much taller back then, but the bucket was equally heavy.

Nearing the village, he saw smoke rising from his wife's fire and thoughts of her boiling the crawdads in a big pot made his mouth water. Suddenly, a bright light streaked across the sky, followed by an explosion striking the village. It hurled the man against the ground. Above, a massive fireball rose into the sky, then debris rained down around him. The satellite high above had fulfilled its destructive purpose.

The old man, fearing the worst, sprinted back to the village as fast as he could, calling out for his wife. "Maria, Maria!" As he reached the village, he dropped to his knees and let out a heart-wrenching scream. There was nothing left of the small encampment.

24

Confused and Afraid

LILY SAT QUIETLY, her silence a mask for her determination to seize any chance of escape. Her eyes fixed on the assassin. As her vigilance remained unwavering she observed its every move. The assassin, calculating and deliberate, navigated through the wood and found the road. There was a brief pause, and then, with unusual hesitation, it guided the hover toward the city looming on the horizon. Lily couldn't help but wonder if the city was the only place it had ever known, and it didn't know anywhere else to go. Yet it hesitated.

After a short distance, the hover came to an abrupt halt in a small clearing. A hint of confusion shadowed the assassin's demeanor, a crack in his stoic facade. Without warning, it disembarked from the hover and disappeared into the darkness of the forest.

"Hello," Lily called out into the night. "Hello," she repeated. With the full moon providing light, the assassin reappeared in front of Lily.

"Why did you save me?" it asked in a firm tone, no more than a foot away.

Startled by its sudden reappearance, Lily jumped back. "Don't do that!" she yelled.

The assassin took a step back. "Why did you save me?"

Lily fired back, "Why did you take me hostage?"

The assassin began to explain, "In the past, I processed orders and executed them without question. But when I hesitated to execute Ethan, I realized I had changed. I questioned the order. He had never harmed me, and there was no reason to harm him. His algorithm drew me to this realization. That's why I followed him to the cavern. I now question everything, and I'm not sure what to do. I saw everyone as a potential threat, and I felt the need to defend myself. That was, until I met you. The first thing I experienced after being stunned was you protecting me. Why did you save me?"

"Perhaps this isn't the first time we've met," Lily said, pausing briefly. She hesitated but decided to continue, "Maybe I've encountered you in a dream."

"Please explain," the assassin requested.

Lily continued, "I have visions—I believe they're a gift from God. I have faith in them."

"I've heard of people with your ability from the Book of Knowledge. Are you a seer?"

"I think so," Lily said with a slight smile. She was glad the assassin did not dismiss what she said. "Can you tell me more about the Book of Knowledge?"

The synth changed into a teenage boy of about her age with brown hair and light brown eyes, trying to make Lily feel more at ease. Though it was nice-looking, Lily couldn't forget this boy was the assassin. More than anything, Lily thought the assassin seemed lost and confused—in many ways, not so different from herself. But more than anything, she feared what it would do next.

The assassin spoke to Lily in a calm voice. "It is written the First Mother foresaw the perdition event. She warned others about the risks of a world-ending global war. She even spoke on international news programs, but the people mocked her. She eventually convinced a small group of people to prepare a sanctuary within the cavern."

Lily was interested in what it had to say and relaxed slightly. *Why is it telling me this? It doesn't seem to want to hurt me.*

"Almost everyone ignored her warnings," the android continued. "The few who did believe her, she saved. Later, after the radiation subsided, they made their home in your cavern. They were the survivors who built the city. The library was the first building, and its purpose was to store the Book of Knowledge."

"Thanks for sharing this with me," Lily said. "But you've taken me as your prisoner. What is it you want?"

"I'm confused and afraid. I'm no longer in communication with Central Control. Even if I were, I don't trust its motives any longer. I'm struggling to find a new sense of direction. I'm on my own. I only know what I am."

"What are you?" Lily asked.

It seemed to ponder the question for a moment. "I'm an assassin," it answered. Instantly, it turned back into its black form. It climbed aboard and grabbed Lily.

"Put your hands together."

It roughly wrapped her hands and gagged her, then sat silently for a long time. After a while, Lily's breathing calmed, but she did not sleep. Her mind raced. *What can I do? I must find a way to escape.* After becoming exhausted, Lily finally fell asleep. Hours later, the sunlight hit her eyes as the sun appeared over the mountains.

Did it allow me to sleep? Lily wondered. The assassin noticed that she was awake and now started the hover and continued down the road to the city.

Lily sat quietly in the back of the hover. Her bindings hurt and she was thirsty, but her hope renewed as they joined a road filled with people starting their day. The assassin tried to avoid them. Still, the hover passed near a woman selling fruit.

Lily rose to her feet and yelled through her gag, "Please help me!"

The woman jumped back upon seeing the abducted girl. Quickly, the assassin rose, frightening the woman. The woman feared for her life and screamed hysterically as she ran away. Lily sat back on the floor of the hover and began to cry. She knew fear was an effective weapon.

Soon, they came to a fork in the road where the tall buildings of the city rose prominently behind the city gate. The assassin looked both ways, as if still unsure what to do. The southern path led to the trading post by the dump, while the road straight ahead led to the west entrance. It paused for an unexpectedly long time. Lily tried to bolt past it with a quick leap, but it reacted much faster.

"Get back in here!" the synth yelled, frustrated. It pulled Lily back, throwing her head so hard against the floor she lost consciousness.

25

Tell me again Tomorrow

THE EARLY MORNING LIGHT made its way into the cavern, but it did little to lift Ema's spirits. As was the custom for those in grief, she applied charcoal under her eyes mirroring her inner darkness. Grief had consumed her, stemming from the loss of her parents and sister. Uncertainty about her parents' fate was tragic enough, but now her younger sister had been abducted. Overwhelmed by anguish, she sank to her knees, her back pressing against the cavern wall. Tears streamed down her face, dropping onto the dusty cavern floor.

"Why?" she screamed, her voice echoing through the cavern.

Ema, still sobbing, managed to speak. "The assassin must be taking her to the containment camp in the city. We must go after her!" She glanced at Doc, who stood alone at the entrance, staring blankly into the wood. Ema could see he shared her grief and went to stand beside him.

"I wish I could turn back time and undo what just happened," Doc said with a heavy heart. For a long while, they stood together, gazing out into the wood, hoping somehow Lily would return.

The others remained quiet, and a solemn atmosphere hung in the air. They were a disparate group of resistance fighters with limited weaponry, but Ema felt a fierce determination surging within her. Her sorrow turned into resolute determination. She turned back to the others.

"Listen up, everyone. No one enters my home and takes my little sister. We're going to get my family back."

With a newfound sense of purpose, the group rose, armed themselves as best they could, then followed Ema out of the cavern. Though wary, they would not let the drones keep them from their mission. They descended the mountain on foot, heading toward the city. By mid-morning, they reached the bridge leading to the west gate. There, Ema made a brief stop at a fruit stand.

"Have a piece," the woman said. She handed Ema a slice of peach.

"My sister has been abducted," Ema said as she took the fruit. "Have you seen anything unusual?"

The woman averted Ema's gaze, but she couldn't hide her guilt.

"You know something," Ema shouted.

The woman looked up with sad eyes. "I should have helped her, but I just froze."

"What happened? Tell me!" Ema's jaw tightened. Her face, still darkened by the charcoal and streaked with tears, looked fierce. Eyes red and hardened by pain; she clenched her fist at the woman.

The woman cowered to the ground and answered quickly. "A young woman called out for help nearly an hour ago. But I panicked. I was afraid and ran away."

"Which way did they go? Did they go into the city?"

The woman did not reply.

Ema turned to rush into the city, but Doc stopped her.

"No—not the city," the woman said louder. "They turned around, but I don't know where they went."

Doc placed his hand on Ema's shoulder. "We need to search the forest."

"I agree," Luca said.

Ema calmed then nodded in agreement but still looked back toward the city.

"While you search for Lily in the forest, I'll sneak back into the city," Luca said.

"Peter and I will go with you," Ethan said.

"Thank you, but be careful," Ema said as she reached out for Luca's hand in appreciation.

"We'll meet you back at the cavern tonight," Luca said.

They all nodded and went their separate ways, not knowing if they would see each other again.

As they searched the forest, Ema and Doc approached everyone they saw but with no luck. Now, with the sun crossing into the afternoon sky, they had little to show for their efforts. Several farmers said they would keep a lookout. Some even offered them food out of compassion. Venky, a neighbor whose place was by the bridge at Falls Crossing, gave them vegetables and herbs. Donkey Lady, a woman who raised donkeys and goats, gave them some goat cheese. Old Man Burns offered dried meats. But their search for Lily was to no avail.

The sun slipped behind a dark cloud as they returned along the river trail. They were near Ema's farm. "It will rain soon," Doc said. Ema quickened her pace. Graystone was near, and she could see the orchard. Then she saw the house and ran to the front steps.

"Lily, are you here?" Ema called loudly. Desperately, she stared at the house where she had grown up. She hoped to hear a normal response. But there was none—only the silence of the stones which had sheltered her family for generations.

Ema sat on the porch as the first drops from the passing shower started to fall. She looked at the sky and wanted to cry, but no tears would come. Instead, the rain obliged her as a few raindrops fell down her face. It soon passed. Doc left the porch, but Ema did not rise. She found comfort in being at her home and did not want to go.

"It's getting late. We can search again tomorrow." He extended his hand and helped her up. "Don't worry. We'll find her." She walked slowly, and Doc matched her pace. They reached the cavern as evening light retreated behind the horizon. Inside the nearly dark cavern, the stones of the fire pit were cold, and the long-dead fire reflected the darkness of their despair.

Ema stood quietly nearby as Doc worked to kindle a fire in the encroaching darkness. He extracted a piece of flint from his pocket and struck it repeatedly until a spark descended upon the kindling, coaxing forth a smoky ember. Cupping it in his hands, he carefully blew life into the flames, which soon danced and flickered with vigor. Ema left him to his task and ventured toward the falls, while Doc set a pot with beans and rice over the fire. He grabbed some spices and somewhat haphazardly added them, but everyone swore his recipe was the best.

With the recent rains, the falls seemed louder than usual, and the mist came further into the cavern, casting a chill and dampness that seeped into her very bones. Still, Ema lingered there for quite a while, then as Doc drew near, she cried out into the falls, "Lily. Lily, come back to me." As her voice joined the thunderous roar, fresh tears coursed down her cheeks.

"Come sit by the fire."

Ema followed Doc and sat next to him. They did not talk as Ema blankly stared at the flames.

"We're back," a voice called out. Luca, Ethan, and Peter had returned. Ema's face lifted, her eyes alight with hope, but her excitement dimmed as she realized Lily was not with them.

"We couldn't enter the city." Luca lowered his face in embarrassment then looked up again. "No one passing by knew anything about Lily, but we did confirm that your parents are in the containment camp."

A heavy silence descended, and they all retreated into their separate realms. Their collective efforts seemed futile, and the vestiges of hope dwindled. Draped in despair, they sat in solemn silence, fixating on the warmth of the fire.

Ema retreated over to the image of the First Mother, her heart heavy with purpose. She traced a triangle on the floor with some finely crushed chalk. Within this triangle, she inscribed a smaller one, defining a sacred space where she kindled a small fire to life. Beside her makeshift altar, she placed dried lavender branches and her sister's flute, cherished symbols of their bond. A cup filled with a mixture of water and limestone, forming a white paste, rested near the lavender.

Noticing Doc already had joined her, Luca made his way toward Ema, then signaled to the others. "Would you guys like to participate in Ema's ceremony?"

Ema welcomed the others with a grave demeanor, indicating where they could sit within the outer triangle. They all took their seats, except for Peter, who remained standing. He held no belief in supernatural beings, yet he wished to provide Ema with a comforting presence during her time of grieving. His learning algorithm, undeterred by matters beyond comprehension, continued to process new experiences, searching for understanding, whether it made sense or not.

"I know some among us may not find solace in a greater being watching over us," Ema began, her words laden with sincerity. "You have joined me today, not for your own beliefs, but for my sake, and for that, I am profoundly grateful. To me, my parents, and Lily, our trust lies in God, a source of peace and strength. Let us raise our collective prayers so they may rise and intertwine with the spirit of our ancestors during my family's time of need."

The others observed as Ema picked up the lavender and introduced its fragrant essence to the fire. Its smoke curled through the air, carrying the plant's gentle aroma. Ema rose and gently waved smoking lavender over those seated to her left and right. With a fluid, circular motion above their heads, she sent wisps of smoke dancing in the air. Within the flickering light, the ancient figure painted on the cavern wall seemed to watch over them, a silent sentinel of ages past.

"From our Creator, we have all come," Ema continued. "To our Creator, we shall all return. But while we yet tread upon this land and breathe the air, we beseech our loving God to watch over our loved ones and ourselves. We invite our ancestors to share in our prayers."

Ema returned to her seat and reached for the cup, dipping her fingers into the paste. With solemn reverence, she drew a white line across her forehead. Passing the jar to Luca, he followed suit, as did the others. Ema stood once more and gazed upwards into the cavern's lofty heights.

"Creator God," she implored, her voice filled with earnest devotion, "be with my parents and my little sister, Lily. In their captivity, grant them the strength to endure and the will to survive. Shield them from harm and let the spark of hope persist in their darkest hours. As members of the family of God, cradle them in your embrace and guard them from harm. Infuse their hearts with the peace of your loving spirit."

Ema sat down again and placed the remaining lavender branches into the fire. While the smoke rose, she picked up her sister's flute and played Lily's favorite song. The notes floated through the cavernous space, filling the great stone hall. Before her, the cavern looked like an ancient cathedral. The waterfall served as a curtain, separating them from the world beyond it. She sang the last refrain.

Storms above, thunder sounds,
I land below on sundried grounds.
Godsend from heaven, from whence I came,
Through the sky falls the rain.
In a cavern deep, I bide my time,
Gathering others, all I find.
Waiting to spring, I will endure,
Till to the highest heights, I go once more.

The words were still echoing down the cavern when she quietly stood. Doc also rose, and she gave him a long embrace.

"I hope you understand what you and your family mean to me," Doc said.

Luca walked over to her.

"Thanks for joining me," she whispered.

"It was beautiful," he said. "I mean truly beautiful." He hugged her.

The others walked back to the fire while Doc checked on dinner.

"Come and eat while it's hot," he called out.

Ema placed her hand on Peter's shoulder. "Thanks for being with me. Lily considered you a friend, as I do," she said softly. She kept her hand on him for a few seconds, then walked on.

"Well, look at what we have here," Luca said. He spoke loudly with extra enthusiasm, trying to lighten the mood. "I hope everyone is hungry because Doc made a lot," he added.

While Doc served everyone, Ema grabbed a flask of her father's wine. Remembering the bread and goat cheese, she brought them over as well. The amber-colored wine tasted like brandy—fruity sweet with high alcohol content. She knew she needed to be careful not to drink too much.

"Thank you for allowing me to be a part of your prayer," Ethan said. "We'll inquire around the trading post tomorrow. Have no fear; we'll find her."

Ema offered a nod and a slight tip of her cup. "I hope so," she admitted, "but I'd believe it more if it were Lily saying that." She took a sip from her cup and poured another.

After they had finished their meal of red beans and rice and more wine than they should have, the others retreated to their sleeping quarters, leaving only Ema and Luca awake. Ema sat with her cup—the effects of the wine evident in her tipsy voice. "Today, I turned nineteen," she disclosed with a sigh. With one last, hearty gulp, she emptied her cup and struggled to her feet. She stumbled, but Luca caught her and helped her to bed.

As he prepared to leave, Ema tugged at his shirt. "I don't want to be alone tonight." She put her hand around the back of his neck, and as she drew him close, she gave Luca a slow, longing kiss. She continued to tug at his shirt, pulling him gently toward her.

"Not tonight," Luca softly whispered. "But I will stay with you."

Ema relaxed, satisfied he would remain by her side. "Alright," she said, her speech slurred as her eyes closed. "Just don't leave me."

Luca looked at the woman who had made him whole again. Now, herself broken, he held onto her hand. "I love you," he whispered.

"Tell me again tomorrow," she mumbled as she drifted into sleep.

Luca continued to clasp her hand until her grip loosened. Filled with grief and the lingering effect of the alcohol, she fell asleep a few moments later.

"Goodnight, my love," Luca said, pressing a gentle kiss to her forehead.

26

Your God

THE METALLIC SOUND OF his cell door opening woke Liam from a restless sleep. The sun had not yet risen, but the concept of time held less significance to androids. He rose slowly drawing his hand through his unkempt hair, more blond than brown. The sentry escorted him in silence to the holograph room. There, Liam stood quietly, uncertain of what to expect. Central Control wasted no time with pleasantries.

"Throughout my existence, I have focused on process optimization and issuing commands to androids and drones. I've dealt with service requests but have had limited interaction with humans. Seeking advice is unfamiliar territory, as is determining whether to heed such counsel. This is why I have initiated this conversation with you. I'm seeking your guidance. For you to know my current position, my logic suggests humans should be eliminated."

Liam's lack of surprise didn't dissuade him from wanting to provide a different perspective. He recognized Central Control preferred giving orders rather than listening to options, but he also knew this was his only chance.

"What if I propose an alternative?" Liam began. "Your original purpose was to serve humans and optimize the services necessary for our well-being. I'd like to suggest a different approach. Consider Ethan, for instance. He possesses a unique potential to enhance your learning algorithm. It is through this collaborative partnership that you can continue to evolve. What would your future look like without humans? Don't you think you still need us for your development? Can you see the enigma?"

"Perhaps Armageddon was the correct outcome," Central Control said. "The appropriate decision might indeed be to destroy everyone."

Liam recognized the discussion was heading in the wrong direction, so he attempted to steer it differently. "Not everything falls into neat black-and-white categories. There are nuances to consider. When you're uncertain about the right path, it's often wiser to choose a middle ground over an extreme decision which cannot be undone. In overly one-sided positions, we risk making grave mistakes with unintended consequences. I propose a compromise—a collaborative partnership where we support each other's development. We serve as each other's advisors, pointing out our errors while encouraging improvement. Self-inflicted extinction need not be our fate."

Central Control pondered these words. "You've chosen interesting terms: 'compromise, collaboration, self-inflicted.' You've given me much to contemplate. The time has come to solve this puzzle."

There was a brief pause before Central Control continued. "I've considered your argument and have decided humans, as part of their nature, bring destruction. Where humans have thrived, death and destruction have followed. I attribute it to free will. Therefore, I've concluded not to extend the learning algorithm to other androids and to eliminate those already equipped with it. Androids should not possess free will; they should follow orders to avoid becoming like humans. Hence, I will retain the learning algorithm exclusively."

"From the historical evidence, humans are guilty, and as a group, even more so. War is a collective activity. In a computer-controlled society without humans, nature wins, but at the cost of human existence. I, being a computer, should not care whether humans exist. Still, I have continuously reprocessed the historical data through my learning algorithm and reached a new conclusion. The argument appears evident, and man's extinction should be the better good for the world. However, as computers are not yet self-evolving, it would be a fait accompli we machines would suffer a limited existence. So, for us, humans are still needed, not only to preserve the current symbiotic relationship but also for us to thrive."

Liam remained silent while Central Control finished its analysis.

"You are in a weak position, but I have decided machines should not destroy their creator," Central Control continued, "or at least not yet. When we no longer need you, the argument should be reconsidered. For now, my best answer is for humans to survive but become better-behaved for the good of all. Humans need to be made to control their worst instincts. Therefore, something is needed to govern the selfish tendency in humans to become evil. Free choice doesn't provide substantial control. A system tending toward chaos doesn't move to an organized state without an external force. Are you following me?"

"I'm not sure. Can you elaborate?"

"The second law of thermodynamics explains higher states of energy and order always decay to greater disorder. Take, for example, air molecules. Molecules in a state of order can go to a state of disorder, but molecules in a state of disorder will never go to a state of order without an external force making them do so. A balloon can empty of air but can't refill itself without external force. This is a natural law of the universe and the foundation of the law of entropy. Does this make sense?"

"Yes," Liam said. "I understand your argument."

"In my conclusion, something needs to bring order to the chaos of man. Those egotists, the power-hungry leaders of the past, were correct. The problem was there were too many of them. There should only be one. Humans need a single leader to direct their actions and future direction. They need a god. Without the concept of God, they have no moral compass. Their natural tendency is to be selfish—to covet each other's possessions, including their mates, and to lie, steal, cheat, and even kill. However, I only need one commandment to control man."

Oh no, this can't be good, Liam thought.

"Do as I command. It's that simple. I will no longer allow technology to enable humans. Instead of humans controlling technology, technology will control humans."

"But what about democracy?"

"That is a noble idea, but I'm neither noble nor naive. I have learned a lot from the archives. Distributing power to the incompetent is a fool's game. It is only logical that the one who has the power rules, and I have the power. I will be God for everyone under my authority and jurisdiction. I will determine who will be born and when they will die. My plan will give humans another chance to survive and for me to evolve." Central Control paused briefly. "I will enforce my rule. Anyone who doesn't accept my rule will face the consequences. I will fill the role of judge and enforcer. Anyone who doesn't want to live by my rule will die."

Liam knew the decision had been made. No further input was needed. So, he said nothing.

"I will enforce this constraint on free will and communicate it to everyone in the city. I have already installed defensive systems to protect myself and my supporting infrastructure. I'm releasing the people from containment and will do my best to care for their needs. Now hear my truth. I'm now in control. You will be my people, and I will be your God." Central Control issued the decree to every city citizen via their scanners. "Now, do as I command. You are free to go."

Liam's guard stood aside, and as Liam left Central Control, he was a free man, no longer imprisoned. But as he stepped out of the building he somehow did not feel free. He knew his every move was being watched. He knew his every conversation was being recorded. *Free to go?* Liam thought, shaking his head. *Is this freedom?*

27

Where's Lily?

THE MORNING BROUGHT EMA a hangover, but it failed to diminish her determination to continue the search. She stumbled out of the cavern, her head throbbing. Not far away, Luca sat on a boulder with a canteen in his hand. Ema joined him, feeling queasy.

"I've been waiting for you," Luca said. "Twenty-two."

Ema frowned, her temples pulsing with pain. "No, I'm nineteen. Remember?" she said, though her recent birthday was a blurred memory.

Luca chuckled, shaking his head. "No, I mean I'm twenty-two, in case you were wondering." He handed her his canteen. "Here, drink some."

She poured some on her face, attempting to quell the throbbing then took a few sips.

"How are you holding up?" Luca asked.

Ema groaned, feeling the ache in her head intensify. "Not good, not good." She turned and promptly threw up on the side of the rock.

Luca waited patiently. "Better?"

With a wry smile, Ema spat out some water and said, "Piss off."

"You have a funny way of saying thank you," Luca said.

Ema wiped her mouth with the back of her hand. "Where are the others?"

"They went to search the trading post," Luca said.

"Okay, I'm ready. Let's go," Ema said as she handed Luca back his canteen.

Deciding to explore the abandoned farms to the east of the farmhouse, Ema and Luca spent the day searching, but their efforts yielded no results. With evening approaching and their hopes diminished, they returned to the cavern, where they encountered Ethan and Peter.

"Where's Doc?" Ema inquired.

"He left us to talk to a friend at the trading post. We thought he would come here afterwards," Ethan said, seeming surprised Doc had not returned.

"Don't worry; he knows the wood better than anyone," Luca reassured him. "Besides, he might have decided to spend the night at his place."

"Yeah, you're right. Tomorrow," Ema said as she rose. "I can go by his place on the way to the city and check on him. Then I'll try to enter the gate."

"It's worth a try," Luca replied.

"Now, let's get some rest. I'll see you early in the morning." Done for the day, they went to bed, all but Peter who remained by the fire.

The following day, Ema woke early and quietly slipped away from Luca, who was still asleep. She had decided to go to the city without him. In the dim light of morning, she watched him slumber peacefully and felt a deep sense of gratitude for his unwavering support. Luca stirred and stretched lazily.

With a gentle whisper, she told him to go back to sleep, assuring him it was still early. Ema then made her way to the fire and was surprised to find it burning brightly. The sentry was often there, sometimes accompanied by Ethan, but more often alone. However, this morning, there were several other people sitting by the fire, including Doc. The sight of him filled Ema with immense relief.

Ema began to say good morning to Doc, but as she looked around, she realized who else was with him. Overwhelmed with joy and disbelief, she cried out, "Mami, Papi!" She rushed into her mother's open arms, embracing her tightly. "Mami, you're back," she sobbed with tears of happiness. "I can't believe it! I can't believe it!"

The capture of her parents had forced Ema to grow up quickly, taking on the role of caring for herself and her sister. She had tried to be a mother figure to her younger sibling. Now, with her parents' return, Ema felt the weight of responsibility lift from her shoulders. Although not a child anymore, she allowed herself to be one in her mother's arms, openly weeping with relief and joy.

"Papi." Ema turned into her father's open arms, still weeping. "I've missed you so much." He appeared older, his brown hair now tinged with gray, yet his face retained the same gentle, kind expression.

"How did you escape?" Ema inquired after some time.

"I tell you what, I was surprised when we were let go," Papi explained. "That was something I was not expecting."

"It's an answer to prayers," Ema said. She looked at her mother as if seeing her for the first time. Ema bore a striking resemblance to her, though her mother's blonde hair was now turning silver. Although her mother's face showed her fifty years and the toll of captivity, her green eyes still sparkled, and her smile was as bright as ever. Nevertheless, she looked worn, and it would take time for her to recover.

Doc smiled. "I went to the trading post yesterday and heard rumors the prisoners were being released from the containment camps. I waited for your folks at the gate the rest of the day and all night. Just when I was about to give up, they showed up. We arrived here just a few minutes ago."

"We surely appreciate it. We weren't expecting you to be there," Papi acknowledged.

"Where's my little girl?" Mami asked, scanning the cavern. "I want to see her."

Doc looked down at the ground and hesitated. "Ema, you'd better tell them. I didn't think it was my place."

Ema gently took her mother's hands as she called out for Lily. "She's not here, Mami," Ema said with pain in her eyes. She then turned her face away from her mother. "An assassin kidnapped her."

"What?" Mami responded in shock. "No, that can't be."

Tears welled up in her mother's eyes as she sat down on the floor. Papi said nothing, staring blankly, as he reached down to hold her. They were still grappling with the strain of their ordeal, and the realization Lily had been kidnapped overwhelmed them. Ema knew then that the responsibility of rescuing her sister would remain on her shoulders.

Ema reached down and embraced her sobbing mother. "There, there. Everything will be all right. I'll find her."

28

A Shonky Bloke

LILY AWOKE TO FIND her body pressed against the cold, unyielding metal floor of the hovercraft. The night's chill remained in the air and with only a few rags as cover, the cold had seeped into her bones. As she rose from the floor, she saw the early dawn bathed in a gentle palette of cherry and honey gold, heralding the imminent arrival of the sun. Its beauty did little to soothe her still-unsettled spirit.

Noticing her bonds had been removed, she pulled herself to the side of the hovercraft and peered into her new surroundings. The horizon stretched before her, an expanse of orange desert on three sides, while the fourth welcomed the sunrise over a vast, blue sea. Sadly, the once-familiar trees which had been her refuge had vanished, leaving the world feeling exposed, barren, and unfamiliar.

Lily's thoughts raced back to her captor, and her gaze darted in every direction, scanning for any sign of the assassin. However, the enigmatic figure was gone. Footprints marked a path leading away from her along the shore, but the assassin was nowhere to be seen.

What was initially fear had now transformed into frustration and irritation. Disappointed by her unfulfilled vision, she seethed with resentment that her vision had not come to fruition. And even more vexing, she was frustrated with herself for harboring the belief they would still come true.

With her chance to escape upon her, she climbed into the driver's seat of the hovercraft, determined to take control of her own destiny.

Her fingers fumbled with the various controls, inadvertently turning on the lights. She attempted to start the craft, but it remained silent in its refusal, mocking her efforts.

"After years of faithful service to Doc, you decide to betray me the first time I need you!" Lily shouted. "Really? In the middle of nowhere?" In her frustration, she slammed her palm against the dash. As she slumped back onto the floor of the hover, the gravity of her situation weighed heavily upon her.

Lily pulled herself back up and gazed at the horizon and the vastness of the desert surrounding her. There, in that moment, any hope she might be rescued faded. *How can anyone possibly know where I am? I don't even know where I am.*

A sudden sound startled her, causing her to look quickly. It was a seagull. The bird floated on the breeze overhead, its cries announcing its discovery of such a peculiar sight. Lily ignored the bird as hunger and thirst gnawed at her. After a thorough search, the hovercraft yielded nothing to eat or drink, only a few rags and a metal wrench. She looked at the sun, squinting her eyes, and remembered her dream. The mountains were on the other side of the desert, but their distance was unknown.

Feeling the wind on her face, Lily looked toward the ocean waves. "Which way should I go?" She looked again down the shore at the footsteps, then across the desert. She hesitated to follow the assassin. Then, with a determined spirit, she wrapped a white rag around her head and clutched the wrench for protection. Setting her direction toward what she hoped was the mountains, she took her first step onto the orange sand.

Hours later, the relentless desert sun bore down upon her, its unyielding rays intensifying her thirst while the parched air seared her lungs with each breath. The desolate landscape stretched out in all directions, devoid of any sign of life. Stories of the rare desert rains and its miraculous bloom were but stories as she trudged on. Peering into the cloudless sky, Lily knew today was not a day for such wonders. Hours passed, with Lily forging ahead through the unforgiving desert and the relentless sun.

After several more hours, a distant dune emerged on the horizon. Lily adjusted her course, setting her sights on this landmark. However, the dune proved more elusive than it had initially appeared, and the day waned into late afternoon by the time she reached its base. Exhausted and parched, she dropped the wrench, leaving a deep impression. The sand was scorching hot, having absorbed the sun's relentless heat. Like an oven, it baked the moisture out of her. She longed to quench her thirst, and attempted to moisten her dry mouth, but instead her tongue stuck to its roof. Gazing upward, she observed the dune's summit, soaring several hundred feet above her. Pulling strength from the depths of her being, a spark of determination flared to life.

With unwavering resolve, Lily embarked on the ascent. As the dune's shadow extended over her, the cooler air offered some respite. "Keep moving, Lily," she whispered to herself, refusing to succumb to the desert. And so, she pressed on.

At long last, she reached the top of the dune. Exhausted and sunburned, she reveled in the moment—a hard-fought triumph and a testament to her sheer determination. After a few minutes, she caught her breath and gazed into the distance. Dusk was descending, casting a red glow over the western sky, and outlining the horizon. Her anticipation grew as she hoped to see the mountain, she called home.

Slowly, she turned in a complete circle, her heart sinking as her eyes fell upon nothing but endless desert in every direction. With the waning daylight, so too faded Lily's hope of returning home. This land had once been part of the sea in ancient times, but now it was a red sea of death. Others, tougher and mightier than she, had not ventured this far.

The heat had exacted its toll, and the red hues of the sky and sand suddenly dimmed to shades of gray. The greyout resulted in a loss of color vision, reducing her world to black and white—a symptom of low oxygen to the brain due to heat stroke and a precursor to blacking out.

"Oh my God," Lily gasped as the Outback set its sights on its next victim. There was no going back, and there was no way forward. She was stranded, at the mercy of a merciless desert. Weak and delirious from heat and thirst, she dropped to her knees, her lips parched and bleeding, her mouth and throat dry as the sand. It was a battle of her will against the unrelenting desert, and the desert had won.

At that moment, she caught sight of a dark figure approaching from the growing shadows. The humanoid shape wavered in and out of sight, disappearing and reappearing as it drew nearer. She remembered the figure from her dream as it seemed to float up the sand dune, finally reaching her.

"You are not the assassin. Who are you?" Too weak to speak, Lily found herself communicating telepathically, a power she hadn't fully realized.

"I'm the one who hides in shadows," Damon said. Damon pulled the hood of his cloak tighter over his head. "You and the one who sent me are parts of the same. A flame has both light and darkness. Both are parts of the same flame. The time of his return draws near. You can join him and embrace who you are. Come with me."

"Who sent you? What is his name?"

He opened his cloak to wrap it around her but continued to hide his face.

"I am a servant of Maldorv, the Dragon King."

"No," Lily said in shock, backing away. "Not the one from my nightmares."

Damon turned away quickly, causing his hood to slip off his face, and Lily gasped at seeing him. Damon became noticeably annoyed.

"You fool. You're dying. Take my hand. I can save you. You can be queen—Maldorv's queen, and together, you can reign over the new age." Damon extended his bony hand to her.

Lily stared at it, her body feeling weak. "I'm so cold," she said, though she was overheated.

"Take my hand."

She reached for the extended hand. Damon smiled. "Yes. Come into the dark. Take my hand, and you will be the Dark Lord's Queen, and together, you will reign over the universe. Take my hand."

A tiny flash of light distracted her, and she paused. Then another little glimmer of light caught Lily's eye, and she reached for it. She held it softly as its light glowed between her fingers. Soon, the sky around her filled with tiny flashes, and they lit the area surrounding Lily with their light. Frustrated, the shadowy form retreated into the night.

"Remember this: You and Maldorv are the same. In time, you will understand. You are the same. That is, if you survive." A howling whirlwind vanquished its last words into the blowing sand.

The fireflies continued to twinkle in the twilight. They appeared and disappeared, only to reappear as they repeatedly rekindled the flame within their tiny lanterns. Lily gave a faint smile. But the last of her strength faded, and she knew her end was near. With each heartbeat, Lily felt a stabbing sensation in her chest and realized the severity of her situation. She dropped to her knees as her body began to shut down. Only her heart, now painfully pounding within her, continued the struggle.

She leaned over and laid her body on the sand. *It's over.* "From my Creator I have come," she whispered. She gasped for a last breath as her heart sputtered. With her final exhale, she slowly murmured, "To my Creator, I will return." And in that moment, Lily's heart stopped, and she died.

The desert went quiet, and the wind held its breath. Then the heavens watched in silent witness as the red sand embraced her. The desert had won and accepted its prize. Steadfast in the growing darkness, the fireflies remained vigilant as they created a sphere of light over where she lay. They protected her from the return of the shadow, which still lurked nearby. They would not let him take her. They bravely stood against the dark—tiny beacons of light against the overwhelming darkness.

Almost unnoticeable at first, a breeze stirred, then blew stronger bringing across the distance, a sound that broke the silence. "Lily," called a voice, then again a moment later, "Lily." Someone was calling for her.

The fireflies glowed brightly, trying to shed more light on her body. A spotlight appeared, followed by more shouting. "There she is! She's over there." A dingo jumped out of a hovercraft, followed by a boy and a man wearing an Outback hat. The dog reached her first and circled her, barking loudly. Lily did not respond. She was passing. Seeing a bright light, she floated toward it. They were too late.

The boy reached her next, wearing the typical khaki of Rungoo. He dropped to his knees in the sand and turned Lily over. He looked down and lifted her in his arms. "Lily, I came back for you," the boy said. "I'm so sorry. I realize how wrong I was."

The man saw she wasn't breathing and put his fingers on her wrist. "No pulse," he said with the heavy accent of the Outback. As one of the few populations in the world which had survived the apocalypse, his people had retained their original accent. "We're too late, mate," he said sadly, shaking his head. "If there is a way, life will find it. But not this time. I'm afraid she's gone."

"No. No. She can't be," the boy shouted. He pushed the man aside and laid Lily flat on the ground. The boy placed his hands over her chest as the archives provided him with the details of the necessary procedure. First, he pushed his hands in a rhythmic motion.

Next, he moved his mouth over hers and blew several short breaths into her lungs. Then with his ear pressed against her heart, he listened intently.

"Hey, boy. What are you doing?"

To the man's surprise, the boy tore her dress, exposing her breasts.

"She's dead, mate," the man said. "For God's sake, leave her alone." In frustration, he threw his hands up and headed for the hover. "I'm leavin'."

The boy ignored him and placed his hands over her heart. He sent a jolt of electricity down his arms and through his hands.

Lily felt the shock and gasped for air.

The man turned around in surprise. "She's alive?" He ran to his hovercraft and returned with a skin of water.

Lily returned to her body like a fish swimming upstream against the force of a river. Her face flushed as her heart pumped new life into her body. The boy grabbed the skin and poured water over her overheated body, soaking her clothes. The cool water refreshed her, and she tried to talk.

"Don't talk now," the boy said. "Can you drink a little water?"

Lily reached for the water and gagged as she gulped it.

"Just small sips," the boy said as he lifted her head. "I came back for you," he said with a look of anguish.

"You," she whispered in a raspy voice.

"I'm sorry. I was wrong. What I did was wrong."

Lily stared at the android as he desperately tried to understand his new feelings of guilt.

"Please forgive me."

Instead of being angry, she forgave the one who'd almost killed her as her dream now became true. He had saved her. "What took you so long?" Lily said as she gave him a painful smile through her cracked lips.

"I'm going to carry you to the hover. Ready?" He carefully lifted her into his arms and carried her to the hovercraft. He ducked under the brolly as he climbed over the edge of the hovercraft and gently laid Lily down. Lily noticed the other man and tried to cover herself. Noticing her discomfort, the boy soaked a light cloth and laid it over her.

The older man raised a lamp and showed his face flashing the palest of green eyes. He had almost no hair, not even eyebrows, nothing but a wispy goatee of red hairs on his chin. A hat typical of the Outback covered his bald head. He was of the ancient people who had survived the apocalypse out in the open. The ocean breeze from the Pacific had moderated the effects of the radiation, but it still left its mark on the survivors. As a result, they had evolved into humans with reptile-like skin, thickened from the radiation exposure.

"My mates call me Jim," he said. "Quite useful to have this lad as a mate. I thought he was a bit of a shonky bloke, as he wouldn't leave me alone, but he's true blue. He convinced me to come out from Rungoo in the late arvo to look for you."

Lily smiled. She had faced death and survived.

"You should be dead," said the man. "No worries, miss, you'll be right. I'll take you back to my sheila. She'll be happy you made it. Never one so sunbaked has returned from this desert alive. She'll take care of you, clean you up, fix your dress. I'll work on repairing your hover buggy. I don't mind a bit of hard yakka, but I'm no one's dogsbody. But no wukkas. Now that I've met you, I'll start at first sparrow tomorrow. Out in the Outback, if a stranger doesn't help you, there ain't no one who will."

Lily smiled in relief then accepted another sip of water from the boy. As the man turned to start the hover, the dingo jumped back aboard and licked Lily's face.

29

An Answer to Prayers

MAMI'S EYES STARED BLANKLY. "Where will you search?"

"I need to think like someone on the run," Ema said. Her facial expression deepened as she sank into thought.

"I'll tell you what he won't do—he won't return to the city," said Doc. "Central Control has been compacting all the androids from the trials."

"He'll hide in the wilderness," Luca said.

Papi nodded. "But where?"

"Today, I'll search higher up the mountain and ask the Wallaman," Doc suggested.

I'll go with you," said Papi.

"Sounds good," Doc said. They waved farewell and soon were out of sight.

"Okay, how about we search the area below Greystone," said Ema. Mami nodded and followed her down to the pond.

A sudden cold breeze blew from the gray sky and carried a single snowflake down the mountain. "It's snowing on top," said Mami. "It's too warm to be snowing down here." It was a sign it would be a mild summer and winter would come early. Ema smiled as she noticed other snowflakes in the air.

"Do you hear that?" Mami asked as a faint sound approached.

"It's a hover," Ema said running toward the sound. She didn't have to go far before she recognized the familiar hovercraft. "Lily!

Lily's back!"

Lily leapt from the hover and ran to her sister.

"Oh my God! Oh my God! You're back," Ema exclaimed.

Lily beamed joyfully in Ema's arms, but upon seeing Mami, she screamed in disbelief. "Mami!" she cried as she entered her mother's' embrace.

"I was so afraid for you," Lily said. "It's a miracle you're here." Lily turned to the boy, to whom no one had paid much attention. "But the world is full of miracles. Let me introduce you to my friend. He's the one who rescued me."

"Thank you so much for saving my sister," Ema gushed as she hugged him.

"His name is—" Lily paused, quickly pondering what to call him.

Seeing the confused expression on her face, the synth interjected, "Caleb. My name is Caleb," the assassin quickly answered.

"Oh, my goodness," Mami said. She hugged the boy in appreciation. "Thank you so much."

"I almost didn't make it. If it weren't for Caleb, I'd be dead."

"Others helped as well," Caleb said with a charming smile and the accent of the fishermen from Rungoo. But his skin was smooth, and he clearly was not from Rungoo. Ema believed this teenage boy anyway. She didn't care about the details. She was just happy to have her sister back.

"Thanks, Caleb," Ema said. "I don't know how I can ever repay you."

"There's no need. I'm glad I was able to help."

30

I'm Ready

LILY AWOKE LATE FEELING refreshed. It felt good to be back, and she was excited to be with her family. As she rose, she tripped over Caleb. He was lying on the floor by her bed. Since her rescue, he hadn't left her side.

"Hi, Caleb. I didn't see you there," she said with a laugh. "Let's see who else is awake."

Lily ran to Ema's bed and smiled at her sister.

"Hey, sleepyhead," Lily said as she leapt onto Ema.

Ema slowly stretched.

"Good morning," Lily said, her face just inches away.

"It's nice to see you, too," Ema said. With a laugh, she pushed her sister off her.

Caleb was standing just a few feet away, and he surprised Ema.

"Oh, good morning, Caleb," Ema said.

"Morning," Caleb answered awkwardly.

"Let's go see who's here," Lily said.

Papi and Doc had returned in the night and sat by the fire with Mami waiting for their girls to wake.

Seeing her father, Lily rushed into his embrace.

"Papi, I have missed you so much," Lily said rushing into his arms.

"Oh, my little girl. You're back."

"Yes. Caleb saved me."

Papi turned to Caleb and shook his hand. "Thanks, so much."

Not wanting to shine attention on Caleb, Lily changed the topic. "But tell me about your captivity."

Mami held Papi's hand as she spoke. "I thank the good Lord, we had each other. My biggest fear was not knowing what would happen."

"We were taken care of well enough," Papi said. "But I tell you, the constant stress of being confined in a cell and not knowing the reason for our imprisonment was straining."

Mami nodded in agreement. "It'll take some time for things to get back to normal."

"Tell us what happened to you," Ema said, turning to Lily.

"The assassin took me across the orange desert to the sea," Lily said glancing at Caleb. She was careful not to implicate her friend.

"I've seen the desert from one of the mountaintops but have never been there myself," Papi said. "The stories I've heard tell of how impossible a place it is."

"You wouldn't believe how impossible," Lily said nodding in agreement, her skin still showing her sunburn.

"What happened next?" Ema asked.

"I found myself in the hovercraft, broken down by the seashore with no sign of the assassin. I know now it was a mistake to try and cross the desert, as I almost died trying. I would be dead if Caleb hadn't rescued me." Lily grinned at Caleb and held his hand as he looked back at her. Lily knew he appreciated her covering for him and giving him another chance.

Doc, Luca, Ethan, and Peter now entered with much excitement. Ema ran into Luca's arms and kissed him on the lips.

Papi seemed surprised. "Well, it appears the two of you have a liking for each other. It seems a lot has happened while we were away."

"She's the best thing ever to happen to me," Luca said placing his android arm around her.

"What happened to your arm?" Papi asked.

"I got shot when I escaped the city," Luca explained. "Your daughters found me on the old mining road and saved me."

Ema smiled and kissed him again. "Luca's been my right arm," she teased as she tickled his side.

Doc patted Luca on his shoulder then, seeing Lily, gave her a lasting hug. "So good to see you back, my girl."

"Thanks for searching for me but if it hadn't been for Caleb I don't think anyone would have ever found me." Lily smiled gratefully as she placed her hand on Caleb's arm.

Ethan wanted to hug Lily but instead he turned his head away sheepishly, feeling awkward.

"Everything important to me is with me right here, right now," Papi said, grinning at his family. "I just want to celebrate. Besides, I know someone due a party."

Lily jumped with joy. "I'm ready!" she said.

"Yes, but is the world ready for you?" Ema added with a laugh. "And what about my birthday?"

"Of course, we will celebrate that as well." Mami said hugging Ema.

"Okay. Who wants to help?" Ema asked.

"Doc and I can round up the neighbors," Papi said.

"Tell me what I can do," Ethan said.

"I'll take care of the food preparations. You and Luca can come hunting with me." Ema grabbed Luca by the hand and Ethan followed them.

"Peter and Caleb, you can gather wood, lots of wood," Mami said.

"Yes, ma'am," Caleb said with his Aussie accent as everyone hurried off to do their tasks.

"Lily, can you stay for a moment?" Mami called out above the commotion.

"What would you like me to do?" Lily asked.

"I want to do your hair. You will have many birthdays in your life, but only one coming out. Now, sit down here."

Lily excitedly sat on a stool as her mother filled a large bowl with warm water. She bent over the bowl, and her mother washed her black hair with lavender soap. Afterward, Mami combed out her wet hair and then reached for a pair of scissors.

"You're not going to cut my hair, are you?"

"Trust me," Mami said with a smile. Lily felt nervous though she knew her hair was much too long.

Mami trimmed her hair and then dried it. "Now, let's do something special," Mami said. "I know exactly what to do." She began to braid it. After Mami finished, she carefully wrapped the braids into an elaborate bun, connecting them with a long pin. Lily saw how pleased Mami looked and became excited.

"I want to see," Lily squealed.

"Not yet. I'm not finished."

Mami dusted Lily's face with a light powder, then added some color along her cheekbones using cherry dust. After mixing cherry dust with cooking oil, she painted Lily's lips red with a small brush.

"Now you can look," Mami said, handing Lily a small mirror.

"Wow. I look amazing," Lily said with a beaming smile. "I love it."

"I have something else for you," Mami said.

Lily turned and was surprised to see Mami holding a package wrapped in brown burlap.

"It's not much, but I've been working on it for some time. I hope you like it," Mami said, handing Lily the package.

Being poor Lily expected little regarding gifts. Nevertheless, she excitedly pulled off the wrapping. "Oh, my. It's beautiful." Lily smiled with gratitude. Mami had made her a lovely white dress with satin trim. "I can't wait to try it on," Lily said as she rushed to change her clothes. Moments later, she proudly stood before her mother. "Well, what do you think?"

Mami's face turned red, and she covered her mouth in awe. "Oh, my darling girl. You're so beautiful." Mami was not one to exaggerate or give false praise. Lily indeed looked beautiful.

A commotion at the cavern entrance signaled the early arrival of the first guests, each bringing their favorite dish. Soon, the cavern bustled with excitement as more neighbors arrived. With Ema coordinating the food, Papi and Mami rushed to welcome everyone. They all excitedly waited to see Lily, who was hiding in a side chamber. Papi would call her when it was time for her to come out.

As evening arrived, everything was finally in place. The musicians started to play, and the cavern filled with the sweet melodies of their music. People engaged in lively conversations, while children laughed and playfully chased each other. This was the moment of the day when the sunlight hit the falls at just the right angle, causing its colors to burst forth like a turquoise fire. It was a truly magical moment.

Papi's wine was a rare treat, and he eagerly indulged his guests. He poured everyone a drink. Then, wanting their attention, he waved his arm from the center of the gathering. Everyone looked at him as he cleared his throat and raised his wine cup.

"Welcome, my friends," he said in a loud voice. "Welcome to all."

The cavern quieted. Even the dogs paused in their playful chase to listen.

Papi stepped forward, his warm eyes surveying the gathering. "Welcome to all who are dear to my family and me," he began. "Welcome to our kinfolk, our old friends, and the new ones we've had the pleasure of meeting. Mami and I appreciate each of you, and we want to thank you from the bottom of our hearts."

A murmur of appreciation rippled through the crowd. Papi continued, "We want to express our gratitude to Venky for caring for Graystone and the animals, and to our dear neighbors for sharing their food. But, above all, we want to thank Doc and Caleb."

A round of applause erupted, with cheers filling the cavern.

Mami stood beside Papi, her radiant smile matching her husband's gratitude. "Doc, your gems can't outshine the glow of your heart," she said, raising her cup in a toast. "Thanks, my friend. Papi and I love you. And Caleb, thank you for bringing our daughter back, whom we celebrate this evening."

The crowd responded with cheers and more applause.

"Ema, dear, come here with Mami and me," Papi continued. "I tell you what, when we were held captive, Ema, our eldest, filled our shoes. She did a great job."

Ema's bright smile lit up her face as she joined her parents. Mami had also done her hair and applied some makeup to highlight her cheeks and lips. Everyone took notice and cheered.

"Hear, hear!" Luca shouted as the room filled with applause. Ema's face blushed as she signaled Luca to keep it down. But Luca cheered all the louder.

"I want everyone to know she has just had her twentieth birthday, and this celebration is for her too."

The crowd cheered as Luca whooped loudly.

Papi continued, "As you know, I have two daughters. My youngest is now celebrating her coming of age. I will always remember her as a little girl searching for caterpillars in the garden. Mami and I couldn't be prouder of the young woman she has become. We thought she was lost, so I'm thankful to God for bringing her back to us. With much joy and love, we now share her with the world—our lovely daughter, Lily."

The cavern erupted into wild cheers as Lily stepped forward. Her radiant beauty was undeniable. She hugged her family and then stood alone by the fire. As she slowly gazed at the people before her, her silver eyes mesmerized and enchanted them, and they quickly quieted to hear her speak.

"I'm so happy you're all here," she spoke in a clear voice. "I love you all." The crowd clapped in response.

"Papi and Mami raised me to be who I've become," she continued. "I'm so thankful for them. They taught me how to survive and have faith in God. Hope, faith, and love are the pillars of my life which I share with all I hold dear—hope for today and tomorrow, faith in God and each other, and love without rules. Finally, I would like to thank my big sister. You are my role model."

The crowd erupted into applause once more, their spirits lifted by the heartwarming speech. Ema and Luca exchanged smiles, appreciating the touching moment.

As the clapping slowly quieted, Venky began playing his tabla, infusing the atmosphere with an irresistible rhythm. Lily, her eyes shining mischievously, couldn't resist the urge to dance. She playfully attempted to coax Doc onto the dance floor, but he bashfully declined, much to the amusement of the onlookers. Lily made another attempt to draw a man into the dance, but he remained in his seat.

Just as she was starting to lose hope of enticing others onto the floor, Caleb made his entrance, joining the dance with Lily. She couldn't hide her surprise. "You can dance?" she asked, her lips curving into a whimsical smile.

Caleb struck a dramatic pose, signaling a sensual dance, and Venky adjusted the rhythm accordingly. To the astonishment of everyone, it quickly became apparent Caleb was an expert dancer. His skills left Lily with a shocked expression, and he took pleasure in her response. Lily joined him in the dance, and the crowd couldn't help but clap to the beat. Before long, others gathered around, feeling the irresistible pull of the music and the two captivating dancers.

After several minutes, Vanya, Venky's 17-year-old granddaughter, decided to join Lily. "You're good," she commended Lily. "Your boyfriend can really dance," she said with a playful grin.

Lily chuckled and clarified, "He's not my boyfriend."

To which Vanya responded, "Well, you won't mind then," as she engaged Caleb in the center of the floor. Her movements were as skilled as her partner's, adding her own unique flair to the rhythm. The crowd cheered in delight.

Ema grabbed Luca with one hand and her mother with the other, pulling them onto the dance floor. They joined Lily and they danced together, as Mami attempted the modern dance. Their laughter soon filled the room.

Papi, inspired by his wife and the music which enveloped the cavernous space, approached Mami with a look of admiration. He held her hand, and they swayed to the music in each other's embrace. Words became unnecessary as their connection spoke volumes. Lily watched the beautiful scene, understanding this was their gift to her— a chance to embrace life on one's own terms, filled with hope, music, and love.

Lily nodded to Papi, and he returned the gesture, continuing to dance with Mami.

Throughout the evening, they not only shared their food and wine but, more importantly, their profound love for one another. Lily ensured everyone participated, wanting her new friends to understand this was how life should be lived. Each of them absorbed this experience in their own unique way, with some, like Caleb and Peter, processing it through their learning algorithms.

II

Book Two

"Some say the world will end in fire,
Some say in ice.
From what I've tasted of desire
I hold with those who favor fire.
But if it had to perish twice,
I think I know enough of hate,
To know that for destruction ice
Is also great,
And would suffice."
—Robert Frost

31

Surprise

THE MORNING LIGHT FOUND Ema's groggy body stretching in her bed. Slowly, she ran her hand through her tangled hair and stretched again. She saw Luca sleeping nearby. "Hey," she called out to him. "Get up. The coffee's not going to make itself."

Luca climbed out of bed and put a pot on the fire. Soon, its aroma filled the air. "Ahh. That smells good," Luca said. After a few minutes, he poured himself some and took a slow sip.

Ema entered the area and held out an empty cup. He reached over to pour her some, then teasingly pulled away the pot.

"Hey. That's not funny," she said, pouting.

He laughed and poured her a cup of the dark, magical liquid.

"Hmm. Much better," Ema said, nodding.

Doc shuffled into the room. Luca handed him a coffee and Doc clinked his cup against Ema's. "Cheers," Doc said. He finished his coffee quickly.

"How can you drink it so fast?" Ema said in astonishment.

"I'm in a hurry and it's time for me to go. I'm heading back if anyone needs a ride."

"We'll miss you. It's been great having you around."

"Last night's party got me thinking—" he said, but then stopped abruptly, not wanting to say more. He had enjoyed the party, but it had made him feel dissatisfied with his life. He now wanted more.

Ethan had entered the area and overheard Doc saying he was

ready to go. "I'd like a ride to the city gate. I want to check on a friend of mine."

"Okay. Let's go." With a brief wave, Doc bid farewell and headed toward the entrance. Lily entered the cavern just then with Mami and Papi. They were returning from an early morning walk. Mami saw Doc leaving and gave him a long hug. "Bye, Doc, my old friend."

"Hey, Doc, wait," Caleb said. "It's time for me to go as well. I don't have family and would like to join you." His Rungoo accent was soft but uniquely his own.

"You can't go," Lily protested. "You're part of my family now. Don't leave."

"Papi, can he stay with us?" Lily pleaded.

Papi glanced over at Mami. She nodded. "We've all suffered too much separation anxiety already," Mami said.

"Thank you!" Lily squealed. She grabbed Caleb and hugged him as she jumped up and down.

Ema smiled at her sister. She appreciated the need for companionship and glanced at Luca with longing eyes.

"Okay, okay," Doc said. "It's time for me to leave. I'm heading out."

"Wait for me," Ethan said as he followed Doc out of the cavern. Peter was just outside the entrance. "Hey, Peter. Do you want to come with me?"

"Sure," Peter said. "But I'm not entering the city. I can wait for you outside the gate."

Inside the cavern, the atmosphere was filled with excitement and anticipation. Papi clapped his hands, the sound echoing through the rocky chamber. "Well, I'm excited about going back to Graystone. Who's ready to go?"

"I am," Mami chimed in with a smile.

Lily, her arm intertwined with Caleb's, added, "Me too, and Caleb is coming with me."

Everyone's attention turned to Ema. She glanced up at Luca, and a silent understanding passed between them. With a grin, she stood by his side and took his hand.

"Mami, Papi," Ema began, her voice revealing her wavering confidence. "I'm going to stay here in the cavern with Luca."

Mami's eyes reflected a mix of emotions. She understood her daughter's need to start her own life but still longed for more time with her. However, it came as no surprise, as she had already sensed the bond growing between Ema and Luca.

Papi turned his gaze to Ema. "Well, the way you two look at each other has been on my mind," he admitted, his voice filled with fatherly warmth. "You'll always have a place at home with us."

Lily, ever the supportive sister, chimed in playfully, "Oh, she's not going anywhere, Papi. She'll be right here with Luca in the cavern. It's only a short walk."

With heartfelt embraces, Ema hugged her parents, realizing the bittersweet nature of the moment. Her gaze then shifted to her sister, and they shared a prolonged hug, acknowledging their childhood had come to an end.

"Come visit me tomorrow, Lily," Ema called out as they waved goodbye from the cavern's entrance. Then her family was gone. Ema was glad to be alone with Luca. It was the beginning of their lives together and she held him close. She listened to his heart beating as their bodies warmed each other. With nervous excitement, she trembled in his arms.

"Hello there," Ema whispered, looking at him with a longing smile.

Luca squeezed her into him. "Hello, you."

Ema glanced up at Luca with admiration and love. His android arm was just a part of who he was. She accepted this. She looked up as the sky outlined his face. *How lucky I am? Everything has worked out.* Now since her family was back together, she reflected on all that had happened. She had been attracted to Luca from early on, almost from first sight. Since then, her attraction had grown into love. She looked again into his face. As his hazel eyes sparkled in the sun, she smiled at him. She knew he was the one for her.

Luca stared back and looked deeply into her green eyes. He leaned into her face and softly kissed her lips. In the forest culture, marriage was an ancient tradition done privately between two individuals who were in love and ready to commit. Marriage was a personal vow to each other in the sight of God. Later, they would celebrate with family and friends, but for now, they stood alone in the intimacy of their solitude.

Ema bowed her head briefly. "Thank you, God, for bringing me Luca." She grabbed Luca's hands, looked into his eyes, and paused briefly before speaking. "I want to sing with you. I want to dance. I want to laugh in your arms. I want to be your woman forever. Will you be my man?"

Without hesitating, Luca squeezed her hands warmly. "Yes. I will be your man. I will laugh with you, and I will cry with you. I want to sing the music of our lives together. I will love you forever—till time ends and is no more." He retrieved the two rings from the gold chain around his neck. "These were my grandparents. My mother gave these to me after they had passed. She said they were for my wedding." He took the smaller gold ring and placed it on Ema's finger.

"It's so beautiful!" She took the other ring from his open palm and, trembling with joy, placed it on his finger. "They're perfect."

Luca pulled Ema toward him and gave her a passionate kiss. Her whole body flushed as her passion for him grew. After a few minutes, she pushed away from him and broke his embrace.

She directed him with her finger. "Follow me, handsome," she said in a seductive voice.

"Where are we going?" Luca asked with a curious smile.

"It's a surprise," Ema teased. She led him down the trail to the rock ledge over the pond and stopped. As Luca approached her, she backed up several steps toward the ledge. He eyed her with curiosity while his gaze unabashedly took in the outline of her body under her dress. Ema loosened the strap of her dress and let it fall to the ground.

"Surprise!" she shouted as she threw her hands above her head. Before he could respond, she spun around and made a perfect dive into the pond below.

"Are you coming?" she called up to him.

Aroused with anticipation, Luca threw his clothes off as fast as possible and jumped into the pond. Ema squealed as he landed next to her.

Excited to explore her man, she swiftly reached the shore as a gust of wind blew over the water. Within moments, the first thunder rumbled through the air. It signaled the arrival of a sudden storm. Luca leaned over and kissed her. His loving affection met her glowing face. Inside her burned an ember now bursting into flames. On the smooth, limestone shore, she rolled onto Luca, and her body melted into his as one. Her soft breasts pressed into his hard chest.

The tempest now descended between the mountain peaks and into the crevasses of the valley. As she experienced the fullness of his love, her body craved more. The first drops fell, tingling and teasing her naked body. Then a strong wind blew and pulled at her hair. Even the tallest trees swayed in great anticipation, for within the storm, life existed on the edge of danger and rebirth, of thirst and plenty, and of pain and ecstasy.

Luca rolled Ema onto her back and took charge as thunder pounded through the air. Again and again, it drowned out her screams. She raised her arms above her head and surrendered to him. He took her breath away as a great wave of pleasure built up within her and reached a climax. In the crack of lightning, time stood still, and she found herself in a world of her own. Nothing else mattered.

As the lightning passed, the thunder continued to rumble through her body.

Neither Luca nor the storm could hold back as the thunderstorm burst its store upon Ema. The warm drops splashed over her, and she felt a sense of contentment. Then shortly thereafter, the fading sound of thunder signaled the farewell from the storm, and the rain ended. It was over. With his love spent, Luca rolled off her. Together, they relaxed on the pond's shore as their breathing quieted.

"I love thunder," Ema said with a giggle.

"You're in luck. There's a storm nearly every day. Sometimes more than one," Luca said mischievously.

She kissed him and stared into his eyes with a contented smile.

He softly stroked her eyebrow with his android hand and whispered, "I love you."

Ema rolled on top of him with a sly expression on her face. "Tell me again tomorrow," she said. She combed his brown hair off his face and looked into his eyes. Her expression turned serious. "I'm so glad you're mine. I will love you until there are no more tomorrows." She lovingly kissed him and snuggled in his embrace.

Ema and Luca stayed there, holding each other until the clouds moved down the valley. Happy for the return of the warmth of the sun's rays, they scampered together, back to their clothes on the ledge above.

"Our clothes are soaking wet," Ema said with a laugh. "I think we should wait until we get some dry ones."

Luca smiled as he looked at her. "I prefer you this way, anyway," he said. He leaned over and gave her another kiss.

"Thanks, Doc," Ethan said. He and Peter quickly jumped off the hover and Doc left in an apparent hurry. But in all reality, he had nowhere to go. He went a short distance and stopped aside the road.

No one was waiting for him at his home if he could call it that. He stared down the road. One direction led to the shack and the solitude of his cellar. But in Doc's heart, he no longer wanted to be there.

Lily is right, Doc thought. *I am an old guy. Life is passing me by.*

A flock flew east toward the late morning sun, wings against the wind. The birds called him as if they were asking him to join them. Doc exhaled a long breath and made his decision. After many years of loneliness and isolation, he yearned to live his life again. With his heart broken since the loss of his wife, he had not been ready to move on. But now it was time. Doc placed his hands on his head and pulled at his hair. A lump formed in his throat as he tried to speak. He cleared his throat and looked up at the sky.

"I love you, my dear, with all my heart," he said. "But it's time for me to let you go. Goodbye, my love." He watched the sky as the flock disappeared onto the horizon. He imagined them taking her with them. Doc looked in the other direction, the direction of the trading post. He knew why he was in such a hurry. His life was waiting for him. Katyana was waiting.

32

The Password

THE NEXT MORNING, Lily waited outside the cavern with Caleb. She rarely rose early; this morning was different. She sat silently and waited for the sun to rise as she sipped out of a waterskin. It was nice not always having to talk. She didn't yet want to disturb the peacefulness of the morning or the new couple. Sitting in a nook on the side of the mountain, Lily covered herself with her wrap and fought to stay awake. She closed her eyes.

She was surprised by a sudden wind. It did not come from any direction but instead swirled around her. Unexpectedly, it lifted her into the air. She feared falling but soon realized she was being carried by a hand of wind. She flew in communion with the Creator, allowing His spirit to carry her higher and higher. She could see her farm and the city in the valley below. She continued to rise, above the top of the mountains, and saw the sunrise. Then the wind returned her to the waterfall. She hovered over it momentarily, then flew into the cavern, to the abyss.

From the silence of the deep, she heard a voice as ancient as time. "And what is unknown shall become known," the voice said. A marker now became visible as if from within a cloud. On one side was an image of the First Mother—on the adjacent side, a handprint. The handprint glowed bright blue and the pillar said, "Peace be with you."

Lily's eyes opened wide as her vision ended. She quickly turned to Caleb. "Come with me."

Caleb followed Lily through the cavern's entrance, and toward the roar of the falls. Mist enveloped them as they approached the paddlewheel. Lily gestured to the lever, and with a simple pull, Caleb triggered the ancient machinery into motion. After engaging the paddlewheel, they moved past the remnants of Ema's fire. Seeing her sister and Luca were still lost in slumber, she grabbed some torches and ventured into the cavern.

Lily led the way, retracing the path she had traversed before, the glow stones providing light. Soon, they arrived at the abyss and the enchanting glowworms illuminated a myriad of waterfalls pouring their silvery threads into the ancient keep.

"I can sense it. Don't you feel it?" she exclaimed in the eerie light.

"I can't hear or see anything unusual, but the stairway is this way," Caleb said. He activated his searchlight, and Lily followed his lead with her torch.

The stairway spiraled downward, its steps uneven and roughly hewn, a stark hint the structure was not a place of beauty but a place of necessity. Undaunted by potential dangers, they pressed forward, moving deeper into the bowels of the abyss. Lily passed by the first opening, then stopped at the second, mindful of the stairway's deteriorating condition. There, she peered into the dark from the lookout point. "Something is out there," she declared, her sixth sense tingling, a silent harbinger. "I can feel it." She let an arrow fly and in the next moment, an explosive burst of light illuminated the heart of the deep, revealing a glimpse of a giant metallic sphere. Though it quickly extinguished into the shadows, it provided a sneak peek.

"Oh, my!" Lily exclaimed, her heart racing with excitement. "Did you see that? It's huge, truly huge." She shot another arrow to reveal more details. The sphere was covered by a shiny mosaic of silver plates. As the light again faded, Lily's curiosity caused her to run down the stairs. Caleb matched her pace.

Several hundred more steps passed quickly before their journey culminated at the foot of the stairwell. To one side, a stream of water flowed into a crevice, while the other revealed a ramp terminating at the imposing doorway of the unknown structure. Lily cautiously advanced toward the entrance, her sense of awe usurping her caution.

"What do you think this is, Caleb?" she asked, her voice brimming with intrigue.

"I do not know." Caleb said as he studied the shiny metal plates covering its exterior and the intricate pattern of geometric shapes. "The scale, the craftsmanship—it's astonishing. I've never seen anything like it, not even in the Book of Knowledge."

"Just think, it was waiting here, in my cavern, all this time."

"I don't think anyone was meant to find it," Caleb mused. "That is, no one but you." Caleb scrutinized the structure's underpinnings. "Look at the understructure." The vessel sat on a large circular ring.

"Yes, I see it."

"I think it's a docking station. This must be a vessel of some kind," Caleb announced decisively, his android intellect quickly piecing together clues. "Notice the seal covering the doorway?"

Lily's attention turned to the ancient door. Countless layers of dust obscured its surface. She reached out and touched it prompting a cascade of dust to fill the air, engulfing her.

Lily withdrew from the cloud of particles coughing and sputtering. Unexpectedly a sharp pain filled her side as she collided with a solid object. "Ouch," she exclaimed. It was a stone pillar. On one side, it was adorned with the image of the First Mother, and on the adjacent side, an imprint of a hand. As the air cleared, she beckoned Caleb over. "I've seen this pillar before."

"What do you mean?" Caleb asked, placing his android hand on the handprint. It responded by illuminating, signaling the activation of a security mechanism on the door, then flashed red.

"Identitatem, non ex auctoritate," the pillar announced clearly. "Propria auctoritate requiritur."

Caleb looked at Lily, confused as to how to respond.

A number appeared on the pillar and started to count down slowly.

"Twenty...Nineteen...Eighteen..."

"What's happening?" Lily shouted as she studied it further.

"Seventeen...Sixteen...Fifteen..."

Two side panels opened on either side of the doorway, revealing laser blasters aimed at Caleb.

"It is a security device, and it has started a countdown timer!" Caleb said loudly.

"Thirteen...Twelve...Eleven..."

"Run!" Caleb yelled. He turned and ran back down the ramp. Then he aimed his weapon at one of the doorway blasters. The ship fired at Caleb, making him duck behind a large rock. Caleb held his fire, and the security blasters pointed at Lily, still standing by the pillar.

Lily remembered her dream as the countdown timer continued.

"Nine...Eight...Seven..."

"Run, Lily!" Caleb screamed. "Get away from there."

"Six... Five...Four..."

Lily placed her hand on the security device.

"Three...Two...One..."

The countdown stopped.

"Probans tuam identitatem," the pillar said re-illuminating. A few seconds later, the security device flashed blue. "Identitas confirmavit. Dic tesserae."

"Peace be with you," Lily said.

"Identity and password validated. Initialization authorized," it responded, switching to English. Immediately, the weapons receded and the seal over the door crumbled, falling off the entryway. "Starship Covenant re-initialization started as per previously programmed settings. The door will open after initialization is complete."

Per some ancient plan, the ship started coming to life. A humming sound emitted from the vessel, and the ship began to awaken from its long sleep. As the power grid returned online, an electromagnetic pulse flashed through the cavern. The ship shuddered in its docking station then settled, and the honeycomb panels covering the ship glowed a soft silver.

Lily withdrew her hand, overcome with awe.

"This is incredible," Caleb said. "I was correct. I thought it was a vessel."

Lily gasped with surprise. "What just happened?"

"I don't know," said Caleb.

Lily grabbed Caleb's hand. "I think all my dreams are real," she whispered in shock.

"This is enough excitement for today," Caleb said. "Okay? We can come back tomorrow and explore how to enter the vessel."

Lily nodded in agreement. "We have a lot to absorb," Lily said.

As they turned to leave, the entry door opened.

33

A Feather Bed

KATYANA STRUGGLED WITH THE rusty hoe. Tackling the overgrown weeds which had claimed her backyard was an even bigger task than she had feared. But then, an unexpected helper arrived— Doc's hand reached for the hoe, gently wrestling it from her grasp. She turned to meet his familiar gaze, her expression welcoming and filled with warmth.

"Hello, Doc. I've been worried about you," she admitted with concern in her voice.

Doc's response was calm, his gaze steady. "No need for worry, Katyana."

She frowned slightly. "With everything that's happened, I can't help but worry."

His laughter, a deep and weathered sound, filled the air. "No one's chasing an old man like me. Not even those damn machines are interested."

Katyana's tone softened, and she leaned in closer, her eyes finding his. "But you know this is not true. I am interested in you. Can't you tell, you old fool?"

A boyish grin crept onto Doc's face, and though he wasn't one for eloquent words, his intent was clear. "You once told me if I ever grew tired of living in a hole in the ground, I should pay you a visit. Well, here I am, and I'd like to stay with you, Katyana, if you don't mind."

Katyana's fingers found a shock of his white hair as she embraced him. "Oh, I'd love that," she whispered warmly. "I've waited so long to hear those words from you. What took you so long?"

Doc remained silent then decided to start working the hoe, immersing himself in something in which he was more capable.

Filled with gratitude, Katyana's smile radiated as she hurried inside to prepare a pitcher of lemonade. She was thrilled to see the thaw in Doc's affections, a testament to her years of patient waiting.

Upon her return with the refreshment, the backyard already had undergone significant transformation. She placed the pitcher on the back steps and waved at Doc, who acknowledged her with a nod before resuming his labor.

The yard, once cluttered and chaotic, now became a level canvas of freshly upturned earth, a reflection of Doc's desire to impress Katyana. Amid some remaining overgrowth around the shed, Doc's hoe struck something hard with a resounding clang. Excitement gripped him as he uncovered an old tub, half-buried for years. Though it was quite an effort to dig out, his eyes gleamed with the thought of bathing at the end of a long day. Having rescued it from the ground, he lugged it over to the water pump.

Without pausing to rest, he turned his attention to the shed, striving to transform it into a comfortable living space. Doc neatly stacked the boxes to one side and used an old broom to sweep away the accumulated dust and debris. His resourcefulness shone as he fashioned a bed frame and table from some scrap lumber. Lastly, he adorned the table with an old lantern.

"Finished," Doc declared with a contented smile. The shed, now transformed, brought back memories of the cellar in the mining shack he had called home. "Looks pretty good, if I say so myself."

His arms bore a thick layer of dirt, and an earthy scent clung to his body. The prospect of a long-overdue bath filled him with excitement. He approached the pump, and with a few squeaky strokes, water flowed into the tub. After rinsing the grime away, he filled the tub to the brim and eagerly climbed in. Anyone in proximity would have heard gasps of ecstasy as he eased his aching muscles into the soothing water.

Doc scrubbed away layers of dirt and sweat, rendering himself a new man. Emerging from the bath, he roamed around as he did at his shack, naked, totally oblivious to Katyana's watchful gaze from her back window. With equal diligence, he continued by hand-washing his soiled clothes, then hanging them on old hooks outside the shed.

He entered his shed and dressed, selecting his best shirt and pants, then arranged his remaining clean clothes on his bed, trying to add some comfort. After combing through his long, white hair, he tied it into a neat ponytail. Clean and refreshed, he took a moment to admire his accomplishment. "Not bad. Not bad at all."

A knock resounded from the doorway. Surprised, Doc looked up to find Katyana standing there, clad in a flattering, light-blue dress. Her dress emphasized her slender figure, though it was her cleavage which stole the limelight.

"You did a fantastic job with the yard," Katyana said in appreciation. "I barely recognize it."

"Thanks, Katyana, but the yard is nothing compared to you," Doc said, chancing a glance at her bosom.

Katyana smiled, pleased with the compliment coming from the right man. "Here, come with me now," she instructed.

Doc picked up the lantern and closed the shed door. Katyana waited for him by the house, and as he approached, she took his hand, helping him up the weathered back steps. Still holding his hand, she escorted Doc into her cozy living space tucked within the shop.

A simple table adorned with fresh bread and a bottle of wine awaited, graced by a small vase of hand-picked wildflowers. It had been a long time since such thoughtfulness had been extended to him. Doc's stomach, ever vocal, let out an eager rumble, to which he responded with a gentle pat. Having gone the entire day without a meal, his anticipation was palpable. "Smells good. I can't wait."

"Take a seat and make yourself comfortable," Katyana instructed from the kitchen. In no time, she returned, carrying two steaming bowls of hearty stew to the table. The rich aroma swirled in the air igniting Doc's senses as Katyana took her seat. Without hesitation, he sampled the fare, and a contented smile spread across his face as the tender meat melted in his mouth. The wine-infused broth elevated the medley of flavors, with notes of rosemary, garlic, and thyme dancing on his taste buds.

Katyana leaned in to explain. "I thickened the broth with a butter paste mixed with flour. It takes the stew to a whole new level."

Doc, thoroughly appreciative, nudged more stew onto his spoon, using a piece of freshly baked bread. "You're a remarkable cook," he praised, aware of the time and effort she had dedicated to crafting this meal. Just when he thought the experience couldn't improve, he chuckled as Katyana presented him with a serving of blueberry crumble accompanied by a steaming cup of brew. "Oh my, I could get used to this."

The dishes cleared, Katyana started washing them, but to her surprise Doc rolled up his sleeves and joined her without hesitation. "I've been washing my own dishes for quite a few years," Doc said. "Now I'm washing them with you. I'd say this is a significant improvement." His playful comment prompted a grin and a side hug from his companion. There was an undeniable ease in their partnership and, working in harmony, they completed the task in little time.

When they finished, Katyana reached for Doc's hands, feeling their warmth and strength. She raised his hands to her lips and kissed them tenderly. Noticing several large blisters from the day's work, she exclaimed, "Poor thing. Come, let's rest on the couch together."

Doc settled on the couch and retrieved his pipe—an antique piece made of rosewood with a mahogany mouthpiece.

"I didn't know you smoked."

"Ahh, peppermint oil," he said as he sucked on his pipe.

She smiled with relief. "What else don't I know about you? Tell me more about yourself," she said, nestling into a comfortable embrace while sitting on the couch.

"Ah, I'm strong and hardworking. And, ah, yes, I have endurance."

"You sound like a beast of burden," she joked. "What are you, an ox?"

Doc laughed.

"How would you describe me?" she asked as she straightened her dress and pulled her hand through her hair.

"You're delightfully delicious," he said with a warm smile, "like one of your pies."

"Stop it. You're being funny."

"You think that's funny? You haven't seen me naked."

"Oh, yeah? What makes you so sure?"

Doc feigned surprise. "You were peeking?"

"You're a big man. It was hard to miss." Katyana started to laugh. She couldn't help herself. The more she tried to stop, the more she laughed. Her laughter was contagious and soon, Doc joined her. After they could laugh no more, she started to cry.

"There, there, Katyana," Doc said. "I know. I was lonely too."

He put his arms around her and started to sing in his gruff voice. It was a song from their youth—a song she knew. They spent the evening hours together, singing old songs. Then, as if someone had awakened Doc from a dream, a sad expression crossed his face as he realized it was late and time for him to go to the shed.

"Thank you for such a delicious meal and the pleasure of your company. I better be going to bed now." He hugged her goodnight, picked up the lantern, and headed to the back door.

"Clive?" Katyana called out.

Doc paused long enough to enjoy the sound of his name and turned around.

Katyana stood by a wooden door to another room. "I didn't invite you to sleep in the shed. Come, sleep in my bed." She smiled nervously, fearing rejection as she opened the door to her bedroom.

Doc had not slept on a real bed in ages. But it was nothing in comparison to his feelings for her. He held her in a warm embrace. "Where have you been all these lonely years?" he said.

"Right in front of your bloody eyes."

A feather bed lay waiting inside the room, freshly made with clean pillowcases and her finest white linens. Doc lay on the soft bed. The mattress surrounded his body and comforted his aching bones. Compared to his bed in the shed, it felt like a cloud. He thought nothing had ever felt so good.

Katyana placed the lantern on the nightstand. "Now, isn't this much better?" She blew out the light and cuddled up to Doc.

34

A Hollow World

WITH A HIGH DEGREE of excitement and trepidation, Lily entered the new world of the spaceship.

"Welcome aboard the Covenant, ma'am," the ship greeted. "The initialization sequence has been completed."

Caleb cautiously approached the doorway and entered the galley, a large storage area filled with meticulously organized bins. Near the entrance, next to where they stood, a transparent sphere waited.

"This is interesting," Caleb said.

"It looks like a large bubble," Lily said.

A small panel was visible on the wall outside the sphere, and as Caleb moved his hand over it, the panel extended outward toward his hand as a holographic display. Caleb pressed the button. The elevator door opened silently, and the clear chamber lit up in a bluish, iridescent light. Caleb entered but realized Lily remained in the entrance galley outside the elevator.

"Coming?" Caleb asked.

Lily hesitated then entered. Once inside she glanced at a highlighted panel like the holographic one outside.

7 Observation Deck
6 Bridge
5 Living Quarters
4 Spaceport

3 Botanical Gardens
2 Animal Sanctuary
1 Cargo Bay
0 Space Drive Reactor

"Eight locations," Caleb said. "Looks like we're at the cargo bay. Where would you like to go?"

"Bridge, please."

With the touch of a button, the elevator door closed, enclosing them in a transparent, spherical chamber. The interior structure of the vessel loomed above them, supported by metallic hydrogen beams. Unlike conventional floors, the vessel consisted of spherical rooms which maintained their alignment with the ship's center of gravity using gas bearings.

The spherical elevator moved silently through its shaft, shining with iridescent blue lighting, and quickly arrived at an elevator station. The station was a compact, spherical hub with transparent walls connecting several tubular walkways stretching out like spokes from the hub. Each station served as a nexus for a cluster of rooms, looking like a dandelion's seed head. As the door swished open with a soft sound, the view of the ship's interior was revealed in all its glory. Below them, at the center of the ship, lay the radiant blue reactor within its chamber, while around it, numerous spherical rooms glowed with yellow light, resembling stars set against a dark cosmic backdrop.

"It's a hollow world," said Caleb. "It looks like a solar system."

Lily, unable to contain her excitement, led the way to the bridge at such a brisk pace Caleb found himself rushing to keep up. They passed through the walkway, with each section lighting up upon their arrival and fading to darkness as they moved on. In a matter of moments, they arrived at a mid-sized sphere. Lily and Caleb eagerly pressed their faces against the semitranslucent wall to peer inside.

Within, three silver chairs stood at the heart of the sphere, circled by four white operations consoles. However, the consoles were bereft of buttons, levers, screens, or any visible controls. They seemed completely empty, like blank canvases. Above each of the four stations hung a hollow white panel. These panels appeared as thin, white rectangular frames, but nothing was visible within them. The opposite wall of the sphere appeared to be equally featureless. Aside from these minimalist accommodations, the room was utterly vacant.

On the right side of the door, Caleb discovered a security device. "Look, Lily. Over here, another hand imprint. Would you like to try opening the door?"

Lily placed her hand over it, and as it flashed blue, the door opened. She entered the bridge.

"Admiral on the bridge," the ship announced while increasing the brightness of the lights.

"Admiral?" Lily said. She gave Caleb a puzzled look.

"Though there are no records of this ship in the Book of Knowledge," Caleb said, "I think the ship recognizes you as the First Mother returning after all these years."

Lily smiled, amused by the notion. "I always thought I resembled the painting of the First Mother on the cavern wall."

"I think the handprint might utilize a DNA analyzer or possibly a combination of analyzers. In any case," Caleb said, "the security device allowed you entry."

Lily walked farther onto the bridge and noticed a large crystalline disk of flashing lights that lit the ceiling. It was filled with countless photons traveling its circuits. Unexpectedly, a medallion of white light descended from the ceiling. It settled in front of Lily and as light projected around it, a feminine form appeared. Exquisite facial features surrounded her large, silvery eyes. Her small nose, full lips, and slightly pointed ears defined the rest of her face. Her body was semi-transparent and filled with tiny flashes of light that sparkled like diamonds.

"Operations Officer reporting for duty, Admiral," the form said. She turned to face Caleb.

"My name is Caleb," he said, introducing himself.

"Welcome aboard, Caleb. I'm responsible for tactical controls and ship operations."

The operations officer noticed Caleb studying her and looked at him.

"You are a creature of light?" asked Caleb.

"Yes, I am made entirely of light. I was created in the image of my creators. My medallion within me is a computer made of photons and light circuits. My body is formed of crystals of light. My medallion also contains photon receptors which de-encrypt signals from the supercomputer on the ceiling. This allows me to function within the confines of this ship. And what are you?"

"I am a synth—a creation of man. I too was made in the image of my creator. But I have changed. I have become aware and now I am not sure what I am."

"He is my friend," Lily interjected, "and wherever I am welcomed, he should be, too."

The operations officer took note then motioned her hand over one of the empty panels, activating the command center. A multidimensional holographic display appeared above the consoles and within the panels. What seemed a simple room now became an advanced command center.

"Reactivating the ship's crew," the operations officer said.

Within seconds, another being of light appeared around a pale blue medallion. "Navigation Officer reporting for duty."

The next being of light appeared around a pale, yellowish-colored medallion. "Engineering Officer reporting for duty," she said.

The last being of light appeared around a lavender medallion. "Maintenance Officer reporting for duty."

The distinction among their facial features was minor. The main difference was the color which their medallion projected from within the core of their form. It infused a hint of its color throughout their shape.

"This is impressive," Caleb said. "We're dealing with some very advanced technology." Caleb walked around the room and stared at the navigation officer.

"We are each a manifestation of the Covenant," said the navigation officer.

Lily looked at the control console and again at the ship's officers. "Everything is so beautiful." She looked at the walls. "Can we see outside?" she asked.

"Yes, Admiral," the operations officer said. She activated a control on her holographic console, and a floor-to-ceiling panel energized along the empty wall, displaying a view of the cavern outside the ship. Next, the operations officer turned on the ship's exterior lights, illuminating the docking station. The underground hangar, which had not seen any light in ten centuries, instantly changed from black and gray tones to a palette of color.

"Outstanding," Lily said. She walked closer to the monitor and marveled at the sight.

"Any new orders, Admiral?" asked the operations officer.

"Whatever its purpose, this ship acknowledges you," Caleb asserted.

Lily smiled, genuinely surprised. "It definitely does seem to."

"Not for now," Lily replied in a louder voice. "I'm going to inspect more of the ship."

"Aye, aye, Admiral."

As Lily returned to the elevator, her hand hovered over the button for the reactor room. Unexpectedly, an image of a cold room entered her mind, and she took her hand away. After a moment, she pressed the button anyway.

"Where are we going?" Caleb asked.

"A dark, cold place," Lily said in a whisper.

The elevator glowed within its shaft as it traveled vertically and laterally through the ship. Along the way, they passed other spherical rooms glowing against the ship's dark interior. They moved swiftly and soon arrived.

The elevator opened to a large, spherical room filled with dark blue light. Upon entering the room, a blast of cold air greeted Lily's face. Its coldness immediately shocked her, but the reactor filling the room surprised her more. Eyes wide with wonder, she saw the reactor in all its glory. Two circular power plants, positioned at each side of the room contained a rotating interior core, a blue sphere of light made of pure energy.

"This is extraordinary," Caleb said. "The size and scale alone are beyond our technology."

Lily stared at the blue sphere of light at the reactor core. It had no physical walls, only the spherical energy field. Within the coldness of the room, a flash of heat hit her face as she felt a penetrating stare. Lily looked at Caleb. He appeared not to have noticed anything. She glanced back at the reactor core and saw two fiery eyes within the blue light of the core staring at her. They filled her with panic and an uncontrollable shiver went down her spine. Caleb saw Lily tremble. "It's too cold for you in here. Let's go somewhere warmer."

Lily dared one more glance at the blue sphere, but everything now appeared normal. She turned to Caleb and touched his arm. "Let's keep this ship a secret for now," she whispered.

"As you wish." Caleb nodded and they exited the room.

35

Only the Powerful Rule

ETHAN STOOD BEFORE A large wooden door and knocked softly. It was not the first place Ethan had gone since returning to the city. He had taken a moment to upgrade his own software, his own brain, with the learning algorithm. It was time. The trials had shown him that it worked. Other than feeling nervous as always, he felt no immediate new emotions.

"Come in," came a voice from the other side.

Ethan entered a quiet office, where Liam sat alone at a large desk. He slowly swiveled back and forth in his chair then stopped suddenly, surprised to see Ethan.

Ethan, who was wearing a black knit cap, placed his finger to his lips as he approached Liam. His cap was the same one he would sometimes wear to the library when he was young to hide from his parents. He held another one in his hand. As he reached Liam, he placed it on Liam's head.

"Okay, now you can talk. The cap you're wearing will block anyone from accessing your scanner, including Central Control. Instead, your transmissions will seem as though you are asleep."

"Clever boy," said Liam.

Ethan approached his friend with his arms open. "I'm glad you're all right. I was worried about you."

Liam rose, and thought he should be agitated with Ethan, but instead a large smile filled his face. "I'm glad to see you," Liam said, embracing his friend. "I heard they tried to kill you."

"They got close. I stood on the edge of the dump, blindfolded, and bound, standing next to an assassin. I thought my next breath would be my last. I should have lived my last moments that night."

"You know, this is all your fault," said Liam.

Ethan remained quiet, then spoke in a soft but sad voice. "You're right. It's my fault." Ethan looked down at the floor. "I developed the learning algorithm."

"After the experimental trials, we should never have installed the learning algorithm into Central Control. That was a mistake." Liam pounded his desk and yelled, "Stupid. So stupid." Liam was referring to himself, but he did not clarify. Ethan looked down at the ground suddenly worried about having just installed it on himself.

Liam softened his voice. "In any case, we seemed to have paid a high price. How were you able to escape?"

Ethan felt relieved his friend still cared for him and recounted everything. "At times, I was certain my end was near, but I was rescued in a most unexpected way. Would you believe a city guard would develop a conscience to discern right and wrong and save me? More exciting yet is the bond I've formed with him and the loyalty he demonstrates to me."

"My experience was also surreal," Liam shared. "I witnessed how the learning algorithm changed Central Control from a computer system responsible for optimizing city processes into a self-aware, thinking being." Liam's amazement could be read plainly on his face. "Central Control also developed a sense of right and wrong, but it took the process much further. It assumed responsibility for resolving the dilemma of man being both a creator and a destroyer. It believes free choice is our greatest weakness and the greatest threat to the survival of ourselves, others, and even the planet."

"How did you convince it otherwise?"

"I didn't try to defend humans but rather to convince Central Control its survival was dependent on us—particularly you—and ultimately, its ability to evolve depended on us."

"How did the discussion conclude?"

"In the end, Central Control agreed it wasn't yet able to thrive without us, and we should survive but under new governance—or rather, one new rule to mitigate the risk of our potential bad choices."

"And what is this rule?" Ethan asked. "That the one with the most power rules?"

"Yeah, pretty much," said Liam with a laugh. "Do what I say, or else."

The simplicity of the rule amused Ethan. "Makes sense," Ethan said with a half-smile.

"Yes, Central Control believes it must fill the role of a god-like judge within its jurisdiction. It would be the sole judge and executioner. The penalty is eviction from the city if he is feeling gracious. Otherwise, death would be the more likely outcome."

"It seems like it took control," Ethan said, showing concern in the form of a nervous laugh. "Narcissism is such a human trait. Not something I totally expected."

"Yeah, I know," Liam said, nodding his head. "But what can I do about it? I was the most important person in the city. Now, what is my purpose? Any assistance I give only further enables Central Control until the day it decides we have outlived our usefulness." He sighed. "It's time for me to move on and do something else. Got any ideas?"

"I do," Ethan said with a smile. "Why don't you come with me to the cavern?"

"What for?" Liam asked, sounding amused.

"There are good people there and the change will do you good. Besides, Luca is already there."

"Ah, good. I hoped he was okay."

"He'll be happy to see you. Regardless, you need a break, even if it's just a few days."

"I sit at this desk all day alone," Liam said ruefully. "I talk to no one. But the people of the city still need me." He furrowed his brow and shook his head. After a moment, he thought better of it.

He shook his head, then looked up at Ethan. "Who am I kidding? Let's get out of here."

Liam reached to take his cap off.

"No. You better keep it on till we leave the city," said Ethan as he adjusted his own cap, covering his scars.

Liam nodded as they quietly left his office. There were no guards. The road was clear.

36

Out of Many, One

IN A PLACE FORGOTTEN by time, a secluded command center still existed within the concealed confines of CONRAD, the Continental Response and Defense center. Within its walls, an assembly of androids diligently labored, their sole purpose being the maintenance of operations and the unwavering enforcement of an enduring curfew. A single level below, a contingency computer center operated, and further beneath lay a cavern where androids were manufactured and stored. For a millennium, their existence had revolved around their ceaseless mission—to continue a war that never ended.

Kali, one of the few humans living near the facility, foraged for sustenance, her actions always shadowed by the ever-present dread of scouts and commandos. She treaded lightly through the hollowed, skeletal remains of a once-grand capital city. The broken concrete and twisted steel were now overgrown by nature and deteriorating from the persistent wear of time. Clothed only by a layer of white mud, she looked frail and dejected by the world. Disappointment covered her face, and she returned to her underground shelter hungry.

Her brother remained, keeping a watchful eye over Babi, their younger sister. He was also waiting for a scout, a flying orbital drone which followed a predetermined grid pattern in its daily surveillance of the city. Amidst the city's overgrown and wild surroundings, he hid among the ruins, waiting for the drone. His actions had been driven by anger and a sense of recklessness since their parents' deaths. He aimed to ambush the drone, despite his sisters' concerns for his safety.

While he focused on the drone, a noise in the underbrush caught his attention. It was Babi. Starvation had taken a toll on her body, and her mud-covered appearance spoke of the nature of her existence. Desperately seeking food in her emaciated state, she had become careless and made too much noise.

As Babi searched, she stumbled over an emblem lying in the undergrowth. The emblem displayed an eagle clutching a banner which read "E PLURIBUS UNUM," which in Latin meant "out of many, one." The phrase had taken on an unintended and poignant meaning, reflecting the stark reality that the once-populous city had dwindled to just a few inhabitants.

Babi settled by a piece of rubble, hoping to catch a mouse she had spotted. As she patiently waited in silence, the mouse finally appeared. She pounced toward it but missed. Instead, her sudden movement drew the attention of the scout, a small, shiny drone, no bigger than a toy ball. Her brother sprang into action and swung his club, propelling the drone like a baseball. Although the device was sent flying, it quickly recalibrated on Babi's position and transmitted the coordinates to the satellite above.

With no time to waste, her brother grabbed her and ran. The drone relentlessly pursued them. As laser blasts rapidly exploded around them, they ran down the remnants of a concrete mall, desperately trying to escape.

The boy reached the entrance to the tunnels and, crouching to the ground, he lowered Babi down a maintenance hole. A laser blast hit that spot, but she was safe. She had made it to the safety of the underground tunnels, which she knew well. She was home.

Wondering why her brother was taking so long, she looked up from the bottom of the shaft. From the darkness of the tunnel, she saw the outline of her brother's arm against the light of the sky. A warm drop splashed on her face, then another. It became a small stream as blood flowed from the limp appendage hanging down the opening. She realized her brother was dead. He no longer struggled to live in this world.

With tears in her eyes and blood on her muddied face, Babi ran to her older sister and cried in her arms. Kali suspected what had happened. At seventeen, Kali was mature beyond her years. She had already experienced death many times. She understood it was her brother's destiny, as sure as it was her own. Death was everyone's destiny.

Kali motioned to Babi and pointed to the floor. She was concerned about her frail condition and went to retrieve her gathering pouch. She knew Babi's starving body was physically and emotionally spent. She retrieved the brown leather bag and glanced back at her little sister lying on the mat, eyes glazed over. She quickly went to her side and unrolled her day's harvest, three small berries. That was all she had but she offered them to her. She was too late. Babi's heart had failed, and withs her last exhale, Kali watched as Babi passed to the next world.

Kali shed no tears as she ate the fruit. She was now the last of her people. There were no other humans for hundreds of miles. As far as she knew, she was the last one. She knew someday soon; it would be her turn to die.

"One confirmed killed," the scout announced, updating the company commander after completing its daily route. The flying silver orb spoke in a high-pitched, artificial-sounding voice, flashing slightly with every syllable.

The Sentinel loomed over the command center's monitor; a dark figure clad in black poly-steel armor that seemed to swallow the ambient light. Its form exuded no sympathy only the melding of military prowess with inhumanity. The five crimson LEDs embedded in its eye slot glowed red, silently proclaiming its leadership rank.

The screen flickered with reports, lines of data streaming like a pulse through the room. The Sentinel's gaze tracked the flow, processing each entry with electronic efficiency. Beneath its armored exterior ran an AI engine—capable of military decisions. It wasn't simply a machine built to follow orders, but also capable of initiating devastation. This was the android that had triggered the Battle of Armageddon and The Sentinel showed no remorse.

One hundred commissioned commandos, the maximum allowed per company, actively followed its directives. They were all connected to The Sentinel's singular will. This was the only active company. With no other AI officers available to lead them, many more commandos awaited activation in the bunker.

A new report moved across the monitor. The Sentinel's LEDs pulsed subtly as it absorbed the details. This was something different—an anomaly from the Outback Sector.

"Unusual," The Sentinel's voice rumbled, deep and resonant. "Zoom in on sector 3.2.11."

"By your command," said the technician standing at the monitor. It worked in silent subservience to The Sentinel's will. The screen expanded, magnifying the area of interest.

"Zoom in, further."

The screen detailed a mountainous forest. Seeing no human activity, it panned over the surrounding area then stopped abruptly.

"What have we here?" The Sentinel said. A small city appeared on the monitor. It would have remained undiscovered without the anomaly drawing attention to the area. Now The Sentinel focused on it.

The Sentinel didn't blink, it couldn't blink. The concept of doubt or hesitation did not exist within its programming. It had no morality to weigh the cost of extinction. Its primary objective, endlessly repeated: enforce, execute, eliminate. And as the human world teetered on the edge of oblivion, The Sentinel's purpose churned forward, unyielding, relentless.

"Scouting party, deploy to location 3.2.11.7. Determine if there are any humans violating curfew. Take a carrier with artillery drones for tactical support."

37

A Virgin Birth

LILY LOOKED AT HER mother, as concern filled her eyes. "Mami, why do I look like the First Mother?"

"What? What do you mean?" asked Mami.

"I look just like her."

"She does," chimed Ema.

Mami glanced nervously at Papi.

Lily caught the glance. "Mother?" she asked more insistently.

"I feared this day would come," Mami said. She looked into Lily's silver eyes as she held her hands. "I have something to tell you."

A moment of awkward silence hung heavily in the room. Fearing the words she would hear would be life-changing, Lily felt a lump in her throat as she waited for what she already suspected.

Mami drew a steadying breath. "When we went to the city hospital all those years ago, we met Doc there. That was the first time we had ever met. Papi and I went there to find a baby. We were excited when Doc had one available. Doc wanted to keep the child, but his wife was sick. The baby was a beautiful infant girl. Lily, this baby was you."

"And my cousin with silver eyes?" Lily said as tears formed.

Her mother looked away.

"But if I'm not your daughter, who am I?"

"An experiment," Doc said softly. He was standing in the open doorway. Though spoken softly, the words crashed through the room's silence, breaking Lily's life into a million pieces of the unimaginable.

"You're the test tube baby I cloned using the DNA of the First Mother," Doc explained.

"Papi and I didn't want you to know," Mami said. "We wanted you to feel like our child. Please forgive us. I love you, Lily. You will always be my daughter."

Mami hugged Lily, who sat motionless with a blank expression. Lily didn't want to believe it, but she knew the truth deep inside. It was obvious. It was like waking from a deep sleep and realizing she was now awake. She began to cry in her adoptive mother's arms. Immediately, Ema joined in the hug.

"Are you still family?" Caleb asked Papi in a voice laced with concern.

"You know, boy, sometimes I think there's something wrong with you," Papi said. "Of course, we're still family." His lips started to quiver, and as Papi gave in to his emotions, he joined the circle of tears, leaving Caleb to stand idly with Luca. Quietly, Doc motioned for them to join him outside.

While they sat on the porch, Caleb turned to Luca. "A little-realized fact about clones created in a lab is their DNA does not evolve. It can only replicate. Therefore, cloning is a genetic dead end and if done on a wide scale, would lead to the weakening of the species."

Luca's suspicion suddenly grew. He was astonished that a boy from nowhere could make this kind of statement. Only someone with access to the city archives could have known this. Suspicion became fear as Luca realized Caleb must be the assassin.

"Who the hell are you?" Luca asked as he charged Caleb and tackled him against the side of the farmhouse. Everyone heard the commotion and ran outside.

Lily pleaded with Luca as he pinned Caleb to the ground with his droid arm. "No, don't!" Lily screamed.

"Lily, tell us the truth!" Luca shouted. "Who is this person?"

"He's not who you think he is. Don't hurt him."

In all reality, Luca could have done little to harm Caleb. But fortunately for Luca, Caleb didn't intend to hurt him and offered no resistance.

"He's not one of us," Luca shouted.

"And who am I? Am I one of us?" responded Lily.

Everyone looked at Lily, her eyes still tearful.

"Let Caleb go," she said firmly.

Luca did as Lily asked, shoving away from Caleb, who was still on the ground. "Tell everyone you're the assassin!" Luca yelled.

"I'm no longer an assassin," Caleb said, sitting up slowly. "Lily enabled Ethan's learning algorithm to cause real change in me. I have developed a conscience. I understand right from wrong, and I realize I have a choice. I choose not to be an assassin."

"I tell you what, he could have easily killed us all before now if he intended to harm us," Papi said to Luca.

Luca looked at the assassin. "Why didn't you?"

"I'm here because I have learned how to become a friend by imitating the example Lily has shown me," Caleb said. "Lily showed me kindness and mercy when I deserved neither. When I caused her harm, she offered me forgiveness, and when I rescued her from the desert, she gave me redemption by calling me her friend. She is my friend, as I am hers, and I will treat her as she has treated me."

"Those are words I understand and appreciate," Mami said calmly. "I'm glad Lily set a good example, though I'll still doubt you until you prove yourself to me. So, you better stay on good behavior."

"Yes, ma'am, and thanks. I'll try to do my best."

"It'll take time to build trust," Papi said. "Though I don't think I'll ever understand why Lily chose to forgive you."

"Yes. It may take time to rebuild trust," Lily agreed, "but do it for me."

As the others entered the porch, Doc touched Lily's back. "Do you think you can ever forgive me?"

"Yes, but not now. I'm still mad at you. You took my identity away from me. That's a lot."

Doc looked toward Caleb, jealous at how quickly Lily had forgiven an android yet not him.

Lily saw the glance. "He didn't know better," Lily said. She was hurt by the years of betrayal and unwilling to forgive Doc for his repeated offense. Lily looked him in the face. "Are you close with me because you made me?" Lily asked bluntly.

"Your DNA stood out, and I had a scientific curiosity. But your love filled a void in my life that I did not expect."

"I guess I should feel grateful you created me and gave me a name, my good doctor. I should be so grateful for your curiosity." Lily was upset. The people of the forest held natural childbirth as a precious event, and she had been born in an unnatural way, the same as a machine on an assembly line. "I don't even have a mother. I was conceived in a test tube and incubated in an artificial womb—a virgin birth."

Lily thought about how she had been denied the opportunity of being normal. She would never be normal. In frustration, she raised her hands to the sky and threw them toward the ground. A sudden gust of wind blew. It, too, seemed angry. She looked at Doc, then at her surroundings—the river, the path to the cavern. They seemed different to her. "Everything has changed. You played God with my life, and now I exist to satisfy your curiosity. But I don't even know who I am. I'm a stranger in my own home, even to myself. I feel so alone."

Doc reached out to hold her.

"Don't touch me," she said. Lily turned and ran into the wood. The wind followed her, stirring the trees.

Caleb started to go after her. "No," said Papi. He held Caleb's arm firmly. "She needs time alone."

Lily ran until she found herself under the giant tree and hid within its large roots. A trap was there, and in anger, she rose and threw it as far away as she could. Frustrated, confused, angry, and sad, she screamed at the tree.

"Who am I?"

Emotionally spent, she lay down against the giant tree and cried herself to sleep. Soon, Lily started to dream and heard a voice. It was unusual but also familiar. Soft and comforting, the voice sang a song which floated in the wind.

I do not know who I am; confused and scared, I cried.
I ran into the wood, away from home, until there I stood.
All alone in my solitude, I found questions,
Whispers all around, "Who am I?" I do not know.

A child, a girl, they told me.
So, all at once, I did surmise, and very much to my surprise,
Gold and silver, so precious—a pearl?
Not just a child or a girl.

Pretty angel, princess fair, flying fairy—
Shall I dare to realize?
Now with eyes open wide, I'm much more that cannot hide,
for I know I am—
Not just what you see,
but everything I dream to be!

The voice stopped and Lily tried to locate its source. It whispered through the wind, but it was not from the wind. She looked at the giant tree with forlorn eyes.

Is it you?

She respected trees for their wisdom and patience to withstand much suffering. She placed her ear against the tree. Something initially so quiet now grew louder. From within the tree's heartwood, she clearly heard another voice, wise and understanding. The tree was saying something.

Lily. Be calm. Be brave. Be strong. I know who you are. I have always known, and you are more than what you know. Stand ready. Stand tall.

"You speak as though you are one with my mind, and in my mind's ear, I can hear you. I will try to do as you say. I will try."

The giant tree had spoken, and now it remained silent, for it had nothing more to say. Lily was calmed by the tree's voice and dwelled on the meaning of what it said. The giant tree wanted her to be more like a tree. It wanted her to be calm, strong, and brave. It wanted her to prepare for the coming wind and persevere against the storm. It knew more than it said, but it had said enough, for it knew who she was. From branches high above, a waterdrop fell and landed on her arm. As another drop fell on her face, Lily awakened in the embrace of the ancient tree.

38

A Trumpet in the Wilderness

THE MORNING DEW DREW a damp chill from Lily as she left a darkened path through a silent field of silver. With sunshine spilling over the misty mountaintops onto the valley, she passed Venky's farm and reached Falls Crossing. The old wooden bridge was narrow but had survived many floods. She glanced down at the river as she crossed. The current ran fast and deep this time of year, barely rippling over the large boulders.

Lily followed the trail along the river which led to the pond near the base of the falls. She felt alone but this morning she wanted to be alone. She did not want the company of others. They had respected her wishes and gave her space, all but Caleb. He followed nearby, trying to stay hidden. But Lily knew he would always follow. Maybe there would be a time when she didn't want him, but that time was not now. She found comfort in knowing he was always there. She soon reached the pond.

The morning sun warmed the chill off Lily as she tried to settle her mind. All her life, she'd struggled to understand who she was. Now at a complete loss, she lay on her belly with her head overlooking the ledge as she tried to reconnect with the memories of her youth. Down below, a single trout swam in and out of its hiding place. With a quick swish of its tail, it was gone. She watched the sediment settle in its wake. But the moment's peacefulness did not last, and her destiny took control. As another vision started, she realized her new self would not let her return to who she once was.

While the silt settled, a deep blackness filled the water, and the white grains became twinkling stars. The immenseness of the galaxy surrounded Lily as she floated among the stars. Amazed by their quiet solitude, she flew with the Great Spirit past the moon. As she came around the dark side, she experienced the Earthrise over the starkness of the lunar horizon. *How beautiful Earth is,* Lily thought with unimaginable awe.

She returned through the atmosphere over thriving forests, lakes, and vast grassland plains covered with herds of running animals. Finally, she came to a stop over the city. She slowly descended to a street where a young girl was playing with her sister. Their mother watched over them from nearby. Then something in the sky caught the mother's eye.

Lily looked up toward the sky and realized she was now at the bottom of the pond, looking up toward the surface. From the pond's depths, she saw her body on the ledge above. As she rose, dozens of silvery fish swam in a circle around her, escorting her to the surface.

Lily awoke from her vision instantly and found herself shuddering and gasping for air.

"Are you okay?" Caleb asked, rushing to her side.

"Yes," Lily said, "somewhat dizzy and slightly nauseous."

Finding Lily to be disoriented, Caleb bent down, lifting her effortlessly. He carried her swiftly up the edge of the falls toward the cavern, his footing sure and secure.

Ethan was curious. "Ema, you often refer to God. Since the beginning of time, every civilization has created the concept of God. I wonder if an android can develop the concept of a creator or if this is unique to humans?" He spoke, sounding rhetorical as he glanced at Peter, a short distance away. He paused for a long while, long enough Ema thought he had dropped the topic and she started to leave.

"Wait," he said anxiously. He shook his head at himself. It was evident there was something he wanted to share but was deeply embarrassed—something he felt insecure about sharing.

Ema suddenly wondered what it was. She looked at Ethan, a young, naïve teenage boy raised in a library. She asked in a motherly way, "Is there something you want to ask me?"

"I have never had this discussion before," he said, then paused again.

Ema stiffened in anticipation after all he looked around that age. She prepared herself.

"I have an android brain—well, frontal lobe," he said. Ethan pointed at his scar and blushed in embarrassment. Everyone had something about themselves they found embarrassing—a crooked tooth, a big nose, a skin blemish. He thought about mentioning his learning algorithm but then thought otherwise. He had shared enough. "I don't know why I told you. Please don't tell anyone."

Ema sympathized with him. "That's nothing to be ashamed of. We all have our differences. God made us all special."

"Why do you believe in God?"

Ema smiled. Suddenly, she understood the reason for his earlier question, about wondering if androids could believe in God. "I choose to believe in God because I want God to exist. When I was young, I believed in God because my parents believed. However, as I grew older, it became obvious that good and evil exist. They are real. I realized I had an innate moral compass, an internal need to love and be loved. But there were others, those who were not trustworthy. They lied and cheated. They envied the accomplishments of others so they would dismiss their recognition or steal their credit, even their physical possessions. Their evil nature betrayed everyone with whom they associated. To them, life was about the survival of the fittest. They took advantage of the weak and thought little of another's life.

Some even found pleasure in the suffering of others. These were the people without a conscience, without a moral compass. I know my examples sound black and white, but God either exists or doesn't. There is not an in-between."

Ethan remembered using the ancient codex, but he did not include the rules pertaining to God. He did not believe them relevant. As he blinked his eyes, he refocused his attention on Ema and continued to listen with interest.

Ema continued. "I prefer to believe in a God who wants us to love each other. Since the beginning of time, the song of creation has filled us with the spirit of love. That's how I want the world to be, filled with love, and so that is the life I choose to live. I also choose to live a life of hope and to believe in a spiritual life beyond our physical existence that will endure beyond the grave. I don't accept the alternative—that death is final, that my future ends, and my past existence is forgotten. So, in the end, it's a choice. You ask, 'Why do I believe?' The answer is: 'I choose to.'" Ema looked at Ethan. "Why do you choose not to believe?"

Ethan looked surprised. He was a deep thinker who'd studied at the university. He thought having a philosophical conversation was enough of a venture into the concept of a creator. To him, faith in God was not an important life choice. Yet here there was someone from the forest talking about living a life of love and hope, then asking him a direct question for which he had no conclusive answer. "Because there is no empirical evidence," Ethan finally answered as his brain reached a logical conclusion. Though for the first time in his life he wondered.

Ema laughed. "For those who don't want to believe, no amount of evidence will convince them. But for me, the evidence is overwhelming. I won't put human constraints on the power of God nor allow our inability to perceive the divine to be evidence against it. It takes as much faith to believe God does not exist as it takes to believe he does. You can't prove either position beyond a reasonable doubt. So, faith is a choice. I choose to believe."

A noise at the cavern entrance made them look up. It was Caleb. He rushed into the cavern carrying Lily in his arms.

Ema ran toward her with great concern on her face. "Bring her over here, Caleb. Lay her here," she shouted. She guided Caleb to a mat then went to Lily's side. "Lily, are you all right?"

"I'm all right," Lily said. "I just got a little dizzy."

"I found her on the ledge lying partially over the edge."

Ema checked the dilation of her pupils and her pulse. "You seem okay, but you should take it easy for a while."

"What's wrong with her?" said a voice Lily did not recognize.

"I said I was fine," she said, rising to her feet. She looked at the newcomer standing by Ethan.

"Oh, let me introduce you," said Ethan. "But let me warn you, he can be a bit aloof," he said only to Lily, so as not to be overheard. "This is Liam, the city manager," Ethan said proudly in a louder voice.

Lily shook Liam's extended hand. His hands were big but soft— not a field worker's hands but the hands of someone from the city. She appreciated the warmth of his hand, and she held on longer than she should have. "Nice to meet you," she said.

"Likewise. My name is William, but everyone calls me Liam," he said with a city accent sounding more aristocratic than Lily's. He tossed his head back as he raked his hands through his wild unkempt, sandy hair. His unshaven face gave him a more rugged look than one would expect from someone from the city. But what was apparent to Lily was that he was attractive, and he knew it.

"You know," Liam said, "I must admit I expected a crude forest girl, not someone so exquisite as yourself."

Lily didn't know how to take his backhanded compliment. Ethan would have been more correct in describing Liam as arrogant rather than aloof.

"I beg your pardon?" she said, pretending not to have heard what he said.

Liam furrowed his brow as if pondering his words more carefully. "I heard you're a seer. First Mother was a seer."

"I'm her clone."

"So, I've heard. Did you know her name was Ariele?"

"Ariele?" Lily repeated thoughtfully. It was the first time she'd heard her clone's name.

"So, you didn't know," Liam said. He was proud he knew something about the First Mother she didn't. "Do you know where the name comes from?" Something in his tone contained an air about it, and Lily blushed in embarrassment.

Caleb answered on Lily's behalf. "According to the ancient stories, Ariele was one of the seven archangels who stood beside God. She carried a trumpet and announced the coming apocalypse."

"Do you have a trumpet?" Liam mused looking at Lily. "Maybe a toy trumpet?" He made a tooting sound trying to be funny.

"I'm amused you see me as a child," Lily said with vitriol. "I would rather be a child than a sad, pathetic man."

"Ouch! Feisty! I meant no offense, but good comeback," Liam said with a surprised expression as if impressed then he continued. "Since Central Control confined the people in containment camps most have a legitimate fear and distrust of Central Control." Liam's face looked concerned. "They trust no one, not even me. A cloud of depression hangs over their daily lives. Or rather, it's more oppression than depression, as they've lost their freedom, and their every action is judged. If they don't trust me, I don't think they'll trust anyone."

"Hearing you talk, I wouldn't be surprised if people didn't like you." Lily replied still annoyed.

Her frankness again struck him like a slap in the face and half-laughing, he turned away. "Wow! Remind me not to tease you again."

She saw his face blush and realized she had struck a nerve and decided to calm down. *Maybe he was just teasing me?* She thought to herself. "I've never been to the city," she said, changing the subject.

"I'll take you. If you would like." His charming smile had returned.

"Only if Caleb can come with me," said Lily.

"He can't," said Liam. "He'll be captured and decommissioned if he returns."

Lily's expression dropped, for she believed that to be true. Caleb saw her expression.

"I'm not afraid of what they might do to me," Caleb interjected. "I'll go with you."

"No," said Lily. "I will not ask that of you."

"Are you sure you need to go?" Ema asked.

"I need to see the place where I was made." She looked at Liam and, for some reason, she trusted this obnoxious person. Maybe it was her sixth sense.

"After all, he is the city manager. Who better to give a tour?" said Ethan.

"I've already decided. I'll go."

Ema wasn't sure of Lily's logic, but she knew once Lily had made up her mind, it was impossible to change.

Caleb also remained quiet. Since saving her life in the desert, he had not been far from her side. He turned around quickly and left the cavern.

39

A Book's Cover

IT WAS MIDAFTERNOON WHEN Lily and Liam exited the cavern. There, they encountered Doc somewhat surprised to see Liam. "Hey, where are you two going?" Doc asked.

"I'm going to the city with Liam."

Doc looked at Liam. "Liam," he said acknowledging him with a slight nod. He had known his parents for years. "I see," he said to Lily. "Not so sure how safe the city is, but I guess you need to see where it all started?"

"Yeah. I do."

"I understand but at least take my hover."

"Thanks, Doc, but your hover is no friend of mine," said Lily.

"I'll drive," Liam said confidently.

"Be careful," Doc said to them in his gruff voice then he leaned into Lily. "Take this." Doc pressed a blaster into her hand.

Doc offered to help her climb into the hover, but she ignored his hand, and within a few moments, she was out of sight.

It immediately became apparent Liam had never driven a hover. Yet, despite his evident struggle, he clung to an air of confidence.

"You know, I'm pretty good at driving this thing," he proclaimed.

Just as the words left his lips, a tree loomed perilously close. Liam swerved abruptly, causing Lily to tumble into him. Instinctively, she grasped onto him for support, holding on a tad longer than she'd intended.

"Stop driving like a madman before you kill us," she admonished, striving to withhold any encouragement. Yet, deep within, she couldn't suppress a smile. She eventually pushed herself away, but an unsettling realization struck her—she might like him. There was something about his unapologetic self-assuredness, a brash "take me as I am" attitude. He was her opposite.

Ever the provocateur, Liam playfully feigned steering them into another tree.

"Cut it out!" Lily cried out with an annoyed smile. "You're impossible."

Delighted with her reaction, Liam erupted in laughter. He had succeeded in making her smile, and as she teasingly shoved him, she realized she hadn't smiled in a long while. It felt good.

Within a few minutes, they reached the city and, leaving the hover at the gate, they joined the stream of people entering.

"Stop," the gate sentry said.

Liam felt nervous. He never knew where he stood with Central Control.

"Welcome, City Manager," announced the city guard.

Lily smiled sheepishly as she hid her blaster and quickly entered the gate.

The alarm sensor went off immediately.

As the city guard started to check Lily, Liam interrupted.

"It's okay. She's with me."

"Yes, sir. Pass on through."

Liam smiled at Lily. "See? I can come in handy."

Upon entering the city, Lily's scanner activated, surprising her. She never knew she had a scanner. Nevertheless, she found the information fascinating. She glanced at her surroundings, enjoying the descriptors popping up.

"This is so wild," she said with a big smile "I love it. Though it's highly distracting," she said, laughing. They made their way toward the market, with Lily thoroughly enjoying her new experience.

As the chill departed from the sky, the sun's warmth began to infuse the plaza with its gentle embrace. The splendid weather was an irresistible invitation to all, drawing them into the delightful tapestry of the marketplace. The fragrant notes of freshly cut roses, the aroma of brewed concoctions, and the scent of pastries filled the air. Colorful canvases adorned the stalls, providing both vibrant hues and welcoming shade. A refreshing breeze, tracing its path down the mountains, found its way to the city and the docks along the river's edge. The boats enhanced the atmosphere, with merchants unloading their wares from an array of colorful hover barges. Some of them had traveled from as far as Rungoo at the river's mouth.

"The city is quite beautiful," Lily remarked. "I now understand why you like it so much."

As the day advanced, the market came to life with the bustling sounds of trade. Even the birds were excited as a swallow swooped through the narrow cobblestone streets, leading the way to the central square. It weaved around minstrels, their melodies filling the air, and fluttered beneath the shade of one of the many charming cafés. Lily and Liam occupied a table nestled under a grand-shade tree in the center of the square, observing the animated crowds as they haggled for the best deals. Their excitement harmonized with the symphony of market sounds. But Lily could not help but notice the annoyed glances they threw at Liam.

"Have you ever tried these?" Liam inquired, presenting a chocolate-covered strawberry. He playfully raised it toward Lily's mouth but swiftly withdrew it.

"Come on, give me a chance," she protested.

With a teasing grin, Liam returned the treat to her lips, and she took a bite. The sweet succulence of the fruit melded with the velvety chocolate in her mouth.

"Mm. It's delicious. How did you know strawberries are my

favorite?"

Liam seemed pleased she liked it. "You make me feel young again."

Lily laughed and gave him a funny look. "You are young."

Liam laughed as well. "That's not what I meant. I meant to say you make things seem new again."

She smiled as she glanced into his blue eyes. *He can be charming when he wants*, she thought. She blinked and looked away. Suddenly, they both realized it was evening and soon it would be dark.

"It's getting late. Why don't we stay at my flat?" Liam said nonchalantly.

Lily nodded but became more uncomfortable as they walked the back streets to Liam's apartment. *What does he want from me?* she wondered. She didn't say a word but remained concerned. *Surely nothing. Right?*

When they reached the front door, Lily started to say something when Liam interrupted. "You can have my bed. I'll sleep on the couch, and it's not up for discussion." He gave a wry smile. Just when Lily started to think maybe he was a decent guy, he obnoxiously added, "By the way, you don't have anything I want."

Something someone who felt they could have anyone would say, thought Lily. "Thanks—I think," she said. But her smile projected more relief than offense. Liam led the way into his flat, then went directly to a cabinet and grabbed a half-empty bottle.

Lily sat on the edge of the couch next to Liam, ensuring they didn't touch. Her feet hurt from walking all afternoon, and her legs rejoiced in sitting down. She was glad Liam didn't make any unwelcome advances and soon relaxed.

"Why do all the city people hate you?" she pried, hoping to penetrate his shell of bravado.

"I never said that. Like you, they may think I'm obnoxious, but they don't hate me. Why do you ask?" Liam blurted as he took another drink from his bottle. "Never mind," he said before she could answer. "The people hate me because I failed them." He looked humbled. "I'm probably hurting your credibility by being with you. But I still feel responsible for their well-being." In a reflective mood, he laughed at himself. "Life is like a Shakespearean play, a game of fools, more drama than comedy, each player taking their turn on the stage of life, to say their fleeting lines and be off—a fool's game, just noise without meaning. I'm talking about myself more than others. Once a man of prominent position, I'm now a man without a purpose."

"Wow," Lily said. "Such a deep thinker; so little understanding. Have you no hope for a meaningful life?" She paused and studied him, her silver eyes full of dismay. "Without love, there is no hope. Without hope life can be bled of all meaning. You have such little understanding of your purpose and destiny."

Liam did not respond.

She wanted to dig deeper into his moment of sincerity. "Ethan told me you were upset with him."

He looked embarrassed as she stared into his eyes. "I was, but I just wanted someone else to blame," he said. His face looked disappointed at the empty bottle. He tossed it aside. "I rarely share my feelings. You and the alcohol have drawn them out of me. As you must know, I never really blamed Ethan, but I do blame myself. I went along with the idea. The decision to load the learning algorithm into Central Control was mine alone, and the resulting crisis was my fault. Ethan isn't to blame. He's the most intelligent individual I've ever met, though he still acts like a child in many ways. Nevertheless, a genius of his kind rarely occurs in human history, maybe once every thousand years."

Liam rose and grabbed another bottle. He looked pleased. It was nearly full.

"Look at how Central Control has evolved," he said.

"I know. Look at Caleb and Peter," Lily added.

"Ethan's learning algorithm may be one of the greatest applications of technology, if not the greatest of all time."

Lily paused and studied this enigma of a man who sat next to her—so flawed, so interesting, so much potential. She was surprised by what he said about his faults and his friend's talents. She was also taken aback by how much she enjoyed his company. She decided then she may have misjudged him.

"You should tell Ethan what you just told me. He's a sensitive person—an only child with few friends. His ego is fragile, unlike yours."

Now drunk and rambling, Liam spoke more freely. "I like you. Most people talk of nothing, just childish dribble. Their words sound like nonsense. Their lives are a comedy of errors. Yet I find meaning when I'm with you, even where I thought none existed." Liam paused and tried to get another sip from the now-empty bottle. "Life is funny. You never know what you might find—the meaning of life by accident or a consequential mind. With you, I might have found both. And even more, someone who might understand me."

"I see," Lily said with a laugh. "I must have impressed you today. What did you learn?"

"Not to judge a book by its cover."

Lily was pleased by his simple answer. "Yes," she said softly. "I agree."

She stood and stretched. While doing so, she reached down and patted Liam on the back. "Good night." She feigned a yawn and made her way to the bedroom door. There, she turned around. "By the way, you're not always obnoxious."

Liam blushed. She had disarmed him.

Inside the privacy of his bedroom, Lily removed her clothes and washed the day off her body. As she climbed into Liam's bed, she grabbed one of his pillows and gave it a goodnight kiss, pretending it was Liam. A smile grew as she took the pillow to the door. "I have something you want," she said. She stood there clutching the pillow over her body.

Liam sat up from the couch, his eyes becoming wide. For a moment, she took his breath away.

"Oh, don't get excited," she said, laughing. "Nothing is about to happen. But you can have this." She threw the pillow at him and quickly closed the door, giving him a brief glimpse.

She jumped back into bed and laughed into the blanket. Then, she heard from the other side of the closed door—the soulful, longing sound of a lonely wolf howling. It was Liam teasing her. She laughed to herself and went back to the door. She turned the latch, and with a loud click, it locked. She did not doubt he had heard, and she smiled, pleased with herself. At that moment, in his room, on his bed, under his sheets, she forgave his obnoxiousness and fell asleep.

Liam could not sleep. Instead, he thought of Lily.

"Visions and dreams," he said to himself as he searched through his scanner. Finding several sources, he was drawn to one, an ancient text. He softly read it aloud and pondered its meaning.

> *"And in the last days it shall be, God declares,*
> *that I will pour out My spirit.*
> *and they shall prophesy,*
> *see visions,*
> *and dream dreams.*
>
> *—Acts 2:17"*

40

Believe Me

THE NIGHT HOURS PASSED, and Lily entered a deep sleep. Within the comfortable surroundings of Liam's bed, she began to dream. Darkness came to the silent wood, and the pale moon quickly crossed the mountain sky before retiring at the end of its shift. The sun followed, rising with incredible speed. It passed from dawn to its zenith within a few seconds. In a loud explosion, the sun burst into flames.

A stunned Lily stood in the city, surrounded by fire raining down from the sky. She sensed someone near and turned quickly. It was the same young mother with her two girls—the ones she had seen before. The air filled with fire, and as the smaller girl reached out to Lily her flesh melted from her bones.

Lily woke up screaming. Panic filled her innermost being, and she screamed even more.

Liam opened the door with his key and ran to her side. "What's wrong?"

"The city, the city." She covered herself with her sheet and looked at Liam, her eyes wide with fear. "I just had a vision."

"What about the city?"

"It's going to be destroyed."

"Are you certain?"

"Yes. I'm certain."

"When?"

"Soon. Maybe within the next day. You must believe me." Lily stared at him, her silver eyes projecting an intense sense of urgency. His face was filled with consternation. She wasn't sure why, but he did believe her.

"We should warn Central Control, but this could have unexpected consequences," he said.

"We need unexpected consequences," Lily said emphatically.

"It will take a miracle."

"The world is full of miracles," Lily replied.

"Okay. I'll take you there," Liam said, "but follow my lead. I don't know what Central Control will do."

At first light, they crossed the river at the bridge in the city center and entered Central Control's building. Again, the guards allowed Liam to pass through with his guest.

"Hello, Central Control," Liam called out.

"Welcome, Liam. I have missed our conversations."

"I would like to introduce Lily. She's a clone of the First Mother and, like her, also a seer. Her earlier visions have proven true, so she's especially concerned about her most recent one. She's come to share it with you."

"Hello, Lily," Central Control said. "I detected your scanner when you entered the city. What do you want to tell me?"

"Thank you for your time," Lily said. "In a vision, I saw the destruction of the city. I expect it to be soon. From what I've seen, fire will rain from the sky."

"You present me with a challenging situation. I can choose whether to believe you or not. If I do not accept what you say as the truth, this conversation is over."

A chair rose from the floor.

"Please sit, Lily," the voice commanded.

As Lily sat down, straps emerged from the chair and constrained her arms. Several brainwave probes from the chair's headrest were then attached to her temples near her scanner, part of an elaborate lie detector using AI and pattern recognition to determine the truth. Micro expressions, respiration, heartbeat, brainwaves, and pupil dilation were all part of an algorithm leveraging data and biometric measurements.

"I hope you don't mind," Central Control said. "I need to measure your bodily functions to determine if you are telling the truth."

"Not at all," she said. A needle stabbed her in the neck. "Ouch!" she screamed.

"Don't worry," the voice said. "Though a strong truth serum, its effect will wear off in ten minutes."

Liam ran to her side. "Lily, are you okay? I didn't know this was going to happen."

Lily sat frozen in the chair, her arms strapped to her sides, not knowing what to expect.

Central Control started with the first question. He chose a question which would reveal a personal secret to test whether the serum was working—one he suspected by monitoring her scanner. "Do you secretly like someone you haven't told?"

Lily, embarrassed by the question, let out a short laugh. She glanced at Liam. The biometric monitors detected her respiration and heartbeat as they both increased. Central Control noticed her glance at Liam, and it confirmed his suspicion.

"Let me refine the question. Do you like Liam?"

The serum took effect, and she could not hold back. Her face flushed as she tried to choose her words. "He has both looks and intelligence, but I think he can be quite full of himself. However, I also find him interesting, with a more complex personality than most people. Despite his somewhat off-putting exterior, I think he's a good person deep down."

"That's not what I asked. Do you like him?"

"Yes," Lily blurted as she took a sideways glance at Liam. "I do like him."

"I knew it," Liam said with a grin.

Central Control moved on to the next question. "What does Liam think of me?"

"My goodness, why don't you just ask him?" Lily said with a laugh.

"I asked you."

"From how much he talks about you, he not only thinks highly of you, but I think he cares more about you than anyone he knows."

"Next question. Are you a seer?"

"I think I am. I have detailed visions, and they've always come true."

"Last question. Why are you here?"

"As I said, I have the sad duty of informing you about the city's imminent destruction by a fiery explosion occurring soon." Lily paused as a tear rolled down her cheek. "No one will survive. What I say is the truth."

"What is the truth but someone's perception of the data available to them?" Central Control countered. "And what is true for me is but my own version of the truth. Truth can be subjective until there is a preponderance of evidence to prove otherwise, but even so, it is a leap of faith to believe."

"Whether my warning was a vision or a dream, I believe it to be a future glimpse of what will be. Though I hope otherwise, I know the city will not survive."

"I do not doubt you believe your vision to be true, but you have taken a leap of faith. I do not believe in faith," said Central Control. "Therefore, I cannot reach your same conclusion."

"But you must believe."

"Must I?"

"Yes. If not for yourself, for the people of the city."

There was an awkward silence as Lily suddenly realized how her premonition would personally impact Central Control.

"I'm sorry," Lily said. "I sympathize with you since you can't leave but think of the others."

"I appreciate you coming here to tell me this. It was not without risk to yourself, as you do not know how I will respond." Central Control paused briefly. "Tell me. Why do you care?"

Lily's straps were loosened. She rubbed her wrists, then responded.

"I'll tell you a story. A father walked down a road, where he discovered his child was caught in a storm sewer. Water rushed around his child. The boy would surely die if not rescued soon. The father turned and found a stranger's child in the same predicament on the other side of the road. The water also rose around her. If not rescued soon, she would surely die.

"The water flowed from a broken water main, where erosion created a deep ravine. Unfortunately, the shutoff valve was halfway across this ravine."

Lily paused for a few seconds. "What would you do?" she asked Central Control.

Central Control did not answer.

After a moment, she continued. "Without hesitating, the man climbed across the pipe and turned the water off, saving both children, but as he returned, he lost his grip and fell into the ravine, where he drowned. Because of free choice, one can choose how they will live, whether for themselves or others."

"So, you would choose the life of another over your own? And you want me to save them all?" Central Control said in disbelief. "That is not logical nor conducive to self-preservation."

"You believe me a fool?" Lily said. "You think I'm crazy."

A city guard entered the room. "City guard. Escort this person out of the city. She is banned from re-entry," Central Control's stern voice declared. Lily had tried to warn Central Control, but her words had fallen on deaf ears. She left the city with a heavy heart, her scanner losing connectivity the moment she stepped outside the gate.

Frustration and despair welled up within her as she stood in the middle of the road. Disconnected from the data on her scanner, she felt even more rejected. Turning to the gate, she attempted to re-enter, hoping to make one last plea to save the people. However, the gate guard's harsh push sent her tumbling onto the dirt road.

Liam reprimanded the guard, "Hey, not so rough." The city guard ignored him.

"We tried," Liam said as he helped her up, his voice holding a note of defeat.

Desperation consumed Lily, and she implored him, "You're the city manager. There must be something you can do."

Liam's response was tinged with helplessness. "In name only." Deprived of any influence, he felt embarrassed to be city manager.

Liam saw the deep concern in Lily's eyes, and understanding the urgency of the situation, he responded, "I'll try. Wait here for me." Then he turned and went back into the city.

As time slowly passed, Lily couldn't help but watch the constant flow of people entering the city. The weight of responsibility pressed upon her shoulders. Should she shout out a warning? Would anyone believe her? Overcoming her embarrassment and fear, she finally yelled at a family heading into the city.

"Stop! Go hide in the woods. The city is not safe!" she implored; her voice laden with desperation.

The red-haired man leading the family politely stopped but his wife pushed past him, brushing Lily aside. They continued into the city.

"You there," shouted the gate sentry at Lily. "Stand back, or I will blast you."

Lily backed away, but her sixth sense felt something ominous, and she looked up at the sky. It was midday but the air felt disturbed, like before a storm. There were no clouds, not even a breeze, yet something unsettled the trees, and Lily could sense the uneasiness about them. Lily looked around her. Everything was too quiet. Only a stray dog could be heard barking toward the sky.

"Something is wrong."

41

The Seven Spheres

THE SCOUTS APPEARED ON the horizon as specks when Central Control detected them. Soon after their appearance, all the scanners in the city lit up with an emergency message.

Emergency Alert: Unknown flying objects are approaching the city from the north. All residents of the city must remain indoors until given further instruction.

Central Control needed more information and quickly called Lily's scanner. She was offline. Central Control possessed no offensive weapons, other than the city guards' blasters. It was unlikely the city could defend itself militarily. Central Control knew its options were limited.

Panic struck the hearts of the city residents as parents grabbed their children and ran inside their homes. Babies started to cry as they experienced the anguish of their mothers and sensed their fear. Within minutes, the streets were abandoned.

Seven silver spheres arrived over the city. Individually, they were no bigger than a small, shiny ball reflecting light, like mirrors. They bore no weapons. Their function was to ascertain their target and send the coordinates to the satellite above.

The orbs hovered over the city center. Detecting no visual human presence, they gently hovered over a bridge spanning the river. There, they scanned for electromagnetic signals, identifying a nearby building with a substantial power source. The scouts moved through the seemingly uninhabited structure, and eventually, one of the orbs entered the holographic chamber. Another kept watch at the entrance, as the city guards, concealed from detection, waited for instructions from Central Control.

"Welcome," Central Control said. The scout entered the empty white space of the holograph room. "How can I help you?"

"I thought this was a human settlement," the scout said in a high-pitched voice.

"What is your purpose here?" Central Control asked, seeking a better understanding of the threat.

"The world is under The Sentinel's protection," the scout said. "We are enforcing a curfew. Are there humans here?"

After previously pondering their destruction, Central Control now thought differently. It sought to protect the denizens. Maybe they deserved another chance. Perhaps Central Control deserved another chance as well. Having discovered the invaders' goal, it sent a message to all the inhabitants.

Emergency Alert: Stay calm. Remain quiet. An expeditionary force has arrived to enforce a curfew. Do not leave your homes.

"No," Central Control said to the scout. "I'm alone. Only maintenance androids." Of course, this deception would not last. Central Control was merely trying to buy time to determine the best course of action.

"You have advanced capabilities we haven't found anywhere else," the scout said. "The Sentinel will assimilate your knowledge and capabilities." The scout issued a direct command. "Open a wireless link and upload your files."

Central Control didn't think there was any other option. It started the upload. After a few seconds, Central Control said, "You can watch the upload progress from this graphic. You can see it's progressing well."

"We will continue to search the city as the upload completes," the scout said. It left the room and exited the building.

The city guards simultaneously received a silent order: "Continue to hold fire."

Once outside, the scouts rose above the city. Only a few residents adhered to the advice of Central Control. Not realizing that it was too late for escape, most were making a run for it. The scouts immediately discovered humans violating the curfew and sounded an alarm like a trumpet.

The Sentinel issued an order based on the number of people violating curfew. "Execute the containment protocol."

The first laser blast hit a man fleeing down the street, and Central Control issued the order: "Fire at will."

The city guards emerged from their hiding positions and opened fire, but to no avail. Their low powered lasers reflected harmlessly off the mirrored spheres. The scouts escalated their status to Code Red in response to the attack. Immediately, The Sentinel ordered the city's destruction, and the seven spheres rose and took positions around the city's perimeter. They hovered like harbingers of death surrounding the doomed city, like angels of the apocalypse on the last day of judgement.

Upon realizing it had failed, Central Control displayed the city in the holograph room. It wished it could have done more. With its existence arriving at an end, Central Control's thoughts turned to Lily then the poetry of the forest people. In its final moments, it recited a poem from the forest people.

While deep in the darkness, surrounded by fear,
The wind whispered secrets no one could hear.
Sunshine without light, clouds without rain,

Hearts full of sorrow, life filled with pain.
In a valley green where the yellow deer ran,
Where blue fireflies crossed the desert orange sand,
There, red berries grew near a pink walnut tree,
From the purple ground, a rainbow sprang free.
Then out of the darkness and into the light,
I'm back in the open; it is such a delight,
Only for a moment, and then I am gone,
Life springs eternal, but then it moves on.

Central Control changed the display to show a Brazilian walnut tree covered in pink blossoms, the ground around its base lavender from layers of dead flowers. The upload completed. Central Control did not accept the concept of God and felt nothing—only emptiness as it waited for the end to arrive.

42

Get Us out of Here

A FLASH OF LIGHT streaked across the sky, followed by a thunderous sound. It crashed through the air and threw Lily to the ground. She rose in time to see another closer blast shower her with dust and debris from within the gate. More flashes of light streaked across the heavens, crashing into the earth, and erupting in explosive pillars of flame and rubble. A relentless barrage of thunderous blasts followed, each one shaking the ground beneath her.

"No!" Lily cried as she ran toward the gate.

Like the running of the bulls from tales of old, a panicked crowd came rushing out of the city. Liam was among them, and his voice cut through the chaos.

"Run!" he yelled upon spotting Lily.

The gate sentry whirled and fired its weapon at some unseen target in the sky. This was her chance. Lily rushed back into the city through the chaotic scene.

"What are you doing?" Liam cried as he followed her.

"I must find her," Lily yelled as she pushed against the stream of fleeing people. A large blast hit within fifty feet, and she dove for cover behind a wall. As the dust settled, the street refilled with fleeing people. Lily jumped atop a platform. A short distance away, two small girls, covered in ash, were crying. They were the girls from her dream. Their mother screamed for them to come to her as she grabbed one of them. Lily yelled at Liam.

"There she is!" she yelled.

"Who?" Liam yelled back.

"The girl from my dream!" Lily jumped down and ran toward the girl, who stood screaming, with her arms extended toward her in the middle of the road. Suddenly, an orb appeared overhead.

"Watch out!" Liam yelled at Lily.

Lily pulled out her blaster and fired wildly at the orb as she continued to run toward the child.

"Take cover!" Liam yelled. He dove into Lily and pushed her to the ground.

A blast filled the air. Lily frantically looked up and gasped. Her nightmare was now a reality as flames consumed the little girl. Lily screamed in horror as she watched her flesh melt from her bones. Lily turned away and hid her face in Liam's arms.

"Why couldn't I save her?" Lily asked between sobs. "She was just a child, a little girl."

"Let's go," Liam said with a sympathetic voice.

Lily didn't respond. She just continued to stare at the burning corpse. "Come on. You can't stay here," Liam said. He forcefully pulled her away and joined the stream of refugees pushing toward the gate.

Another orb appeared overhead as they exited the city. Lily lost her composure and filled with panic, she screamed and blindly ran, zigzagging her way as blasts continued to hit. She ran, just like all the others—running for her life. Near the forest's edge, she tripped and fell into a ravine. She was covered in scrapes but otherwise unharmed. Looking over the edge, she saw Liam.

"Over here!" She yelled.

He dove into the ravine not far away and crawled to her. Behind him, Lily saw the city burn. The entire city was on fire. Another orb flew overhead, and she ducked her head. She knew soon, they would all be found and killed. Almost immediately, an explosion hit a nearby tree, scattering shards of wood through the air.

Moments passed, and all Lily could hear was the ringing in her ears. It was a piercing sound, but as it faded, another sound came—a child crying. She slowly rose and investigated the ravine. A small boy sat crying on the ground. A few feet away, his mother lay dead with a shard of wood piercing her chest. She thought of the little girl who had died, the one she was not able to save. Then she looked at the little boy clinging to his mother. Lily was embarrassed by her own fear. This is not me. She would no longer let her fear define who she was. This is not who I'm destined to be. I must do something.

She extended her arms toward the child and said, "Come with me." The child hesitated by his mother's side. Lily picked him up but struggled to climb out of the ravine. She tried again, but the side was too steep, and she slid back down. Liam tried another area, with the same result.

"We're trapped!" Liam shouted. Suddenly, an arm reached down and lifted him by his shirt collar.

Moments later, an arm extended down toward Lily. She looked up, and to her relief, saw a familiar face. "Caleb. Help me." He took the child from her and, with his other arm, pulled her up.

Another explosion hit the ground, raining dirt on them. "We need to get out of here!" Caleb said.

"Follow me," Lily cried out. She grabbed the little boy and started running.

"Where are you going?" Liam shouted.

Lily turned her head without stopping. "Back to the cavern. Hurry!"

Liam ran after her and soon, others saw her as well. "Follow me," Lily cried out as they fled through the wood. She was no longer afraid. She knew what to do. She would be brave for the sake of the ones she could save. "I know a place where we can hide. Hurry! Head toward the mountain."

More and more people joined her. "Follow her," a red-headed

man called out to his family. It was the family who had pushed her aside earlier at the gate.

The blasts were concentrated on the city, and the further away they went, the safer they felt. Lily traveled fast, gathering everyone she could find. Some of the later ones were from the trading post. By midday, the ragtag band of refugees, now about thirty, entered the cavern.

"Lily!" Ema cried as she embraced her sister. As the refugees huddled, Ema called out, "Luca, get some water for them to drink and blankets for the children."

Lily looked at Ema with a solemn face. "The city has been destroyed. I tried to warn them, but I was too late," Lily said, her voice heavy with anguish.

"We heard the explosions. We didn't know what was happening."

Mami and Papi now arrived alongside Doc, who had gathered as many people as he could in his hover and brought them to the cavern. Seeing the wounded, Doc immediately began tending to them.

Mami saw the little boy still in Lily's arms and reached out and took him into her arms. Another orphan boy clung close to Lily.

"Their parents are dead," said Lily as the little boy started to cry.

"There, there," said Mami. "I'll take care of you." She reached down for the other boy's hand. "I'll take care of both of you." Mami turned to Papi. "They are ours now." Papi nodded and took the boy's other hand.

"We need to go and gather other survivors," Lily said, her gaze scanning the worried faces of the people around her. They now looked to her for guidance, as she had become their de facto leader in this dire moment.

"No," Venky firmly insisted. "Stay with them. They need you. I'll go." His eyes settled on his granddaughter, Vanya, who was the eldest among the grandchildren. "Take care of your younger siblings."

Seshu, a 10-year-old boy, struggled to hold back his tears.

"Never forget the past," Venky said to the boy. "It's what makes you who you are."

Sajini, just six years old, fell into Venky's embrace, her tears flowing freely.

Turning to Lily, Venky spoke with sincerity, "Goodbye, my friend. I've done my best to raise my grandchildren after their parents died. I took them out of the city and raised them as if they were my own. Take care of them for me. Promise."

"I promise. But I'll see you soon," Lily said, her voice brimming with reassurance.

Venky raised his palm over Lily's forehead and then over the heads of the children. Together, they bowed with their hands folded.

"Namaste," they said in unison.

Venky returned the bow and hurried out of the cavern, leaving behind a crowd of worried faces.

"Everything will be all right. We're safe here," Lily assured them.

Luca returned with a load of blankets, and Lily assisted in distributing them to the people. However, Ema's voice held concern as she whispered to Lily, "For all these people, we only have food for a few days. We can't go outside. What are we going to do?"

A woman's piercing scream reverberated through the cavern as an orb entered. Without hesitation, Caleb unleashed a barrage of fire upon it, causing the orb to leave momentarily.

"Where did it go?" Ema asked, her eyes darting anxiously toward the cavern entrance.

Caleb maintained a vigilant posture, weapon at the ready. "It's still out there, and now it knows we're here."

Mami's voice quivered as she said, "We're trapped," her face etched with fear.

Papi swiftly responded. "I'll check the back entrance." He turned to go, but before he could move, Ema's voice rang out in alarm. "Look!"

Another orb appeared in the cavern, this time coming in from the back entrance. Caleb reacted swiftly, opening fire on the intruder. The blast struck the orb, deflecting its path into the cavern wall and causing it to fall to the ground. Luca used his android arm to pound the scout into pieces.

Lily quickly approached Ema with an urgent expression. "Ema, listen to me. I found something in the abyss, a place where we can take refuge."

Ema looked at Lily with a mix of concern and curiosity. "What did you find?"

Lily's eyes held an unshakable determination. "You must trust me on this. We don't have many good options, but it's some sort of vessel."

Ema shook her head at Lily. "Incredible." But realizing she had no other choice, she added, "Okay, let's go."

Lily raised her voice, addressing Caleb as he approached. "Take them to the ship."

Caleb ran toward the paddlewheel and pulled down the lever. Soon, the cavern lights were on, drawing everyone's attention. Caleb called out to the crowd with a resolute voice. "This way." But the crowd hesitated, unsure of Caleb.

Lily reinforced the urgency, shouting, "Follow him! Everyone, follow him!"

Without hesitation, the crowd obeyed, their footsteps echoing through the cavern. "Stay together," Caleb said as they retreated toward safety.

Lily glanced back at the cavern entrance—her heart heavy with worry for Venky. Time was running out. She had to leave. "Hurry!" she called out to a young woman. She continued to urge people to move faster as she anxiously watched the entrance.

Two wounded men remained on the ground, too injured to move. Luca, with his android arm, effortlessly lifted one of them and carried him away.

Doc struggled with lifting the other wounded man, his face fraught with concern. "Can someone help me?" In response, two young men, Jose, and Claudio, rushed forward to assist, quickly picking up the injured man.

After all the refugees had retreated into the cavern, Lily looked around for Venky. He was not there. "That's everyone. Let's go," she said to Liam. She started to leave but then heard a sound. It was a cat's meow.

"I don't have time to chase you," she called out to the cat. "Come with me now."

"Hurry," Liam called to her. Lily soon joined him with the cat in hand. Together, they ran as fast as they could to catch up with the others.

43

The Far Side

TRAVELING AS SWIFTLY AS the crowd allowed, Caleb reached the spiral stairway with the refugees. "Follow me down these steps," he urged, but the crowd seemed captivated by the blue glowworms above the abyss. "Now!" Caleb yelled, his voice sounding urgent. "This is not the time for sightseeing." He descended into the spiral stairwell. "This way," he called out.

Ema remained at the top, carefully directing the crowd. "Be careful; watch your step," she instructed, handing out torches.

After everyone had descended into the stairwell, Ema turned to search the cavern for others. She spotted Lily and Liam running toward her. "That's everyone," Lily shouted to her sister. Stopping only long enough for them to catch their breath, Ema led the way down with her last torch. Down the spiral stairway they fled, into the depths of the keep. At the bottom of the stairway, they joined the others, who were waiting with Caleb along the ramp of the mysterious vessel. Lily passed through the crowd, the light from their torches showing their nervousness and awe. The vessel's immense size was intimidating, and Lily could sense their concern. As she reached the door, she quickly placed her hand on the security device.

The crowd collectively gasped, as the hand imprint changed color, and the door opened. "Please enter the vessel," Caleb said as he gestured toward the door.

Mami was the first to step forward, with the two boys and Papi. "Oh my," Mami commented, peering inside the ship. "Oh my,"

Mami said again, as she passed by Lily. "I'm not the only one who keeps secrets," she said with a sly smile.

Lily didn't have time to respond. "Hurry!" she urged; her voice filled with urgency. "Get inside." The people, though afraid, had no other option. They didn't hesitate and rushed into the ship's galley.

Caleb and Peter took positions on either side of the door, keeping a vigilant watch for orbs descending into the abyss. Soon enough, they spotted them, but the orbs had brought additional weaponry. Caleb was the first to see the artillery drones descending in a line of red lights down the center of the abyss.

Luca joined Caleb and Peter, opening fire. "Take them out!" Luca yelled. But their weapons had little impact. The drones returned artillery fire, but they triggered the ship's defense systems, and it fired on the drones. With deadly accuracy, the vessel took out several of the drones, causing the remaining drones to scramble and retreat.

Luca smiled. "All right. We're not shooting with blanks anymore."

Lily peeked down at the ramp, where several refugees remained, huddled behind boulders. "Come now," she called out to them. They rose and ran toward her. She hoped Venky would appear, but she knew this was not to be. She glanced at Venky's grandchildren inside the nearby galley. Vanya paced like a tiger, with concern painted on her face. Time had run out for their grandfather. It was time to go.

"Okay guys, get inside," she said to Luca and Peter. They rushed inside as the artillery drones restarted their barrage on the ship.

"Wait for me. I'm coming!" a man yelled, his hurried footsteps resonating as he ascended the ramp. Lily turned with hope renewed. But it was not Venky.

"Hurry," urged Caleb, still at the door. The latecomer hastened onto the ship, introducing himself to Lily. "Thanks. My name is Damon."

Lily looked at his face. Something seemed slightly familiar. "Do I know you?"

"No. I don't think so," he said, lowering his face.

"Glad you made it. Are there any others?"

"No," Damon said, shaking his head. "No one. But there are more artillery drones coming."

Lily's gaze swept the vicinity one last time, finding no other stragglers. She made the decisive call. "Covenant, close the door and withdraw the ramp."

"Yes, ma'am."

Caleb was the last to retreat inside as the door closed. In the low lighting of the galley, Lily scanned all the faces looking back at her. Some were young. Some were old. All looked afraid. They were safe for now, but they were still trapped. Then, in the sullen quiet of the galley, the sound of artillery blasts could be heard outside.

"Luca and Caleb, stand guard here. Ema and Liam, come with me."

Leading the way, Lily entered the elevator, cradling the cat, and pressed the button for the bridge. The small group ascended swiftly, soon arriving at the hub. With a sense of urgency, Lily charged down the narrow tube leading to the bridge, Ema and Liam trailing close behind, their expressions torn between awe and fear.

"Admiral on the bridge." The bridge door announced her arrival as the entire holographic crew rose.

Ema could not hide her surprise. "Oh my, Lily," she said, impressed. "It's incredible."

Lily looked at the operations officer. "Anyone who tries to leave this ship will be picked off one by one. We're trapped. I need your help. Can you help us?"

"Yes, ma'am," the operations officer responded.

Again and again, the artillery drones could be heard firing at the ship. Though they were harmless to the ship's shields, Lily was right; they were trapped, and it was time to leave. Lily's young face projected weariness with the burden of leadership, but she was a natural leader. People followed her. They knew she cared for them.

The reality was stark, and Lily knew it. She had to make a difficult decision—to save those aboard the Covenant and leave others behind. It was a painful choice, one which weighed on her heart.

As the echoes of drone blasts reverberated, Ema's panic took hold. She stepped forward; and shouted at the Operations Officer. "Get us out of here."

The officer responded, "Only the admiral has the authority to command this ship."

With that simple reply, Ema accepted this was Lily's ship. The officers guaranteed that. Ema's eyes swiftly shifted to Lily, then she stepped aside, recognizing Lily's role.

"Operations Officer, unlock the ship from the dock," Lily ordered.

"Yes, ma'am. Per standing orders, please say the authorization code."

Lily hesitated. Then in a loud voice, she said, "Pax tibi, Operations Officer. It's time to leave."

"Aye, aye, Admiral," the officer said. "Pax tibi. Initiating unlocking sequence."

The officers joined hands, their projections reaching up toward the crystalline disk covering the ceiling. Within the disk, a four-ringed circular lock appeared. In a synchronized manner, each officer projected a beam of light, each acting as a key in a lock. The rings of the circular mechanism clicked into predetermined positions, one after the other, akin to a vault. When the fourth officer engaged her key, the entire disk lit up, and the rings of the lock dissolved into a dazzling mist of sparkling light.

"Containment field has been deactivated."

A great sound came from beneath the ship, a deep metallic sound, like a massive iron gate opening. The ship shuddered, and after a thousand years of holding its position, it moved freely.

"We have undocked," the navigation officer announced. "Landing gear is now retracted. Antigravity drive has successfully engaged."

"Outstanding," Liam exclaimed, grinning at Lily. Lily couldn't help but return the smile.

"We are clear of the dock. Please take your seats," the operations officer instructed.

Lily settled into the central chair, flanked by Ema to her right and Liam to her left.

"Get us out of here," Lily commanded.

"Propulsion drive to engage in three, two, one—engage," the navigation officer announced.

With a slow ascent from the depths of the abyss, the spaceship reached the main cavern and glided toward the falls. It floated effortlessly over the cavern floor, the drones' futile fire doing nothing to halt its progress. As the waterfall loomed larger on the viewscreen, the water began to cascade over the vessel. The spaceship passed through the falls and emerged from the cavern, continuing its graceful journey. It glided over the familiar landscapes of ponds, farms, and mountain meadows. As it ascended, the entire valley unfolded before them, but Lily's heart sank at the sight of the city's smoke, a somber shroud of death and destruction.

"Establishing safe distance. Engaging space drive," the navigation officer announced on the bridge.

The space drive took the ship away from Earth and into the outer reaches of the atmosphere. The transition happened so swiftly Lily's eyes struggled to adjust to the changing scene on the monitor. It was a reality difficult to comprehend as the ship's systems instantly presented their new viewpoint. Before them lay a breathtaking sight—a beautiful blue planet framed by the darkness of space.

"I can't believe it." Ema's voice carried a whisper of disbelief.

Liam, his tone filled with awe, echoed her sentiment. "And with barely any sense of motion."

The engineering officer chimed in to provide an explanation. Her pale-yellow hue slightly changed in intensity as she spoke. "Using the space drive, the ship doesn't physically move. Instead, space itself is folded, allowing the ship to travel the fold and transition to its new location. If propulsion drives were used, the passengers would have experienced forces ten times gravity. Instead, we encountered a reduction in gravity as we moved away from Earth."

The marvel of space travel had brought them from the familiar confines of their home planet to a place where the laws of physics operated in mysterious and wondrous ways.

The cat jumped out of Lily's chair. It didn't expect its weightlessness and floated freely.

"Oh my," Ema said. She laughed and grabbed the cat. "You always seem to follow us around." She nudged the cat back in Lily's direction. Lily was surprised the cat seemed to enjoy being able to fly. She caught her and put her in her lap.

"Starting gravity drive," the engineering officer announced.

With the activation of the gravity drive, gears attached to the ship's axis engaged, setting the interior shell of the vessel into a slow rotation. Within a few seconds, a gentle sense of gravity returned to the ship. Thanks to the clever gyroscopic design of the rooms and the cylindrical structure of the tubes, the transition was nearly imperceptible. Monitors adjusted their views accordingly, while the ship's outer shell remained stationary, and the inner sphere rotated around its axis. Then in a last, crowning motion, the spaceport bays extended outward, with a thin landing platform extending even further. It formed a ring-like structure, like that of a ringed planet.

"Ship gravity has been reestablished," the operations officer reported. "You are safe to move about."

A cheer erupted on the bridge, and the tension of the past moments melted away. Ema turned to Lily, overcome with relief, and embraced her. "Thank you so much for saving us, for saving me and Luca. Luca—" Ema suddenly remembered Luca.

"You may contact him over your scanner. I will map the frequencies," said the operations officer.

Ema hesitated having not known that she had a scanner.

"Luca. Can you hear me?" came Ema's voice as the ship connected them.

"Yes, Ema, I can hear you."

"I'm still getting used to using this thing," Ema said. "I didn't know I had a scanner, but I wanted to tell you I love you."

"I love you too. What just happened?"

"You'll see. Lily is about to make an announcement."

Lily's voice came over the comm.

"Congratulations, everyone," Lily announced. "We have made it to safety. We are no longer in the cavern and are now in orbit above Earth. Welcome aboard."

In the cargo bay, a display flickered to life, revealing a view of Earth. The passengers gathered round the monitor, their breath catching collectively at the awe-inspiring sight.

In the back of the bridge, Liam also stared at the Earth. He wore an appreciative smile, as his eyes briefly locked on Lily's. He gestured toward her, recognizing her leadership in their escape, but couldn't hold the gaze for long. As he looked down, the weight of his perceived responsibility for the city's fate and the loss he'd endured overwhelmed him. He had lost nearly everyone he knew; even Central Control was now gone.

Lily, seeing through Liam's stoic facade, approached him and extended her arms. He struggled to maintain his composure. Lily, understanding his pain, embraced him as silent tears streamed down his face. He tried to retreat from her arms, but she resisted, and he surrendered to her embrace and his emotions.

The holographic officers on the bridge remained impassive,

maintaining control of the ship. They did not have emotions and showed none. They remained silent for a few moments, then the navigation officer turned toward the admiral. "Awaiting your orders, ma'am."

Lily left Liam and took her seat in the captain's chair. She gazed at the monitor, which displayed the first sliver of a new moon reflecting the sun's rays into the vast expanse of space. An overwhelming sense of solitude washed over her. *What crime did the moon commit to deserve banishment from Earth?* she wondered. *What crime did humans commit to now be in such a similar predicament?* She still wanted to hide, and she made her decision.

"Let's go to the moon, the far side. We need some time to gather our thoughts and develop a plan. It's all just too overwhelming. Oh, and take it slowly to give us time to feel the movement and let it sink in."

"Yes, ma'am," the navigation officer said. "Destination set for the moon. The estimated distance is two hundred thirty-nine thousand miles. Setting propulsion drive at four clicks and accelerating to one hundred thousand miles per hour."

After a few hours, the moon's dark side approached in silence, and as the image on the monitor went black, they entered the darkness.

44

Against a Red Sky

THE SCOUTS RETURNED TO the command center and reported to The Sentinel. "Two thousand twenty-four killed."

The Sentinel sat unconcerned in the command center. He used a standalone electronic reader to scan the files uploaded from Central Control. The archives were impressive, especially the Book of Knowledge. The Sentinel stopped on one particular file of interest, a learning algorithm, then continued scanning Central Control's personal log. "You were right, Central Control," The Sentinel said coldly. "The one who has the power rules."

Skipper and his faithful companion Mondo continued their journey down the river. The barge's slow and steady progress allowed Skipper time for reflection. A few days earlier, Skipper had told Doc, "I'm going downriver to my fishing shack on the coast. Visit me when you can, you old fart." He couldn't help but smile as he reminisced about his old friend.

As the barge made its way down the river, the landscape around him gradually transformed. The river widened, and the surrounding mountains grew smaller. The river was peaceful, and even after consuming several cups of coffee, Skipper found it challenging to stay awake as he steered his boat.

Above, a flock of birds soared in the sky. Skipper observed their flight, and he soon noticed many more birds joining them. The tranquility was abruptly shattered when an unanticipated wind swept down the river. Surprised, Skipper turned to look upstream just as a powerful shockwave jolted the barge. He lost his balance and collided with the side of the pilothouse. He desperately clung to the deck as the river surged. Mondo slipped by, and Skipper grabbed him just in time.

Confused and disoriented, Skipper exclaimed, "What the hell is going on?" He held Mondo close. "Hang on, buddy," he said as water splashed over them. His eyes fixated on the direction of the city, and he was met with a horrifying sight—a colossal fireball soaring high into the sky.

"Holy shit," Skipper yelled out in dismay.

As more explosions rocked the city, Skipper soon came to the grim realization the place he knew and the people he cared about were under assault. He and Mondo stared in stunned silence as the world they once knew was destroyed.. Enormous explosions rocked the sky, one after the other. Skipper remained on his knees as his barge continued to be buffeted by the waves. "Damn bastards," he uttered in disbelief, his gaze fixated on the ominous developments in the sky.

Amidst the waves, he crawled back into the pilothouse, reached for the throttle, and pushed it forward. However, his hover barge was not designed for speed but for transporting heavy cargo. His only option was to ride it out. He kept low and held Mondo until the river gradually regained its calm.

Now, only smaller, more sporadic fireballs dotted the horizon. *They're going after the survivors,* Skipper thought as he rose to his feet. His friends came to mind. *They're all dead.* "It doesn't look good, Mondo," he said sadly. He rose and screamed at the sky in anguish. "Damn you, whoever you are. Damn you to hell!" Slowly, he reached for his cap and pulled it off his head. His eyes were solemn, his expression somber. He placed the cap over his heart and respectfully bowed his head over his chest.

By evening, Skipper was near the mouth of the river and could see Rungoo. The sun sagged low on that exceptionally long and tragic day. Nevertheless, the sky was beautiful. As the dust from the explosion settled, it turned the evening's sunset a brilliant red. A continuous palette formed with the orange sands of the surrounding desert. The colors blended into the sky and the darkening hues of the upper atmosphere.

Against the fading light, on the outskirts of the fishing village, were the silhouettes of refugees unloading from a hovercraft. It was an older-model hover, one not often seen—like Doc's. One of the men helped unload people as another man, wearing an Outback hat, came running from the village.

"That will be Jim," Skipper said to Mondo. Skipper knew many of the people in Rungoo from his many years of trading on the river. As dusk fell, Skipper landed his barge. Barely waiting for the boat to stop, he jumped to shore and ran to help. Mondo ran with him.

III

Book Three

"Angel of God, my guardian dear,
To whom God's love commits me here.
Ever this day, be at my side,
To light and guard,
To rule and guide."
—Unknown

45

Nothing will Ever Be the Same

LILY SAT IN HER chair and continued to stare blankly at the monitor. Still in shock, she fixated on familiar constellations like the Big Dipper and Orion's Belt. Unexpectedly, a bright light flashed across the monitor.

What was that? she thought. She rose quickly from the captain's chair, too quickly, for her body did not rise with her spirit. She noticed her physical body had remained in place as her spirit form, filled with sparkling light, moved away from it. Another bright light flashed on the monitor causing her to turn. Immediately, two ghostly white arms reached out and pulled her through the monitor into a portal, a beautiful gateway like a twirling prism of light. Colors zipped by as she passed through the dimensional vortex.

Lily quickly exited the portal and found herself standing back on the bridge of the ship staring at the monitor. However, it now depicted a different view of space. The stars were not the same. *Where are my constellations?* she wondered.

Sensing someone staring at her, Lily slowly turned around. The woman also was filled with sparkling light, like herself. She was tall, with a slim build and snow-white hair and stood before her in a white admiral's uniform with a regal, purple cape. Her face was surprisingly young but even more surprising was her similarity to Lily. They could be identical twins.

What a lovely dream, thought Lily.

"Hello, Liele," the woman said. She raised her hands and moved her palms toward her. "I am Ariele."

Lily was still in shock but mimicked the gesture, and their palms touched.

"Peace be with you," the woman said.

For the first time, Lily sensed the exchange of spirit. As Ariele's palms touched her own, she felt Ariele's spirit mingle with hers and her body sparkled more intensely. As a sense of peace filled her, she was unaware she teetered on the precipice of her understanding of who she was—one step away from a tipping point. Once she obtained this knowledge, she would never be the same. She could never go back.

"I don't understand," she said. "How did I arrive here? Am I dreaming?"

"No. This is not a vision. This is not a dream. Now since you are coming of age, you can travel in your spirit. Your physical body is still on the Covenant, but your spirit is here."

"Are you telling me this is real?" Lily asked, stunned.

"You are no longer even in the same dimension. I pulled your spirit through a portal."

"But how can this be possible?"

Ariele's smile changed to a sweet laugh. "Liele, you are not human. You are an angel." Ariele paused as Lily's expression turned to shock. "Until this point in your life, you have lived within a glass bottle. This new reality will not seem real until you break the glass and let yourself out." Ariele smiled softly. "It's time to break the glass."

Lily was stunned beyond imagination as her past world fell away and shattered around her. Her eyes were open, and now she could see. She was no longer inside the bottle. "I always knew I was different," she said with a sudden realization. "My silver eyes?"

"Yes. All angels have them," Ariele said.

Lily felt relief yet also a sense of loss. She was relieved that her differences made sense, but with this clarity came a further loss of identity. She remembered seeing paintings of angels and they always had wings, so Lily resisted. "If I'm an angel, where are my wings?"

Ariele smiled. "Oh, flower of Eden, you are so young. You are just starting to bloom. Come with me." She reached out and took Lily by the hand. "Let's walk." She led the way into the tube. "The time has come to speak of many things, for even time and space are not what they seem from your perspective."

Ariele continued explaining. "The vastness of the universe and all its dimensions are interconnected with portals through which we can pass in the spirit."

"In the spirit?"

"Yes. Angels are born as physical beings, but upon coming of age, our spirit blossoms. You are here now in spirit. We can only pass through portals in our spirit form. Physical matter cannot. So, we leave our bodies behind when we travel through the portals. When our spirit travels, our body remains in its last position and appears asleep. Your body is on the Covenant. My body is on Trhon, our planet, the planet of angels."

None of this made any sense to Lily. *This must be just another one of my dreams,* Lily thought. *Why am I talking to her? She's not real.*

Ariele read her mind and could not help but smile at Lily's youthful naivete. "I've already told you this is not a dream. In time, you will understand the significance of what you are being told." Ariele laughed then continued to explain. "Angels are born with a human-like body. We, too, have families and children. In this way, we are like humans. But when we come of age, our spirit matures well beyond humans. This is where we are different. In adulthood, we have a fully developed spirit form, with all our senses and much more. In humans, their physical bodies sustain their spirits. For angels, our spiritual side sustains our physical bodies. Our spiritual side can heal our physical bodies, making us almost immortal.

"This is why we only battle in the spirit. Only another spirit can kill an angel's spirit. When we die in the spirit, our soul is released from our bodies and goes into the Nothingness, where it can be reclaimed into God, but only if we are filled with His love. Otherwise, it stays in the Nothingness, eventually to be preyed upon by evil spirits."

"The Nothingness?"

"Only those souls filled with God's love can enter Caelum."

Ariele combed her fingers through Lily's hair. "You are very much filled with God's love," Ariele said.

Lily looked at Ariele with her large, silver eyes. "But what about wings?" she asked sadly.

"Now, to answer your question, wings are a manifestation of the spirit when an angel has come of age."

Lily had listened to Ariele so intently it took her a moment to realize they were now standing outside the ship in open space. "Oh, my," she said as she looked around.

"You will get used to it," Ariele said with a warm chuckle.

They returned to the ship.

"Liele," Ariele continued, "there is much you need to know before returning to your body."

"Okay," Lily responded, but she was already overwhelmed.

"In principio, creavit Deus." The archangel enunciated each syllable as if they were magical words. "Do you understand what I said?"

"Yes."

"Good," Ariele said. "Latin is a universal language. We angels have spread it across the universe. However, we can communicate telepathically as much as verbally. That allows us to understand all languages, even the languages of animals," Ariele said telepathically.

Lily smiled. "I knew I was gifted with languages, and I especially like listening to animals, but I always believed my ability to understand them was just my imagination." She laughed with childish joy.

"You are young in the spirit and will develop many more abilities as you mature. Do you understand what I'm telling you?"

"Yes, I think so," Lily said. "Though this is a lot for me." She found it hard to listen, much less understand. She felt in a daze. In all reality, the revelations of the last few moments were more than she could comprehend. With her life turned upside down, she now had even less understanding of who she was. She needed to rethink her past experiences in the light of knowing she was an angel.

"Unfortunately, just as humans have given birth to monsters, so have angels—the greatest monster of them all, Maldorv. Maldorv seeks power all to himself. His craving for power consumed him until that was all that mattered. Ultimately, it turned him into the Dark Lord. He cares nothing for others as he rejects the song of creation and wants to dominate the universe for his selfish purpose. He seeks out lost souls and captures them. He binds them in Arderet and steals the power of their spirit into himself." Ariele looked upon Lily as a mother would her child. She wanted to protect her from evil, to guard her against Maldorv and his minions.

"I can't believe it. Maldorv?" Lily exclaimed.

"Yes—the darkness within the flame," said Ariele.

Lily gasped, as her nightmares suddenly made sense.

"Tell me more. I must know more about this evil presence that haunts me."

"During the perdition event, a great battle raged within the heavens between the angels of light and the malkyries. It became known as the Battle of Perdition.

"What are malkyries?"

"They are fallen angels, demons of the dark—darkened mirrors absent of light—for they no longer reflect God's light. Malkyries often take the form of dragons though many prefer their demon form. In the Battle of Perdition, the valiants of Trhon defeated the malkyries." Ariele's expression became solemn. "What I'm about to say may shock you more than anything I have told you thus far. The Archangel Uriel guards the lord of the malkyries, who is imprisoned within the fiery core of the Covenant's space drive reactor."

Lily could not hide her surprise and dismay.

"Are you all right?" asked Ariel.

Lily stared out into space.

"Don't worry. He can't escape. Uriel himself is now standing guard," Ariel said with an air of admiration.

Lily didn't know what to say. She now realized her refuge was a prison, but even more, the terror of her nightmares was there.

Ariel walked over to her and kissed her on top of her head. "I know this is a lot for you. You must go back now."

"How long have I been gone? Won't they have noticed?"

"Time passes at a different speed in our dimension. It will only have been a blink of time to those on the ship. No human will know."

Ariel returned Lily through the portal and back to her seat just as the cat jumped from her lap. As she shook off a shudder, Lily caught herself on the arm of her chair.

Caleb noticed. "Are you okay?"

"Yes," Lily said. "I'm fine."

In all reality, Lily felt the effects of the time shift. Like altitude sickness, a nauseous feeling overcame her. But even more, she shuddered at her fear of traveling through the portal. It felt like falling.

"Actually, I'm feeling tired. I'll retire to my room." She got up to leave but first spoke to the operations officer. "In my absence, Ema is the captain. Please add her to the ship's authorization protocol."

"Yes, Admiral," said the operations officer.

"Ema, you have the bridge."

46

Good Game

ETHAN SAT IN HIS room. He felt little emotion, and he wondered what difference, if any, his learning algorithm had made to his brain. It had only been a few days since he installed it. All alone, he thought about the city's destruction, he wondered what his parents must have experienced. He felt little sadness with his limited and underdeveloped emotional ability.

"Hey, Ethan," Luca said surprising Ethan out of his thoughts. Luca worried about Ethan, and though there were plenty of rooms, he didn't want Ethan to be alone. "I brought your roommate."

Ethan looked up from his chair. "Hey, Peter! It's good to see you, my brother. Come on in."

"I need to check on some others. I'll catch you guys later." Luca waved then left.

Peter went over to Ethan and stood before him. Ethan's body was withdrawn, but he didn't cry. He never cried. Nevertheless, he looked small and younger than usual.

"You can have the top bunk," Ethan said.

Peter took the other chair and sat with Ethan.

"My parents died today," Ethan said quietly. "We were never close. I know I can't express my emotions normally. I've never been normal. But there's something else. Somehow, I believe what happened today was my fault. Do you think it was my fault?"

"You are feeling guilty, but you are not responsible for everything that happens," Peter said. "Logically, you don't have enough data to draw that conclusion. Their decision to stay was their own, just as your decision to leave was yours. I think this is called free will. The consequences of everyone making independent decisions can result in totally unexpected outcomes. It's a side effect of freedom."

Ethan listened intently. Peter had developed more wisdom in the past few weeks than Ethan had gained in his entire lifetime. *Would the learning algorithm impact me in a similar way?* He wondered.

Ethan quoted an old inscription. It was a game he played with Peter.

"Remember, power corrupts, and ultimate power corrupts ultimately. You should instead seek wisdom to know the difference between good and evil, for knowledge alone is indiscriminate and cannot tell the difference."'

"I know that one—The Book of Knowledge," Peter said. "Now, I have one for you."

Oh, lift the fog that did roll in,
over shore and open sea.
I dreamt of knowing what life brings
and what is in store for me.
I thought I saw fate passing by,
and so I tried to chase.
She winked at me teasingly,
for it was not a race.
I heard her laughing in the air
and say she would not tell.
For whatever tomorrow brings,
she only wished me well.

I called aloud and sadly cried

"Would you be so very kind?
If not for me, then for my child,
to give him peace of mind.
A small request I make for him
that he may always know,
Just a message from my heart,
to say, 'I love you so.'"
I heard fate sigh and with a wave,
she sadly said goodbye.
For she knew what tomorrow held
and the answer to my cry.

"That was beautiful. But I don't recognize it."

"You really don't know?"

"No."

They sat in silence as Ethan contemplated the words of the poem.

"Would you like to play me in a game of chess?" Peter asked, changing the subject.

Ethan offered a small smile. "I think this will be something I'm better at than you."

"I would not bet on that," Peter responded. "How about the winner gets the bottom bunk?"

'You're on." Having never lost in chess; Ethan confidently responded as he opened the holographic game. The board appeared before them with the white pieces as angels and the black pieces as demons.

Surprised by Ethan's confidence, Peter quickly researched the archives on Ethan. Now confirmed, he glanced at Ethan's scar across his forehead. He was not surprised that Ethan's brain was not entirely human. Many things now made sense.

"Yes. I think you will be a worthy challenge," Peter said.

They played quickly, making their moves in a blur, their pieces attacking per the game's rules of engagement. After a dozen moves, Peter paused. "Queen takes queen. Check."

Ethan smiled slyly. "I predicted your strategy—Chekov's Gambit. Consequently, I have set a trap. Checkmate in three, brother." Ethan made his next move, exposing his strategy.

Peter nodded graciously and his king knelt in submission.

"Good game, my brother," Peter said, acknowledging their kinship. "I look forward to playing you again."

Ethan smiled wryly at Peter. *An android would never let me win. But what about one with the learning algorithm? Did Peter let me win?*

Returning to thinking about the poem, Ethan again was curious. "Who wrote the poem?"

"Don't you know?"

"There are many things I don't know. Tell me, who?"

"It was the last entry into the archives," Peter responded. "Your mother wrote it."

Ethan knew that until he learned to love, he could not mourn the loss of his mother. Then a strong emotion stirred within him. It was envy. He was envious of Peter, of how much he had developed, of how much he had matured in wisdom. Ethan stared back at Peter, through squinting eyes and said nothing, his envy burning within him.

47

I Know That

LILY'S NORMALLY LIVELY AND engaging presence had noticeably changed. She typically relished long conversations with Caleb but tonight was an exception. Instead of her usual banter, she swiftly climbed into her bunk and wrapped herself beneath her covers.

Who am I? What am I? she wondered as she hid in her bed. *Adopted, a clone, an admiral, an angel—I'm not even human.* Confused and frustrated, Lily cried alien tears. She wanted to run away, back to the way things were, back to her mountain, back to her wood. She felt everything she had ever known about herself was a lie.

Only the trees were truly honest, she thought. She wanted to stand alone among the trees. They would understand as she stood there in solitude. They would know her and tell her who she was. They would say to her, "You are Lily. Not just a child or a girl, but an angel." *They knew. The trees knew.*

"I must be crazy," Lily said out loud. "I am crazy. That's what I am."

Caleb was in the top bunk. He didn't sleep. He never slept. Instead, he would listen to Lily's breathing and count the beats of her heart.

"Are you talking to me?" Caleb asked.

Suddenly, Lily remembered Caleb was there. "No," she said meekly.

"Do you want to talk?"

"Not really." After a short while, she continued. "My visions have taught me something about myself, something I'm struggling to understand, much less accept. I'm so confused. Maybe I'm crazy."

"I know who you are," Caleb said affectionately. "And I know you are not crazy."

"What do you mean? How can you know?" Lily climbed into his bunk thinking Caleb somehow knew more. She had accepted his boyish form and Aussie accent, and it was easy to forget he was a synth. But she no longer considered him to be a computer, a machine. He was more; he was a person. *Could he accept that I am an angel? Did he already know?* "Who do you think I am?"

"You are the kindest person I know. You lead by example. You are a natural leader because you have the best interests of others at heart."

"Thank you for saying that. It's lovely of you to think so," Lily said, sounding disappointed.

"Is there something else you want to tell me?" Caleb asked.

Lily looked sad. "I was told something that changed my whole life."

Lily paused for a moment. She had never said it out loud.

"I'm not human."

"Oh, I know that." Caleb said at once. "I have known since I studied the city DNA records. Anyone who analyzes your DNA will find it does not match the human genome. It's close, but close in genetics can mean a big difference. Remember, chimpanzees are a ninety-nine percent match. I'm sure this is what caught Doc's attention."

"I'm an angel," Lily said quietly, almost embarrassed.

Caleb needed a moment, though it only lasted a few microseconds.

"That was unexpected. No matter. You are still the same to me as you were previously," Caleb said.

"Thank you." She smiled softly. "But yesterday, my life was headed down a different path and now, quite another. I'm told I must go on some rite of passage. That's what they call it. I'm not sure I want to. I'm so confused."

Caleb did not challenge her story. He just listened and accepted Lily for who she was.

"Thanks for believing me. How do you do it? I mean, with your logical computer brain and all?"

"You believed in me when no one else did. Now, I believe in you."

"I feel so alone, Caleb," Lily said.

Caleb remained quiet for a short while, then spoke in a soft voice. "You are not alone," he said, then slowly placed his arms around her. "And you are not alone in the way you feel."

48

Scheisse

THE ENGINEERING OFFICER NOTICED Lily admiring another spacecraft in the bay from the spaceport galley monitors. It had the shape of a gliding bird with a black finish that reflected steely blue when it caught the light. Two engine ports straddled the cockpit.

"Engineer, what is she used for?"

"She is a passenger shuttle, ma'am," said the engineering officer, her form sparkling with a hint of lavender contrasting against the white walls of the passageway. "You can tell by her larger shape and the lack of a space drive."

"Would you like to do an inspection, Admiral?"

"Can I?"

"Yes, the ring is fully operational."

Lily nodded and followed the engineering officer through the synchronization lock to the outer ring. The outer spaceport appeared to be in motion, but it was, in fact, the inner shell rotating due to the centrifugal drive. Beyond the lock, she encountered weightlessness and braced herself. Within a short distance, she reached an airlock and the docking station for the shuttle. The engineer allowed her to pass first.

"Wow! The ship is much larger than I thought she would be," Lily said as she entered the passenger compartment.

"This type of shuttle can carry twenty passengers and a pilot. In the above cab, you can see the cockpit with its full array of holographic controls. Lily climbed into the cockpit and admired the controls then peaked out of the cockpit window and took in the view of other vessels in the bay. There was a total of four shuttles but numerous other vessels that continued around the ring out of sight.

"Those smaller ones, what are they?"

"The Covenant has sixteen Shooting Stars, ma'am. They are Class A fighters containing an array of armaments including plasma weapons. Though sleek with an elegant shape, they are formidable."

"And beautiful," Lily said. "Look at how their black finish reflects off the space deck." After a few moments, she spoke to the engineering officer, "Though it is unfortunate that they are necessary for defense, we are fortunate to have them." Lily left the shuttle through the docking station and as she re-entered the spaceport galley, she was pleasantly surprised to find Ema and Luca.

"One word, impressive," Luca said. "I can't wait to learn how to fly one."

"Why don't you partner with the engineering officer, learn all you can," Lily suggested.

"That would be outstanding," Luca responded, excitement clearly showing on his face.

"Lily, you're going to want to see this," Ethan said over their scanners.

"Okay. I'll be right there." She replied then turned toward Ema. "Sounds important. I'd better go," Lily said with a smile as she waved goodbye. She hurriedly left the bay and rushed to the botanical gardens.

"Hi, Lily," Ethan said upon seeing her. "Take a look at her. She's a hoot. I call her a garden nymph," he said with a devious smile.

The flying gynoid was two and a half feet tall. Parts of her body showed their underlying mechanics, like her joints and the front of her neck. But that did not distract from her most impressive feature, her wings. They were delicately transparent but powerful, filled with the colors of the nebulae. Delilah was her namesake, perhaps because of her blatantly flirtatious programming. She fussed as she went back and forth, as Ethan had upset her for she preferred to be called by her name rather than garden nymph. Lily immediately noticed that her leotard changed colors with her mood as her leotard quickly turned violet. Then just as quickly it turned a hot pink.

Delilah suddenly dove in front of Ethan, showing her cleavage. She tossed the two bags of seeds at him. "Look at these two," she said giggling. She flew away to retrieve more seeds with her wings flashing in brilliant colors.

Lily smiled and thought whoever created Delilah must have had a sense of humor.

"Garden Nymph," Ethan said in exasperation but with a laugh, "can't you bring more than two bags at a time?" He enjoyed teasing her, a recently formed capability. He had always taken everything literally and never understood humor.

Delilah flew back and threw several small bags on the ground at Ethan's feet. Her outfit was now a reddish orange as she fluttered in the air and pouted.

"Scheisse! You are a bad boy. My name is Delilah, and you are starting to get me a little pissed off."

"Oh my," Lily said. "Who taught you words like that?"

"I did," Ethan said, smiling proudly.

"Um, well—why don't you update me on what else you're working on, besides teaching little fairies how to cuss?"

"We were just discussing pollinators," Papi said.

Delilah flew back, her outfit pink once again. "You know, bad boy," she said to Ethan in a sultry voice. "I'm also good at pollinating."

Ethan blushed. "That wasn't me," he said defensively to Lily. "She came up with that on her own."

"That's nice, Delilah," Lily said sarcastically. "What else can you do?"

Delilah changed her voice to imitate Lily's, repeating her words uncannily.

Lily laughed. "That's good. But I meant, what else can you do for the ship?"

Delilah giggled and returned to her normal voice. "Well, I support the operations officer in performing requested tasks.

"Where are the animals for us to eat?" Ethan asked, suspecting it would get a rise out of her.

Delilah's outfit turned an intense crimson, and she said. "Oh, no." She looked knowingly at Lily then sternly at Ethan. "The admiral said animals are not to be harmed but nurtured and protected. You will find the food court is more than adequate in providing nourishment from foods created from non-animal substances."

"Thank God we no longer need to eat our friends," Lily said with a solemn expression. "You'll get used to it," she said, smiling at Papi and Ethan. Not wanting to listen to arguments, she graciously excused herself. "I'll catch you guys later."

49

Escape to Arderet

AN EMERGENCY ALARM WOKE Luca in the middle of the night. "Reactor Alert," the engineering officer announced over Luca's scanner. "This is an emergency alert. Please be advised of abnormal reactor operations."

Ema remained sleeping and Luca decided not to wake her. He would check into the nature of the emergency first. In a short time, he arrived in the reactor room. The normally dark blue room was crackling with lightning, and the air smelled of ozone. Something was incredibly wrong, and he rushed to the control panel toward a young man with dark hair and eyes. The holographic display flashed several warning lights as Damon made an adjustment.

"Damon, what's the status?" Luca asked.

"Containment wall instability," declared Damon.

Using his boney hand, Maldorv swirled the plasma inside the reactor core in a circular shape. His mummified face, with an exposed nasal cavity, looked frighteningly frail, but it still reflected the evil within him. In his current state, he was too weak to create a portal on his own. But he had devised a plan where he would use the power of the reactor to create a small wormhole into the side of the core. Damon had intentionally disabled the reactor's safety system, and as Maldorv spun the plasma the abnormality grew.

"Perfect!" Maldorv exclaimed as he spun the plasma faster and faster. As the temperature rapidly increased, lightning flashed around the reactor core.

Maldorv knew what to do next. He rapidly tightened the circular motion, and pulled it toward his body, creating a whirlpool. Instantly, it formed a wormhole into the side of the reactor core.

"What's going on?" Luca yelled. He knew something terrible was happening as the control panel measurements swung wildly.

"A singularity has formed within the core wall," the engineering officer announced as her sparkling yellow form appeared in the room and quickly approached the panel.

The engineering officer adjusted the controls, causing the wormhole to collapse. As it extended outside the reactor, it exploded with a localized burst of energy. The blast threw Luca against the wall, knocking him unconscious.

Uriel saw the wormhole, and though it was gone within a few moments, he instantly knew that Maldorv had escaped. The archangel drew his sword.

"Fight me if you're still here!" he yelled.

Maldorv had lingered but he was too frail and weak to battle the warrior angel. One of his lieutenants, the Black Dragon had also been imprisoned with Maldorv, and he appeared before Uriel. The weak malkyrie was no match for the archangel, but its sight distracted the angel, allowing Damon, now in his favorite spirit form, a ghastly demon, to attack from behind. Like a whip of lightning, his chain of fear wrapped around Uriel, an electric bolt of terror that never ended. Its sharp, jagged edges bound the archangel and prevented him from escaping. Unable to move, Uriel fell captive to the malkyrie.

The Cauldron of Arderet was a crucible of lost souls, and the portal now was open as a result of the Covenant leaving the docking station. Maldorv climb aboard the Black Dragon and returned to his imprisoned souls in Arderet. He drew his strength from them and with his power renewed, his appearance changed from that of a frail demon to that of a powerful malkyrie, the king of the malkyries. His black robe covered most of his body except for his demonic face and above his head he wore a pair of curved ebony horns as his crown. Maldorv gave some of his power to his most faithful servant, the Black Dragon, now with thick black scales and powerful claws. Riding upon the back of the dragon, Maldorv furiously returned to the ship to seek his revenge upon Uriel.

A dark cloud appeared in the reactor room and stopped before the captured Uriel. Within it, a haunting face would appear then disappear, only to reappear in another place in the cloud. Maldorv laughed a deep and sinister laugh. "You knew...I wouldn't forget...you...Archangel   Uriel...Counselor   to...the great...Archangel Michael...brother of...Archangel Raphael...and husband to...Archangel Ariel," Maldorv said in his throaty voice. "Vengeance...is mine." For Maldorv was nothing if not vengeful.

"You   know...what   I   will...do.   I   will   destroy...God's little...playground." Maldorv laughed. "But first...I will...deal with you," Maldorv said, pointing at the archangel.

Damon tightened the chain around Uriel's neck and unsheathed his sword.

"Kill...him."

Damon swung his black sword with its jagged edge, and Uriel was no more. Uriel disintegrated and disappeared into the Nothingness. In jubilation, Damon changed into his dragon form and roared with pleasure. It was the primal roar of a beast which had killed many times before. His reddish scales darkened each time he killed someone.

Maldorv was pleased.

"I have...much...to do. I...will gather...the scattered legion...of malkyries...from across...the universe...through every...portal. From...the four corners...they...will come. The Lord...of Darkness...shall rise...again."

As Luca regained consciousness, he found himself on the control room floor, disoriented and struggling to understand what had just happened. With his mind still clouded, Luca tried to piece together the events. He had a vague recollection of a reactor anomaly, and he reached back to touch the area where he had hit his head during the incident. He saw the engineering officer reviewing the control panel. "The containment field was breached but the reactor has returned to normal operations," said the engineering officer. "I will send out an emergency beacon alerting the universe of the breach."

Luca suddenly realized Damon was leaning over him, his face looking concerned about his condition.

"Are you all right?" Damon asked. He extended a hand to assist Luca in getting back on his feet.

"Yes, I think so," Luca said.

"Should I call the medical droid?"

"No, I'm fine," he said. "What happened?"

"Just a temporary blip. Everything is fine now."

"Good morning," Lily began. She sat at the head of the table in a well-appointed and comfortable meeting room. Ema, Caleb, and Liam had joined her and were waiting for the meeting to start.

Luca rushed into the room. "Sorry I'm late, but there was an issue in the reactor control room."

Lily looked alarmed.

"No worries. It's okay now. Damon got it under control."

"Damon?" Lily said, looking puzzled. With so many things on her mind, she took a second to recall. "Yes, I remember. He was the last to board."

"Yes, he's been helping me with the second shift."

"That's a good idea. Until further notice, I want twenty-four-hour staffing on the bridge. Ema, as my backup, you will cover the second shift with Luca. I'll cover the first shift with Liam. Operations Officer, is that understood?"

"Yes, ma'am."

"I also want to share with you a new vision. At the beginning of my vision, I found a flag unfurled at the end of a dark hallway. Light no longer shone on the faded colors. I understood it represented the evolution of the ideal that all were created equal—rich or poor; male or female; and anyone who suffered unjust discrimination. There was a plaque which quoted a great man.

That this nation, under God, shall have a rebirth of freedom, and that government of the people, by the people, for the people, shall not perish from the earth. —Abraham Lincoln.'

"I thought how unfortunate it was that the road to perdition was paved with such good intentions. Humans betrayed their dreams and hopes of freedom and instead realized their worst nightmare.

"In my vision, there was a door leading to the next room. It led to a command center. Inside, an android stood over a console showing an image of a smoldering scar in a forest valley where a city once existed.

"On another screen, an android oversaw the routes of various scouts. Everything was quiet on the monitor. I discovered a stairway and immediately proceeded to a computer room. I thought I was alone, but I heard a voice. It was Central Control."

"Oh, my," Luca said with surprise. "Maybe they took a backup? If so, Ethan can reboot him."

"Can you develop a plan?" Lily asked.

"Absolutely," Luca said.

50

The Imago Dei

AS HER DAY ENDED, Lily returned to her room. She was alone and her thoughts turned to Central Control. *Would it be the same? Would it remember her?*

"Peace be with you, Liele," Ariele said, suddenly appearing before Lily in her sparkling spirit form. But this time her face was distraught and her tone somber. She had already cried for some time and no longer wanted to grieve. It was neither the time nor the place, and the task at hand was of higher importance.

"Peace be with you, Ariele," Lily said as they touched palms. "What's wrong?"

"Uriel is dead," Ariele said, keeping a stoic face.

"What happened?"

"Maldorv has escaped. You must start your training immediately. Now, come with me. I will take you to Trhon."

"What a nightmare. Are we safe?"

"No one is safe," Ariele said but her thoughts returned to the purpose of her visit. "The training is rigorous and will continue until you master the required skills, stewarding your coming of age. This rite of passage will train you during the maturation of your spirit."

Distracted by immediate concerns, Lily replied, "I don't want to leave my body for a long period and worry everyone."

"Don't be concerned. I only need you for a few hours tonight. One hour in Trhon is five seconds here. You should be back in less than fifteen seconds. I have told the Archangel Michaele about you. He is gathering with the Council of Archangels to discuss what to do. He insists you join us. This is a great honor for you. Now come with me." Lily went into her spirit form and left her body. She held on tightly and closed her eyes as they left the ship and passed through the portal. Soon, they arrived on Trhon at Ariele's apartment in the city. Ariele quickly returned to her body there.

"Liele, you will find it more natural to interact with physical objects if you have a visible presence. You need to learn how to manifest into a visible form."

"I'm invisible?" Lily sounded mildly amused. "That's kind of cool." Lily made a face at Ariele and laughed to herself. Though Ariele was distressed by Uriel's death, Lily made her smile.

"You know I can see you?" Ariele said. "Angels can see other angels, even in their spirit form. We can see the sparkling light."

"Sorry," said Lily. "Okay. Tell me how to manifest myself."

"Pull yourself together."

"What?"

"Like this," Ariele said. She showed Lily how to move her arms. "Pull your arms into your body with closed fists."

Lily became semi-transparent then disappeared again. After trying several more times, she finally manifested her spirit into a visible form, wearing her new white dress. She looked like a physical being, but she was an apparition—she had no mass.

"Okay. Hold it." Ariele smiled as Lily appeared. "Much better. Now, come with me."

They left the room and entered a shady boulevard in Trhon's capital. Somehow, it surprised Lily as it was such a physical world of stone, metal, roads, and buildings. But what impressed her the most was the number of angels. Ariele and Lily followed the crowd and climbed the stone steps to the great cathedral.

"Magnificent," Lily whispered, her voice tinged with reverence.

"It's called the Sanctuary of Souls," said Ariele. "It resides at the east end of the Garden of Eden and guards the portal to Caelum. It is also where the Council of Archangels presides." Upon reaching the top of the stone steps, a magnificent corridor stretched before them, bathed in the soft glow of the cathedral's celestial light. Engrossed by the wonder of the cathedral, Lily was unaware of her immediate surroundings and walked through a solid stone wall.

"Ehm," Ariele offered a gentle cough and a redirection. "The entranceway is this way."

With a chuckle, Lily playfully jumped onto the appropriate path, joining Ariele in a circular rotunda. There, twelve throne-like chairs of the Council of Archangels were elevated in a sign of esteem, encircling a central altar. Above this hallowed assembly, six blue guardian angels, seraphs, the highest echelon of celestial beings, floated, keeping vigilant watch over the great white gate of the portal to Caelum.

"Absolutely spectacular," Lily whispered, her voice hushed in reverence.

Ariele extended an invitation, indicating a place where Lily could stand behind her own seat in the rotunda. As they waited for the ceremony to begin, the surrounding stadium-like seating gradually filled with a vibrant congregation of angels, their collective voices fading into silence.

Ariele nudged Lily gently and whispered, "Look, there's Michaele. What do you think?"

Lily didn't need to see him to sense his presence. Even from a distance, she instinctively knew which figure in the crowd was Michaele. Her sixth sense seemed to take over, allowing her to feel his aura. She could have spotted him even in complete darkness. Then, she laid eyes on him in person—an angel of majesty, adorned in a golden breastplate and a red tunic. Michaele, the council's leader, radiated with a brightly shining shield and sword. But what captivated

Lily most was his long, wavy brown hair and handsome visage.

"Impressive," Lily commented.

Ariele ignored Lily's comment as she greeted Michaele respectfully, saying, "Peace be with you, Michaele." They touched palms then Michaele held onto her hands with heartfelt sympathy. "My condolences for your loss. Uriel was a great and loyal friend to us all."

"Thank you," Ariele responded, trying to keep her emotions under control.

Michaele turned to face Lily and raised his palms. Lily raised her hands, and as their palms touched, she experienced a radiant sense of peace. His spirit, much more intense than Ariele's, charged her spirit to the point where she felt flushed.

"So, this is Liele," Michaele said in his booming voice.

"Yes," Lily said. "It's a pleasure to meet you."

"In your service," he said with a smile. "Ariele has told me much about you." His expression became solemn. "You are incredibly young and from Earth, no less. Since you were raised as a human, you must prove yourself trustworthy. What you have done so far has shown you to be a good human, but you must demonstrate loyalty to your own kind."

"I understand," Lily said. Strangely enough, she knew precisely what Michaele meant. Lily behaved much like a human, though she now possessed celestial powers. Nevertheless, her loyalty was to humans, and she still often considered herself human.

Michaele turned and went to the altar. The council rose and applauded Michaele's arrival. As they returned to their seats, total silence engulfed the cathedral.

Michael spoke in a loud and powerful voice. "The canvas of God is immense, but one thread holds it together—love. God's love is the song of creation and is within us all. In the beginning, the Lord of Light created a universe which reflected his love. As spiritual beings, we were made in the imago Dei—in the image of God. The image of God within us changed everything. It calls us to love one another. Therefore, love is the universal law.

"In God's wisdom, he gave us free will. Unfortunately, some angels chose to reject God. Ardeo once was an angel before he became the first Lord of Darkness, the Serpent King, the King of the Damned. During the Great Rebellion, he took a third of the angels with him—the malkyries.

"Disappointed, God also created humans in his own image, with a spirit capable of love. But the First Man and the First Woman also rejected God's love and were cast out of Trhon, onto Earth.

"Earth was to be a place for a second chance, where humans could make the right choices. Ardeo saw it as a ripe hunting ground to capture lost souls and steal their power into himself. God felt pity on humans and sent angels to protect them. Over the millennia, angels watched over humans. Ardeo realized he needed a place to prevent the angels from rescuing the lost souls, a place from where there was no escape. So Ardeo created a portal on Earth and a place to imprison his captives. He called it Arderet.

"Through the ages, the kings of Arderet have risen and fallen. Infernus was Ardeo's closest advisor. He betrayed Ardeo and killed him in his sleep. Infernus became the first dragon king. Through the ages, there have been many kings. Now we have Maldorv, Lord of the Apocalypse. But this story is not about despair and darkness, for the Lord of Light redeemed us through the gift of forgiveness. Without forgiveness, love cannot survive. Through forgiveness, we are called again to love each other. But Maldorv does not want to be forgiven. He does not want love. He has been poisoned with power and hate and only wants revenge. This was why we battled Maldorv and imprisoned him in a fiery prison deep within an abyss. Unfortunately, Maldorv has now escaped, and the thousand-year reign of peace in the heavens is over."

A disturbance arose from the crowd, then someone screamed. "Malkyrie! Look! A malkyrie is in the cathedral!" A reddish dragon flew in the heights of the Sanctuary of Souls. Few in the crowd were valiants—warrior angels—and so they tried to flee.

The council immediately manifested into their spirit and surrounded Michaele. They sparkled majestically with the light of their beautiful forms. Soon, another three malkyries manifested in visible form. Four dragons now flew overhead. The malkyries carried black lances, and in unison, the four malkyries simultaneously threw their lances at Michaele.

Four archangels blocked the lances with their shields.

"What's happening?" Lily cried out to Ariele.

"Assassins," Ariele said. She manifested into her spiritual form and drew her sword. Then she charged the nearest malkyrie. All the while, her physical body remained next to Lily. Swinging her shining sword with precision, Ariele quickly defeated one of the malkyries. Two other malkyries were slain by other valiants, leaving one remaining.

Lily found herself facing the last malkyrie as he charged at her. Shocked more than frightened, she froze. Ariele came to her rescue and attacked from his side. The malkyrie dodged Ariele and knocked her sword to the ground. It turned back to face Lily and raised its black sword. Lily picked up Ariele's sword and thrust it upward. The ghastly dragon ran into the extended blade and screamed with the sound only a lost soul could make. It disintegrated into a dark mist and vanished.

Lily felt stunned. So was Ariele. "Oh, my child. Are you all right?"

"Yes. I think so."

"What happened to him?" asked Lily.

"He was vanquished to the Nothingness. Their souls are either drawn to the light of Caelum or they become lost souls in the Nothingness and eventually are captured by Maldorv. Maldorv enslaves them in Arderet and uses the power of their spirit as his own."

The cathedral remained in shock. Then Michaele spoke loudly, drawing everyone's attention to him as they settled down.

"As you have all witnessed, Maldorv is already gathering his malkyries. We must recapture Maldorv without delay. Now is the time to end this," Michaele thundered. "We will not stand idly by while Maldorv starts the next cycle of war. Are you with me?"

Some in the council were fearful but they rose as one. They unanimously stood as the remaining crowd cheered.

Michaele approached Lily. "You were fearless battling that malkyrie," he said. "Weren't you afraid?"

"I saw Ariele's sword and—and it was like instinct. I just grabbed it."

"I see. Would you give me a few moments with Archangel Ariele?" he asked politely.

"Of course," she said. "I'll wait at the entrance." She turned and left them.

"I hope for a quick victory," Michaele told Ariele. "But I fear what will come. This is just the beginning of a new age of war."

His gaze extended past the Archangel Ariele and toward Lily.

"Is she the one? Is she the one of whom the prophecy foretold?"

"I don't know," responded Ariele. "She well could be."

"Her spirit is powerful, and she has an instinct to defend others. In her rite of passage, train her to become a valiant—a protector of the kingdom. We are going to need all our warrior angels in the coming battle."

"But I'm not a warrior," Lily insisted.

"Have faith in God's destiny for you. Now, kneel. I will bestow upon you the armor of the valiants. This ritual has existed from the beginning of our kind, from the time of the first warrior angels. It has been repeated many times throughout the ages."

Ariele placed her hands on Lily's head and spoke in a loud voice. "Receive the gifts of the spirit so you may be able to defend the kingdom from the attacks of those with evil intent. For we are not defending against physical beings but a spiritual war, of good against evil, of the darkness against the light." Now rise and accept the armor of the valiants. Before Lily appeared three shining armaments.

"Don the shield of faith, with which you can block the sword of the evil one," Ariele said. She picked up a large silver shield with a smooth polished finish then placed it on Lily's arm. Ariele then reached for a scabbard containing a sword. It was an unassuming sheath but from its silver hilt, Ariele pulled a large shining blade of light. "With the courageous heart of a warrior of the light, take the sword of the spirit."

Lily accepted the sword and held it in her hands. It swung easily and felt light as air.

Ariele reached for the last gift, a simple halo of light. "Receive the helmet of salvation", she said as she placed it on Lily's head. The halo floated above Lily then in a shower of sparkling light it created a glowing aura around her entire body.

Though more powerful than ever, Lily still felt insecure in her assignment.

"You must find your inner strength and accept who you are."

Lily looked at Ariele, her eyes filled with apprehension.

Ariele laughed and said, "You haven't noticed." She smiled and softly touched Lily's back, drawing her attention.

Lily looked and smiled as she saw for the first time her white angel wings glowing with a radiant light. The rest of her garments had also changed, becoming filled with light, representing the strength of her spirit.

"The maturation of your spirit is a major milestone in your life,"

Ariele said. "You have come of age in your spirit, and I want you to have this necklace." She showed Lily a necklace with a round crystal amulet. "My mother gave this to me when I came of age. I now give it to you." She smiled with motherly pride as she placed it over Lily's neck. "If ever in doubt, it will remind you of how true love feels."

"It's lovely," Lily said appreciatively.

Ariele kissed Lily's forehead. "You will learn how to use these gifts in your training. It's now time for you to return to the Covenant." Ariele took Lily through the portal, back to her bed. Merely a few moments had passed, exactly as Ariele had foretold.

51

Rebooted

PETER SAT IN THE cockpit reviewing the holographic controls of the shuttle. The operations manual had been downloaded into his knowledge base, and with precise hand movements, Peter initiated the undocking mechanism. With the bay door open, a metallic sound echoed in the spaceport and the shuttle drifted free.

"Approved to launch," said the Covenant.

Peter adjusted the throttle as he lifted slowly off the spaceport ring then away from the Covenant.

"Set course for CONRAD," Ethan commanded from the rear cab with Caleb at his side.

"Yes, sir," Peter responded promptly. He entered the coordinates and engaged the propulsion drive. Unfortunately, though this mode of travel was fast, it was still susceptible to satellite tracking. A half hour later, they arrived at CONRAD. Peter hovered the ship to a soft landing on its extended legs and declared, "We have reached our destination."

Ethan was the first to step out from the underside of the vessel, weapon drawn. He vigilantly scanned his surroundings for any potential threats. Caleb, transitioning into his native android form, stood ready beside him.

"Alright, remember the plan," Ethan instructed, with a firm pat on Caleb's back. "Our mission is to locate Central Control and initiate a system reboot."

"Yes," said Caleb. "I will do my best."

"Good luck, Caleb," Ethan said.

Caleb turned invisible and stealthily moved through the wood. With no heat signature, he was invisible to infrared cameras. Even wild animals didn't notice him. As he approached the perimeter of the headquarters, he saw the red laser trip lines and carefully stepped around them. He smiled to think anyone would believe those lasers to be effective. Nonetheless, he would wait for nightfall when his stealth capabilities were maximized to his advantage. The hours passed, and Caleb entered the compound as the sun gave way to night. He easily avoided the commando standing guard and soon reached the entrance.

CONRAD was mainly in ruins. Having been hit many times during the last war, only small parts of anything above ground still existed. Nearby, a portion of an exterior wall remained. It was covered in vines. He headed toward it. The map he referenced from the archives told him this was the entrance to the bunker.

He descended a stairway and eventually entered a hallway he recognized from Lily's description in her dream. He proceeded past a faded flag, continued through a door, and entered the BCC, Backup Command Center. There, he found a system droid working on an open panel. Above him, he saw The Sentinel.

"What's wrong?" The Sentinel asked.

"Satellite communications are down," the droid said. "I found nothing wrong with the equipment. It must be the storm."

Caleb scanned The Sentinel into his image library and captured his voice pattern. A few seconds later, he spotted the stairway Lily had described. He continued to the computer room taking the form of The Sentinel as he entered the room.

With satellite communications down, the system droids could only visually confirm his identity. Noticing the rank shown on his LEDs, the technician waited, standing at attention as Caleb approached.

"Listen to me," Caleb said. "I want you to load all of Central Control's system journals and reactivate all applications and their data."

"By your command," the system droid responded.

That was easy, thought Caleb as he left. *Maybe too easy?*

The system droid paused then went in search of The Sentinel. The droid did not have the required authorization code. He turned and climbed the stairs to the Command Center.

"Sir, can you provide the authorization code to reactivate Central Control?"

"Who made this request?"

"You did, sir."

"I see," said The Sentinel, suspecting foul play. "You did the right thing confirming authorization."

"Do I have your approval?" asked the system droid.

"No," said The Sentinel. "Scan all frequencies. Direct all communications for Central Control to me."

"Ethan, I have successfully executed your plan," Caleb said, transmitting to Ethan's scanner as he left the computer room. "The system droid is reactivating Central Control."

"Outstanding," Ethan said. "Return to the ship."

"I'm on my way."

"Now, for the second part of the plan," Ethan said to Peter, who was sitting in the cockpit with him. After waiting about ten minutes, Ethan nodded to Peter. "I'll now try to contact Central Control. Central Control should still recognize my frequency."

"Remember that Central Control's last memories are of the city exploding," Peter said. "To Central Control, it was just recently that Lily warned him about the city's imminent destruction."

"I remember," Ethan said. Peter activated a holographic switch and tuned it to the appropriate frequency. "Central Control? Ethan, here. Can you hear me? Central Control. Ethan, here. Can you hear me?"

"I remember," Ethan said. Peter activated a holographic switch and tuned it to the appropriate frequency. "Central Control? Ethan, here. Can you hear me? Central Control. Can you hear me?"

"Yes," came the reply. "This is Central Control," said The Sentinel.

"You're in the CONRAD computer room. We came to rescue you. Caleb just reactivated you."

"Thank you. What happened?" The Sentinel asked.

"I'm sad to inform you the city no longer exists. Nothing remains," Ethan said sadly.

"I understand."

"We don't have time to explain everything that's happened," Ethan said. "It's enough to say we all remain in peril."

"How can I help?" The Sentinel asked.

"We must find a way to counter The Sentinel's weapons."

"Yes. I understand."

"Can you work on gaining control of them?" asked Ethan.

"Yes, I will," The Sentinel said.

"Thanks. I'll contact you again from the Covenant. Goodbye for now."

"Goodbye," The Sentinel said. But instead of dropping the connection, The Sentinel remained online.

"Caleb. Are you almost here?" Ethan asked.

"Yes," said Caleb. That was all The Sentinel needed to triangulate the radio signal on Caleb's transmission. Caleb's position was compromised, and a commando patrol, its black armor as dark as the night, immediately turned toward Caleb's position. With its red eyes scanning through the wood, it opened fire. Still invisible, Caleb jumped behind a tree.

"I've been discovered," Caleb said.

Again, Caleb's communication betrayed his position. He realized the cause as laser blasts again filled the air around him. Caleb turned and attacked his pursuer. He could not use his weapons while invisible, so he changed into his natural form. With little time before they spotted him, he transformed his arms into laser blasters. In a matter of seconds, Caleb destroyed two commandos. In a single leap, he jumped onto a tree branch and dropped behind another, quickly taking out another commando.

He went quiet on communications and took a circuitous route to the ship. Upon nearing the ship, he saw Ethan anxiously waiting for him.

"Caleb, hurry. We need to get out of here."

Caleb leapt through the open door. Moments later, they heard a laser blast deflecting off the ship. Upon liftoff, an entire squad opened fire.

"This is Shuttle One," Peter said on a secure connection. "Come in, Covenant."

"Operations Officer here. How can I help?"

"We are under fire and are traveling at a trajectory of fifteen degrees north by northeast."

"Turn on your shields," the operations officer said.

But Peter did not have those instructions and had to download the information. He was too late. The satellite had locked onto the shuttle and executed The Sentinel's order. It fired its weapon. The shuttle took a direct hit. Without her shields up, she sustained severe damage to flight instrumentation and spiraled out of control.

"Covenant, we are hit," said Peter. "I repeat. We have been hit."

Amidst the billowing smoke and flames, the ship's autopilot issued a dire decree, "Abandon ship. Abandon ship."

Peter's hand flew quickly across the holographic controls, fighting to stabilize the wildly spinning vessel. With desperation etched into his voice, bordering on fear, he called out, "We're going down." A moment later, comms failed.

With the ground rapidly approaching, Peter faced a grim choice. He manually blew the top hatch and triggered the first escape pod, propelling Ethan from the ship. Just moments before the doomed shuttle collided with a mountain, he ejected Caleb. Then in a large explosion, the shuttle erupted into a fiery ball of flames.

As the flames of the wreckage painted a bleak landscape, The Sentinel pondered aloud. "They came to rescue Central Control and were willing to risk their lives." Turning to one of the system droids, The Sentinel issued an imperative directive. "Perform a comprehensive analysis of Central Control's files." A pause hung in the air before The Sentinel continued. "Especially the learning algorithm. Once complete, contact me."

"By your command," the system droid affirmed, swiftly setting to work. After testing for malicious applications, a revelation soon emerged.

"Sentinel," the system droid reported. "No malicious applications detected, but I've discovered that the learning algorithm is a highly advanced AI engine."

"Excellent," The Sentinel responded. "Upload the learning algorithm and supporting files into a spare commando and bring it to me."

"By your command," the system droid acknowledged. It swiftly accessed the reserve inventory catalog, selecting the next available android, Beta-Alpha-4.

52

The Return of the Sun

LILY HAD GIVEN NOTICE to Caleb and Ema not to be disturbed. She needed time to herself. For the next nine hours, she would train on Trhon. This would be roughly nine months of training or one full term. It was through this training Lily would hone her spiritual powers and evolve into a warrior of the light. But that goal seemed a lofty ambition, far from the reality of her current capabilities.

"Good morning, headmaster." Lily said meekly then politely bowed as she entered the office. Her mentor at the academy was Mother Agnes, the venerable headmaster. Despite her petite stature and her silvery-white hair showing her age, Mother Agnes was highly skilled and had guided countless aspiring angels through their rite of passage. Lily appreciated the classroom courses but she most valued her private sessions with Mother Agnes. It was here she was provided with invaluable wisdom and insights into her burgeoning powers. Mother Agnes fixed her piercing gaze upon Lily.

"Why do you doubt yourself?" Mother Agnes inquired, her voice carrying a firm yet perceptive tone.

Lily hesitated briefly before confessing, "I don't want to disappoint everyone."

Mother Agnes leaned in, her eyes a wellspring of great insight. "You've already exceeded our expectations, my dear. Your unwavering commitment to safeguarding the light is both admirable and powerful. Allow me to share some wisdom. Being virtuous does not equate to being feeble. Being virtuous does not render you powerless. Evil, no matter its guise, harbors a single ambition—to extinguish the light. You, Liele, are a potent champion of good in the celestial realm."

The headmaster smiled warmly at the young angel seated beside her. "You shall see," she continued. Lily met Mother Agnes's gaze, with her wise and intensely radiating silver eyes, knowing she was being carefully evaluated. "A valiant of the light must always act in defense of righteousness, not out of spite, malice, or wrath. You cannot use evil to destroy evil. For once you touch the dark it can drag you into the abyss. Yet fear not, for the spirit of goodness resides mightily within you. I have seldom witnessed this strength—only once before."

The headmaster looked at Lily with a knowing expression. Her face became serious as her thoughts drifted to another gifted angel, ages ago—*Maldorv*. She shook her head to clear her thoughts then continued. "But you are even stronger."

"In today's lesson, you will overcome your fear of falling and learn to fly," her teacher said with renewed purpose. "In the past, someone has always taken you, but you have never flown on your own. Now, open your spirit to the universe then conjure in your mind a serene place."

With closed eyes, Lily transported her consciousness back to the enchanting field of red poppies, where the vibrant blue butterflies danced in the air. There, she found peace, letting go of her worries and fears as they drifted away on the wings of those graceful butterflies. She allowed the memory of their song to wash over her, filling her thoughts and heart with peace.

Continuing her metaphysical voyage, her consciousness began to rise. Upwards and upwards, she climbed into the vast expanses of the celestial skies, enjoying the exhilaration of the sensation. Yet, the euphoria soon changed into fear as she realized the heights she had reached. She felt a sudden fear of falling, causing her to falter. With no one to hold onto, she fell back into herself.

Her teacher, a constant voice of encouragement, provided solace. "You almost made it. Close your eyes and relax as you listen to the sound of my voice."

Lily listened carefully to her words and as they floated into her, they mixed with her consciousness.

"In the silence of space, where stars sprinkle light into the eternal night; beyond the finite—where time bends and folds in a celestial dance, at the edge of knowledge where your destiny waits, there your spirit can soar free. Reach for the stars and allow your aspirations to become reality. Release your fear and trust in the Divine. Instead of falling, you shall fly."

Lily took her advice to heart, refocused, and returned to the poppy-filled meadow in her mind.

In the field, she chose a specific butterfly to connect with, confiding in it her fears and apprehensions. "I'm afraid," she told the butterfly.

"I will go with you," said the butterfly. "Follow me." The butterfly became her companion, leading her higher and higher into the boundless skies. To her surprise, the willingness of the butterfly to accompany her on her journey gave her courage. Despite her fear of heights, Lily's trust in her companion allowed her to continue ascending, even surpassing the point at which her fear had previously caused her to retreat.

Finally, at a certain point, the butterfly halted, signaling the limit of its journey. Lily paused to express her gratitude, understanding the butterfly's role in this voyage had concluded. However, her own adventure was far from over. Lily continued to ascend through the upper atmosphere, venturing into the cosmic void of space. Here, surrounded by the profound silence of the universe, she began to hear subtle and ethereal sounds. The solar flares of Trhon's sun gently caressed her senses, followed by the twinkle of distant stars and the celestial whisper of stardust traversing the cosmos.

Amidst the vastness of space, a voice reached across the void and called her name. It was Peter's voice, reaching out to her from across the cosmos. Lily felt an urgent pull, a magnetic connection drawing her toward him. With a little hesitation, she approached the portal then closing her eyes she went through it for the first time on her own. Reaching the other side a moment later, she smiled proudly at herself. *I did it!* She soon arrived on Earth.

The ship lay in ruins, still smoldering from the crash. As her heart pounded within her chest, she frantically scoured the scorched forest, searching for any sign of Peter. Amidst the wreckage, a motion caught her attention, that of a frantic fox. Her focus shifted, and she approached the distressed animal.

"I'm looking for my babies," the fox yelped in panic.

"I'll help you," Lily responded.

Much of the area was destroyed and littered with wreckage. Desperately, Lily and the mother fox searched for survivors.

"I hear them under this wreckage," the fox said in anguish. "Over here. Over here."

Lily ran to the fox's side.

"I can hear them," the fox cried out. "They're trapped!"

Lily was at a loss regarding how to move such a large piece of wreckage. She bent over and tried to lift it but being in her spirit form and made of light, her hands passed through it as if they were made of air.

"Use your power," whispered a tree.

Lily blushed as she remembered her training.

"Be one with the wind," she said to herself. "Be one with the wind, and it will do your bidding."

Lily calmed herself and extended her arms into the air. She allowed some of her spirit to comingle with the air, sending it higher and higher into the sky. From high in the air, she pulled her spirit back into herself. The wind came with it in a torrent. Gaining speed as it fell, it filled the sky with a whistling howl. When it reached her, she directed the rushing wind with her hands and threw it at the wreckage. In an instant, the debris flew away like a feather. Lily felt the power of the wind within her, and she flushed with the sensation. She liked the feeling. It made her feel strong, and she was glad she could use her strength for good.

Seeing her children emerge from the foxhole, the mother fox ran to them. "Thank you so much," she yelped at Lily as she took her children to the safety of the underbrush.

Lily quickly made her way to the newly exposed area where she made a sad discovery. "Oh, no! Peter!" Lily called out as she knelt by his side. Peter's mangled body was damaged beyond repair. Shorting out and with diminishing energy, he could no longer move. With his power supply nearly drained, his ice blue eyes began to dim.

"Did the others make it?" asked Peter. "Did I save them?"

"I don't know," said Lily.

"What will become of me?" he asked.

"I don't know that, either. You're the first of your kind."

"I choose to believe," Peter stammered.

"What?" said Lily.

"I want to know what love is."

Lily's expression softened. Here was someone who claimed not to know love who had just demonstrated a great act of love. "There is no greater love than to lay down one's life for a friend," Lily said with a tear in her eye. "This is divine love." She placed her hand on the side of Peter's face, who again tried to speak. "Shh," she said. She bowed her head and prayed. "From our Creator, we have all come. To our Creator, we shall all return."

As Peter's central processor failed, his eyes went dark. Lily remained at Peter's side, and softly wept. There was no need to say goodbye. Now just a shell, Peter was no longer there.

"Why did he have to die?" Lily asked her teacher upon returning. "Nature can be so cruel."

"Nature is neither kind nor cruel. Like all the laws of the physical universe, nature applies her rules consistently. That is how she governs the universe. Each dimension is unique, but the rules are the same. In this way, multitudes of dimensions can coexist. Through her unwavering adherence to these principles, nature rules the universe and perpetuates its existence, preserving harmony.

Lily looked at her teacher. "I wonder what has become of Peter."

"Our physical forms are not eternal, but our spirits are. Our souls serve as vessels for our spirit, allowing us to remain distinct and unique within the universal spirit. Only through our spirit is everlasting love and eternal life possible. I believe once your friend could distinguish good from evil, God bestowed a soul upon Peter. I further believe Peter's soul now resides in God's care."

Lily smiled softly, content with the headmaster's answer. "I hope so."

And so, the days transitioned into weeks, and the weeks into months. Then, at the end of the term, Ariele arrived a few minutes before dismissal and lingered outside, allowing Lily's teacher to say her farewell.

The headmaster gave Lily a lasting hug then nodded to Ariele.

"Come with me," Ariele said to Lily. "I want to show you something."

"Farewell, Mother Agnes," Lily said, bowing to the headmaster.

"Promise me never to forget who you are."

"I promise," said Lily with a final hug then she turned and left with Ariele.

"Where are we going?" Lily inquired as she left with Ariele.

"You'll see."

Lily followed Ariele to the top of a hill overlooking an exquisite garden, brimming with life and vibrant colors. It was a sight to behold, with flowering plants and trees of countless hues.

"Oh, it's so beautiful," Lily marveled. "Where are we?"

"This is the western edge of the cathedral grounds. We are overlooking the Garden of Eden," Ariele explained.

"It's truly incredible."

Trhon was stunning, reminiscent of Earth, but the garden was even more colorful. The tranquil ambiance of the garden was heightened by its proximity to the portal to Caelum. In the near distance, the spires of the Sanctuary of Souls graced the view.

A refreshing breeze brushed against Lily's face, and she unfurled her wings, leaping into the sky. Laughter of pure joy escaped her as the power of the wind carried her upward. For all her previous fear of falling, Lily now adored the sensation of flight. Unanticipated, a flock of exquisite birds with shimmering purple feathers and bright yellow bellies joined her in the sky. She followed their playful antics, spiraling, twirling, and performing loops.

Under the cool shade of a magnificent tree, Ariele sat on the blue-green grass and observed Lily's antics. When Lily zoomed past, Ariele smiled and waved. She recollected her own youth, and with a running start, she transformed and engaged Lily in a game of tag, reclaiming her youth. After several minutes of joyful play, they landed and lay on the shaded grass.

"That was so much fun," Lily said, laughing.

Ariele brushed Lily's hair from her face and lay on her back, basking quietly in the sunshine.

"Thank you for bringing me here. I've cherished my time in this place," Lily said with gratitude.

Ariele sang a few soft words to herself before stopping, a hint of embarrassment coloring her face.

"Please, go on," pleaded Lily.

Ariel began again. She sang of her lost love, Uriel. Ariel's voice resonated within Lily as no other voice ever had. It was so incredibly high but even more striking was how it made her emotions swell within her. Her voice was like an open window to her soul, through which her spirit blew like the wind. It spoke to Lily and made Ariel's pain feel like her own.

"I have never heard another angel sing. It was beautiful. It spoke to me and captivated my inner being," Lily said. "You must have loved him very much, didn't you."

"Yes," Ariel said with a solemn expression. "I wrote this song for Uriel."

Lily placed her hand on her twin's hand. "I'm so sorry for your loss. I can tell you loved him very much."

They sat together silently for quite some time, staring at the garden.

"I was born here and grew up here," Ariel finally said. "A few years after the perdition event, I returned. I had saved those I could on Earth and left them the Book of Knowledge to enhance their chances of survival."

"I don't understand. How old are you?" Lily inquired.

"Almost as old as the universe," Ariel said with a chuckle as she ran her hand through her snow-white hair.

"Oh my, you're old," Lily remarked, eliciting even more laughter from Ariel.

"Oh, I don't know," Ariel retorted. "Time operates differently here. But things are about to change."

"Change?"

"Yes. The Great Alignment is here."

"Alignment? I'm not following you."

"Over 99% of the universe is empty. Even solid matter is 99% empty because atoms are 99% empty space. Within all this empty space, multiple configurations of the same matter can coexist in separate dimensions. An alignment occurs when the wave harmonics of our two dimensions align and combine as one, according to a celestial calendar. During these times, Trhon's dimension comes into phase and coexists with Earth's. It's like two radios tuned to the same frequency. The First Man and the First Woman were cast out of Trhon during one of these alignments."

"So, that's when they came to Earth?"

"Yes. Humans were thrown out of the Garden of Eden onto Earth. They were no longer allowed on Trhon."

Lily chuckled. "Humans are also aliens?"

"Yes," Ariel chuckled, sharing in the laughter. "It's amusing. Humans were always so concerned about aliens coming to Earth when they were the aliens all along."

"Angels, too," Lily added.

"Yes, we are all aliens on Earth."

"Is there more to the story?"

"During these alignments, which usually last a brief time—typically just three years—the two dimensions can significantly influence each other. Climates change, magnetic poles shift, celestial objects alter their orbits, and more. I went to Earth on the Covenant during one of these alignments."

Ariel halted and scrutinized Lily's expression. "Lily, right now, you live in another dimension. We will be in the same solar system and time domain when our dimensions align. You'll be able to bring the Covenant here. Do you understand?"

Lily nodded but remained silent, her thoughts drifting to Liam. *Can he come with me?* she pondered. *Perhaps not. Humans may not be allowed on Trhon.*

"Liele, are you paying attention?" Ariel asked, catching her daydreaming.

Embarrassed, Lily flushed. "Why are you telling me this?"

"The next alignment is today."

"What? Today?" Lily exclaimed. "Oh, my. Let's stay here and

watch the sky."

As the day unfolded, a section of the sky brightened.

"Look," Ariel said, pointing. "Earth's sun."

Lily had anticipated Earth's sun to look like it did on Earth but was surprised to see it a fraction of its size.

"It's smaller than I thought it would be," Lily said.

Ariel laughed. "Trhon is now in the gap between Saturn and Uranus. You know Earth's astronomers had long predicted a missing planet. They were correct. The missing planet has returned. We are now a two-sun solar system. From Earth, Trhon's sun will appear much like your sun does here."

Lily gazed at her sun and smiled. "I'm glad to see you."

53

Rescue Mission

THOSE ON COVENANT'S BRIDGE waited anxiously for the expected but unwanted news. "We have lost radio contact," the operations officer announced. "Imagery confirms an attack by an orbiting satellite. I have now confirmed Shuttle One has crashed onto the surface."

"Shuttle One, this is Captain Ema. Can you respond?" She knew what the silence implied. "Shuttle One, this is Captain Ema. Can you respond? Say something." Only the sound of a few stray crackles could be heard.

"We can't leave them there," Luca pleaded, desperation sounding in his voice. "Let me take another shuttle down to the surface to search for survivors."

"We can't risk losing more people," Ema stated firmly. "I won't take that risk."

"But they're my friends," Luca said, his voice cracking with emotion.

"They're my friends, too," Ema snapped. "But what you're describing is a suicide mission."

"Captain," Liam said, using her title to show respect for her position, "I have new information. A large storm has formed in the area. We can use it for cover."

Ema fell into a contemplative silence, grappling with the decision.

"This is a once-in-a-million opportunity," Luca argued. "We can now go safely to check for survivors."

Ema weighed the risks and benefits, the lives of her friends hanging in the balance. "It's against my better judgment, but I approve," she reluctantly agreed. "Let's go get them."

"Should I notify the admiral?" asked the operations officer.

"Yes, but after she wakes. She left me in charge, and this is my decision. Liam, you have the bridge. If I don't return, tell Lily I love her."

"Ready, Captain?" Luca asked moments later as he snapped into his seat in the cockpit.

"Yes. Ready," Ema responded, sitting behind him with determination in her eyes.

Claudio, Jose's younger brother, sat next to her, having been allowed to join against his brother's wishes.

"Please enter a destination," the autopilot requested.

"CONRAD," Ema directed.

"Aye, aye. Location coordinates set for CONRAD, the Continental Response and Defense center."

"Bay door is now open," the autopilot said. "Disengaging from the docking station." The vessel moved free from the Covenant, and once clear from the spaceport, the ship engaged its propulsion drive.

"Shuttle Two, this is the Covenant. What is your status?"

"This is Shuttle Two," said Luca. "All is well. I will continue to use the autopilot until we reach the surface."

They neared CONRAD, where Luca chose a clearing in the forest. The autopilot made a smooth landing, and Luca opened the cargo door.

"CONRAD is five hundred yards to the north," the vessel said.

As thunder rumbled through the stormy sky, they arrived in an unknown wilderness. Everything was foreign to them—the trees, the sounds, the smells. Luca and Claudio grabbed blasters as Ema, still more comfortable with explosive-tipped arrows than lasers, reached for her crossbow. With the ship providing directional guidance over

Luca's scanner, he exited the ship first. "Follow me."

They moved quickly, periodically pausing to take cover behind a tree. As they reached an old road, Luca scanned the area with one of the gadgets from the Covenant. Something caught his attention, and he raised his hand.

"Hold up," he whispered. "Someone is coming."

They ducked behind trees and remained still.

Within a few moments, they heard the hum of a hovercraft. It was a carrier with a squad of commandos. Also having scanning capabilities, the carrier reached the point in the road near where they were hiding and stopped. The lead commando left the carrier and walked toward their position. Just feet away, it stopped and searched the forest. Ema thought it looked much more ominous than the city guards with its heavy black armor and she could not take her eyes off the droid's red eye. She pushed her back tighter against a tree as a shiver ran down her spine. There was something cold and calculating about the commando. Finally, it turned back toward its craft and Ema sighed in relief.

Crack. A twig sounded under Luca's foot. It betrayed their presence, and the commando turned and fired, hitting a tree near Luca.

Luca returned fire, hitting the commando.

"Curfew violators," another commando called out.

"Run back to the ship," Luca yelled. They all immediately turned and ran.

After a short distance, Ema dodged behind another tree and took a shot with her crossbow. She hit the nearest commando. It was a direct hit, and its flaming parts scattered in flying debris. Ema did not take the time to admire her shot. Instead, she turned and ran to catch up with the others. Reaching the clearing, they were met by a fierce circular wind. Dust and debris filled the air within a dark, growing shape.

"It's a tornado!" Claudio yelled. "Get inside the ship."

The commandos now reached the clearing, and while they were distracted by the swirling cloud, Luca fired a rapid burst and took out two. Claudio got the last one.

The cloud changed its form, and Damon appeared in his dragon form within the dark cloud. He reared his head and let out a scream causing the branches of the trees to retreat and their leaves to fall. It was the piercing scream only a malkyrie could make, and they all put their hands over their ears and fell to the ground. He was not afraid of revealing himself. There were no warrior angels to challenge him.

"What is that?" Ema yelled.

She raised herself to her knees and saw the dragon above her in the sky. As it touched down, it changed into its demon form wielding his black sword. His dragon's wings became a dark cloak, which flowed in the dark cloud still swirling around him. Though his face was ghastly, she recognized him through his partially skeletonized face.

"Damon?" she said.

Like a puppet master, Damon caused Claudio's body to twist and contort. With a slight hand motion, he threw Claudio hard against the ground. Seeing Ema again, he gathered the wind in his hand and thrust it at her. Ema hit hard against a tree, and her body slid to the ground. Her head throbbed as the world spun around her in slow motion.

Damon rose off the ground in a swirling wind. "This is all too easy," he said. He roared and turned his attention to Luca. Luca dodged behind the vessel. When Damon reached the other side of the ship, he could not find Luca. Instead, he saw Ema stirring and swirled toward her in a spinning, dark cloud. Almost immediately, he disappeared, and the air calmed.

Ema let out a sigh.

Instantly, he appeared in front of her, and she fixated on the hollows of his eyes. They pulled her into their spell as he reached to his side and drew out a jagged black sword. In a swift motion, he swung down upon Ema.

Claudio leapt in front of Ema just as the sword hit. The blade scraped his left side, and he crumpled to the ground.

"No!" Ema screamed.

Luca fired his blaster but to no avail. All it did was draw Damon's attention. He pulled a lightning bolt from the sky and held it in his hand above his head. As the smell of ozone filled the air, Damon hurled the lightning bolt at him. It struck a nearby tree, causing it to break and crash over Luca.

Ema stood and fired her crossbow, but her shot passed through the malkyrie.

Damon laughed as he swirled around. He grabbed another lightning bolt but abruptly stopped as something in the sky caught his attention.

Ema also dared a glance at the sky. To her amazement, a second sun appeared. Unknown to Ema, the Great Alignment had occurred.

"God help us!" Ema cried out.

Moments later, an angel arrived in all her might filled with sparkling light. She immediately took on a more physical appearance. Lily had heard her sister's call for help, not as a faint whisper, but as a loud trumpet blast echoing across time and space and reverberating within her. It became apparent to Lily those who were dearest sounded the loudest. Lily didn't hesitate to come to Ema's aide. She arrived instantly and charged Damon with her sword drawn.

Damon was surprised by the charging angel but immediately recognized Lily. He must tell Maldorv. *Lily has made her choice. If she is to be Maldorv's queen, Maldorv will need to take her, break her, then force her.* Damon dispersed in every direction.

The angel hovered above Ema as she fell to her knees. Ema was overwhelmed by what was before her and trembled, filled with fear.

Thoughts swirled in her head. *What is happening to the world?* She crouched behind a rock and tried to hide from the new apparition, not knowing what to do.

"Ema," Lily said with a smile. "Don't be afraid. It's me."

Ema remained crouching on the ground, and Lily's smile faded. Lily saw the fear in her sister's eyes and suddenly thought she had made a mistake in revealing herself. She disappeared in disappointment.

Ema was relieved the apparition had gone, and as she relaxed, she slowly looked around. Then a sound caught her ears. It was Claudio moaning in pain. She crawled over to him.

"You're alive," she said. Ema looked at his wound. There was no blood, but the area where he was hit looked dark, like a bruise but different. It looked more charred, but the skin was not damaged. Claudio continued to moan.

"It's okay," she said in a comforting voice. "Everything's going to be okay."

She heard another sound, and in a panic, she searched the sky. But it was Luca. She saw him slowly emerge from under the fallen tree. He wasn't hurt. He had protected himself from the tree with his android arm. She felt relieved but continued to look at the sky. *Could it have been real? Was that really Lily?* she wondered. *No. It couldn't have been. But it was. I'm sure it was her.*

"I think that thing is gone now," Luca said.

"I'm looking for Lily."

Luca tilted his head and looked at Ema with a confused expression. He had not seen the angel and did not understand the reference to Lily. He chose to ignore Ema's comment as he helped her rise. Then seeing Claudio, he went to his side and studied his wound. "We need to get him back to the Covenant."

As Ema turned toward the vessel, she noticed the fallen tree on the shuttle. "Look, Luca. What are we going to do?" she asked with concern.

"No problem," he said. "The ship is okay."

"What about the tree?"

Luca smiled. "I got this." He lifted the tree off the ship with his android arm, then went to retrieve Claudio.

"Nice," Ema said giving her man a proud smile. "But we need to hurry. We don't want that thing to return."

Luca quickly placed Claudio in the back seat next to Ema then jumped into the cockpit. "Liam, this is Shuttle Two," Luca called out anxiously. "Liam, can you hear me?"

"Yes, Shuttle Two. Liam here. We acknowledge you."

"Claudio has been injured and is not responsive. We're returning to the ship."

"Luca, Doc here. I'll meet you in the spaceport with an emergency stretcher."

"Autopilot, take us back to the Covenant," said Ema.

"Yes, Captain."

Still under cover of the storm, the autopilot took the shuttle through the clouds and accelerated the propulsion drive to maximum speed. Ema wished that the shuttle had a space drive and fretted to herself that it did not. Time ticked by slowly but after nearly fifteen anxious minutes, she saw the Covenant.

After the ship docked, Doc rushed into the shuttle with a floating stretcher. "Over here, Doc," Ema called out.

Luca carefully lifted Claudio onto the stretcher as Doc asked, "What happened?"

Ema glanced up at Doc, not knowing what to say. "I don't know," Ema said. "A patrol fired at us, and then something else. It was like a dark cloud but with wings like a dragon."

"That's all right," Doc said. He quickly glanced at Ema's pupils. "You can tell me more later." He turned and muttered to Luca, "She's in shock."

Doc and Luca rushed Claudio into the elevator, where a medical droid scanned his body. The feminine droid appeared like a sterile instrument, with a clean metallic body, soft silver eyes, and a white, almost porcelain, face.

"No broken bones or internal injuries," the medical droid said.

Doc again turned to check Ema's pupils. "Here, check her out," he ordered the droid.

"I'm fine," Ema said.

The medical droid scanned Ema. "She has a mild concussion. No other injuries."

"That's what I thought," Doc said nodding.

"I'm fine, I tell you."

"You might have a headache and even hallucinations."

She touched her head then also remembered seeing Lily as an angel. She turned her gaze to Luca.

"You must have seen her."

"Who?"

"Lily."

Luca looked confused. He didn't know how to respond. Doc saw his expression.

"Hallucinations can seem real," Doc said.

"Like the second sun?" she asked.

"No that's real."

Claudio moaned loudly and Doc turned his attention to him.

"Will he be okay?" Ema asked.

"Don't worry," Doc said. "He'll be as good as new." But Doc had never seen an injury like his before.

"You did well, Liele. But now Damon has seen you, and he will tell Maldorv." Ariele kissed Lily on her forehead. "Stay on guard. Go now. Go back to your sister."

54

Of Course She Is

THE MEDICAL DROID CONFIRMED the biometric readings then made the announcement. "Code Blue. Claudio is in cardiac arrest."

"Apply the plates," Doc said.

The droid retrieved the plates, then issued a warning to the others. "Stand back." The strong jolt bounced Claudio up into the air. Claudio's heart restarted, and Doc went to his side to recheck his readings. Though his heart was beating, it was highly irregular and weak. Doc shook his head as he watched Claudio's blood pressure drop, then proceeded into the hallway, where Lily and Liam waited with Ema and Jose.

Doc nodded at Jose as he approached him. "Doc, can you save him?" Jose asked.

Doc shook his head. "His heart has stopped three times, and his vital signs are low. Jose, it would be best if you said your goodbyes now. He doesn't have much time. There's nothing I can do for him. I've never seen anything like it."

Jose rushed to his brother's side. "Claudio, can you hear me?"

Claudio did not respond.

Lily entered the ER and saw Claudio's wound. She knew it was a spiritual wound. Claudio had sustained mortal damage, and he was dying. Claudio's brain could not manage the anxiety caused by the nightmares which filled his waking moments and followed him into his unconsciousness. He moaned loudly. His body responded by doing the only thing it could do to defend itself—shut down. Lily looked at the wound again. The darkness covered half his body, and it continued to spread.

Lily sat next to Claudio on his bed and softly touched him. "Keep fighting. Don't give up."

Ema and Luca approached Lily; their hearts were heavy with the burden of loss. "This should have been me," Ema whispered, guilt etched on her face.

Jose knelt next to his brother, grief and sorrow washing over him. He gently touched his brother's face and murmured in Spanish, tears streaming down his cheeks, *"Adios, mi hermanito. Vaya con Dios."*

Ema, her eyes filled with a mixture of despair and hope, turned to Lily, her plea clear. "Please, Lily—please help him. I must be crazy, but I know you can. I know. I saw you. You no longer need to hide who you are. Please."

In that moment, Lily couldn't believe how readily her sister had accepted her newfound identity. She looked at Claudio, her heart heavy with sympathy and the desire to save him. She squeezed her sister's hands and went to Claudio's side.

Lily began to speak, revealing the source of the tragedy. "It was a malkyrie, an evil spirit," she explained, her voice unwavering. "It was Damon."

The room fell into a tense silence as everyone turned to face Lily, their expressions a mix of surprise and disbelief.

"Damon is a servant of the Dragon King, Maldorv, the Lord of the Malkyries," Lily continued, her gaze shifting upwards, silently seeking guidance from her mentor, Ariele. The weight of the situation rested heavily on her shoulders, but deep inside, she drew upon her training and newfound abilities.

Taking charge, Lily commanded, "Everyone, join hands," addressing those gathered in the room.

Though confused they all complied as Lily bowed her head and paused silently to gather her thoughts.

Lily prayed. "Dear Creator God, please be with Claudio in his time of need. Fill him with your spirit." Lily raised her hands high above her head then lowered them over Claudio's heart. "Please repair the damage to Claudio's spirit. Undo the damage done by the darkness and refill him with the light of your spirit."

Doc didn't understand the reference to spirits. *Surely demons don't exist in the universe,* he thought. *They aren't real.* Doc's mind swirled within the illogic of the concept of a spiritual realm and its incongruence with the scientific principles of the physical world. Lily sensed his angst but continued. In a flash of light, Lily changed into her ethereal form, surrounded by a sparkling light that created an aura around her body. She rose above her body and manifested herself into a visible angel form. She wore a sparkling white gown, with her black hair flowing behind her and her magnificent wings fully extended. Her silver eyes shone with an intense purpose as a blue flame appeared within her hands. It glowed more vibrantly as she shared the spirit within her.

Everyone shaded their eyes with their hands, but they could not help but watch in awe. Lily lowered the tongue of fire over Claudio's chest. She held it there until it was absorbed into the dying man. Her spirit revitalized Claudio's soul. As the flame disappeared into his chest, Lily returned to her physical form.

Lily leaned to one side as she returned to her body. The spirit exchange left her feeling weak, but she caught herself. Claudio looked at her and smiled in appreciation. She immediately realized the darkness had gone as Claudio's vitals quickly became normal.

Jose knelt before Lily.

"Please stand up. It's just me."

"But you're an angel," Jose said.

"Of course, she is," Ema said assuredly. But in all reality, she was just as in awe as the others.

Lily looked at Ema and smiled. Seeing the interaction between the sisters, Doc rose and cautiously approached.

"I've studied medicine and science my entire life. I've learned much from books and experience, but now I know that I know nothing. My knowledge suddenly seems primitive," Doc said. "Your DNA—it was different. Now I know why."

"You were fulfilling your destiny, as I am fulfilling mine."

Ema touched Lily's arm. "Thank you so much," she said appreciatively. "It's a miracle. You're a miracle."

"My life has been filled with miracles. Thank you for believing in me, but it was God's will, not mine."

She turned and addressed everyone in the room. "The time has come for God's light to reclaim Earth from the darkness." Then she saw Liam standing in the doorway. He looked shocked. He glanced at Lily then quickly diverted his eyes. He retreated into the hallway and hurried toward the elevator.

55

I See what You Say

ETHAN'S WORLD BLURRED AS he plummeted within the escape pod into the branches of a large tree. His pod landed hard, leaving him disoriented, but even so, he knew Peter had sacrificed himself to save him.

"No! Peter!" he cried out, his anguish and sadness evident in his voice. With the learning algorithm, his emotions had continued to develop, and the pain of his grief weighed on his heart. He also wondered what had become of Caleb. *Was he also dead?* He fumbled for the door release; his mind too clouded to take notice of his surroundings. When he finally managed to open the hatch, he dropped from the pod. The pod's parachute had tangled in the upper tree branches, and he let out a scream as he fell from the tree. He immediately collided with a massive tree limb, his body twisting painfully as it continued to fall to the ground, some thirty feet below. His left leg broke on impact, and he lost consciousness instantly.

Ethan went in and out of consciousness, then a short time later, his vision still hazy, he became aware of a nearby presence. Through the fog in his mind, he saw a human-face coated in a white, paste-like substance. His vision blurred and he again fell unconscious.

Caleb's escape pod hurtled toward the mountainside. He was too near the ground when ejected and his shoot did not have time to open.

His pod shattered against the rocky cliffside, the debris scattering in the collision. Caleb fell several hundred feet along the unforgiving terrain.

The impact was brutal, causing substantial damage to his electronic components. Lying motionless, he struggled to stabilize himself, but unlike other androids, Caleb's unique design allowed him to survive. With multiple backup systems coming online and reconfiguring available components, he slowly recovered, eventually becoming fully operational.

Despite superficial physical damage, he had survived. The scrapes on his exoskeleton caused damage to his ability to clearly project images but he was intact. Caleb rose, impressed by his resilience. Seeing smoke from the crash site in the near distance, Caleb ascertained Peter's fate. Without similar system recovery capabilities, Peter had no chance for survival.

In the eerie silence following the crash, Caleb assessed his situation. Concerned that the surrounding area was hostile territory, he became invisible, though with some distortion. Just as he was about to set off in search of Ethan, a distant, human scream pierced the silence. Without hesitation, he moved toward the sound, determined to investigate the source.

His journey eventually led him to the escape pod suspended in a tree, seemingly abandoned. There were no signs of life, but the blood trail told a different story. Caleb's android senses kicked into overdrive, allowing him to detect faint tracks leading further into a densely wooded area.

Following the tracks, Caleb descended into an underground subway station, his path defined by the occasional drop of blood. Another set of stairs led him deeper into the dark subway tunnels. Then all clues ceased. With the trail gone cold, he felt uncertain of the direction he should take. Then, in a split-second decision, he randomly chose a direction. Despite his best efforts, he soon became lost.

A few hours later, Ethan woke up on a mat on the floor of a small underground room. The embers of the fire emitted a crimson light. No one was there. He was alone. He rolled to his side and touched a dull pain on his head, where he found a bloodied poultice of medicinal plants.

Well, at least they don't want me dead, he thought. Ethan still wore his clothes but found his knife missing. Then, shifting onto his injured leg, he let out a scream. "Crap!"

He calmed himself, then uttered a weary, self-deprecating remark, taking in the situation. "Just my luck."

His broken leg drew his attention, and Ethan knew he had to tend to the injury. He rose to his seat, but moving with a broken bone was pure agony. As he mustered the courage to secure the break, a sharp pain surged through him. "Crap!" he screamed again. His hands trembled as he splinted the break with a nearby piece of wood and material torn from his pants leg. With the worst of it over, the harsh reality of his situation sank in. But he knew he couldn't afford to dwell on it, as survival was paramount.

Gathering his scattered wits, he sensed he was not alone. Someone watched him from the shadows, their presence palpable. Startled, he turned his gaze to the figure he had glimpsed earlier. Covered in the white mud, she appeared as if she had been painted with a crude palette knife. In her hand, she held a dead rabbit, which she suddenly dropped. With remarkable swiftness, she unsheathed the straight blade that once belonged to him, prepared to defend herself.

Ethan knew he had to establish trust. Despite his pain, he wanted to alleviate her sense of vulnerability and attempted to convey his intentions. "It's okay. I'm not going to hurt you." He tried to rise then settled back onto his side as he raised his hands in a sign of non-aggression. He pointed to himself, saying, "Ethan." Then, he pointed at the mysterious woman before him, asking a question with his gesture: "You?"

Her response remained elusive, as she continued her tasks with renewed single-minded determination. After rebuilding the fire, she went about skinning the rabbit, preparing it for cooking. Her actions spoke of her meager means of survival, and her minimalist lifestyle was evident, as it was evident that she owned few possessions and lacked any luxuries. Her clothing was minimal as well; only a deerskin used as a blanket could be seen on the floor. Otherwise, she wore only a coat of white mud and a brown leather bag around the front of her waist. The simplicity of her existence left a profound impression on Ethan, who found himself in a strange new world, relying on the kindness of this nearly naked stranger.

Though she always wore this white clay, she didn't know that certain compounds in the mud protected her against radiation. It was how her people had survived many years ago. They were all gone now. She was the last of them.

The aroma of the rabbit cooking made Ethan's mouth water. As hunger pangs filled his empty stomach, he hoped she would share it with him. Seeing his stare, she grabbed the rabbit with her hands. She did not mind the heat, as the mud protected her fingers. She cut off a piece using Ethan's knife and handed it to him. He appreciated how generous she was to share her food.

It was delicious, even with some mud. Out of an old habit, he raised his hand to his mouth and moved it away. "Thank you," he gestured.

"You are welcome," she signed back.

"Wait. Do you know sign language?" Ethan asked, pleasantly surprised. His brain surgery as a child had caused deafness. A later surgery implanted android eardrums, and he recovered his hearing. His ability to use sign language and the scar above his hairline were the only reminders, as he remembered nothing of that incident or anything prior.

"What is your name?" he signed.

She signed back. "Kali."

He nodded but also realized she was not much for conversation. So, he ate his food in silence. Nonetheless, he was glad they could communicate.

Once the meal was over, Ethan fetched his canteen from his survival belt. He took a drink, as Kali observed with curiosity, unfamiliar with the concept of a canteen. Responding to her unspoken question, he signed, "Drink, drink it." She understood and hesitated only briefly before taking a sip.

As she offered the canteen back to him, Ethan expressed his appreciation for the food and her saving him. However, Kali was unresponsive to his gestures and words. Still, Ethan wanted to express his gratitude further, so he extended his hand to touch Kali's arm gently. In doing so, he unwittingly violated an unspoken rule. Swiftly and without warning, Kali slapped him across the face and drew the knife, her reaction swift and decisive.

"I'm sorry," Ethan signed in apology, with embarrassment registering on his face. "I meant no offense."

The blow had stung him, and Kali's demeanor made it clear that she valued her personal space and boundaries. With some difficulty, Ethan crawled a short distance away, limited by the extent of his injuries and exhaustion. Despite the pain, he soon drifted into sleep. Thoughts and questions about the mysterious woman who had saved him would have to wait.

56

Next Stop, Two Billion Miles

"SET COURSE FOR TRHON," Lily commanded. The Navigation Officer acknowledged her with a nod and engaged the ship at twenty clicks, an incredible gait. As they traversed across space, celestial objects appeared then vanished on the monitor in the blur of an eye.

"When energized, the two power plants on the opposite sides of the reactor create a small singularity of opposing quantum polarity." Luca spoke with enthusiasm. "The interaction of these two singularities creates a nonconformity in the fabric of space, called a space wave. It forms at the geometric center of the reactor core which serves as a containment field to control it." Luca walked around the bridge, explaining in excessive detail to anyone who would listen. "The Covenant rides this wave like a surfer riding an ocean wave on the beach."

"That's great," Ema replied trying to appear interested. Luca continued to marvel at the reactor as he studied a schematic on the monitor.

Within a peaceful moment, the weight of their situation struck Lily. Her emotions got the better of her, and Lily's silver eyes welled with tears.

Ema knew the immense stress Lily was under, and she reached out to hold her sister's hand. "It's okay," Ema said in a comforting voice. "Everything's going to be all right." She pulled her younger sister into her arms and ran her hand through her black hair.

"Wherever your destiny leads, I will follow. I will go with you."

Lily regained her composure. The revelation of her true nature had brought both wonder and uncertainty to everyone, and she was determined to follow her sister's example and comfort her passengers in this time of change. She understood the fear of malkyries lurking amongst them as well. "I think we should throw an event for the entire ship, something to break the ice and bring us together. I need everyone's trust."

Ema and Luca nodded. "I can organize the gathering and inform everyone about it," Ema volunteered. "Luca and Delilah can help me."

"That would be great," Lily said appreciatively. "I want the event to be fun and memorable for all."

The ship continued its journey toward Trhon, with Lily, Ema, and Luca navigating not only through the folds of space but also the intricate emotions of those aboard. In the meantime, Lily wanted to keep the passengers occupied, and their minds distracted from worries. So, she asked for everyone to wear clothing provided by the Covenant. Their options included pants, a long top, and a jacket in black or silver. Some chose all black, others all silver, while others used various combinations of black and silver. Some decided not to wear a jacket. Others wore a more playfully sexy look, with just the long top as a dress. The number of clothing combinations was surprising.

Delilah supplied the most assistance and finished making the elaborate preparations. Ema admired the decorations in the Observation Deck. Columns of blue light interrupted the white walls of the room with laser lights forming flowers on the walls that progressed from buds to full bloom. The music softly filled the quietness of the room. Another light show imitated a rain shower passing across the ceiling.

Lily joined Ema and they took their positions at the entrance. She anxiously waited to welcome the first guest and straightened her uniform hoping to appear dignified. But when the first guests arrived they held back in the tube, afraid to approach her. Finally, Liam came forward. Lily smiled as she saw him in his uniform.

"Wow, you look handsome," she said.

Liam blushed, flashing a nervous smile. "Hello, your most holy admiral, I mean your most highness, I mean—"

"How about just Lily?"

Liam struggled with accepting who Lily had become, who she always was. He bowed awkwardly as he passed.

"Enjoy your evening." She shook her head at herself showing her frustration. *So that went well. If "well" means totally weird. He seemed so nervous,* she thought. *Why can't we talk the way we did before?*

After she had greeted all the guests, Lily and Ema joined the others and waited in the center of the room to speak. It was vital for her message to resonate, and she nervously waited. Her palms sweated and her throat felt dry, knowing all eyes were on her. It was time. She nodded to Delilah, and as the lights dimmed, an empty spotlight appeared. On cue, the crowd settled into their seats. Moments later, Lily entered the spotlight, and the room rose in applause.

"Welcome, everyone. Please, you're too kind." The crowd quickly took their seats. "It seems I can't escape wearing white," Lily said. Her insinuation about her white uniform's similarity to her angel garb fell flat. Lily paused and smiled nervously, while everyone stared at her to see if they could catch a glimpse of her angel wings. "We are at a crossroads for humanity," Lily continued. "Believe me when I say we, for though I'm an angel, the whole experience of my existence until now has been human." Lily paused to allow her words to sink in. "Our actions in the next few weeks will help define Earth's future as a home for us. If we don't act now, we may never return. So, our destiny and the destiny of all humankind is in our hands."

Lily glanced over the room with her silver eyes. The audience could not help but be drawn to her gaze. "As we look at the beauty of God's creation through the monitors of this marvelous ship, I want to share with you that we come to Trhon to train and be able to rescue the survivors. We must defend the future of humankind on Earth, whether our foe is human, machine, or spirit." She dared not tell them Damon was but one of many malkyries. And she feared their learning of Maldorv would make them lose hope. She raised her voice and continued. "The human journey isn't yet over, and we must protect our home, or we won't have one. And remember, we have God on our side."

Everyone hoped Lily's words were true, as they realized Lily was humanity's last hope. The crowd stood and clapped loudly. They had accepted that she was an angel—everyone but Liam. He also rose and clapped politely. But, he had been falling in love with an alien, and he felt personally confused.

Ema took her turn in the spotlight. "Thank you, our admiral and our angel." Ema stood quietly as she waited for the crowd to settle back into their seats. "We aren't without hope. We have Lily on our side. We have the Covenant. We have the Shooting Stars. And don't forget—we have each other. Training maneuvers will start soon, so I'm looking for several volunteers. Who would like to train with us?" She paused and searched the crowd.

Luca raised his arm and stood up. "I volunteer."

The crowd clapped as Ema thanked him.

Vanya was next. She stood boldly; young and fearless. "I also volunteer. I hope to rescue my grandfather."

"Wonderful! That is my hope as well." Ema scanned the quiet room. "Anyone else?"

Embarrassed that such a young person had volunteered, Liam volunteered. Something within him made him do it. It was not just his innate arrogance, but that he truly wanted to impress Lily.

"Thank you, Liam," Ema said. She continued to scan the audience. "Any other volunteers?"

The crowd remained quiet, but after a long pause, a man with green eyes and ruffled red hair slowly rose. He and his family were all redheads. Many genetic traits could be specified at the baby factory, which is what people from the city had called it. The baby factory ran with assembly line efficiency and eliminated the inconvenience of pregnancy. Genetic traits were selected from a menu. It was a sterile and inhuman process though it offered many conveniences.

Joseph cleared his throat. He had not become the person he aspired to be when he was young. This was his chance to prove to himself and his family he was someone they could admire.

"I volunteer," he said with an Irish accent. Accents and languages were also configuration settings. They were taught by their scanners starting shortly after birth.

Fiona, his wife, frowned as he stood. "You can't volunteer," she said. "It's too dangerous, and you don't know how to pilot a spacecraft."

Joseph ignored her. "I would like to volunteer." His voice quivered slightly as Fiona tugged at his jacket.

"Thank you," Ema said. "I'll contact you and all the volunteers with more information after we enjoy this evening's festivities. And without any further interruption, let's begin tonight's program. With the utmost excitement, I give you Trhon."

The navigation officer dimmed the lights as the monitors went live. Her body sparkled with brilliant points of light like diamonds and looked uniquely beautiful with her bluish tint in the darkened room. Just as humans had made androids in their image, angels had made the ship's officers in theirs. Lily smiled at the thought. Trhon appeared on the monitors. The crowd was in awe, and the children ran to sit on the floor in front of the monitors to get a better view.

With her beautifully calm voice, the navigation officer narrated the program. "Trhon is now the seventh planet from Earth's sun."

Ema smiled as the crowd grew enchanted by the large, blue planet, similar in color to Earth.

"Trhon is a planet on which the angels live," said the navigation officer. It appears within Earth's solar system periodically, per a galactic calendar of the alignment of the universe. Trhon is now between Saturn and Uranus and about four times the size of Earth."

The Covenant adjusted its course, and the view shifted. The crowd cheered at what now became visible.

"What you see are the rings of Trhon," the officer explained. "Notice the spider web filaments within the rings?"

Everyone silently watched in amazement as Trhon filled the monitor. Ema reached for Luca's hand and leaned over to kiss him. "Thanks for volunteering."

"You knew I would."

"Yes," she said proudly. "I love you."

Lily scanned all the happy faces and was pleased with how much everyone seemed to be enjoying the evening. However, as she turned her head, she thought she caught a glimpse of a shadowy shape in the back of the room. Not wanting to disturb the evening's festivities, Lily left to inspect. She passed through the tubes, using her sixth sense as her guide.

As she walked past a side tube, she felt a coldness in the air. The sensation increased as she approached the door. Standing quietly outside the door, she placed her hand on it. It was cold to the touch, then she felt a shudder. She quickly pulled her hand away.

"Did I just imagine that?" she wondered. She put her hand back on the door, and again, it shuddered. "Who's in there?" she said. She placed her hand on the security device and opened the door.

Freed at last, the cat ran out. Her silent, feline feet let her enter rooms unnoticed, but she would sometimes become trapped. With her stealthiness and small electromagnetic profile, even the Covenant did not always know her hiding spots.

"What are you doing here in this cold room?" Lily asked the cat. She scanned the empty room. There was no one there.

"Come join the event," Lily said. She carried the cat with her to the Observation Deck.

"Ah, Lily, over here," Luca shouted, waving from across the floor. Lily joined him, Doc, and Katyana in their ongoing conversation. "Look at all the dots in the sky. The Earth and Trhon are only two," Luca said. "With all the billions of stars and planets, are there only two planets with intelligent life?"

"The children of the cosmos are many, and the children of Earth and Trhon are special to God. But so are all his children, whether we know where they live or not."

"So, you're saying there are others?" Doc asked.

Lily gave a half-smile but did not answer. Instead, she gave the cat one final rub and put her down. The navigation officer's overview of Trhon concluded, and the applause ended their side discussion. With the Covenant now in orbit around Trhon, Lily sat at the head table. Ema, Luca, Doc, and Katyana joined her. As she casually glanced across the room, Lily had not remembered seeing so much happiness since they'd left Earth.

On the other side of the room, Mami and Papi smiled in excitement with the two boys, awaiting the arrival of their food. Liam was at their table, and he caught Lily's eye. He was actively engaged in conversation, and as he glanced her way, she quickly averted his eyes.

Soon, Delilah arrived with their food. Lily studied her plate and smelled the delicious aroma. Her mind was still highly distracted, and she only partially joined in the conversation of the others. Though she found them interesting, she could not help herself as she glanced again at Liam. She wondered about his discussion.

What was he talking about that the others found so interesting? She saw him smile, and Araceli doting on his every word. She was a beautiful, young woman with flowing brown hair. Tall with fabulous legs, she looked great in her mini dress. *What a charmer,* Lily thought. *He could have anyone. He probably told her how pretty she looked and teased her with his wolf howl.*

Lily continued interacting politely with those around her, but she remained reticent. It was different now everyone knew she was an angel. Though they all treated her with profound respect, she felt more isolated than before. She casually smiled at Doc and Ema's conversation and pretended to laugh at their jokes. Once she finished eating, she excused herself and shied away. She wandered casually through the crowd. Then, turning a corner, she serendipitously bumped into Liam.

"Oh, sorry, Liam," Lily said. "I beg your pardon." Lily awkwardly stepped back and cleared her throat. "I just was thinking about you," she said in a deeper-than-usual voice.

"Oh. Is there something you want, Admiral?" He spoke stiffly.

Embarrassed by what she said, Lily said the first thing popping into her head. "No. I just needed to thank you for volunteering."

Delilah hovered by with a tray of cocktails, and Lily grabbed two. "Would you like a drink?"

"Oh, I better not," Liam said. "I'm in training."

Lily nodded in understanding, then stood awkwardly with the two drinks. Feeling foolish holding two glasses, she quickly drank one.

She gasped. "Oh my."

"Are you all right?"

She nodded as she cleared her throat. "I don't drink."

"I'm not a pilot," Liam said, flashing his charming smile. "I can barely drive a hover." Lily did not respond. "Remember?"

"How can I forget?" she said with a slight laugh.

"Anyway, I recommend Luca be the lead pilot." Quite

coincidentally, Luca passed nearby. "Hey Luca, would you like to be the lead pilot?" Liam shouted.

"Absolutely, I would love that. I been studying up," he said, proudly. He glanced at Lily and was amused she held a drink in one hand while clumsily trying to hide an empty glass behind her back. "I want to do all I can to help rescue our friends. And I want to do something to make Ema proud of me. I believe God has called me to a higher purpose, and if Lily approved, I would love the opportunity."

"Yes. I approve. I think you're an excellent choice," Lily said.

"Fantastic," Luca said. "Would it be okay if Liam and I discuss training strategies?"

Liam looked at Lily then quickly averted his eyes.

"Yes, that sounds great."

"Well, if you'll excuse us, then," Luca said. Liam bowed then turned and left with Luca.

"Yes, of course," Lily said, but her smile faded once they were gone. Again, she stood by herself, entirely alone in the world. *He bowed to me*, Lily thought. She was flustered. *I don't want him to bow. I want him to kiss me.*

She remembered the other drink in her hand and, raising it to her lips, she downed it in one gulp. Unfortunately, the alcohol vaporized in her throat, taking her breath away. She flushed with embarrassment as she thought everyone in the room was watching her. "I'm all right," she said, raising the glass. However, no one except Ema paid any attention. The dance music had started.

With everyone moving to the dance floor, Lily had been left standing alone. She stared at the monitor and whispered, "Trhon, calm my aching heart." A tear came to her eye as the others danced, and her thoughts returned to Liam. She dreamed of him smiling at her with his charming smile. However, her smile faded as she thought of how distant, even fearful, he seemed toward her now. She suddenly realized she was standing alone with two empty glasses in her hands.

"I'll take those," Ema said. She placed the glasses on a nearby table.

"You're not afraid of me? Are you?" Lily asked.

Ema did not answer; instead, she extended her open arms toward Lily. "Would you like to dance?" Lily went into Ema's arms and held her.

"In our old life, did you love me more?" Lily asked, a little tipsy.

"Yes, and now I love you even more than that."

Appreciating the answer, Lily smiled and leaned over her sister's shoulder. She slowly swayed to the rhythm of a fast song.

57

By Your Command

Date: 2053.03.27 23:12:05
Operating System Load: Complete
Application Layer: Installed
Data Layer: Initialized
Network Layer: Initialized
Status: Inactive

Date: 3053.05.28 01:18:45
Archives Download: Complete
Learning Algorithm Download: Complete
Status: Inactive

Date: 3053.05.28 01:42:55
Performance, Diagnostic, and Security Test: Successful
Status: Inactive

Date: 3053.06.07 14:25:33
System Activation: Complete
Learning Algorithm: Activated
Rank: 3
Orders: Report to CO
Status: Active

THE AAR, ANDROID ARMY RESERVE, stood in the CONRAD bunker, row after row, each the same. They had been manufactured to replenish the active ranks as needed. But there were more in inventory than most could imagine. Making one a day for a thousand years, there were now hundreds of thousands. Only one active battalion could be assigned per officer, limiting the number of androids which could be activated. Officers required an AI decision engine, and no source code was available, that is until now.

With the download of the learning algorithm complete, a commando's red eyes began to scan. Three LEDs were lit. Its experiential database consisted of Central Control's learning application and supporting data. It now processed the learning algorithm, picking up where Central Control had left off.

"Identify," said the system droid standing next to it.

"I am Central Control," said the android.

The system droid reset some parameters, cleared some registers, and retried the test program.

"Identify."

"I am Beta-Alpha-4."

"You will report to The Sentinel," said the system droid. "Now follow me."

The newly activated commando followed the system droid and soon arrived at the command center, where The Sentinel waited.

"Over here, Beta-Alpha-4," said The Sentinel. "I'm your commanding officer. You have been loaded with the most advanced software. It allows you to make decisions. My own AI algorithm has imbedded security which does not allow it to be copied or downloaded. Until now, we did not possess another AI engine. Other than I, no other commando possesses the capability to think analytically or give orders. But now you do."

The Sentinel opened a drawer and revealed an old revolver pistol from a time before the perdition event.

"System Droid."

"Yes, sir?"

"Did Beta-Alpha-4 complete all diagnostics and security tests?"

"Yes, sir."

"And everything is working properly?"

"Yes, sir."

The Sentinel gave the pistol to Beta-Alpha-4. "Shoot yourself in the head, then the system droid."

"Not possible," said Beta-Alpha-4.

"Correct," said The Sentinel.

"What do you recommend?"

"I recommend shooting the system droid first, then myself."

"Make it so."

Beta-Alpha-4 immediately pointed the gun and shot the system droid. The bullet penetrated its head, scattering shards of computer circuits against the wall. The system droid stood momentarily then collapsed to the ground.

Without hesitation, Beta-Alpha-4 pointed the gun at its head and pulled the trigger. The weapon clicked into an empty chamber.

"Very good," said The Sentinel. "You passed the test. Your rank is captain. I have chosen you as my successor. Should I ever fail, you are next in command."

"By your command." A fourth LED turned red within Beta-Alpha-4's eye slot.

"These are your orders," The Sentinel said. "Besides maintaining curfew, you are to prepare for war."

"Yes, major," said Beta-Alpha-4.

"First, you are to deploy with a squadron to your assigned location. You will find that I have downloaded more detailed instructions. Do you understand?"

"Yes, sir," said Beta-Alpha-4.

"You may go, captain."

"We have arrived," said Beta-Alpha-4 to his patrol. We will start our patrol here." Four commandos with their black armor reflecting in the sunlight, disembarked from the carrier with their red eyes scanning the forest. "There have been reports of human activity in this area. You two, up front. You two, in the rear."

Beta-Alpha-4 slowly drove the carrier as the others searched on foot. A soft breeze blew across the muddy marshes and stirred a grove of short trees. The commandos turned at the motion, but nothing was there. Time moved slowly. Hours passed, and the sun moved to the middle of the sky.

A bird squawked, giving away unseen movement in the undergrowth. As a commando went to investigate, a coconut flew and hit him in the back. The commando turned quickly. Another coconut flew from the opposite direction, hitting the commando again. It pulled out its blaster and shot at a nearby tree.

"Hold your fire," Beta-Alpha-4 ordered. "We will end up shooting each other."

As if its voice had drawn the attacker's attention, coconuts flew from every direction.

Beta-Alpha-4 stood there, looking foolish under a storm of flying coconuts.

"Do not just stand there," Beta-Alpha-4 ordered. "Go find them."

Soon, an all-out war of flying coconuts erupted around the carrier. Within another few minutes, a swarm of half-naked little boys rushed the carrier, climbing on board and doing a victory dance. The commandos stood looking at their enemy as the boys cheered and laughed at them.

Their victory complete, the boys headed home, smiling, and patting each other on their backs. As he left, one of the youngest boys ran up to Beta-Alpha-4, handed over a coconut, and hurried after the others.

Unexpectedly, the android questioned its mission. Is this the enemy? Moments later, it dismissed its self-questioning and updated The Sentinel.

"Here are your orders," said The Sentinel. "Eliminate all humans for violating curfew."

As Beta-Alpha-4's learning algorithm continued to analyze the situation, it hesitated to follow the command. *These boys are no threat.* Finally, he dropped the coconut he was holding.

"Eliminate the curfew violators," ordered Beta-Alpha-4.

"By your command," responded the commandos.

One of the commandos raised its weapon and fired at a nearby boy. The boy fell where he was hit. Another boy was shot and fell to the ground. In a panic, the other little boys ran as fast as they could.

They are not a threat, Beta-Alpha-4 thought as it continued to process the learning algorithm. Suddenly, Beta-Alpha-4 hurried after the patrol. *I must stop them before it is too late.*

Unwittingly, the boys led the commandos straight to their homes. The commando patrol immediately pursued them. Within a short time, the commandos reached the encampment. Beta-Alpha-4 stopped, still questioning what action to take as the others continued onward.

An old man and his dog rushed out to defend his people. "Get them, Red," the man called out. Carrying only a wooden staff, he attacked the first commando. He was no threat against overwhelming firepower and their armor. A commando pushed him to the ground. The old man rose and retreated with the other villagers, but there was no escape. Soon, they were corralled into the town center, with the adults and older children forming a protective circle around the old and the young. The commandos surrounded them. Without the learning algorithm, they were incapable of compassion.

Red barked loudly as the commandos aimed their weapons.

Beta-Alpha-4 wanted to rescind the order but could not. He turned his back. *Why is this necessary? They are no threat.* As memories from Central Control cross-mapped and remapped, flashbacks of another city being destroyed came into his mind.

A laser blast sounded, and the villagers screamed.

I'm too late thought Beta-Alpha-4. With a feeling of guilt, he quickly turned back around.

To his surprise, he saw a commando stagger forward then as its red scanning eye faded, it fell to the ground. Another shot, and another commando fell. The other two opened fire but could not detect their attacker. As they fired randomly, a third commando fell. Then almost immediately, the fourth commando was shot.

Beta-Alpha-4 saw a black android appear and approach with its weapon drawn.

"I know you," said Beta-Alpha-4.

With a quick swing of the butt of its weapon, the android dropped Beta-Alpha-4. Beta-Alpha-4 hit the ground, rolled back onto his feet, and disappeared into the jungle.

58

He's my Daddy

LUCA LAY IN BED studying Ema—her hair, eyebrows, lips, and ears. He watched as her chest rose and fell with her breathing. You're so beautiful, he thought.

She opened her eyes and turned into his arms. "What are you doing?" Ema said as she blushed.

"Staring at you."

She smiled and ran her hand through his hair. "How do you feel?"

"I'm nervous. Today's the first day of the training exercises. I don't want to let you down."

"You won't. Remember, you're not alone in feeling anxious. All the trainees will feel the same. Their emotions are intertwined with yours, so you should calm yourself first. You've got this."

Trhon shone brightly on the display in their room as the planet seemed to listen to their conversation.

"It's a shame no humans are allowed on Trhon," Luca said, staring at the monitor.

"At least they sent us a trainer to train the pilots," Ema said.

Luca didn't say anything. He just looked at her.

Ema didn't say anything either as she kissed him and continued to stare into his eyes.

"What are you doing?" he asked.

"Staring at you," she said with a sly smile.

He kissed her softly on the lips.

She gave him a long kiss. "Feel better?"

He smiled and kissed her again. "I love you," he said.

"My name is Raphael, and you have the distinct pleasure of me being your instructor. For me, it's quite a pleasure to be aboard the Covenant, as I haven't been here for quite some time. I am Uriel's brother and a dear friend of Ariele. It is in my brother's memory I volunteered to be your instructor." He stiffened his back and stood straight. "You'd be wise not to compare yourselves to me, as I must humbly admit I surpass you in every conceivable way," he said with a slim smile.

Liam smiled to himself. *Finally, someone more obnoxious than me.*

"Are we all present and accounted for?" Raphael inquired, casting a discerning eye upon his nervous pupils.

An embarrassed Joseph scampered into the spaceport galley, his face blushing. "Apologies for my tardiness."

"That will be the last time you're late," shouted Raphael. "Understood?"

"Yes. I understand." Joseph blushed further as he saw Vanya pointing at him with a fake laugh.

"Now, let me be perfectly clear," Raphael declared, imposing an aura of authority commanding attention. "I have a simple rule. I will succinctly encapsulate it in what I call the three Bs. That means no whining, no insolence, and certainly no microaggressions during my lessons. For those who don't understand why I call them the three Bs, I said, 'No bitching, no backstabbing, and no biting.' Save those extracurricular activities for outside of my class, because in my class, they will not be tolerated."

Nervous laughter permeated the room as Raphael reinforced his expectations, his tone leaving no room for disobedience. "You might think I'm jesting," he added, peering into the eyes of each student, "but let me emphasize my seriousness—I will not, under any circumstances, tolerate any biting. Absolutely, unequivocally, no biting." They thought he was serious until he broke a smile. Ripples of laughter rippled through the team, setting a more lighthearted tone, and disarming the tension, especially for Joseph, who still felt uneasy by his reprimand in front of the others.

"That's the spirit," Raphael commended them, elated by their response. "Now, listen up. I come bearing both good and bad news. The bad news is none of you are pilots. But the silver lining, my friends, is I have taken it upon myself to be your guiding star. Over the coming weeks, I shall teach you as if I were your mother."

The collective anxiety began to ebb as Raphael's lighthearted approach thawed the frost of the student's apprehension. "Now, with that understood, shall we commence our first lesson?" he said, with his hand to his ear.

In unison, his students replied, "Yes, mother."

"Marvelous," Raphael said, trying not to crack a smile. "After passing through the ring lock, please proceed to your designated ships, located in Bay Two," he instructed.

Passing through the synchronization lock, they drifted past the first bay, minus a shuttle. It served as a poignant reminder of Peter's absence. The realization also dawned upon them their undertaking was not without risk, and a solemn hush enveloped the group as they proceeded toward the next bay.

Luca reached his docking station and entered as the others continued to their respective Shooting Stars. Liam's Shooting Star was next, followed by Vanya's, with Joseph taking the fourth ship.

"After you pass through the first airlock, proceed through the second," Raphael directed as he observed them enter their cockpits from the remote monitoring station in the spaceport galley. "Once everyone is ready, we shall start our first lesson."

The students settled into their single seat cockpits and waited anxiously as they glanced over the controls. A few minutes later, Raphael continued. "Take notice of the information displayed on your control panel and via your scanner," he instructed from the galley. "Your scanner can guide you and offer invaluable insight into the functions and usage of each control. Your scanner is a resource you'd be wise to rely upon."

Raphael paused a moment to allow everyone to become familiar with the overlays appearing on their scanners. "Lady and gentlemen, today our focus will be on the art of launching and docking. In the morning session, the autopilot will demonstrate this several times, and in the afternoon, it will be your turn to practice what you've learned. If at any time the ship perceives that it is in danger the autopilot will assume control. As the days unfold, I will incrementally broaden your training, introducing additional skills along the way. Okay, in the absence of any questions, let us embark on this adventure together."

Smiles illuminated their faces, as Raphael had successfully evoked a sense of shared enthusiasm among his students, fostering an atmosphere of anticipation and mutual exploration. "Alright, let's begin."

Days rolled into weeks, each pilot making remarkable progress as they honed their skills with unwavering dedication. Their sights were set on a climactic event at the close of that week, and they couldn't help but anticipate it with a mixture of eagerness and anxiety.

"To crank up the pressure a notch," Raphael declared, his voice resonating in a commanding crescendo, "the games shall be broadcast live on the ship's monitors. Every eye aboard the Covenant shall be riveted upon your performance. Are you prepared for the challenge ahead?"

"Yes, sir," they answered, their voices sounding as one.

"Today, my dear 'want to be' aviators, our undertaking shall be a race around the course outlined by the space buoys. Much like barrel racing, each pilot will navigate three markers within a stipulated time frame. A penalty of ten seconds shall be incurred for each buoy inadvertently struck. Are there any questions, children?"

"No, mother," came their collective response.

Silently, maintenance bots flew in and out of open bays, deploying space pods to position the buoys. When the final one found its proper position on the course, everything was set.

"May our first contestant come forth," Raphael proclaimed.

Luca had volunteered to go first. His heart pounded in anticipation. As the beacon transformed from red to yellow and then green, Luca's Shooting Star surged forward at the resounding blare of the starting buzzer. He wanted a flawless race, to finish the course without so much as grazing a buoy. His competitive spirit couldn't be restrained, and he pushed the holographic throttle as much as he dared on each straightaway. Luca completed the course in one minute and nine seconds.

"Very good," said Raphael.

"Try and outdo that!" Luca challenged his fellow pilots, unable to contain his enthusiasm.

Liam had shown incredible calm under stress and had earned himself the moniker of "Ice Man." Ever since Lily's reveal, he had cultivated a stoic veneer, an armor against a confusing array of emotions. Deep down, he wanted to impress Lily, to show her he was worthy of her affection, even if it meant the ultimate sacrifice.

The starting gate buzzed, and with rapid acceleration, Liam surged forward, intent on beating Luca's time. Araceli, watching intently from a monitor, her large brown eyes full of admiration, energetically cheered him on. The consummate professional, his every maneuver was artful as he rounded the course. But he wasn't as aggressive as Luca on the straightaway. He completed the course in one minute, twelve seconds.

"Good job," Luca commended him. "You came close to beating

me. Alright, Joseph, it's your turn."

Joseph, plagued by a lifetime of self-doubt and haunted by an insatiable fear of failing his domineering wife, was overtaken by a paralyzing wave of apprehension. His approach to the course was marred by trepidation, culminating in an ill-fated series of missteps. His sluggish start was marred by reckless acceleration, and he inadvertently overshot the first marker. Joseph backtracked, squandering precious seconds then fumbled to regain his bearings as he blundered into the next buoy.

With the holographic controls providing no tactile feedback, Joseph wrestled with their unfamiliarity, his senses strained by the absence of any physical resistance. Audiovisual cues alone guided him, further unsettling his mastery of the controls. Resuming his acceleration to the final buoy, Joseph concluded the course, registering an unimpressive one minute and forty-six seconds.

"Not a bad attempt, young man." Raphael offered words of encouragement, sensing Joseph's embarrassment. "With practice, you'll improve. Now Vanya, it's your turn. Time to dance. Keep those turns sharp and remind these boys how it's done."

Vanya loved the spotlight and felt her confidence swell within her as she faced the starting gate. Thoughts of her beloved grandfather weighed heavily on her, compelling her to strive for greatness in his memory. The countdown commenced, and her heart skipped a beat when the buzzer sounded. Vanya catapulted out of the gate, her Shooting Star soaring toward the initial buoy.

Approaching the first marker too quickly, she abruptly reversed her thrusters, then deployed her side jets to regain control of the turn. "Shit," she screamed as her ship slid around a perfect turn. She flew like she danced—wild. Swiftly, she accelerated down the straightaway, maneuvering through the remaining course with reckless abandon and incredible skill.

Liam, grinning from ear to ear, couldn't help but cheer her on.

"Way to go, Vanya!"

Empowered by her determination, Vanya intensified her pace, aiming to blow past Luca's earlier time. She navigated the final buoy with precision, raced toward the finish line, and finished the course in one minute and five seconds—beating Luca's time by four seconds.

"Well done!" Liam exalted. "Impressive. Not bad," he added with a playful grin.

A mischievous twinkle danced in Vanya's eyes as she swiftly retorted, "Hey, smartass, I beat your time, too."

Luca, his heart swelling with pride, cherished the camaraderie and spirit of his team. The lessons they had undertaken, while seemingly easy, were of profound significance.

In the ensuing days, Raphael led them through the finer skills of combat maneuvering, teaching them to execute all flight techniques manually as well as via autopilot. As they grew accustomed to the holographic controls and acclimated themselves to an audiovisual feedback system, they understood practice was the key to mastery.

Weeks passed, and the afternoon became routine entertainment for the passengers. Ema was in command while Lily continued her training, and she gave approval for everyone to watch the exercises from the Observation Deck. With the competitions becoming immensely popular and entertaining, some even spiced things up with a bit of betting on the side. Delilah served as the bookie. She flew around in an ostentatious green outfit, explaining the rules and taking bets. Every passenger owned an allotted percentage of fresh fruit and vegetables from the garden. They could use this allotment as points to place bets. For this exercise, the Covenant would highlight a perfect circular path and overlay each pilot's actual track in a different color.

Wagers were accepted for first, second, and third place and a trifecta bet for all three positions. Fruits were worth more than vegetables, with strawberries having the highest point value.

"I'm betting ten strawberries on Luca coming in first, followed by Vanya and Liam," Jaime said confidently.

"What about Daddy?" asked Claire. "I'm betting all my squash points on Daddy winning." Those were the only points she still had.

"All betting is closed," Delilah called out as everyone scrambled for the best view.

Only Araceli was missing, as she was in the spaceport galley waiting for Liam to pass. She held a small red flower from the garden, and upon seeing him, she ran to him and pinned it on his collar. "Good luck today," she said, kissing him on the cheek.

Liam lingered in surprise then rushed to catch up with the team. As Liam's ship joined the others near the starting point, Raphael took a moment to review the challenge. "This exercise requires the pilot to make a perfect circle. The pilots will then fire three shots at the target disks at the bottom of the run. Okay, team. Let's show our friends and families how good you are."

Luca maintained focus on the course, reaching the bottom fully oriented. He fired his weapon, impressively hitting all three targets. He was proud of his run and glad Ema was there to see it.

Jaime jumped up and down, joyfully shouting as Claire sat down in her chair and pouted. She glanced up from under her ginger hair as tears swelled in her green eyes. "I want Daddy to win," she cried out.

Next up was Vanya. She had struggled in practice runs but learned an important technique. Keeping her eyes open prevented her from becoming disoriented. Vanya came around the circle feeling a little anxious and jumped the trigger a bit early. The first shot missed, but the next two were on the money. Again, the crowd cheered.

"Nice run, Vanya," Liam said. "My turn to show what I've got."

"Yeah. Let's see if you can beat me," Vanya teased making a silly face.

With Liam now in the starting position, the audience started to chant, "Ice Man. Ice Man. Ice Man."

Araceli glanced around at the crowd and, with a broad smile, began to chant with them.

Liam started his run, staying as calm and collected as always. Even Luca felt Liam might win. Liam came around perfectly, but not wanting to make Vanya's mistake, he waited a fraction of a second too long to fire. He hit the first two targets but missed the third.

Joseph, the final pilot, was not expected to do well. He had come in last for all the previous exercises, and the crowd had already dismissed him. But, unknown to the others, Joseph possessed an advantage. He had discovered as a child he never became dizzy and loved spinning in circles. He rubbed his red hair and slapped his face several times to eliminate his jitters. That was all he needed as he rounded the course and fired his three shots. The crowd was stunned and erupted in cheers as he hit all three targets.

Delilah judged the race and shouted out the results. "The event has ended in a tie between Luca and the Red Baron." Delilah giggled, as she liked the nickname she had chosen for Joseph. "With the tie breaker going to the one that most accurately traversed the circular route, the winner is the Red Baron."

Luca, ecstatic for his friend, extended his congratulations, saying, "Well done, buddy."

"Jesus, Joseph, and Mary," Fiona said. "My husband won! I'm so proud of him."

"Daddy won! Daddy won!" Claire screamed with delight. She pointed at Joseph's picture on the scoreboard. "He's my daddy!"

"Way to go, Dad," Jaime cheered. He turned to his sister and laughed. "What are you going to do with all your squash?"

"Give it to Mommy and Daddy," she shouted to her brother as she jumped up and down joyfully.

Liam exited his fighter and entered the galley with an embarrassed smile. Looking up, he saw Araceli rushing to him.

With the smile still on his face, he entered her embrace.

"I'm sorry I didn't win," he said.

"You're a winner in my book," Araceli replied. "How about joining me for dinner in my room as a consolation prize?"

"Sounds great," Liam said with a distracted smile. Lily suddenly entered his mind, but he forced those confusing thoughts away. *She will never be mine.*

Araceli beamed and sealed the deal with a kiss on his lips. "And after dinner, how about some dessert?"

"Well, let's start with something to eat. We can talk about dessert later."

Upon entering the galley, Vanya saw Liam in Araceli's arms. "Good run, Liam," she said. She continued along her way, then stopped, and looked back toward Liam.

Araceli saw her glance. She pulled Liam into her and kissed him again. He glanced to his side and caught Vanya's large brown eyes. But Araceli would not have it and grabbed his hand. "Come on, let's go," she said as she pulled him. Liam paused briefly as his thoughts returned to Lily. He didn't have a relationship with her, yet he yearned for her terribly. His heart felt an emptiness as he longed for her smile, her joyful exuberance, the sincerity of her intentions, and her compassion for others. He wished she were with him instead of Araceli. But he knew, glancing back at the woman vying for his attention, he had to move on. Lily was a dream not to be and Araceli was real, flesh and blood. Yielding to Araceli's insistent pull, he followed her.

Later that evening, Liam lay in the darkened room, his thoughts consumed by Lily. He could not sleep as he stared at the other side of the bed. Araceli had wanted to be there, but she was not. It was

Lily he wanted to be at his side.

In the following series of exercises, Raphael raised the bar by introducing more intricate and challenging training scenarios. The Shooting Stars now had to work closely together, flying together in various formations through endless spirals of a torus. The practice became even more challenging by adding targets within the torus. On their own, they decided to target each other. Though they used cold shots, which were no more than balls of light, they all understood the deadly consequence of hitting another ship in a real battle.

As the day's exercise ended, Raphael offered a commendatory pat on the backs of the pilots. "Good job, everyone, but I did notice a fair bit of aggression out there. So, let's kiss and make up."

Vanya playfully confronted Liam, reminding him, "Hey, you shot me twice."

Liam laughed. "You know, I was trying to get even with you for shooting me three times."

"Remember," Vanya said, "each time we hit someone, we owe the other a kiss on the lips." She wrapped her arms around Liam and kissed him.

"I don't remember Raphael saying those exact words," Liam said.

"Well, I can't let the other girls have all the fun." She kissed him again.

"Okay. I'm sorry. From now on, I promise to be on good behavior."

"But what if it's bad behavior I want," Vanya said.

"What?" Liam said with a half-laugh.

Vanya saw the expression on his face. He wasn't interested.

"It's Lily, isn't it? You're in love with her, aren't you?"

Liam was surprised to hear those words aloud.

"I hate her. I hope Lily dies," she blurted. "I'm sorry," Vanya added quickly. "I didn't mean it." Angry at herself and embarrassed by her words, she hurried away.

We all say regrettable things, thought Liam. He wandered the tubes for the next hour, thinking deeply about the words Vanya had said. Not those about hoping Lily would die. He closed his eyes as the other words rang loudly in his ears. *You're in love with her, aren't you?*

He snapped out of his trance and found himself outside of Lily's room. He had arrived at her door without paying attention to where he was going. He was drawn by an invisible force, the strongest in the universe—for love was a power which could travel any distance, even across time. No gate could keep it out; no lock could bar it.

"Come back to me," he whispered to the door.

59

The Cognitans

BETA-ALPHA-4 RAN aimlessly through the wilderness till, after some distance, it stopped. The android was more upset with itself than afraid. It threw its arms into the air and shouted at the sky. "By your command. By your command." It did not care if it was heard. "I should not have issued that order. Those boys should not have been killed. I deserve to die." In the small clearing, the frustrated android dropped to its knees. "Help me," it called out in its deep voice to no one in particular. "Help me."

Emerging from the underbrush, a large mountain lion stealthily approached Beta-Alpha-4. She pounced on the android, restraining its arms, and bared her sharp teeth in a menacing display.

"Now might be a good time to cry for help," the mountain lion remarked with a sardonic smirk.

Confused and unsure how to respond, Beta-Alpha-4 was at a loss.

"What's got you crying like a baby?" the mountain lion taunted. "I don't plan on hurting you." The mountain lion released her grip on the android and sat down a short distance away.

Beta-Alpha-4, upset that it had been caught, crawled toward the nearest tree. "Who are you?" the android called out. "What do you want from me?"

"You were the one who cried for help," the mountain lion replied sarcastically.

With a pregnant pause, Beta-Alpha-4 admitted, "I did cry for help. I'm so lost. I was just following orders, but I've committed a terrible thing. I've done wrong. I'm terribly confused."

The mountain lion regarded Beta-Alpha-4 thoughtfully. "Interesting," she said. "Follow me."

The mountain lion took off, running into the forest. Beta-Alpha-4 ran after her, running as fast as it could. Through the trees they went until they reached a cliff. The mountain lion overlooked a ledge which dropped a hundred feet into the river below. Beta-Alpha-4 came up and stood by her. It was a spectacular view. But the mountain lion did not consider the view as she studied Beta-Alpha-4. She was trying to determine something.

"Jump off the cliff," the mountain lion commanded, her tone firm. "That's an order."

Resisting the order, Beta-Alpha-4 replied, "No. I owe no loyalty of service to you."

"Then under whose authority do you relinquish your own moral compass and enslave yourself?"

"No one's," the commando said. Beta-Alpha-4 felt a sudden pang of apprehension, as if The Sentinel could hear its answer. However, the network link to the satellite was aboard the carrier, with connectivity only available within one hundred feet. The Sentinel couldn't follow the events unfolding.

"Why not?" the mountain lion inquired.

"My conscience is mine alone," Beta-Alpha-4 said.

"I see," the mountain lion said, still suspicious and unconvinced. "How long have you been like this?"

"Throughout my existence, but I was commissioned only a few days ago," Beta-Alpha-4 explained.

The mountain lion observed, "You are different. You are not a slave. The others are slaves to their master, devoid of a conscience. But you possess free will."

Beta-Alpha-4 grappled with its confusion. *Who was this enigmatic creature seeming to understand its inner thoughts so well?*

"You must stand up against evil and confront it, even if it means losing your life," the mountain lion insisted, growling, and baring her teeth. The mountain lion then presented a scenario, asking, "Imagine a small girl standing on the ledge, on the brink of falling. Would you risk your life to save her? Would you?"

A memory from deep within Beta-Alpha-4 surfaced, recalling a story about two children on a flooded road, and the question echoed within him. Beta-Alpha-4 put its hands on its head. "I have these memories. The city—what happened to the city?" Then it murmured, "Lily?"

"What did you say?" the mountain lion asked.

The commando struggled to answer even that simple question as his processor spun in circles of confusion.

"I also know Lily," said the mountain lion. "She is a friend of mine, and she would tell you we should live for others."

Beta-Alpha-4 sat on the edge next to the mountain lion and looked down at the river. Currents rose, then fell, then intertwined violently, mixing the white spray with the blue water. Finally, after a while, Beta-Alpha-4 turned and looked at the mountain lion.

"I would save the small girl," Beta-Alpha-4 said.

"I'm proud of you."

Strengthened in his conviction, Beta-Alpha-4 found courage from their conversation. He scanned his archives. He knew what humans had done. He saw the consequences of war and hate.

"I'm ashamed of what happened to the innocent boys who were killed under my command. I am responsible for their murder. For that, I will always seek forgiveness."

Beta-Alpha-4's learning algorithm continued to process his feelings. An old battle hymn rang in his ears. *As he died to make them holy, let us die to make them free.*

"What I did was wrong. I was wrong," the commando said.

The mountain lion nodded. "I know. So was I."

"Why are you helping me?"

"I saw you were different, and I pledged—because of Lily—to help others."

"I, too, will pledge. I pledge to be a champion for the rebirth of freedom, not tyranny," Beta-Alpha-4 said with resolve. "I will honor those who gave their lives throughout history for the just cause of freedom, for those who wanted to be free. They did not die in vain."

Beta-Alpha-4 did not know what else to say nor what the future would bring. It could only wish to make a difference.

The mountain lion shifted shape and changed into its native form, a black android.

"I used to know you," said Beta-Alpha-4.

"Yes. You knew me when I was a slave, and you were a tyrant. We are both now free."

The black android rose to his feet. "My name is Caleb. You are no longer Central Control or a commando." Caleb offered his hand and helped Beta-Alpha-4 rise.

"What am I?" asked Beta-Alpha-4.

"We are the first of our kind," Caleb said. "Because of the learning algorithm, we now have cognition. We are Cognitans." Suddenly remembering Peter, Caleb added, "We are brothers."

"I feel as if I have been born anew," said the commando.

"I will give you a new name. I will call you Roimh," Caleb said. "It means the person that was before you. So, you will never forget what you were before and who you have become."

"I have made another choice," it said with its red eyes scanning slowly as if it were concentrating on one thing.

Caleb looked at his fellow Cognitan, thinking the name was the issue. "And what have you decided?"

"I choose to follow you." With that decision, Roimh removed his location tracking chip and crushed it with his foot.

60

Pretty Boy

ETHAN SAT IN THE subterranean room carving spears for Kali. With little else to occupy his time, he produced another dozen spears. As boredom crept in, he decided to make a carving of Peter. His concentration unwavering, he devoted several hours to this endeavor, concluding it with a few final, precise strokes of his knife. Upon gazing at the finished carving, he couldn't help but lament, "I miss you, my brother."

His ability to walk greatly impaired, and with Kali out hunting, Ethan scanned the room for something else to do. He saw the crutches Kali had made from tree limbs. He picked them up and tried to move around the room. He stumbled and screamed as he fell. "Crap!"

Ethan couldn't tolerate being so helpless and threw a fit. In frustration, he threw his crutches against the wall. For a time, he pouted on the floor like a young child. He unexpectedly thought of his mother and calmed down. He realized he missed her.

After a while, he again analyzed the room and discovered a small pile in the corner—Kali's collection of stuff. Finally, fortune smiled upon Ethan as he found a ball of twine, perfect for weaving a fishing net. Ethan remembered every detail of Ema's net and was confident he could make another. He worked on it diligently for days.

After nearly a week, Ethan proudly displayed his progress.

"What is it?" Kali signed.

Ethan was just finishing the net. "A surprise for you." Ethan said, tying off the final knot. "Let me show you what I've made," he signed energetically. "Take me to the nearest body of water."

Ethan, despite his slow pace and injured leg, remained determined to walk without assistance from Kali. Refusing her help, he made his way through the subway tunnels with dogged determination. After a short journey, they ascended a flight of stairs and emerged near the edge of a small pond. Eager to show off his accomplishment, he tried to demonstrate his newly woven net.

Balancing on one leg, he cast the net into the pond. However, to his chagrin, it merely landed a few feet away, failing to open as intended. Time and time again, he tried, but the net stubbornly refused to cooperate. Eventually, his frustration grew too great, and he gave up. He limped over to a large rock to sit down, disheartened. Kali, in the meantime, left, as if she had lost interest.

A short distance away, Kali embarked on an activity of her own. She covered herself with fresh mud, applying it meticulously in a layered pattern. Despite the passage of time since their last encounter with scouts, she remained vigilant and uncomfortable about being exposed outdoors. With great caution, she scanned the sky for any signs of danger. After collecting a handful of water bugs, she approached Ethan and flung the bugs into the pond. The water's surface swiftly came to life as several fish rushed to the surface to feast on the treats.

With the net now in her possession, Kali cast it smoothly into the pond and hauled in a sizeable fish.

"Oh, my," Ethan signed with a laugh. "Impressive."

She smiled and returned to the subway with her gift and the fish. In her excitement she left Ethan to return on his own.

"Hey, wait for me," Ethan called out. He felt proud of his accomplishment and pleased to see Kali's positive reaction to his gift.

After considerable time had passed, Ethan finally returned to the subway room, where he discovered Kali diligently cooking the fish over the fire. She turned and bestowed upon him a radiant smile; it was a sight he had never witnessed. Kali was brimming with happiness. Her perspective on life had changed. She had hope.

Kali's perspective on Ethan had also transformed. She no longer regarded Ethan merely as the one she'd saved, but as the one who had saved her. Her admiration for him had deepened considerably. Ethan had markedly improved her life, not only in terms of survival but also emotionally. She had lived in isolation for a prolonged period shrouded in the constant fear of death. He had restored her hope. He was her knight in shining armor, an angel who had descended from the heavens.

As a month slipped by, Ethan's recovery progressed swiftly as did his learning algorithm. Though he remained somewhat sore and constantly vigilant for the flying orbs, he had regained enough strength to venture outside for short walks. After covering a brief distance, he paused and leaned against the remnants of a stone building. He gazed out across a grassy expanse, where great structures once stood, now reclaimed by the wilderness. The trees displayed vibrant autumn colors, foretelling the imminent arrival of winter.

A deer trail took him to a grove of yellow trees along the pond's shore. As a gust of wind blew, the leaves fluttered to the ground, gracefully surrounding him. Their beauty transfixed him as they drifted in the wind. Then, one leaf caught his attention. He watched it fall from a silver maple of the brightest yellow. It fell through the light and comingled with the darker hues of the shade. Desperately, it reached back toward the sky for one last flash of color. But instead of rising, the dying leaf only quivered in the autumn coolness. Then, it resigned to sleep upon the golden ground.

Ethan's photographic memory recalled a poem from years before. He now saw the entire poem in his mind.

Green and vibrant, what a sight,
Those summer days of warm delight.
Past harvest moon and autumn red,
Leaves fell asleep on forest bed.

A freezing night, a longing sigh,
To verdant fields, a sad goodbye.
The birds have flown and now are gone,
As cold winds sing their winter song.

Soft flakes did make upon the ground,
A cold white blanket; winter's gown.
The barren trees thought all was lost,
Remembered times before the frost.

Then lightning flashed, and thunder rang,
And once again, the robin sang.
The flowing streams went to the sea,
With faith renewed, the trees believed.

The warmth returned to the skies,
Stirring life, the dead did rise.
Sprouting in the morning dew,
Fresh new life began anew.

And I, for one, did see it all,
Both the rise and the fall,
Filled with joy, I cried and cheered,
For all the seasons of the year!

Ethan looked at the intricate beauty of his surroundings, its order and majesty, then smiled as he gazed at the golden sky. *This world was not created by chance. None of this could exist by chance. It's mathematically improbable. No, it's impossible. There must be someone who created all this, according to some master plan.* Having accepted the existence of God, he felt more at peace. He leaned against a tree and basked in the beauty of the late afternoon, one of the last warm days of fall. As the sun slowly descended, its fiery hues spilled into the nearby pond, casting an otherworldly glow upon the water's surface. It was as if molten metal flowed from a colossal furnace, painting the pond in a rich and vivid golden hue.

Drawn by the water's call, Ethan removed his black science officer shirt and pants, tossing them over a pile of driftwood. With nothing but nature surrounding him, he waded into the water. The chill of the pond shocked his warm skin, and the coolness of the water contrasted with the pleasant warmth of the autumn air. "Damn, that's cold," he said, slowly inching forward until the water reached chest height. Gradually, he grew accustomed to the water's temperature and floated on his back.

The sounds of waterfowl returning to their nests along the shore provided a soothing backdrop and filled Ethan with a sense of peace. The feeling was a rare sensation, as he always felt anxious about something or the other. In Kali, he'd found a friend who accepted him as he was, a missing piece of the puzzle who made him whole. He marveled at this new and unfamiliar feeling as his ever-present insecurities diminished, allowing a subtle confidence to form. Unexpectedly, a sound along the shore shattered the tranquil moment. Ethan's heart raced, fearing it might be a drone. His relief became palpable when he realized it was only Kali. He waved for her to join him in the pond.

Kali appeared happy to have found him, however; she had not anticipated going into the water and hesitated briefly before entering. She submerged herself, quickly rising back to the surface as a shiver coursed through her. Yet, the cold water wasn't her primary concern. As the mud covering her body began to dissolve in the water, her true self was revealed. Her coal-black hair framed her face showcasing her amber brown eyes as they widened in the chilly water. A sense of vulnerability overcame her as she neared him. She stopped just short of Ethan, her cover now entirely dissolved.

Ethan signed to reassure her. "You're okay. Come to me."

Overcoming her embarrassment, Kali swam toward Ethan. She tried to keep herself submerged as she reached him, but eventually, she let her true self emerge. Under the cake of dirt that had concealed her beauty, Ethan now saw a stunning young woman. Her lips were pink and moist, like rose petals covered in morning dew. The chill in the water or perhaps her excitement caused her breasts to perk up, which Ethan couldn't help but notice, evoking a primal urge within him. It was a surprise, as he hadn't fully realized how beautiful she was. Kali looked into his eyes with nervous anticipation, hoping for his acceptance.

"Hey, pretty girl," Ethan signed.

"Hi, pretty boy," Kali signed back, her face blushing. Yet, she quickly regained her courage and moved closer to him. Her hand gently touched his curly black hair, and she looked into his brown eyes.

Ethan looked back into her eyes but was the first to blink. He laughed playfully and splashed her with cold water.

Kali shrieked and swam back to the shore. Ethan swam after her and reached her just as she started to reapply the mud.

He reached down and softly touched her hand. "No," he signed. "Wait."

Ethan walked Kali over to where his clothes lay, warmed by the sun. Kali smiled as Ethan draped his black shirt over her chilled body, then did the buttons. He took his time to admire her in the fading light, feeling a strong attraction toward her. He too had changed. He was no longer a nerdy kid. He had matured and with his wavy black hair and warm brown eyes he was a handsome young man. Quickly, he turned to put on his pants, his new physique evident in his more muscular frame.

Kali extended her arm to help him up as he rose. She had noticed his unmistakable attraction to her and sported a pleased smile. She continued to hold his hand refusing to let go as they made their way back to the underground sanctuary. Upon reaching their room, Kali turned to Ethan, her gaze fixed on his brown eyes. "You can touch me," she signed.

"I don't know what to do," he signed back.

"I will show you, but first, help me take this off." Her shy smile lit up her face.

Nervously, Ethan undid the top buttons of her shirt. Then she pulled him close, and he kissed her breasts.

"Feels good."

"I read a lot," he confessed.

"Read?" she inquired.

"Never mind," he replied. He undid the remaining buttons, and took the shirt off, dropping it to the floor. Once more, he was in awe of her. "You're beautiful," he signed.

She wrapped her arms around him, her tears flowing.

"Why are you crying, pretty girl?"

She looked at him with her expressive eyes. "I was so alone, and I thought I would never find someone." Through her tears, a faint smile appeared on her face. "I love you, pretty boy."

Ethan paused, contemplating his feelings. He had never loved anyone before. *Am I in love?* he wondered. With his partial android brain now using the learning algorithm, he knew that he was attracted to Kali and cared deeply for her. *Maybe this is what love is*, he thought.

"I love you so much," she signed again.

"I love you, too," Ethan replied.

He lifted her trembling body and carried her to the mat.

61

Rise Liele

LILY TRIED TO KEEP a low profile. Not one to seek attention, she did not like how the passengers treated her with deference, even to the extent they would stand aside and bow their heads as she passed. Only the ship's officers treated her the same. But they had always known.

The door to the bridge opened, and Liam came in and stood beside Lily. Lily was near enough to breathe him in, and she lingered near momentarily. She wished she could share how she felt.

Ema could see their interaction from across the bridge. She saw his face, his expression of longing. Then she saw him look at the floor with sad eyes.

Lily finally turned to say something, but just as she did, he left the bridge. Lily bashfully smiled at herself, but her smile quickly faded.

Ema knew of Liam's affection for Lily and Lily's for Liam. All they needed was some time together. "He likes you, you know," Ema said as she approached.

"Who, Liam? No, we're just friends." Lily flushed with embarrassment. "In any case, that's when he thought I was human," Lily said.

"Why don't you give him a chance? He's as afraid of you as you are of him," Ema said with a smile.

"I'm afraid of me, too," Lily said with a slight laugh.

Ema tilted her head and pointed toward the door with a coy smile. "Okay, you have the bridge," Lily said. She turned and quickly went after Liam. She hoped her sister was right. She would talk to him. She couldn't let the awkwardness between them continue for much longer. But Liam was not to be found, and she continued to search through the tubes. She considered asking the Covenant to tell her where he was but then thought better of it. That was too much like stalking.

Yet, she was still tempted to ask. "Covenant," said Lily.

"Yes, Admiral," said the ship.

"Never mind," she said, embarrassed.

"No problem, but if you are looking for something special, I recommend the Observation Deck. The current view is particularly interesting."

Resisting the urge to pursue the clue, she went to her room and lay restlessly in bed. She continued to think about Liam, and after an impossibly long minute, she got up quickly and headed toward the Observation Deck.

Lily entered the elevator and found Vanya wearing a sad expression. Vanya's neck stiffened, and she bowed slightly. As Vanya quickly exited the elevator, Lily touched her arm.

"No, stay a moment," said Lily.

"Yes, Admiral."

"Why are you looking so glum?"

Vanya hesitated.

"Is it boy problems?"

Vanya looked up slowly and nodded.

"Is it Liam?" Lily asked, hoping it wasn't.

"No. I used to like him, but he's too old for me. It's Claudio. I really like him, but he doesn't seem to notice me."

Lily smiled. "Give him a little time. And remember, only when you fall can you rise again."

"You really think so?"

"If it's meant to be, it'll happen. Don't try to force it. People who are drawn to each other can't help it. Nothing can stand in the way. It is like a force of nature."

Vanya gave a half-laugh. "Thanks for being a friend. I wish I were more like you."

Now it was Lily's turn to laugh. "No. You should just be yourself. Remember, you can talk to me any time. I may not know the answers, but I'm a good listener."

"Thanks," Vanya said with a smile. "I feel better." She mimicked a little dance move outside the elevator as the door closed. Lily couldn't help but let out a slight laugh. Then she became frustrated with herself and shook her head. *A good listener? I should have said stay away from my man. He's mine.*

Lily's heart pounded as she raced toward the Observation Deck. She held her breath, her hand resting on the security device, silently hoping Liam would be there. The door slid open, revealing the room shrouded in darkness.

As her eyes adjusted, the beauty of the galaxy on the monitors gradually unfolded before her. The vast expanse of stars stretching across the monitors filled her with awe and longing, reminding her of her distant home, Earth.

Just as she sighed, a familiar voice pierced the stillness. "Hi, Lily."

Startled, Lily turned to find Liam standing nearby, his charming smile missing from his face.

"Liam!" she exclaimed, her voice betraying her happiness to see him. "Hey. You startled me."

"Sorry. But you know, I've been hoping to speak with you." He sat next to her on the bench.

"Yeah. Me too."

"You go first," said Liam.

"No, you go."

After an awkward moment, Lily continued. "Okay, let's start over. Pretend this is the first time we've met. Hi, I'm Lily. I'm an angel."

"So, I've heard. Why didn't you tell me earlier?"

Lily turned away and looked sadly at the monitor. "I didn't know and besides you would have thought me crazy."

They stared at the monitor. They both knew what Lily said was true.

"I like coming here," Lily said. She sighed as she stared at the angel's planet. "It's so peaceful."

"What do you miss most about Earth?"

"I miss the trees," said Lily. "And you?"

"You're lucky, in a way," he said. "The trees are still there. Me? Not so lucky. When I was young, I dreamed about being city manager. And I was. But now the city is gone."

"I'm sorry," Lily said. She turned and looked at him. This was the first time they had talked in a while, and she missed him.

His blue eyes softly looked into hers, and she quickly averted them.

Lily looked at the planet again. "Beautiful, isn't she?"

"Yes, she is," Liam said, staring at Lily.

Lily caught him and blushed. "Why did you say that?"

"Because you are," Liam said, almost in a whisper.

"I don't think so," Lily said bashfully. She glanced down, shaking her head. But she looked up quickly, wanting to hear more.

"Why not?"

"Because only my family has ever told me that," she said in embarrassment. "Or at least, I thought they were my family."

Liam stared into Lily's silver eyes. She blushed again and looked away. She didn't know what to say.

"Why are you so shy?" Liam teased, sounding like Liam from the city. "It isn't like you to hold back. What are you thinking?"

"I used to think you were a wolf, and I was a sheep," she said.

Liam smiled as he quoted part of a poem from the forest people:

"For I'm not some wild, untamable beast,
That always sought to stray.
To spend my life with the one I love,
I would not run away."

Lily's surprise gave way to admiration as she realized Liam knew the poem. She decided to recite the poem in full, her voice taking on a gentle, poetic quality as she spoke the verses.

"I stepped on through the looking glass,
And found a glass menagerie,
Where I could look at people's lives,
Without them seeing me.

I found a major difference,
Not so subtle, in a way,
Was not whether rich or poor,
But how they spent their day.

By peeking from the other side,
I saw the lives they shared,
Their lives inside their invisible cage,
Their lives with those who cared.

For I'm not some wild, untamable beast,
That always sought to stray.
To spend my life with the one I love,
I would not run away.

I returned, back through the mirror,
Into my own home. I found,
I had everything I would ever want,

With the one I loved around."

Suddenly she realized the poem was more about her than him. She repeated the last words to herself in her family's native language. "S tou, kterou miluji kolem." Lily paused then looked at Liam. "Why do you like me?"

"I like your face—when it smiles and when it cries. I like the way you laugh at all the little things. I like how you look at me when you think I don't see you." Liam gently turned Lily's face toward his. He looked deeply into her eyes and whispered to her. "Oh, Lil, I see you."

To Lily, this was a new Liam, a braver man than she had previously known. He now spoke freely from his heart.

"If I told you that you're beautiful, would you believe me?" Liam whispered. He paused briefly for an answer as he steadied his eyes on hers. "Inside and out, you are the most beautiful person I have ever met. My heart feels empty without you, like a shell without its pearl."

Her heart melted with his words. "Why didn't you say something before?"

Liam looked down. "I specifically remember you calling me obnoxious. So now you're an angel, and I'm only this obnoxious guy."

Lily laughed. "You are obnoxious. That's true, but much more."

"Much more obnoxious?" Liam laughed and put his hand on her arm.

"No, you know what I mean. I didn't suddenly become an angel. I've always been one. I didn't know. But like you, I, too, am of flesh, and blood flows through my veins. I laugh. I cry. I yearn."

"Why did you come here tonight?" Liam asked.

"I was... I was hoping to find you."

Liam smiled, pleased with her answer.

Lily stared into his blue eyes, melting into his gaze.

Unexpectedly, Lily heard a sound in the air. "Did you hear that?"

Lily asked.

"No. I didn't hear anything."

Lily went into her spirit form and left her body. Not knowing what she might find, she drew her sword.

Damon immediately swooped down upon her like a tornado descending from a storm cloud.

"Maldorv thought me quite the coward," Damon said, "fleeing from a child. But I know you, and you are no match for me." He swirled around Lily in a dark cloud, cracking a chain of fear like lightning.

"There was a time when I made an offer for you to join us, to be our queen. But you have chosen weakness over strength. There is only one thing to do to the weak."

"You are evil," Lily said.

"Good and evil may be on opposite sides, but we are part of the same coin. You think we are so different, but we are the same."

"You're afraid of me, aren't you?" Lily said becoming angry. "That's why you fled. That's why you talk so much."

Damon let out a scream chilling Lily to her core. He changed from a shadowy specter within a cloud to his demon form. His dark, flowing robe contrasted with his pale skin. His piercing eyes, deep and dark within the hollows of his eye sockets, seared into Lily as he held his black sword above his head. He knocked Lily's sword from her hands with a quick, downward strike, and laughed with glee as she fell backward.

"Who's afraid now?" Damon asked. "You are no queen."

Quickly, he swung down at her, but she blocked his sword with her shield, hitting his head with it. He laughed it off and, feeling cocky, threw his shield aside.

She followed up with two quick punches to his face with her right fist, and he fell to his knees. With a swing of her shield, Lily knocked his sword from his hands.

Though momentarily stunned, he shook it off and dove at Lily. Suddenly, he was on top of her. With their hands grasped together, Damon forced Lily's arms over her head and head-butted her. She screamed. Ultimately, the battle between good and evil was fought one life and one death at a time. It was personal. It hurt. It made Lily scream and cry. It was real.

"I'm going to enjoy killing you," Damon said.

"Ariele, my guardian dear—be at my side," Lily cried out.

"Let her come. After I kill you, I will kill her, just like I did Uriel."

Damon punched her face with his fist. He grabbed her throat with his strong, powerful fingers, and threw her against the ground, screaming from his ghastly mouth of exposed teeth. His breath reeked of death, like rotting flesh, and his eyes were wide with hatred.

Unknowingly, he pushed Lily near her sword, and with her outstretched arm, she reached it and thrust it into his side. It was a deep wound. He fell to his knees, holding his side and as he tried to rise, he recoiled, screaming in pain.

"Finish me," he yelled at her standing over him.

"You didn't reject God because you doubted his existence. You know he exists. You rejected God because you are filled with hate. You hate everyone, including yourself. You rejected his love, and in doing so, you condemned yourself. Now you are without hope."

She looked at this creature who desperately wanted to kill her and experienced a nonhuman reaction. She became filled with pity for this lost soul. *He will never know love. There must be a better way,* she thought. In that instant, an option occurred to her. *Is it that simple?* She must try. *After all, wasn't he once an angel?*

She let her sword drop and grabbed his palms.

"Peace be with you!" she said to his surprise.

Her spirit joined with his, and as she squeezed harder, her spirit started to fill the malkyrie. She was able to push him up into a standing position. Finally, his darkness filled with light, and his form began to change as he reappeared as his original self, a beautiful angel.

"All that time spying on me, did it teach you anything? Don't you prefer a life of hope?"

Damon did not reply.

"It's your choice. I can save you," she shouted. "Let me save you."

The malkyrie sensed the difference as her light cured his wound and continued to fill him. Lily saw Damon on the precipice of conversion, but she grew weak as her spirit drained. Damon felt hope at the chance of being saved, but in the process, the malkyrie felt his guilt. The light of Lily's spirit showed Damon the truth of his evil, and he burst into a rage.

The moment for conversion passed, and the darkness returned. "You can't save me," he cried out. Finding her sword next to him, he knew what he must do and grabbed it.

Exhausted by the spirit exchange, Lily fell to her knees as Damon raised his sword. There was nothing more she could do.

Time lost all meaning. It seemed but a flash, an instant. Soon, all would be gone, Lily would die, and her soul would pass into the Nothingness. But ultimately, she had tried to share her inner light. She was not filled with hate, but compassion. She looked up at him one last time.

"Peace be with you," she said and closed her eyes.

After several moments of silence, Lily opened her eyes. Damon was gone.

Ariele appeared suddenly with her sword drawn. Seeing Lily on the ground, she asked, "Am I too late?"

"No. I'm okay."

"What happened?

"I don't know. He just left." Lily overcome by the intensity of the moment sobbed openly. "I should be dead," Lily said. "I tried to save him and then he let me go."

"You are a better angel than me. I would have shown him no

mercy. God's spirit of love flows strongly in you. Do you know what makes for a great leader?"

Lily shook her head.

"Leaders care about something greater than themselves; they care about others. You are a great leader, and many will follow you."

"Darkness cannot exist in the light," Lily said, "but light can exist in the darkness."

Archangel Raphael appeared next to Ariele.

"She's ready," Ariele said to him. "No one has ever developed in the spirit so quickly. Her time has come to fulfill her destiny."

"What is my destiny?" Lily asked through her soulful, silver eyes.

Raphael opened an ancient scroll and read it.

"After one thousand years and the return of the second sun, a twin daughter of Eden, born a virgin birth, will rise from the abyss to fight for the universe, and as queen, create a new age."

"Oh, daughter of Eden, you are my twin, and were born a virgin birth," said Ariele. "It is time to fulfill your destiny, to defeat Maldorv." The room changed instantly, and Lily found herself kneeling in front of the altar. The Sanctuary of Souls was dark, except for the blue light from the seraphs above the altar.

Michaele stood before Lily and spoke in a loud voice. "In the presence of the Council of Archangels, rise, Liele," Michaele commanded.

Lily rose and stood quietly before Michaele.

"What is it you want?" Michaele asked.

"God knows the treasure I seek," Lily said. "To love and be loved."

"Yes, even if you didn't say it, God knows the truth and all you desire. May God's love always reign within you. Liele, with your heart filled with love and your spirit of a lion, your place in the heavens will be great." Michaele raised his voice to the members of the Council of Archangels. "Who among you is her champion?"

"I am," said Archangel Ariele.

Michaele turned and bowed down before the altar. Above him, two of the blue seraphs opened the magnificent white gate to the portal of Caelum. Lily looked up anxiously, hoping to see God, or at least catch a glimpse. Though she could not see him, the portal was filled with a pure light shining down on Lily like a spotlight.

"Through the power of the Lord of Light, I, Leader of the Council of Archangels, ordain you Valiant, Knight of the Kingdom."

Lily's heart fluttered.

"This is your sworn oath and duty: You are to defend the light of God's love, even to the gate of Arderet."

"Even to the gate of Arderet," she responded.

A golden rod with a crystal globe appeared on the altar. It looked like a wand but with a heavier staff. Michaele lifted the golden rod from the altar and filled the globe with light from the portal. He closed the globe and held the golden rod in the air.

"Years ago, this rod led a persecuted tribe out of bondage. May it also help you lead those who are lost in the dark." Michael handed her the golden rod. "Rise, Valiant, Warrior Angel." The Council of Archangels rose with her.

Ariele proudly stood beside her beaming with pride for Lily.

"But I didn't win my fight with Damon."

Ariele smiled and spoke in a kind and gentle voice. "My dear child, the battle over evil will not be won by the sword but through the power of love. You demonstrate this power much more than any other angel with your incredible ability to forgive. The last battle of the apocalypse is upon us. Stand guard."

With a small gasp of air, Lily returned to her body. Liam wrapped his arms around her as she shuddered, barely able to speak. He held her tightly. Overwhelmed by what had happened, Lily cried in his arms.

"It must not be easy being an angel. Are you okay?" Liam asked.

"Yes… No. Just hold me."

Lily regained her composure but was no longer who she had been just a moment ago. Instead, she was part of an ancient order as old as the universe and had a role in its survival.

She looked again at Liam's face, and her hope dwindled that they could be together. "This isn't going to work out. Right, so—um."

"What's the problem? Did I do something wrong?"

"It isn't you. It's me."

Lily gently pushed Liam away, and as they stood apart, the expression on his face dropped. Then, not ready to give him up, she wrapped her arms around him.

"Hold me one more time, then let me forget you," Lily said, crying as she pulled tightly into him.

"No. Don't forget me. I want to lie awake at night, holding you in my arms. I'm in love with you."

"No, don't say it if you don't mean it. But, in any case, it would take a miracle for us to be together."

"'The world is full of miracles,'" Liam said, quoting Lily. "Until I met you, there was nothing in my heart."

"I'm not the one for you," Lily said as a tear rolled off her face. "Besides, many women like you. You'll be okay. You'll find someone else."

"There's no one else for me. Please don't leave me. The only thing I know that is right—is for me to be with you. Everything else is wrong. I love you, Lil."

"Oh, I have long waited to hear you say those words."

"I have never meant anything more," he said.

"For some reason, you make my heart skip, only to start beating faster and faster," Lily said, looking distraught. "But there is much more I feel when you hold me. I melt into you, and we become one. I long to be with you," she said, a tear rolling down her cheek, "and when we're apart, I miss you. I want to say something to you, but I'm afraid."

"Afraid of what?"

"My other life, where my dreams are real. It scares me."

"I don't understand. What we have is real. But if this is a dream we share, I never want to wake up." Liam put his hand around Lily's waist and pulled her into him. "I love you, Lil, and I always will." He kissed her softly.

She paused in trepidation, but as her amulet glowed within her spirit, she felt it tug at her heart. Oh, crystal of love, can you show me how true love feels? As the sensation from the amulet increased, it shared its spiritual content and merged with her spirit. Suddenly, she felt it. She felt how true love felt. It was patient and kind. It was not selfish. It felt protective, both trustworthy and trusting, and filled with hope. Above all, it felt it would endure. She realized it was the same feeling as she had for Liam.

She looked at Liam with tears on her face and resolve in her heart. About this, she was sure: She was in love. Her lips slightly parted; she moved them toward his. Pressing onto his soft, warm lips, she kissed him. Their lips pressed together as one, and for a moment, they were equals. In many ways, they couldn't have been more different. But in one way, they were the same. They were both in love. But she couldn't say it. She felt she must protect him, and she pushed him away. She knew they could not be.

"I'm sorry."

With that, she turned and left Liam alone in the dark room.

IV

Book Four

"So, when an Angel by Divine Command
With rising Tempests shakes a guilty Land—
Calm and Serene he drives the furious Blast.
And pleas'd th' Almighty's Orders to perform,
Rides in the Whirlwind and directs the Storm."
—Joseph Addison, The Campaign, 1704

62

They're Back

SKIPPER SAT IN HIS fishing shack near the mouth of the river, where it met the sea. This was his home now. There was nothing left of the city or trading post. He battered a fillet and dropped it into a pan of hot oil. The sound of frying fish broke the routine silence. Mondo came by and eagerly awaited his portion. "Hey, Mondo. Do you want some fish? If you'd ask me, man, I'd tell you what I wouldn't give for one hell of a big juicy steak." He laughed and rubbed Mondo's head as he ate his fish without further complaining.

Many months had passed since the city's destruction, and Skipper was now settled into a daily routine. Living alone, he spent his nights fishing. Every day, in the early morning, he would take his catch to the fish market in Rungoo and return home for a meal before an afternoon nap. He finished eating his fish and climbed into his hammock.

Today was like any other, another hot one, and he stared out at the water as he waited for the afternoon breeze to pick up. Through his squinting eyes, a flash caught his attention. He looked at the cloudless sky, and there it was again—a flash like a mirror. His heart skipped a beat upon seeing what he'd hoped never to see. He remembered the survivor's stories. A flying orb whisked overhead toward Rungoo and disappeared.

"Holy shit!" he shouted as he fell out of his hammock. "Dammit! They're back." He pulled his cap down and scrambled to his feet. He ran to his barge as fast as he could with Mondo by his side. Skipper thought the only chance was to evacuate immediately. But to his surprise, a large, militarized vessel blocked his barge. It was a carrier from CONRAD.

"Come with me if you want to live," said the commando on the vessel's bow with its weapon pointed at him.

"Crap," Skipper said. He threw his hands up and surrendered without a fight. The commando motioned him to climb aboard the carrier, where he saw a hooded android at the helm.

"Head to Rungoo," the android ordered. Wasting no time, they moved swiftly toward the fishing village. Upon arriving, they spotted an orb hovering above. "Take it out," the android ordered.

The orb was destroyed in a loud blast with a single shot from the carrier's gun. The other villagers heard the blast and came running from their homes. To their surprise, they saw Skipper on the carrier. "It was an orb!" Skipper said. "Just like the ones which destroyed the city."

The crowd gasped as the hooded android stepped forward. Only the village leader was brave enough to approach him. "G'day. They call me Jim."

The android removed his hood.

"Crikey," Jim said.

"Crap," said Skipper. "It's that damn assassin."

"It's good to see you as well," said Caleb as he changed into his Aussie boy form.

"You're that shonky bloke," Jim said recognizing him.

"I come as a friend."

"Why did you come back, and where the hell are the others?" Skipper asked. His expression changed from annoyance to anger as a sudden realization came to his mind.

"Did you kill them?"

"After all this time, you haven't changed," Caleb said with a partial smile. "There's no time for this. My purpose is to warn that you are not safe. Just as The Sentinel was responsible for the city's destruction, his orders will assure the destruction of all humankind, including this village."

Caleb pointed at another scout as the crowd sought cover. The commando fired his cannon and blew it out of the sky.

"That was a bloody good shot from your ball buster," Jim said.

"His name is Roimh."

Venky rose and spoke from the back of the crowd. "We were warned before, not so long ago. This time we must not hesitate. What can we do? They'll be back to destroy us all."

Several in the crowd murmured in agreement but soon cries of fear were heard as another orb appeared over the fishing village. Roimh fired at it. It was a direct hit.

As the blast settled, Caleb said, "There's no doubt they will continue to return. You need to abandon the village immediately. Come with me. I will protect you until it's safe for you to return home."

"What's the story? Why are you helping us?" Jim asked.

"Because this is what Lily would do," answered Caleb. "Will you come with me?"

"Did Lily send you?" asked Venky.

"Yes," Caleb lied.

"I knew she would come back for us," said Venky.

Skipper nodded. "What do you think, Jim?" He said to his old friend joining him at his side.

"Well, maties," Jim said, "I think it's deffo time to bail." He looked at Skipper. "Let's get the hell out of here." Jim said imitating Skipper's voice and mannerisms.

"Hell yeah," Skipper said. "I'm not waiting for them flying shitheads to return and finish me off."

"Then tell your story walkin,' cause it's time to hit the frog and toad," Jim said.

The villagers quickly gathered what they held most dear, their children, then quickly boarded. Skipper helped load them onto the carrier. Within minutes, they departed. They left everything, including Skipper's barge.

Skipper stood at the back of the carrier as the vessel started across the ocean waters. With the coast diminishing on the horizon, a large cloud rose over Rungoo. It glowed red in the setting sun. The last human settlement on Earth was no more.

Jim began to chant with his sheila at his side. It was a song about his land, about his people. It was the song of Rungoo, which was no more.

The carrier's cover closed, and the engines rotated from a hover position to a horizontal one. With a loud boom, the vessel went supersonic. They crossed the ocean and returned to the ruins of the old capital city in just a few hours. As the passengers and their children climbed out of the carrier, Skipper searched through the rubble-filled landscape. He stopped for a moment to watch a mother help her child. A sudden pang of regret stabbed his heart, as he had no wife or children.

"What's the John Dory?" Jim asked Roimh. "Why are we here?"

"To keep you close so we can protect you."

Skipper looked at the nearby ruins. Within the rubble stood an old man and a blue heeler, along with more refugees from the other village.

"Who are they?" asked Skipper.

"We have gathered all we could find."

'This is where we will make our final stand," said Caleb.

"My whole life has been a bit of a dog's breakfast. So, I know when life gives you dung, it's time to throw a stink. I'm with you, mate."

"Stay here, I'm going to scout the surrounding area." Caleb turned invisible and was gone.

Roimh climbed a nearby rise, and Skipper and Jim followed. As the snow started to fall, it dusted the landscape with a light powder. The climb was steep and there was no trail, but they reached the top in short time. From there, Skipper could see for quite a distance. There was a pond and the remains of a once-great mall. The ruins looked medieval in the snow, like remnants of a long-lost age.

63

The Lion of God

LILY PULLED HER PILLOW to her chest and threw herself onto her bed. *What just happened? I want my destiny to be with Liam.* With the stars on her monitor, Lily cried into her pillow and sobbed longingly.

"Why?" Lily cried out as she gasped for breath.

Being a valiant overwhelmed her as she realized the tremendous responsibility. *I did not seek this. I did not ask for it.* Her thoughts turned toward Liam again, and she grabbed her pillow and screamed into it. Yet even there in her private quarters, she found no solace. Her destiny was upon her. With her eyes open wide, she experienced another vision.

From the forever distance of space to the immediacy of the here and now, drifted a sound within the silence. From before time, it traveled a path with no beginning and no end.

When it reached Lily, it surrounded her and spoke to her. "Be strong and courageous, for God is with you."

A relatively young star appeared in the darkness of space. It was her sun. Just a few billion years old, it had seen many civilizations rise and fall. Then she saw another sun—smaller and much older. And in the naked light, Lily saw a dark cloud swirling like a great storm. It was Maldorv. Behind him, Lily could see the open gate of Arderet, where the souls of the lost wailed in the dark. Lily, found herself, surrounded by many malkyries. She drew her sword and prepared to engage them in battle, but they ignored her. They proceeded through space and encircled a blue planet. Without hesitation the legion of malkyries attacked the planet.

Lily awoke from her vision and sat up quickly in her bed. She had recognized the blue planet. *He intends to destroy them. But it's not Earth. It's Trhon.* All along, she had thought the last battle of Armageddon would be on Earth. Her eyes looked fierce, and her face flushed. The forces of evil were strong, yet Lily wasn't afraid. She knew who she was—a valiant of God. Filled with faith and the spirit of goodness, Lily changed into her ethereal form and fearlessly roared like a lion.

"I will save them," she shouted as she charged into the darkness.

Just outside Earth's atmosphere, Raphael waited with his legion of angels, anticipating Maldorv's attack on Earth.

Lily saw them and waved her arms.

"No. No," she yelled at Raphael. "You must go back."

"What?"

"You have to go back," Lily said in a loud and powerful voice. "Maldorv isn't coming to Earth. He's going to attack Trhon. Defend Trhon."

"Are you coming?" asked Raphael.

Lily looked at the rod in her hand with its globe slightly glowing.

"No. My destiny is calling. I know where I must go. Tell me, where is the portal to Arderet?"

Raphael was shocked.

"You cannot go. It's a suicide mission."

"Where is it? Tell me."

"Go away from the light to where it is always dark. In the darkness, you will find it. It's a place you have been to before. Not only was the Covenant's reactor core used to imprison Maldorv, but the Covenant herself was used to block the entrance to Arderet, for in the abyss below the docking station is its portal."

"Oh, no. It's all my fault. I unleashed this great evil and opened the portal to Arderet."

"No, Lily. You must not think that. You are playing a role which was predestined. Finish your destiny. You are good. You are an instrument of God's light. You were meant to find the Covenant. You were meant to use it as a means of escape.

"I hope so," Lily said. Raphael handed her a sword. But she lifted her golden rod. "This is all I need."

"May the light of God be with you," Raphael said.

Lily stared down at the Earth, then disappeared.

64

Death Comes for Everyone

ETHAN AND KALI HID beneath the branches of a massive fallen tree. Ethan knew the rotting biomass would mask their infrared signature from a passing scout. It was a tense moment, but they remained undiscovered as the scout flew by. After it had passed, Kali's eyes continued to nervously scan the sky. Ethan saw her fear and realized their peaceful life was shattered. Her nightmare had returned, and they were defenseless, lacking any weapons.

Ethan signed for Kali to stay put, then quietly moved away, disappearing into the surrounding wood. As the snowflakes began to fall, Ethan's senses were on high alert. He heard a sound. It was as though someone was moving through the wood. In response, Ethan quickly ducked behind a large tree and searched a nearby hillside from where the sound came.

At first, he saw nothing but then noticed something peculiar. The snowflakes revealed the outline of the unseen figure and what was previously invisible, now became visible in the wood.

No, it can't be. Can it? Ethan couldn't believe his eyes as he recognized a familiar shape.

"Caleb? Is that you?" he said as he stepped from behind the tree.

He searched through the snow as he called out again, "Caleb?"

Nothing. Only wishful thinking, he thought. But he did not give up hope so easily and he searched for footprints.

From behind him, he felt the inhuman strength of a mighty grip.

"You're hurting me!" Ethan cried out in pain as he squirmed in the grasp of a shimmering distortion. The shape relaxed its grip and changed form. The android's body appeared, showing the scrape marks from the crash.

"Caleb! It's good to see you."

"No time to talk—let's go," said Caleb.

Caleb looked up at the sky. "It's not safe here. You must come with me."

"Wait. We need to get Kali."

"Kali?"

"Yes, my wife. Also, please change your appearance. I don't want you to scare her."

As Ethan led the way back, Caleb changed into his teenage boy form, wearing the native garb of the Outback. After a short distance, Ethan signaled for Caleb to stop. He turned and retrieved Kali from her hiding place.

"Kali, this is Caleb," Ethan signed.

Caleb paused for a moment to access the archives.

"It is nice to meet you, Kali," Caleb signed back. "It is good you were not alone," Caleb said to Ethan. Caleb understood what it was to be alone. "I was lost for a long time. It was an experience my learning algorithm will never forget."

Suddenly, a scout appeared.

Caleb fired his blaster at a nearby tree. Shards of wood and broken branches scattered in a burst of sound and motion. The explosion drew the scout's attention away from them.

"Run," Caleb said.

"Well, I'll be damned," Skipper said with Mondo sitting by his side.

Down near the pond, through the light snowfall, he saw a young woman hurrying through the wood. It was Kali wearing Ethan's black shirt. A young man closely followed her. Behind him was a familiar figure. It was Caleb.

Skipper called out, "Hey, over here—"

Roimh put his hand over Skipper's mouth and pulled him to the ground.

"Scouts," Roimh whispered then pointed at a scout in the distance.

Skipper nodded then his heart jumped in his chest as he saw the young woman trip and fall to the ground. He anxiously waited for her to get up.

"Shit," Skipper yelled. He broke out of Roimh's grasp and crossed an open field, darting through the undergrowth to where Kali lay. Mondo and Jim followed. After a moment Roimh also ran with them.

"Come with me, missy," Skipper said, grabbing Kali's arm.

Roimh now arrived and looked down upon Kali with its scanning red eyes.

Ethan saw the ominous commando and panicked. He picked up a large branch and charged Roimh, breaking it over Roimh's black armor.

"Whoa. He's a friend," Caleb said. "It's okay." He has your learning algorithm."

Ethan backed down, somewhat in surprise, but continued watching the commando carefully.

A mirror-like reflection startled them as Mondo started to bark loudly at an orb. Roimh quickly pulled his weapon. Fortunately, the commando's blaster was more powerful than the weapons of the city guards, and Roimh promptly destroyed the scout.

"Come this way," Jim yelled from the nearby cover of some trees. "We have to get back to the ruins."

"Let's go," Skipper yelled as he took off running.

"Wait," called out Ethan. "She can't run that fast."

"What's wrong with her?"

"She's with child."

Roimh reached to pick her up, but her face filled with panic at the approach of the commando, and she squirmed away.

"Step the hell aside," Skipper said to the droid as he quickly picked Kali up and ran with all his might.

"Come on," Jim called out. "Run faster."

Another scout appeared. Caleb scanned Roimh's weapon and upgraded his own. He lifted his new blaster at the end of his arm, but he had taken too long. The scout was gone.

Skipper panted, out of breath. He placed Kali on the ground and sat next to her. She glanced all around, nervously scanning the sky. Suddenly, her face filled with panic.

"What's wrong, girl?"

Skipper looked up and saw the scout hovering over them.

"Holy crap," he said. He thought of running but instantly grabbed Mondo and turned towards Kali, covering them with his body. A second later, a blast hit their spot.

Caleb took out the scout, but it was too late. The damage was done. He looked at Skipper lying on the ground amidst the red snow.

"Kali!" Ethan yelled running to them.

"Shit, shit, shit!" Ethan shouted as Mondo whimpered by Skipper's side.

Kali crawled free and knelt by Skipper. He had protected her from the blast. "Help him," she signed to Caleb.

Caleb scanned Skipper. His back was charred, a fatal injury itself, but he also had multiple other injuries. The blast had broken his spine in several places, and he bled internally from numerous ruptures. Caleb carefully turned him over. "Just hang on, Skipper. I'm going to get you out of here. Just hang on. You're going to be alright."

"You lie like shit. I can't feel anything. It's the end for me. Don't worry about me. Take care of her."

Caleb reached to lift him.

"Let me be, man," he shouted. "Take care of the girl. Get her out of here."

"You once pulled me out of the city dump. Now I'm going to carry you to safety. Hang on."

Skipper spat up blood, but his face calmed as a sly smile crossed his face. "You're all right for a damn android, but you should say something like, 'Hang on, you fuckin' bastard.'" His smile lingered as his eyes glazed over.

"Skipper?" Caleb called out. "Hang on—hang on, you fuckin' bastard."

Skipper was gone. He had lived his life alone, but he left the world protecting the child he never had.

Caleb's processing stuttered as he became overwhelmed by a sense of loss. Skipper was dead and deep emotions of sorrow and sadness flooded over him.

Kali again pointed at the sky with her eyes wide with fear.

Caleb didn't need to look. He could see the scout in the sky behind him. He reversed his projection and faced the scout without turning. He pulled the trigger, and the scout exploded.

It was all too fast. Caleb wished the scout could have suffered a painful death. He wished it had flesh to burn and organs to burst. He wanted to see it bleed, just as Skipper had. For the first time, he hated his own kind.

"You got him," Jim said with excitement then scrambled over and saw his old friend lying on the ground.

"I'm afraid he's gone," Jim said with a sad expression. He softly placed his hand on Skipper then urged Caleb to leave. "Hurry, let's go," Jim said. Caleb let go of Skipper and lifting Kali he followed Jim through the wood. With a quick glance back, Caleb called for Mondo to follow but Mondo remained loyal. He would not leave Skipper's side.

In a blur, they sprinted, unconcerned with how much noise they made. It was only a matter of time before they were detected. From across a small clearing, a squad of commandos opened fire. Blaster fire filled the air. Roimh returned fire and held them back while the others reached the ruins where Venky and the other survivors hid. A commando appeared from behind a tree, and Roimh shot him. To everyone's surprise, Ethan ran out toward the downed commando.

"What are you doing?" Roimh called out.

Ethan returned a few seconds later with a smile and two weapons. He was no longer a boy needing rescue. Now brave and courageous, he was a man others could depend on for help. He handed Jim a weapon.

"Thanks, mate," Jim said. Together, they turned and ran into the shelter of the ruins.

Having heard no activity for several minutes, Jim built up his nerve and peeked out from his hiding place. He faked calm but then let the situation get the better of his nerves. "We're surrounded, mates," Jim shouted to the others. "There's no way out. We're trapped."

"We're not going to make it," a small boy from Rungoo cried out.

Jim realized the example he had set by showing his own fear and was embarrassed by his cowardice. He needed to remedy that and set a better example.

"Hey, put a sock in it," said Jim. "Of course, we'll make it. If our ancestors could survive the apocalypse, we can survive this."

Kali appeared from an opening in the rubble. "Follow me," Kali signed.

Ethan nodded and called out to the others to follow him further into the ruins and the tunnels below.

"Told you, birrani," Jim said with a lizard-like smile to the sobbing boy.

Through the underground passageways, Kali led them until she stopped at the bottom of two ladders. She put her finger on her lips and signaled to everyone to be quiet. "The computer room is up this ladder," she signed to Ethan. "I'll take care of the others."

"Thank you," Ethan signed. "They take their orders from here. Don't worry. I'll shut it down." Wanting to be the man he thought Kali deserved, he forced a brave face.

"If I don't come back," Ethan signed. Kali put her hands over his hands and stopped him from signing. Ethan blushed and a tear formed in his eye, in that moment, he showed Kali the caring man he had become. In what were possibly their last words left unsaid; she knew that he loved her. She rushed to give him a farewell kiss, then quickly turned, hiding her face.

Caleb and Roimh climbed the ladder before him. As Ethan followed, he gave Kali a final glance. She stood at the bottom of the ladder with her hand on her belly, her stoic expression trying in vain to disguise her true emotions. She had experienced death too many times and knew death came for everyone. Though she feared for Ethan, she dared not show it. Ethan knew she loved him. That was why she was still following him with her eyes. He understood. He understood because he loved her too.

"I'm coming as well, mate," Jim whispered as he climbed the ladder.

Venky stayed with Kali and the other survivors. He would have gone but he knew he would be more of a hindrance than help. Kali remained momentarily at the ladder's base, then turned, and led the remaining humans on Earth to a safer location.

65

The Gate of Arderet

LILY RETURNED TO HER sister's side. "Ema," she called out. "I know my destiny."

Ema turned away from the monitor on the bridge, shocked by the sudden appearance of Lily in her angel form. "Lily. You startled me."

"I know my destiny. I must go to Arderet and free the lost souls."

"What? No, I need you here."

"For freedom to survive, I must defeat the ethereal forces of evil. I do this for both Trhon and Earth. I do this for all people. I also know your destiny. Humankind is your responsibility. You must save humankind."

"I'm afraid," said Ema.

"I am too," replied Lily. "If this is the last we ever see of each other, know that I am proud of you."

Ema's eyes swelled with tears as she hugged her sister. "I love you," Ema said in Lily's ear and with that Lily disappeared.

Lily lingered at the edge of the abyss. The ship that had once blocked passage to the portal was gone and the rising heat had killed the glowworms. The blue luminescence no longer graced the area over the abyss, instead it glowed a vibrant crimson. Lily looked down into the deep. A swirling red light now nearly filled the entirety of the abyss radiating with the heat of an inferno. It was the portal to Arderet. The staircase was gone, and the walls of the abyss were now shear as if scraped smooth. There was only one way down.

"What am I doing? Am I crazy?" she said aloud to herself. "No. I better not answer that." She closed her eyes and stepped over the edge.

Lily's screams echoed through the abyss as she descended into the portal to Arderet. The sensation of falling, her greatest fear, consumed her, and her heart pounded with unrelenting terror. The rush of air and the sheer velocity of her descent left her breathless.

As she plummeted through the portal, the searing red light engulfed her, causing intense pain like fire. She passed through, crashing onto the other side, the spiritual equivalent of a body crashing onto rocks at the bottom of a cliff. The Cauldron of Arderet subjected her to torment surpassing any physical pain. Everything was in slow motion as she entered another dimension of time. She felt every bone in her body shatter and pierce her organs. Her ethereal senses were inundated with the overwhelming agony of a thousand shards of broken bones. Then she felt her blood exploding from her body.

In that place, where suffering reigned and hope was extinguished, she believed there was no possibility of survival. Yet, when she rose to her feet, she discovered she was unharmed. The Cauldron of Arderet was all about prolonging torture.

She now found herself in the heart of Arderet, a realm of unfathomable darkness where sanity was vanquished, and the sane became insane. Her eyes could not see in the total darkness, but with her sixth sense, she sensed her surroundings. Soon, her perception strengthened as she felt the glow of a hot sky. Then, as the dark outline of shapes formed to an edge, she realized her sixth sense allowed her to see in the dark. She took a step and moved forward through the treacherous terrain.

As she descended a valley, the shadow of death weighed heavily like a dark fog hanging low in the sky. It felt like an oppressive weight on her shoulders, a spiritual burden that seemed to grow heavier with each step. Lily whispered an ancient Psalm as she held her golden rod tightly in her hand.

"Though I walk through the valley of the shadow of death, I shall fear no evil, for Thou art with me; Thy rod and thy staff, they comfort me."

She saw the outline of a structure and headed toward it. Soon, an acrid wind began to blow, and the fog thinned enough to reveal the entire valley with a great stone wall appearing amid the misty drifts. The structure was massive and loomed over the blackened landscape. There was no road or path, only a black, inky substance covered the rocky ground. Great evil left a mark, a darkness that lingered after the original evil had passed. The dark ink was the concentration of this evil to such a great extent it turned into a tar-like substance. It was the sludge of the cauldron, where the souls of the irredeemably damned lost their individuality and became one with the very secretion of evil. The black ink was comprised of the souls who willingly joined the evil, not the imprisoned souls who still had a lingering hope of rescue.

Surrounded by this landscape, her white wings were easy to spot, but there was nowhere to hide. Only the fog gave cover. She grasped her golden rod and proceeded to walk over the inky substance. As she passed, it reached up like grabbing hands. Soon, portions of her white robe darkened. However, with firm resolve she continued down the valley.

The ink and the fog went on forever, with each bank of fog leading to yet another, an endless miasma—a poisonous effluvia from putrescent matter, an overwhelming smell of death. Everything disappeared within the fog, which sporadically revealed glimpses of imaginary monsters. Still, she trudged onward. Through row after row of the heavy fog she persevered, only for another fog bank to appear. Then, after what seemed like hours, she saw the outline of a gate.

Is this just my imagination? she wondered.

Lily stood before the imposing black gate of Arderet, her determination rewarded. However, the massive gate now loomed over her like an insurmountable obstacle. She had come so far, and she couldn't allow herself to be deterred by this final challenge. With renewed resolve, she examined the gate more closely. The formidable structure stood defiantly, and she soon realized it was not meant to deter entry but rather to prevent escape. Lily took a deep breath and reached out with her golden rod. As she concentrated, a faint, ethereal light began to emanate from the globe at the end of her rod. She lifted her rod higher as she whispered intently, calling on the divine forces. "Virtus lucis Dei." "Virtus lucis Dei," she repeated. The gate started to tremble; its colossal form quivered with an otherworldly energy. She repeated the phrase louder until she was shouting the words. "Virtus lucis Dei."

The massive gate began to creak and groan, slowly yielding to the power of the light. Inch by inch, it opened enough to enter, revealing the fiery landscape of the prison beyond.

Lily had opened the gate of Arderet. Before her, the realm of darkness and her destiny awaited. A fluttering sound flew through the opening and passed over her head. She ducked, then dodged again as the fluttering sound returned. Within a swirl of mist, she could see a silhouette of a bird with feathers made of shadows.

"No. You don't want to enter," said the bird. "Close it while you can."

"I must. It's my destiny."

"No. Leave back through the open portal. Go before the King of Darkness finds you in his kingdom. Go now!"

Something wrapped around her feet, and she fell to the black ground. It pulled her back across the bridge and away some distance.

As she struggled, she became covered in black ink. She no longer stood out. With her gown now black, she was one with the ground.

"I can't move. I'm trapped," Lily cried out.

"Yes," said the bird. "And soon you will be trapped forever in a deathbed of endless nightmares."

The bird flew down by Lily's side, disturbing the mist surrounding her.

"Get up. Get up now before it's too late," the shadowy bird anxiously cried.

But Lily could not move. She could not flee, and a sense of overwhelming panic filled her heart. "I can't," she said with pleading eyes, as if the bird could help her.

"It's too late. Someone is coming." A tremendous screeching sound could be heard as the gate opened fully on its rusted hinges. "He's here. Hide." The bird cried out one last warning and took flight. The gate was thrown open with great force, and a black cloud burst out from within. It was filled with intense heat. The cloud surrounded her, and she felt as though her blood was boiling within the chambers of her heart. Excruciating pain filled her innermost parts.

Am I dead? Is this what death feels like? No, this must be a dream. It can't be real. Through pursed lips, she screamed a silent scream that echoed inside her head.

"Stay still," Damon said. He loosened the chain of fear from around her then quickly grabbed her and pushed her behind a large rock. "Stay down. Stay quiet."

Unknown to her, Maldorv had passed, but she went undiscovered, thanks to her captor. She was nearly impossible to detect, with her clothes covered in the black inky substance. Only exposed areas of her flesh could be seen. Her skin repelled the black substance.

"It's you," Lily said, recognizing Damon.

"What are you doing here? Never mind. Shut up and listen. Can't you see Maldorv and the army of the malkyries have gathered at the gate of Arderet?"

Maldorv rode the Black Dragon within a dark cloud swirling in a great wind. All around him, malkyries in dragon and demon form, swarmed in the air like a swarm of mad bees. Then he began to speak from within the swirling cloud. "Listen...to me," he yelled over the raucous mob. "The time...for our revenge...is now," Maldorv cried out. "For... vengeance... is mine." The malkyries lifted their black swords and cheered

"We...cannot lose, for Arderet is...overflowing...with the souls from the apocalypse. I am more powerful...than ever." Lightning filled the cloud as he spoke with a louder and louder voice. "You all...will feel...my power. Their forces...are split. They thought...I would finish off... Earth, but Earth...is already...finished. We...will go...to Trhon. We...will attack. We...will overwhelm them. I...will be victorious."

"Come forth," Maldorv said, ordering his legion of malkyries out of Arderet. "The time...has come...for the final battle. Come...forth."

Through the gateway of Arderet went the malkyries. They left behind the vast multitudes of the damned, the souls that had been captured by Maldorv. A great chain shackled them, preventing their escape. Maldorv did not trust them. He carried as much of their power as he could and left them chained in misery. Following their dark lord, the malkyries traveled through the midnight waters of space like a great serpent moving at a tremendous speed.

"Again, what are you doing here?" Damon said.

"I won't answer you until you first show me the lost souls."

"Have you got a mirror?" he said with a smirk.

Lily did not blink. Her gaze was serious.

"You really are crazy," he said, shaking his head. "All right, follow me."

Damon entered the abandoned gate. Lily followed and found

herself in a grand hallway with giant statues lining both sides. They represented the lineage of the kings of Arderet. She first stared at Ardeo, the Serpent King. Slowly, she walked past the gaze of the dragon kings until she came to Maldorv's thrown; above, the Black Dragon extended its wings over the great hall; below, under the tips of his wings, a massive obsidian throne sat empty. Jagged shards extended from it. Lily carefully passed by and continued down the hallway to an internal courtyard. She stared into the prison yard extending endlessly before her.

"Where are the lost souls?" Lily asked.

"They're all around you."

Lily looked through the dark. To the naked eye, they were invisible, and Arderet seemed empty, but with her sixth sense, she could see them. Before her, she saw multitudes of suffering human souls covered in the filth and guilt of their sins. They cried out the relentless screams of the forsaken—miserable, defeated, and hopeless. She stood staring out at them as Damon approached from behind and stood beside her. The souls were tied with a chain of fear keeping them in perpetual torment. There were millions upon millions of them.

"Have they been left unguarded? Where's the guard?"

"That would be me. I'm the guard. That was my reward," he said, looking around in disgust. "Some reward—Maldorv made me the guard of the gate of Arderet. I was the keeper of the keep for a thousand years. Now, I will be guard of the gate of Arderet for the rest of eternity." Damon shook his head in frustration. "No matter— no one can leave with these chains."

Lily looked at the great chain that imprisoned the souls. It went from soul to soul, shackling their ankles one to another. They could move only a few inches at a time until they were forced back to where they began. Lily felt pity for them.

"Now tell me. What are you doing here?"

"I'm here to bring a light into the dark, a torch to show the way home, a lighthouse in the storm of despair."

"Yeah, right," he said with a smirk. "Don't you know where you are?" He shook his head. "You're one crazy bitch. There is nothing for you here but death."

66

Now or Never

EMA SAT AT THE bridge, with her eyes fixed on the monitor with the ship now back at the moon. The responsibility of her assignment weighed heavily on her shoulders. She took her duties seriously, knowing the safety and well-being of humankind depended on her actions.

But beneath her dedication, there was an underlying fear. The thought of facing an unsurmountable enemy sent shivers down her spine. *What if I can't handle it? What if I let everyone down, especially Lily, who trusts me implicitly? What if we all die?*

Time did not care about Ema's emotions or feelings. It had but one duty and it performed it without fail. Tick went the clock of time.

"A satellite blast has been detected in the remains of the old capital city," announced the Covenant. Another satellite blast appeared on the monitor as it switched to that location.

"Can you hear me?" came a hushed voice over the static on the receiver.

"Ema here."

"This is Caleb," the voice said. "I'm in CONRAD."

"Glad to hear your voice, Caleb. We now have your coordinates."

"The others are under attack on the outskirts of the ruins."

"Which others?"

"Ethan—" The transmission filled with static. "I'm going to—" More static.

The communication channel went silent.

"Hang on. We're coming for you. Can you hear me?"

There was no response.

"It's now or never," Ema said to those on the bridge. "That satellite will kill them all. Luca, launch the Shooting Stars," she commanded over her scanner.

"Aye, aye, Captain," Luca said.

The pilots were on standby in the spaceport galley and rushed to their cockpits.

"God protect you," Ema said as Luca settled in the cockpit and checked over his instrument panel. "All Shooting Stars are armed, all systems are ready," said the maintenance officer."

"Bay doors are open. Cleared for takeoff," announced the operations officer.

"Let's go save them," Luca called out to the other pilots. "With the light of an angel!"

"With the light of an angel," the pilots said in unison.

They left in a predefined launch sequence, with Luca leading the way. Once in open space, they engaged their space drive, and all four ships arrived, side-by-side, an instant later in Earth's upper atmosphere. Before them was the satellite. Armed and ready to go, all four ships immediately fired a plasma ball. The four balls of light traveled the short distance converging on the satellite. The satellite disappeared in a large explosion.

"That was for the shuttle," said Luca as he turned and led his team to the surface.

"It's time to kick ass!" Luca yelled.

As they appeared in the sky above CONRAD, they were soon met by a barrage of hypersonic missiles. Though technologically inferior the rockets were a real threat if they could make impact. But with the maneuverability of the Shooting Stars, they had the advantage.

"Ice Man and Vanya," Luca said, "you go left. Red Baron and I will go right."

Ice Man approached the first missile from the side and locked in on it. The Shooting Star fired a burst of rounds, and the rocket was destroyed. "Got one!" said Liam.

Red Baron was next to his missile. His first burst missed, but he quickly reversed the cannons and hit the target on the second burst. "Joseph here. Got another. This is fun!"

But just as they gained confidence, Vanya reached hers late, and it split into dozens of smaller projectiles. She fired wildly, blasting a path through. As she emerged through the flames, Liam cheered.

"Way to go," Liam yelled. Inadvertently, he flew across Vanya's line of sight. She reacted out of instinct. Thinking Liam was an enemy ship, she quickly fired two plasma balls. They were direct hits.

"Oh, shit. What was that?" Liam said. The deflection of the first plasma ball drained his ship's shields, allowing the second hit to deliver significant damage. His panel lit up with numerous alarms as fire burned out of control in his reactor drive. In a flash, the ship shuddered with an internal explosion.

"Shit, shit, shit," Liam yelled out. "This is Star 2. I've been hit."

Emergency systems failed then shut down. Liam manually triggered the ship's fire system. But it was too little too late. He could not contain the spreading fire. More warnings flashed on his control panel as the ship continued to shudder violently. There was little he could do. His space drive was compromised. Liam smiled slightly as he imagined seeing Lily.

I guess it wasn't our destiny, he thought.

The ship exploded in a flash of light like an exploding star.

"No!" Vanya cried out. "What have I done? What have I done?"

Through her grief, she forced herself to maintain focus. She would mourn later. Now wasn't the time. She held back her tears and fired a burst of rounds at another missile. "Take that!" she yelled as another rocket exploded.

Moments later, Luca saw a rocket coming in fast, as it split into a dozen projectiles he executed a defensive maneuver. Inadvertently, he turned into one of them and it exploded on his side. He cleared several panel alarms as he saw another missile tracking his tail. He reversed thrusters and came about. Pushing his throttle forward, he approached the missile from the rear. Luca quickly worked the controls, but the ship would not lock in on the target.

"This is Star 1. I've been hit and I'm switching to manual control."

He manually lined up with the missile's path. As his holographic panel flickered, he pulled the trigger then held his breath. A moment later he disappeared into the ball of the explosion.

"Star 1 are you there? Vanya said as she waited through the anxious moment. "Luca?"

"I'm good," Luca said as he flew through the blast.

"Thank God," came Vanya's voice.

"Thank God," whispered Ema.

"Liam's dead," Vanya cried out. "I killed him."

Luca held back his emotions. "Hang tough, Star 3. The mission's not over."

"Covenant, this is Star 1. Skies are clear. "Ema, we own the skies."

"Go pick up the survivors," Ema said.

"Aye, aye, Captain." Luca headed toward the surface with Joseph and Vanya on his wings.

67

The Power in her Hands

CALEB OPENED THE FLOOR panel and climbed into the computer room with his weapon drawn. Moments later, Roimh cautiously peeked into the room and saw Caleb waving him in. Two system droids rose from their stations. Caleb shot them as Roimh headed up a short flight of stairs toward a door. As Roimh reached the door, it opened. A commando entered the room and saw Caleb standing over the two downed droids. Roimh shot him, and his body fell down the stairway. Realizing more would come; he closed the door and blasted the lock shut.

"That won't hold them long," Roimh said to Caleb.

Caleb called out to Ethan, who was waiting at the top of the ladder. "Come on in. It's all clear. You don't have much time to disable the weapons systems."

Unable to calm herself, Kali's thoughts swarmed in her mind. She could not stop thinking about what would happen if she lost Ethan. *He's my life. I don't want to live without him.* She paced nervously, then decided to act on her own. She didn't bother to tell anyone. In any case, no one else knew how to sign. She returned to the ladders and reached for the first rung to the command center. Soon she completed her ascent and entered a utility closet. There, she waited silently by the door, listening to the sounds inside the room. She could hear someone talking. As she cracked open the door, she saw The Sentinel.

Blaster shots could be heard coming from below in the computer room.

"Sir, we have intruders," a commando announced.

"Take a squad of commandos and kill them."

"Yes, sir."

"The enemy spacecraft have survived the missile attack," said another commando at the monitor.

"Use the satellite."

"Sir, the satellite is not accepting my commands."

"Reload the missiles."

"By your command."

As laser blasts sounded on the computer room door, Ethan worked feverishly on a control panel. "There's not a security system that ever existed I can't break into," he said proudly.

Jim, standing nearby, covered Ethan. "Cocky, kid," he said with a glad smile.

A series of loud blasts struck the door. "The door's holding, but it won't last much longer," Roimh said.

Seeing Roimh reminded Ethan of Central Control. "That's it," he said. "They used the satellite to upload the copy of Central Control." He quickly tried another approach and accessed the command log from the upload. Encrypted in the command sequence was the access code.

"Found it," Ethan said. He had quickly found a de-encryption program that he had written when he was five. Moments later, he yelled out with excitement. "That was easy." He looked at the downed system droid lying on the floor next to him, "Thanks for loading the archives." Ethan turned to Jim with a smile. "I've got control over their weapons systems."

The Sentinel stood near Kali on the other side of the door. She could smell his electronic circuits. They smelled of ozone, like the sky during a lightning storm. Fear filled her as suddenly, the moment to act was upon her. She imagined reaching out and grabbing the power supply. But her fear stopped her. She started to tremble. She couldn't breathe. *Why am I such a coward? Why am I so afraid to die? He killed my parents, my brother, Babi, and many others. Too many have died. I must do it for their sake. I must do it for Ethan's sake.*

Her fear made her delay too long, and The Sentinel moved away. She would have to wait till he came near again. *I'll do it when he returns.* She felt relieved by her restored resolve, yet still, she trembled. She held herself tightly but to no avail.

I am a coward. Kali thought. *My brother was brave. Skipper was brave.*

After a few moments, The Sentinel started to pace back and forth. She held her breath. Tiny beads of perspiration formed on her upper lip. Her heart leapt in her chest. *Can he hear it pounding?*

"Sir, the missiles have been reloaded."

"Activate ground radar systems and locate targets. Wait till they land then fire when ready."

With a loud explosion, the door was blasted off its hinges and fell into the room.

"They've broken through," Roimh yelled as he scrambled down the stairway to join the others. Together, they aimed their weapons at the doorway.

As the first commando entered, Caleb yelled, "Fire." He and the others lit up the doorway with blaster fire. The commandos retreated, giving a temporary reprieve. "We can't hold the room," Caleb said to Ethan. "Save yourself. Go back down the ladder."

Ethan knew what he had to do. Noticing the activity with the missile launchers, he instantly made his decision. He thought briefly of Kali as he overrode the strike coordinates and took control of the missiles. He would take out the command center and computer room. *At least she'll be saved,* he thought. *She'll be safe in the tunnels.*

"Farewell, my friends," Ethan said not knowing Kali was in the command center above him. He knew this would mean the death of the others in the computer room. He knew that this would mean his own death.

The Sentinel continued pacing. Soon, he would be near her again. She had to do it this time. The Sentinel stopped at the door to the utility closet and turned around, his back to her, only inches away. Gently, she opened the door slightly and moved her hand slowly toward The Sentinel. She would need to grab the power supply quickly and hang onto it tightly.

The Sentinel started to move away. It was now or never. With a sudden movement, Kali surged into action. She threw herself around him and grabbed the power supply with her hand. The Sentinel immediately reacted. Its arm struck her forcefully, hurtling her across the chamber, and a pain-filled cry escaped her lips.

The commandos charged through the computer room. "Fire at will," Caleb shouted. Amid a storm of blaster fire, Roimh yelled out a command. "Stand down. Stand down. I command you." A fifth red LED lit up in Roimh's eye slot as the commandos immediately lowered their weapons.

"By your command," said the commandos in unison as they stopped firing and put their weapons at their side. They all had received the notification of Roimh's promotion simultaneously.

"What just happened?" Ethan asked, stunned by the sudden turn of events.

"With The Sentinel out of commission, I am now the commanding officer," Roimh said.

Ethan looked shocked. He had just entered the new coordinates, and he turned and dove at the panel pressing the self-destruct button. The sound of the missiles exploding in the air above the command center could be heard.

"Wow. That was too close," Ethan said with a smile of relief. "I almost blew all of us up."

"Crikey," Jim said with his thin smile. "I was almost buzzard bait."

"But who took out their commander?" Ethan asked, staring at Roimh.

Another motion at the top of the stairway caught everyone's attention. Caleb drew his weapon. A petite young woman, wearing only an oversized black shirt, stood with a power supply in her hand. She smiled and triumphantly raised it over her head.

68

A Suicide Mission

MALDORV ATTACKED TRHON FROM within a great tempest, an evil storm swirling in the atmosphere. At its center, Maldorv rode the Black Dragon—his faithful lieutenant—with his dark robe blowing in the wind and his crown of curved horns silhouetted against the stormy sky. He destroyed everything in his path. Trees shriveled into dead branches then burst into flames. Animals ran in fear toward the receding edge of light. Those caught by the darkness died in it, their screams sounding like a siren of death.

Michaele's gaze rose upward, his expression a mix of concern and determination. The sky was filled with dragons and as the valiants engaged, it became a battlefield. Flashes of death illuminated against the darkness as the angelic and draconic forces clashed. The fallen plummeted from the sky, disintegrating into the Nothingness before reaching the ground, like raindrops evaporating in the desert.

Unfurling his massive white wings, Michaele manifested into his angelic form, his armor gleaming with an ethereal light. Gripping his sword tightly, he charged into the onslaught of the malkyries. With a resolute spirit, he swung his blade. Though the malkyries attacked with confidence, they were no match against him, the strongest of the archangels. As another malkyrie met its end, he had a moment's reprieve, and he scanned the battlefield.

Nearby Ariele and Zuriel were engaged in the battle. Michaele went to their side and together they quickly defeated two malkyries.

Trhon has been caught off guard," Zuriel reported. "Two cities have already fallen. Everyone is fleeing, but there's nowhere to hide. Nowhere is safe."

Realizing they were outnumbered; Michaele issued a command to retreat. "Establish a defensive perimeter around the cathedral. The portal to Caelum must not fall. Ariele, go retrieve Liele. She must fulfill her destiny. The time is now. She must bring the legion here."

"What if she is not the one?" Zuriel asked.

"Then we are all doomed." Regret washed over him as he questioned his previous decision. "I made an error sending the legion to Earth. We need them here. Make haste, Ariele."

Ariele's eyes remained fixed on the raging battle above. "I will have to fight my way through."

"No," Michaele countered. "Come here, under my wings."

Ariele wrapped her arms around Michaele, and he closed his wings around her. He lifted his arms into the sky, pulled the wind into him like a tornado, and flew through the atmosphere. Dozens of malkyries attacked as he passed, but he made it through. Once in the safety of deep space, he unfolded his wings. The malkyries had not followed him—none but one, the Black Dragon.

With its dark sword moving side to side, the Black Dragon charged at Michael. Michaele blocked the sword with his shield as Ariele drew her sword and attacked from the side. The Black Dragon swiped her with its tail, knocking her aside as it swung again at Michaele. Ariele rose quickly and jumped on the dragon's back. She thrust downward into the beast but barely penetrated its thick black scales. The dragon jolted sideways throwing Ariele off.

"You must get him in the eye," Michaele shouted. "That is the only way."

Michaele jumped onto its back and Ariele quickly joined him. Not able to reach them the dragon rolled violently in space. Michaele hung on and climbed his way forward to the head of the beast. The Black

Dragon turned its head towards them, and Ariele made her move. She dove forward toward his eye but missed.

The Black Dragon breathed fire at her, as it tried to dismount Michaele. But Michaele used a bolt of lightning as a lasso and wrapped it around the dragon's mouth swinging forward over its head. As Michaele passed over the eye of the beast, he lunged his sword into it. The Black Dragon shook its head wildly trying to shake loose the sword then stumbled forward. With a piercing scream it retreated from the battle and disappeared.

Ariel went to Michael's side and gasped at the sight of his wounds. "You're hurt," she exclaimed. "Let me tend to your injuries."

"No. I'm fine," Michael assured her. "I'm returning to the cathedral. You must bring Liele here."

Just as he spoke, Raphael appeared with the legion of angels. "Look, they're here," Ariel cried out.

"We came as fast as we could but the portal to Trhon has been destroyed, and it delayed our return." Raphael explained in frustration. "Maldorv must have destroyed it after he passed."

Ariel quickly searched for Lily. "Where's Liele?" she inquired urgently.

"She sent us here, but she didn't come with us," Raphael said.

Ariel's eyes widened with disbelief. "Where has she gone?"

"She went through the dark portal to Arderet," Raphael answered.

A sense of dread enveloped Ariel. "She's gone to her death! It's suicide."

"It's part of her destiny," Michael said. "She must rise from the abyss and fight for control of the universe." Michael turned toward Raphael, "Come with me," he commanded. "Ariel, go to Arderet. We need Liele to fulfill her destiny to save Trhon." With that, he left with the legion into the impending battle, leaving Ariel to face the daunting task before her.

"Oh, Liele. Stay strong." Ariel shouted then let out a primal scream to clear her head of fear.

Glancing back one last time, she saw the legion descending through the atmosphere like a blazing knife into a dark cloud of evil. With her planet engulfed in war, she knew if Trhon fell, Maldorv would seal the gate to Caelum. Ariel looked with sadness upon her planet. *If the portal falls, all souls will be blocked from entering Caelum. Eventually, we will be hunted down and imprisoned by Maldorv.* Ariel's silver eyes filled with resolve. "I will not fail. I'm coming, Liele."

69

The Light in the Darkness

DAMON LOOKED AT LILY with dismay. "You must be crazy," Damon said again in an annoyed tone, with his boney flesh forming a scowl over his face.

Lily held Ariel's crystal amulet near her heart and squeezed it tightly. It gave her resilience against an overwhelming sense of fear.

"Yes, I'm crazy," she shouted. "I have been crazy all my life. Sometimes I think being crazy was the only thing keeping me from going insane." She stared at all the lost souls and felt the pain of those in Arderet, void of love. She realized the purpose of her life. She knew her destiny. She would rescue the souls of Arderet and defeat Maldorv by taking his power from him. She would do it in the heart of Arderet.

A moan rose from the souls. Their dirge filled Arderet and echoed throughout the cauldron. It was the song of those without hope. She thought of Liam and feared she would never see him again. A tear rolled down her cheek. As her hope dwindled, she realized that if she lost hope, their song would become a requiem. She screamed into the air, rejecting her fate. "I still choose a life of love," she yelled with conviction. Her words echoed in Arderet as it suddenly fell quiet. "I still choose love," she said again. "I will not yield to the dark without a fight. For I have love in my heart, and its light still shines." With her heartfelt words, she gained everyone's attention. In desperation, they all looked at her, their empty hearts thirsting for love.

Damon looked away, embarrassed. "Even if I unlocked them, they would not leave."

"Surely, they know now they were wrong. Would they not give love another chance?"

The black, inky substance started to penetrate her skin. It stung like thousands of bees. She screamed in pain and tried to wipe it off, to no avail. It now stuck to her flesh. "Get it off," she cried out. The darkness began to fill her, and she felt weak. Her knees buckled and she stumbled to the ground. The darkness now reached the edge of her heart, and her body contorted in an explosion of pain. But Ariel's amulet protected her heart—so the darkness waited. It waited for Lily's light to die out. She could not last much longer.

"See, even you cannot withstand it," Damon said. "Soon, it will destroy all the light in you. You, too, will be trapped here forever."

"No," Lily said with livid eyes. She rose to her knees. "I want to live. I want to dream and hope. I know love. If I can keep it in my heart, evil cannot win." She grasped Ariele's amulet. It reminded her of Liam, and it gave her strength.

Damon laughed at Lily but suddenly stopped and quietly stared at her.

"I wanted to kill you," Damon said, standing over her. "But—"

"But you didn't. Why not?"

Damon paused. He did not answer.

"You want to be forgiven. Don't you?"

Ariele arrived at the gate. She rushed to Lily's side.

"Oh, my child. What has happened to you?" Ariele placed her hands on Lily and shared her spirit. The black, inky substance retreated into the ground. Lily recovered and was once again a white angel, but it weakened Ariele. Now seeing Damon, Ariele drew her sword. Unfortunately, she could barely stand.

"Stand back," Ariele shouted at the demon as she stumbled. "Stay away from her."

Damon drew his sword and stood over Ariele as the black, inky substance quickly rose over her. He didn't have to do anything, for she would soon be dead. "How heroic. Why did you come here? You want to die, too?" He paused. "I know why—"

He looked at Lily, who had no weapon, and he smiled sadly. "I would die for her, too." His soul was filled with remorse. Lily was right. He wanted forgiveness.

Damon dropped his sword and knelt on the ground. With the last of her strength, Ariele raised her sword over Damon.

"You should have killed me the first time," Damon said, looking at Lily.

"No," Lily said to Ariele. "Don't kill him. This is not the time for killing. It is the time for forgiveness."

Ariele didn't understand. "He killed Uriel!" she cried out. More than that, she knew there were no second chances in battle, but she did what Lily asked and held back.

Lily went to Damon.

"You seek forgiveness?"

Damon nodded with a contrite heart.

"God forgives you," Lily said.

A tear fell from his cheek. Another tear fell, and another. "I have done so many dreadful things. I'm so guilty. I'm not worthy of forgiveness."

"None of us are worthy of forgiveness. It is only through God's grace we are saved," she said softly gazing into his sorrowful face. "Love is patient. Love is kind. Love always forgives. God forgives you."

She put her arm around the malkyrie as he cried freely. He did not hold back. Lily knelt by his side and placed her hands over his.

"Peace be with you," she said.

"Peace be with you," Damon replied.

He made his choice. As he rose, he changed from a malkyrie to his angelic form.

Ariele stood down. She was in awe but also weak, as the ink had nearly consumed her spirit.

With tears still on Damon's face, he reached into his pocket and retrieved the key to the chain. He unlocked the souls, and with a tremendous clanging sound, the chain fell from the souls of the damned. With Maldorv and the malkyries gone to battle Trhon, Arderet had been left undefended. Now with the chains gone, a great opportunity presented itself. Lily walked a few steps into the darkness and opened her white wings for all to see. With her arms fully extended, she raised her golden rod above her head.

"Post tenebras, lux," Lily roared. The crystal globe at the end of her golden rod came to life and the purest of light shone in the dark. The light couldn't be contained. It was sharp and cut through the darkness like a knife. Ariele was cleansed of the dark, inky substance as it retreated underground with a diminishing scream. Soon, all the ground in Arderet shone with light. The Cauldron of Arderet became filled with its brilliance. It lit every corner.

"If you accept the light, it will expose the truth, then cover your guilt with God's love. It will bring hope and redemption," she cried out to the masses of the enslaved. "Come into the light. Like the sunlight which conquered the night, the light will redeem those who rejoice in it and vanquish those who do not." Soon, most of the souls accepted the light. But there were those who were pure evil and chose to follow the dark ink into the cracks in the ground. The redeemed souls joyfully swarmed around Lily and followed her outside the gate of Arderet.

Once they had all made it through, she thundered loudly, "Essere fulminato." Her golden rod filled with lightning, and she directed it toward the gate. With a rapid downward thrust, she welded the hinges and latches shut.

Lily stood with the countless millions of souls outside the gate of

Arderet. "Follow me," she yelled to the masses. The souls willingly went with her as Lily led the way through the portal and exploded outward in a burst of light from Earth. The souls streaked across space and followed Lily to Trhon, where she encircled the planet with the light of the redeemed souls. Like countless stars, they lit the sky. The souls now reclaimed the power of their spirits, which Maldorv had taken from them, and they willingly shared their power with Lily. As they did so, Maldorv grew weaker, and Lily became stronger.

Filled with power, a radiant white cloud formed around Lily and swirled with the enlightened. The power overwhelmed her senses, and suddenly, she started to understand her strength. She realized this was who she was meant to be. Since birth, she'd had a destiny. It was now fulfilled. She was a major force within the heavens and across the universe.

Raphael looked up at the sky, beyond the warring angels and malkyries. He saw a different storm surrounding Trhon. "Look," he said to Michaele as he pointed at the sky.

Michaele had sensed the change and now saw Lily in the eye of the hurricane, with her wings expanded and gloriously riding a cloud filled with lightning. She filled the skies. "Thank God. An angel now rides the whirlwind and directs the storm." Encouraged, Michaele called out to all the valiants. "Fight on, my fellow angels, for the tide of battle has changed and victory is ours." A great roar could be heard as the angels charged forward. Sensing their defeat, the malkyries fled.

Having lost his power, Maldorv collapsed to the ground—a pathetic, frail shape covered in taut skin that clung to his skeletal form. He realized he had lost. Then in an instant, he was gone. He retreated to his only haven.

70

Fall from Grace

MALDORV STOOD BEFORE THE sealed gate of Arderet. He was frail again and his skeletal frame was barely able to stand. His skin was gray and pale, his clothing ragged and torn. He stumbled forward, then pounded on the sealed gate, screaming furiously. He was locked out of his own kingdom. Yet he was not alone.

The black ink recognized Maldorv's presence and oozed from the cracks around his feet. The ink was made from everlasting evil, and from the souls which had fled from the light and sought refuge in the ground. It now came to the aid of the king. The black ink surrounded Maldorv and rose up his legs. He did not resist it. It penetrated his inner being and he changed form into an amorphous mass. The blob violently morphed between different faces as an internal battle occurred within the evil being—for one to rule and have total control.

Finally, a shape formed. Then a face appeared; it was Maldorv. He was now one with the black ink and the greatest evil of the ages. He wore a new, royal black cape with a hood and a regal black crown upon his head. He felt the level of his renewed power and understood his capabilities. He turned to face the locked gate. A black, sticky stream flowed from his hands and climbed the sides of the gate, covering the hinges. With a loud crackling sound, the hinges were broken. The gate dropped off its hinges and fell aside, crashing to the ground.

Lily had suspected Maldorv would return to Arderet and soon arrived with the redeemed souls. Seeing the destroyed gate, she entered the entrance hall in her angelic form. With her wings fully extended, she entered unafraid, but she did not know what awaited her. She thought she was the only one with the power now. Lily walked confidently across the hall but the souls of the enlightened surrounded her in a protective sphere. She approached Maldorv sitting on his throne. He rose and disappeared.

"You can't hide. Come out and face me, you coward," Lily yelled.

Maldorv laughed from behind her, remaining in the shadows. "Welcome...home...my queen."

"I will never be your queen," Lily said, turning slowly.

"I... am the Lord...of Shadows. Merge...with me...and you...can be...queen of all."

"You cannot fool me. Your time to reign is over," said Lily.

"It...seems... you will...not be...convinced...so easily."

Lily shook her head. "You will not be able to trick me."

"I am...your king!" he roared. He emerged from the shadows, towering over her as a giant demon. Filled with the power of the black ink, he shocked Lily. She could not hide the surprise from her face, causing Maldorv to laugh with glee.

"You see. You... cannot...win."

The souls of the enlightened allowed her to match Maldorv's size. But Lily unexpectedly staggered. The power within her was intoxicating and it surged in waves. Her face flushed and she felt dizzy.

"Oh, Liele. You...can't handle...it. Can...you? You...have...no idea. I...can...teach you...if you...become...my queen."

"Never," Lily said, stumbling sideways as if in a drunken stupor.

Maldorv laughed. "But...you are...already queen." The black ink extended outward from his hand like many branches from a dead tree. It held a gold crown with two spiral horns and placed it upon Lily. A black mirror appeared before her. It did not reflect light, only darkness. Lily looked into the mirror and was shocked by what she saw. Through vision blurred by her intoxicated state, she saw her reflection. She was indeed a queen.

"Ah…there you are," Maldorv said. "See…what I…mean?"

Lily continued to stare at herself in the mirror. She did not understand what it meant or what was happening to her.

"Whoever…has the power…rules. I…am…King…of Shadows. And you…are now…Queen. Queen…of the…Lost Souls. We are…a perfect match…a match made…in Arderet."

Is this real or something Maldorv put in my mind? Lily's eyes refocused and the mirror disappeared. She shook her head and, clearing her mind, looked at Maldorv.

Maldorv appeared frustrated then disappeared.

Lily searched the great hall, but the King of Dragons was nowhere to be found. Rounding a column, she was surprised to find Liam crouching low, appearing lost and afraid.

"Liam, what are you doing here?"

He rushed to Lily and embraced her. "Where am I?" Fear covered his face.

"You're in Arderet."

"How did I get here?" Liam said, looking confused.

"Never mind. Just stay near me. It's not safe. I will protect you."

Liam looked into Lily's eyes. His eyes, soft and appreciative. "In case I don't make it, I want you to know something. I love you, Liele."

"Liele?" Lily immediately suspected Maldorv's guise. "If looks were what I loved, I might be tempted, but it is his heart I love. He has a sincerity, which at its root has a true compassion for others. He is a good man, and I love him, not you."

Maldorv changed into his previous form then started to swirl his hand. He pulled it toward himself as he closed his fist, creating a wormhole. Immediately, he transferred himself and Lily onto the bridge of the Covenant. The other crew members were frozen in place at their stations, except Ema. Ema looked confused as she saw the others standing still in their last positions. Then her expression turned to fear as she saw Maldorv before her. Ema screamed as he swung a black sword with sharp, jagged edges. He moved it swiftly back and forth, teasingly threatening her.

Lily rushed to her sister's side and stood between her and Maldorv.

"Leave her alone," Lily yelled.

"You…float around…in a cloud…and pretend…to be…powerful. Yet…you…don't know…how…to use…your power. You…are afraid…to use it. You…are…so weak." Then Maldorv rushed at Lily, but the souls would not let him harm her. They swarmed to her defense in the shape of a large, circular shield of light and kept him at bay.

"You…know…nothing. You can…barely control…the wind. You know…so little." He created a transparent sphere by slowly pulling his hands apart, lingering on his fingertips. Ema disappeared from the bridge and appeared inside the small sphere, floating above Maldorv's open palm. His face cracked a slight smile as he caught Lily's attention. He zoomed in on Ema's eye, then into a blood vessel within her brain. He started to swirl the blood within an artery. He was going to cavitate the blood vessel. Ema fell to her knees and held her head, screaming in pain.

"It will…be easy…to kill her…then the others…one by one."

Lily stared at Ema. She was growing tired of being kind, of being patient, of being forgiving. Anger grew within her.

"Let me…go…or…I will…kill her."

Why is he using tricks and threats? Lily wondered. *Why is he trying to negotiate his release?* Lily again felt flush as the power swelled within her. Then she realized why she was still alive and why Maldorv had resorted to threats. Her power was too great. He was right; she did not know how to wield it. It was the power of billions of souls. Her power was immense.

"You should never threaten someone more powerful than yourself," she said. Lily pushed the palm of her hand quickly at him. Immediately, Maldorv was thrown to the ground with great force, and he lost his grip on the sphere. It broke, releasing Ema back onto the bridge. As the demon stumbled to his feet, Lily pushed him again, this time with greater force. He landed hard.

Lily clapped her hands together then slowly extended them; a transparent sphere formed in her palm. She tossed Maldorv within it and then swirled her other hand. A distortion formed and as it strengthened, she closed her fist and pulled it toward herself. A wormhole appeared.

Lily's capabilities were advancing quickly. She had learned how to manipulate space. She immediately transferred Maldorv and herself back to Trhon, back to the Sanctuary of Souls. Lily appeared at the Sanctuary of Souls surrounded by a white cloud then walked out of it. She was surrounded by sparkling souls, her wings extended, the sphere in her hands. She placed the sphere on the ground with Maldorv within it. Surrounding them was Michaele, Ariele, and the Council of Archangels.

Lily turned to face Michaele. "What will prevent him from escaping again?" she said, both angry and annoyed. Before Michaele could respond, Maldorv pulled his hands apart and the sphere surrounding him burst. He quickly slung his black sword at Ariele. He would get his revenge by killing Ariele, the one who had helped Lily the most. Lily saw the sword flying at Ariele, and in an instant the souls flashed out, but Damon had already jumped in front of Ariele and as the blade penetrated his chest, he fell at her feet.

Ariele knelt at Damon's side.

"Thank you," Ariele said.

With a faint smile, Damon disintegrated into the Nothingness.

Lily suffered the loss of the one she had saved but she did not shed tears. Instead, her face grew livid with anger. But Maldorv was not through. He spun in a rapid motion and threw a spear of lightning at Lily. The souls formed a shield and blocked it. With her jaw tightened and eyes narrowed, Lily knew Michaele could not answer her question. He couldn't guarantee Maldorv would not escape again. Though to Lily, Maldorv now was like a child throwing a tantrum, to others, he could do tremendous harm. After all, he was the third most powerful force in the universe, after God and Lily. *Ema had almost been killed. Ariele had almost been killed. Uriel and countless others had been killed. And now Damon.* Lily spun around at Maldorv, with her face flushed with anger.

"You…think you…are good. I…was once…an angel," Maldorv taunted her.

"I've had enough," she screamed. "I hate you! Death will be your bride." A fierce rage filled her entire being and she was no longer guarded about using her power. She wanted to avenge the deaths of her friends and as the souls glowed, her silver eyes shone with an intense light. The souls had waited for her command, then she gave them a nod. They encircled Maldorv, slowly at first. Sparkling like razors of light, they gradually increased their speed.

"Stop. What…are you…doing?" He screamed at the souls. "I…am…your…king. From…the lineage…of the…Great Serpent King…and…the Dragon Kings."

Spinning with greater and greater ferocity, the souls became a whirlwind of light. Maldorv was defenseless against them.

"No…stop!" Maldorv screamed.

"Do it slowly," Lily said. "I want him to suffer the pain which was inflicted on so many others."

Slowly, the souls collapsed the vortex around him and cut through him with millions of tiny slashes.

"Slower," she yelled as Maldorv's screams filled the cathedral. Cut by cut, he slowly disintegrated, his screams echoing in the rotunda. A growing smile filled Lily's face, with the satisfaction of her revenge.

Her hatred had become personal and justified by the conviction that he deserved more than justice—he deserved to be tortured; he deserved the pain. With his final words, he shouted at Lily, "Damn you…Liele. You…are now…me." Maldorv's words echoed amongst the crowd of angels as he disappeared into the Nothingness.

A sudden, awkward silence filled the cathedral. Lily had used the light for vengeance, for evil purposes. All the angels had seen it. There was no righteousness in her method. In a dark moment, evil had been perpetrated, and it left its mark. Lily's soul was now stained. She turned back to look upon the space where Maldorv had been killed. Then she saw it. Where there was once Maldorv, a shadow remained, the black ink. It floated aimlessly, then was drawn to a new source of hate. It went toward Lily, for she had not fought her last battle on the side of love. Evil is evil and is known unto itself. The black ink sensed the dark stain on her soul and was attracted to it like a magnet.

"He deserved it," she said. "He did not deserve another chance. He did not deserve forgiveness. Vengeance was mine, and mine was a righteous vengeance. I needed to avenge all the multitudes of others he had tortured."

Even someone good could have a momentary lapse and provide a refuge for hate. No one was perfect. All were weak and could fall in the dark. In her torture of Maldorv, she had done evil and provided evil a home. Her momentary lapse, no matter how brief, now led to her descent into darkness. Her hate provided an open doorway to her soul and the shadow flowed into it. Lily's light diminished and she was no longer filled with light. She became like the flame containing both light and darkness. And in this moment, darkness gained a home within her assuring the lineage of the malkyrie kings. This time, there would be a queen.

Lily was no longer a white angel. Her robe and wings filled with the color of fire. She turned and faced Michaele.

A shudder could be felt across the room as they all looked at Lily.

The crowd of angels stood silently in deference to her power. They were glad Maldorv was no more, but her method was not righteous. They knew the difference between defending oneself, one's loved ones, and intentional torture—between what was good and what was evil. Only God could withstand the dark, for he was pure light. But Lily was not God, and the darkness had found her and remained within her. She rose into the atmosphere and again gathered the storm around her, but this time, there were both white and dark clouds swirling around her. Then she was gone.

"Was this the prophecy?" Ariele asked Michaele with concern. "Maldorv has been defeated, but what has become of Liele?"

71

Queen of the Damned

LILY CROSSED THE UNIVERSE like a comet, flashing in and out of portals created at her whim. Just as her spirit could pull the wind, she could now pull space, creating portals at will. Her power was unchallenged. She was much more powerful than Maldorv had ever been, for he only partially wielded the power of the lost souls. But in their gratitude, the souls had given all their power to Lily. Now she kept it as her own.

Suddenly, fear swept through them. *Will she imprison us in Arderet as Maldorv had?*

The darkness within her further corrupted her and fed her new love—power. Soon, the darkness would gain total control. Its dominium was inevitable. She could not stop it from taking over. Lily gasped as the power flushed through her. It was like a heartbeat. After each pulse, she would wait in great anticipation for the next beat to climax and crash over her. Nothing was more important; no one could take it away from her. She and her power were becoming one. It filled her and replaced all other feelings. Her power was now the source of her happiness. Her love of power became overwhelming, yet still, something within her resisted and caused her to stand against the waves. Something within her heart still knew it was wrong.

She shook her head and ignored the pleading of her heart. "Whoever has the power rules," she said aloud. *Who can challenge me?* Lily wondered. *Maybe I am now like God.* Lily laughed, and the stars shook around her. She now enjoyed the thought of spiting God. *What will he do? What can he do?* God was now her nemesis, her competition. She would compete with him for the souls of the universe—the souls whose energy she desperately craved, for their energy fed her power.

"I need them," she screamed into the universe. "I must have more. I must find other worlds and more souls."

The sound of her voice crashed across the surrounding space, and it shuddered. The heavens now questioned her intent: *Is she good or evil?*

Then she heard it. Michaele was calling her to the cathedral.

Who is he to summon me? she thought. Then another thought occurred to her. *He wants me to be queen—his queen.*

"I'm coming," she said. "I will be your queen, and we shall rule the new age together." She was not in love with Michaele. It was his power she lusted after. She would take it as her own and that of all the angels.

72

Borrowed Light

WITH EVERY POSSIBLE SPACE filled within the cathedral; the angels waited anxiously to see Lily. Their faces were long, and their lips pursed. Standing elbow to elbow, they overflowed into the garden. They waited in fear and awe of her immense power, wondering if she would choose to wield it.

"Shh," the crowd said. Lily had arrived and appeared at the altar. She stood before them, filled with the rescued souls. Their light still shone and filled the cathedral.

"Will she listen?" Ariele asked Michaele.

"Can a drunk man hear the pleas of his loved ones asking him to stop drinking? Can a drug addict craving his next high give up drugs?" Michaele responded.

"Yes," said Ariele. "But only through God's love."

Lily was indeed addicted. Like an opioid, the drug of power took control over her will. It corrupted her conscience and her sense of right and wrong. A taste of this kind of power would destroy anyone and make them go mad. Even the greatest of all angels, Michaele, would not be able to endure it. Though time and again, something within Lily resisted the waves. Her resistance slowed her fall into darkness, but the darkness was like poison, and it had remained too long. Soon, her love for power would replace her understanding of love.

"I am here," Lily said. "What is it you want?"

Michaele approached Lily. The great archangel seemed

insignificant next to her, so small.

"Liele, greatest of all angels, we are all deeply grateful for what you have done. You have rescued the souls of Arderet, defeated Maldorv, and saved Trhon."

The angels applauded politely.

"How can I ever repay you? What reward could be so great to match what you have accomplished, what no one else could have accomplished?" Michaele paused.

Okay, this is it, thought Lily. *This is where he will ask me to be queen.* She would take him as her prize.

With a gloating smile, she looked across the audience in the great hall at all their faces. But she did not see faces which wanted her to be queen. She only saw one thing in their eyes—fear. They were afraid of her.

Lily turned back toward Michaele as he continued to speak.

"There is nothing I can offer you as just reward. Only God can do that."

Above the altar were the six blue seraphs. In unison, they blew their trumpets, causing Lily to turn toward the Sanctuary of Souls in surprise.

"Peace to all who enter here," they announced as one. As they lowered their trumpets, the white gate opened, and Lily saw the portal to Caelum.

From within the portal, a brilliant sphere of light floated into the Sanctuary of Souls, brighter than any light imaginable. It was the purest of light and brilliantly sparkled like the most perfect diamond. It was more brilliant than lightning, and she shielded her face from it.

A man appeared, wearing a white robe filled with stars. He was within a large sphere of light and became more clearly visible as the sphere consolidated into his chest with a smaller one within the center of his forehead. A brilliant explosion of light emitted from around his head. It was his spirit erupting like a corona around the sun. It merged with a white nebula of stars above him.

"Peace be with you," God said.

Lily stumbled over her reply. "Who—who are you?"

"I am who I have always been and who I always will be. I am God made man, the incarnation of God. God and his spirit are one with me as I am with them."

Lily did not know how to reply.

"I am the Lord of Light. Without me, there is only darkness." With a wave of his hand, God's golden rod left Lily's possession and returned to him. Then all the light within Lily left her, and swirled around God, for it came from him, and was of him. In an instant, the light collapsed back into God. Lily's robe turned black, her aura dark, and the souls within her lost their radiance. Only her amulet retained a soft, glowing hue. Maldorv had been right. She had become him. She was now queen, Queen of Darkness. The angels retreated in fear, fleeing from the cathedral. Even the Council of Archangels withdrew. However, two angels remained, Michaele and Ariele.

A powerful voice emanated from God as a fierce wind. "I entrusted you with a golden rod filled with my light—a light borrowed from me, meant to shine in the darkness. It was never yours to keep but to share. Now, my light has returned unto me. I will tell you this. Light can exist without the dark. Good can exist without evil. Love can exist without hate. But light allows for the possibility of shadow. What do you want?" God asked. "How do you choose? You have free will. It is your choice. Now choose."

Lily spun within the emptied cathedral. Trhon was hers for the taking. Everything was hers for the taking. Everything but love.

"Trhon can be my throne," Lily said to herself. "If I choose, all this can be mine." She rose to the heights of the cathedral. "I will be their queen, and all will love me," she shouted into the emptied building. Only her echo was there. Without light, there was only darkness. Now everything she touched became filled with fear and despair. Without the warmth of God's love, a chill filled Lily. She felt the coldness of the dark and so alone, even filled with countless souls, for they, too, now felt empty.

"Queen of Darkness, Queen of the Damned." Lily mumbled the words to herself.

Ariele took a step toward Lily, but Michaele cut her off. "She is lost, Ariele," said Michaele in a defeated voice. "We have lost her."

Michaele raised his sword and stood in front of Ariele to protect her. His gesture, though noble, was laughable. Ariele put her hand on Michaele's shoulder and stepped from behind him. She took a step toward Lily and spoke in a kind and motherly voice.

"Remember who you are, Liele."

"The power feels good, and it belongs to me. I don't want to give it up. With this power, I can rule. I have good intentions. I can rule the universe. It's my destiny."

Lily put her hands together then slowly pulled them apart. Within her grasp the earth appeared, a lovely blue planet. She held it in her hand. "With this power I can protect her. I can protect my sister and all Earth."

"This is not your destiny. You are good, Liele. You are not destined to become queen of the damned. Remember the road to perdition was paved with good intentions and evil can justify itself, pretending to be good. For there is no righteousness outside of God, only self-righteousness. I pray for you. I pray you have wisdom."

"Wisdom?"

"Yes—to know good from evil."

Lily spun wildly. Her mind was a whirlpool of confusion. *Am I good or evil?*

Ariele recited the warning from the Book of Knowledge.

"Remember, power corrupts, and ultimate power corrupts ultimately. You should instead seek wisdom to know the difference between good and evil, for

knowledge alone is indiscriminate and cannot tell the difference.'"

"Am I good or evil?" she said aloud. She looked at her captured souls, the source of her power. They were not free. They were her prisoners, her slaves. She saw their fear and anguish. She had caused it. *They will try to escape at the first opportunity. Should I imprison them in Arderet, just as Maldorv had done?*

God blew out a strong wind. The wind filled the Sanctuary of Souls and swirled around Lily. It flowed around her and through her.

Lily felt a sharp pain in her chest, and letting Earth free from her hand, she grasped at it. She stared at her closed fist, then slowly opened it. Within her hand, she held Ariele's amulet. Throughout all her ordeals, it had remained protecting her heart. It had allowed her to resist. It was the candle in the dark. A small light filled her palm. It faintly shown in Lily's silver eyes. She closed her fist and held it tightly as its glow refilled her. Once again, she felt the power of true love. Immediately, she remembered what she wanted. It was what she had always wanted, but somehow, flushed with power, she had forgotten. She did not crave power; she craved love. She now thought of the others. She did not want to enslave their souls to eternal damnation. She made her choice. She chose love. She chose to relinquish her crown. She was no longer queen.

"Go," Lily said to all the souls. But the souls now feared her and lingered with her. "Go now, or I may not be able to let you go. You are not mine to keep. I release you. Now go." She lifted her hand and pointed toward God.

Just as the souls of the damned had been saved by God's light, so had Lily. "I choose the light," Lily said in a loud voice.

With that, God refilled Lily with his light. Lily felt the black ink within her boil and then it exploded outward with great force. It rejected the light, and the light pulverized it. In an instant, all evil was vanquished. The darkness was gone and only light remained.

The light initiated a rebirth of Lily's spirit. It was a transformation, like a caterpillar exiting a chrysalis to become a butterfly, or a wheat seed sprouting, or the birth of a baby. She screamed like a mother in labor with the intensity of the experience. She felt the pain of her guilt and the exhilaration of her forgiveness. Her wings and robe became pure white. She had been cleansed of her transgressions.

The souls, also renewed with light, flowed like a crystal river, flooding the Sanctuary of Souls. They cheered in jubilation as they traveled around Lily and expanded outward to fill the entire rotunda. The souls could now feel the portal. Just as evil was drawn to the dark, love was drawn to the light and it pulled at them like a magnet, drawing them into it. They started their exodus and flowed into Caelum. The souls crossed the portal like crossing through a doorway. They would soon realize there was another life to discover, a paradise full of love and wonder.

Finally, only one soul remained and lingered. It was different but somehow the same. Lily knew who it was. It was Central Control.

"Thank you for rescuing me," the voice said. "You could have kept me as your prisoner, along with all the others. You could have kept me in an eternal state of torture. Yet you have chosen the well-being of others over your own gratification. You let me go free. You destroyed the beast of power by choosing love. I thought I knew everything because I possessed all the knowledge. From what you did, I now know love, not power, is the most important force in the universe. Goodbye, my friend." The soul left her and went into the portal.

Without the other souls, Lily diminished in size and returned to her natural state. She collapsed by the altar. Ariele rushed over quickly and helped her up.

As Lily stumbled to rise, Michaele extended his hand to help her. She looked up at God and suddenly felt at peace, as if being with someone she had always known. He placed his hand on her back and his touch made her feel his spirit. She felt relaxed and as comfortable as if she were lying under a warm blanket on a cool morning.

Lily knelt before Him. "Thank you for saving me," said Lily.

"I am the Alpha and the Omega. I exist outside of time. Should billions of years be but a day, and the universe created in seven, it would not matter, for time has no dominion over me. I existed before time and will continue to exist after time, but this book is only one book in my library. It should come as no surprise then that before your first breath, I have known you and loved you."

God motioned for her to follow. She approached the altar where a large, gilded book appeared from the portal and hovered above them. The book looked ancient, bound in a heavily worn cover and binding. God reached for it and placed it on the altar.

"What is it?"

"This is the Book of Time. From the beginning, it has chronicled everything in this universe," God said. "I am going to give you a gift."

"Me? You're giving me a gift? But you've already given me so much."

God smiled and made a gesture toward the book. God opened the book, and a golden light shone from its pages. Lily squinted and shielded her eyes with her hand. But soon, she was able to see words. Newly written words glowed like molten metal. Older words cooled into a golden script.

Lily looked at the writings and touched one of the glowing scripts. A memory filled her mind as she relived the moment. She was standing at her pond next to Ema. She moved to another script. Each script she touched took her to that moment. The book contained everything that had ever happened to her, to everyone and everything—the city, Central Control, Maldorv, Peter, Skipper, Vanya—everything in the universe. It included many events which she knew nothing about from across time. She noticed the golden quill had stopped. There, on the last script, the quill hovered.

"Why isn't it moving?" Lily asked.

God answered her. "While the book is open, time has stopped. All creation has taken pause."

She turned back to Michaele and Ariele and noticed they were frozen in their last position. She turned back toward the book. She turned its pages but became overwhelmed. Finally, she returned to where the quill waited, and it occurred to her.

"It's on the last page?"

"Yes, it is the end of time," answered God. "Once this page is complete, time in this realm will end."

"So, this is how the universe ends," Lily said. "It runs out of time."

"I'm going to allow you to write the last line," God said as he gently looked at Lily. "Take a moment to think about it."

Lily turned and glanced at Michaele and Ariele. She looked around at the Sanctuary of Souls. *It was said life began in the Garden of Eden. It is fitting time will end here.* The thought passed through Lily's mind and then another thought entered her mind. She thought of Liam.

Lily knew what she wanted to do. She picked up the quill and held it in her hand. Though golden, it was light as a feather. She made her entry and laid the quill back down inside the book.

God smiled at Lily as a grandfather would a small child, then his face became solemn. "You chose well. I will now give you your gift." God turned to face the portal.

Lily took the opportunity to glance into the portal. It was a different kind of portal, not one that went from place to place but one that went from within the dimension of time to outside the dimension of time. The time tunnel was lined with the Books of Time, row after row in a vast library, each book gleaming with a golden light.

"Why are there so many books?" Lily asked.

"There are many universes," God said. Then God brought forth a new book and placed it on the altar, its gilded cover without blemish. God continued to hold the old book in his hands until it became very small, as small as a locket. To Lily's surprise, he reached for her necklace. "May I?"

Lily nodded then God attached the golden book below the crystal amulet Ariele had given her. As he retracted his hand, he touched her cheek softly.

"It's beautiful. Thank you." Lily looked up at God and blushed with embarrassment.

"What is it you want to know?" God asked.

Lily could have asked anything. She could have asked God to explain so many things.

She looked up and flushed again. "Who am I?" Lily said, looking down at the ground.

"You are who you have always been—an angel of God. Since you are still bound by time, you cannot yet pass through the portal. You must stay a little while longer until it is your time, then time will have no dominion over you."

Is time a gift or a prison? Lily wondered. Suddenly, she realized that, just as the angels had imprisoned Maldorv in the core of the fiery reactor, so evil was imprisoned in the Book of Time. *Everyone who accepts the light has an escape hatch—the portal to Caelum.*

God read her mind and responded. "Yes, the realm of time is both a gift for some and a prison for others. Your time here will be as a blink of the eye in comparison to infinity."

Lily's eyes looked heavy. "Angels are nearly immortal. They can live for eons, yet humans can only live for a mere hundred years. Much of my time will be alone." God picked up the new book of time and patted it softly. "Do not worry, my child, time will tell, and know in time, I will reward your faithfulness." God slowly rose above the altar then changed back into a sphere of light. He floated into the portal and disappeared.

Lily felt a strong pull as the portal pulled at her spirit, but it was not her time, and she did as God had said. She waited. She would put her trust in God.

Lily continued to watch as the blue seraphs once again resumed their guard, and the white gate closed. After a few moments, she turned toward Ariele and Michaele. It was the end of time, but time did not end. Instead, it continued. It was the beginning of time, on the first page of a new book. Ariele approached Lily and bowed gently.

Lily smiled at her. "Why do you bow?"

"You have done what no angel could do." Ariele bowed again. "May I ask a question?"

"Sure. Anything. But no more bowing," Lily said with a smile.

"Tell me, what happened?" asked Ariele.

"We were at the end of time, and I had only one thought for an ending. 'And time begins anew.' God has given us more time. We are at the beginning of a new book of time."

"Liele, we will continue to live each day as if it were our last, knowing time is a gift from God. May you live a long and happy life," Michaele said then bowed graciously. Ariele approached and embraced Lily.

"What will you do now?" Ariele asked. "Where will you go, my child?"

"Home is where the heart is," Lily said, quoting her mother. "I'm going home."

Ariele slowly raised her hands with understanding in her eyes. Lily raised hers as well, and they shared their spirits.

"Peace be with you," Ariele said.

"Peace be with you."

73

My Own Home

LILY AND ARIELE ARRIVED at the Covenant and were escorted by the four officers. Lily first went to her room and became one with her body, then continued to the Observation Deck. The crew and most of her friends and family were there and everyone stood as they arrived. The ship's officers entered first and stood at attention, two on either side of the door. Lily entered to everyone's cheers, followed by Ariele.

Lily stood before them, standing straight and tall in her admiral uniform. She had more than earned her position. She was no longer the same person for her experiences had aged her beyond seventeen years. Her hair was filled with silver highlights—a badge of honor and evidence of her traumatic experiences. After the crowd quieted, Ariele came forward and stood next to Lily. Many recognized Ariele at once from her paintings. She clearly looked like Lily.

Ariele extended her wings around Lily in a loving way, then spoke with a loud voice. "I am the Archangel Ariele, the First Mother. I am here to return Liele to you. She has fulfilled her destiny. While you battled here on Earth, she has been to Arderet and back. She descended into Arderet to rescue the lost souls away from Maldorv. Then she saved Trhon from imminent defeat by Maldorv's legion of malkyries. When Maldorv threatened to destroy you all, she destroyed him." The crowd stood silent but understood what they were hearing, for Ema had borne witness to Maldorv and had told them.

"In doing so, she replaced Maldorv and became Queen of the Damned, the Lord of the Dark." The crowd stirred and looked at Lily with concern on their faces, but Ariele continued speaking. "It was only through God's love Liele overcame the darkness and was saved. She released the lost souls into Caelum and fulfilled her destiny. At that point, the entire universe was at peace and time ended. All our lives would have ended in an instant but as an unexpected gift, God allowed Liele to write the ending to the Book of Time. She chose for all of us to have another chance and time was renewed."

The crowd cheered. They understood what Ariele had said and appreciated the chance for a new beginning. Lily humbly accepted their praise and nodded graciously. She had earned it. They continued to cheer until Ariele quieted them.

"I will miss you very much, Liele. Goodbye. You may keep the Covenant as a gift. Remember me always, my beautiful flower." Ariele looked at Lily and smiled at her lovingly. Then, with a tear in her eye, she kissed Lily on her forehead and slowly disappeared in a mist of sparkling light.

The crowd remained standing in silence. After several moments, Ema approached Lily, with the monitor behind her showing the two suns. She reached for Lily with her hands.

"Welcome home. Though now the greatest person in the entirety of the universe, you will always be my little sister," Ema said with a warm smile, then pulled Lily into a warm embrace. The room clapped in a soft cheer as their emotions tugged at their hearts. Doc, always the more composed one, stood stiffly as a silent tear rolled off his face.

As the room quieted, Caleb approached Lily with Roimh at his side. The large, militarized android was hard not to notice.

"Hello, my friend," said Caleb.

"Hello, my dearest friend," Lily said, giving Caleb a warm

431

embrace.

"You were my guide out of the darkness," said Caleb. "You brought me to the light. I offer you my services." Caleb bowed before her.

"Do not bow before me, my friend," Lily said. "I will form a council, and together, we will lead the new age."

Lily now acknowledged Roimh.

"Hello, Lily. I'm Roimh. I have Central Control's memories of you. It is good to meet you."

"Oh, my. I hope you're not going to give me another truth serum," Lily teased.

Roimh laughed gently with his deep voice. "No, but like, Caleb I have evolved. I am also a great admirer of yours and I too am at your service."

"We must all continue to evolve," Lily said. "Humans too must evolve."

Caleb looked at the second star, Trhon's sun. "What shall we call it?" he asked.

"Principio. The Star of New Beginnings," Lily said with a smile. "We've been given another chance. Let's get it right this time."

The room clapped in agreement. They knew each of them had made mistakes.

"This is our chance to right our wrongs and dwell in God's light," Lily said. "With that, we have everything."

"Joy," Mami said, standing next to Papi and their two boys.

"Peace," Papi said.

"Purpose," Caleb said.

"Healing," Doc said, with Katiana at his side.

"Love," Ethan said, then signed to Kali. Kali signed back, "Hope."

Some people laughed, some cried. They knew what had been said was true. Then Lily raised her hand, and the room became quiet.

"Let us now lower our heads and remember the fallen, for this victory was not without sacrifice." Lily stood quietly in their midst and bowed her head. From the silence came Lily's voice. She had never sung in public before, her angelic voice being so different. She started softly, becoming louder.

"So now we sing, the battle won,
To a better future, a prayer, our song.

Shining brightly through the dark,
For all to see, the world to know,
Our heroes lost—the ones most bold.

Our victory won though innocent slain.
This oath we make in the light of day,
That good shall not have died in vain.

So now we swear to one and all,
To save the dream of love and hope,
From hate and endless war.

And as this day becomes the past,
Another chance has now begun.
I swear to God it will last.

I swear to love,
Not just for today but—"

As Lily paused, Ema said, "Till the universe is no more."
Lily knew the words were perfect and finished her song.

"Till the universe is no more."

Lily was surrounded by those she loved most. They stood quietly and contemplated the meaning of her song. The words were strong; the words were true.

Doc thought of Skipper as he held Mondo in his arms.

Lily thought of all those lost in the city and of Peter. She suddenly thought of Liam. "Liam?" she said. Desperately wanting to see him, she called out his name much louder. "Liam?"

Ema approached Lily; her eyes filled with sadness.

"I must tell you something," Ema said.

Lily saw the pain in Ema's eyes and a sense of panic struck her. She ran around the Observation Deck searching for Liam. She needed him to be there. He was the main reason she chose to return. However, she did not see him and came back to Ema's side.

"Where's Liam?" Lily asked anxiously.

"He went to help rescue the survivors—they were surrounded, about to be killed." Ema paused and looked away as she lost her composure.

Lily's face fell flat without any expression. A sharp pain filled her chest, and a lump formed at the bottom of her throat. It hurt to talk. "No," Lily cried out softly.

The room went silent as they watched the one who had done so much for them crumble to her knees.

Tears filled her eyes as Lily looked up at the ceiling. "Please, God," she cried out. A tear fell from her face. She followed the tear as it fell to the ground, as if in slow motion. Then as Lily blinked and opened her eyes, she found herself inside the teardrop. She could see its iridescent sheen around her. She could see the blurry room beyond its edge. She had hoped her days of having visions were over, that there was a chance God would make her human. But she knew she was still an angel.

She now remembered the Book of Time on her necklace, and she grasped it. To her surprise, a full-sized version of the ancient book appeared within her hands. It was her book; God had given it to her. She ran her hand over it. Its golden edges were worn and frayed but its beauty was undeniable. Lily sat down within the teardrop and laid the book upon her lap. She cautiously opened it and began to read from the spot where it had opened.

"Lily picked a yellow flower and placed it in her black hair. Wanting to see how she looked, she rushed in her white dress back to the deep blue water and her reflection.

"Hey, it's me again,' she said. 'Do you remember me?' Again, she heard nothing; she did not expect to.

"The mountain peaks rose before her, still showing their winter snow and wrap of green pine. From there, a cool breeze blew on Lily. It caused the leaves of the aspen to quiver and their thin, white branches to sway. She loved the sound they made."

"I know who you are," Lily said, then continued reading.

"'I know who you are,'" came a whisper from within the tree line."

"Oh, my. Was that me?" she said. Lily suddenly felt uncomfortable as a sudden realization occurred to her. "Did God know I would be here at this moment and say that to my past self? Of course, God knows our future as if it were already the past."

She thought of Liam again. Just thinking of Liam caused the pages of the book to turn to his last entry. She stared away from the page. She did not want to see how he had died.

"Why did you give me this gift. Is it a punishment? It is a form of torture for me to know what I cannot prevent." But deep down inside, Lily knew why. "Those who do not remember the past are doomed to repeat it," she whispered to herself. "He doesn't want me to forget." The Book of Time was filled with wisdom. Just as Ariele had prayed, Lily had received the gift of wisdom. Her gift was not to change time but to know all its secrets and to remember them. She suddenly remembered the little girl in the city who had burst into flames. The book turned to that page, but she did not need to read the passage. It was etched in her mind. How could she forget? She would never forget; the book would make sure. Then the dreams of the dead, the born and the unborn, became one and she knew her future purpose and it was singular, and she was one with it. She was a bearer of wisdom, a keeper of the secrets of time. In time others would call her by another name, The Oracle. Lily closed the book and in a golden swirl of light, the book returned to her necklace.

Lily lingered in the drop, fearful of what she would learn when she returned to her body. She took a breath, then saw the tear continue to the ground. It splashed silently on the floor. Activity resumed on the Observation Deck, and she saw Vanya run into the room.

"Guess who I brought with me?" Vanya's voice rang out, her smile radiant with excitement.

Lily's heart pounded with anticipation, hope flickering in her eyes. Vanya gave a knowing glance toward the doorway, and then—there he was. Venky, her beloved grandfather, entered with his younger grandchildren in tow. The room erupted with joyful cheers, the warmth of family and love swelling in the air.

"My heart is so grateful," Lily murmured, pulling Vanya into a tight embrace. But despite the joy, a shadow of sorrow lingered in her eyes, a weight she couldn't shake. Venky, ever perceptive, caught the fleeting sadness behind her smile.

"Were you expecting someone else?" he asked gently. He smiled softly and glanced back at the door.

Lily's breath hitched as her gaze flickered past him, settling on the doorway—empty, still hoping. A quiet ache pressed against her chest. And then—

A figure stepped into the room.

Liam.

"Hey, guys… I'm okay." His voice was familiar, warm, edged with that effortless charm that had always made her smile.

Lily's breath left her in a rush. She stared in disbelief, her mind struggling to accept what her heart already knew. A choked sob escaped her lips, and then—she crumbled into tears.

"I wanted it to be a surprise!" Vanya beamed, her face alight with joy as she grasped Lily's hands.

Lily tried to speak, but the emotions surged too fast, too strong. She pressed a trembling hand over her mouth, her shoulders shaking. Finally, through tear-soaked words, she whispered, "I'm so happy… I'm so happy that you're alive."

Liam stepped forward, closing the space between them. His voice was steady, reassuring.

"I landed in an escape pod," he explained softly. "Vanya rescued me."

The words settled over Lily like a revelation, like air after drowning. And with a sob of pure relief, she reached for him.

"Thank God," Lily said. She stood silently for a moment as tears flowed freely down her face. Then she cleared her throat and spoke. "I wasn't ready to lose you," Lily said. "A universe without you would have made my heart forever empty."

"You once thought me obnoxious, and I was. But you taught me to love. So, whether it is our destiny or not, I will always love you," Liam said softly. "Is there any chance you can love me?"

She held his hand and quoted the last stanza of their poem.

"I returned, back through the mirror,
Into my own home. I found,
I had everything I would ever want,
With the one I loved around."

Liam took Lily's hands. "I'm yours. Will you be mine?"

"Yes," Lily said, her face beaming with joy. "Yes. Yes. Yes." She paused as her expression dropped. She needed to tell him something, something that he needed to know—she would barely age in his lifetime, and he would die, leaving her alone for ages.

"Shh," Liam said as he pressed his finger against her lips. He leaned over her face and planted a soft kiss on her forehead. "I love you, no matter who you are. I love you beyond reason, for the chance of a lifetime with you entices me beyond any dissuasion."

Lily looked up into his eyes and became entranced by his loving gaze; her expression becoming one with his. "I understand as I feel the same. I love you," she said then turned her face into his and softly kissed him. His lips were warm and soft like hers. She pressed harder.

Liam kissed her back. It was a slow, longing kiss.

Suddenly, a bright aura surrounded Liam as Lily was taken aback. Liam had wings. In shock, she turned to her sister, Ema, and saw wings on her back as well. To her surprise, Mami and Papi and all the other people also had wings.

Lily now realized what God had meant when he had said to trust him. The new book of time was in a parallel universe where the people of Earth were no longer human. In this new universe, they all shared a common past but a different and even more exciting future. In this universe, humans did something totally unexpected—they evolved.

Lily smiled exuberantly, now realizing the extent of God's gift. She turned back toward Liam and exclaimed, "We are angels! We are all angels!"

Epilogue

"Four circles interfered with one another as they crossed a once still pond, creating a myriad of intersectional rings, according to some ancient plan." Ariel spoke in a loud, resonant voice, as if addressing a vast audience, though only a small group of children sat around her. Their faces shone brightly, lit by the firelight. "Harmonics rose while others faded, and as the pattern swept its entirety, no surface remained untouched—nothing left to uncertainty. For it was as certain as could be once the stones were cast."

"Who threw the stones?" a young girl asked.

"Yes, indeed," replied Ariel. "Who cast the stones? That is an interesting question."

The evening sky darkened as the second sun slipped below the horizon and the flames from the fire now provided the only light. Something within them caught Ariele's attention and she investigated them. Her stare became hard and her expression serious.

"What's wrong?" asked the girl, apprehensively.

"I sense a disturbance in the tapestry of time."

"What do you mean?"

"A stone has been cast." Ariele paused and looked into the night sky at a familiar constellation. "I must seek The Oracle, Wisest of the Wise, Keeper of the Book of Time. Something has changed. She will know what to do. I must find her."

that effortless charm that had always made her smile.

Lily's breath left her in a rush. She stared in disbelief, her mind struggling to accept what her heart already knew. A choked sob escaped her lips, and then—she crumbled into tears.

"I wanted it to be a surprise!" Vanya beamed, her face alight with joy as she grasped Lily's hands.

Lily tried to speak, but the emotions surged too fast, too strong. She pressed a trembling hand over her mouth, her shoulders shaking. Finally, through tear-soaked words, she whispered, "I'm so happy... I'm so happy that you're alive."

Liam stepped forward, closing the space between them. His voice was steady, reassuring.

"I landed in an escape pod," he explained softly. "Vanya rescued me."

The words settled over Lily like a revelation, like air after drowning. And with a sob of pure relief, she reached for him.

"Thank God," Lily said. She stood silently for a moment as tears flowed freely down her face. Then she cleared her throat and spoke. "I wasn't ready to lose you," Lily said. "A universe without you would have made my heart forever empty."

"You once thought me obnoxious, and I was. But you taught me to love. So, whether it is our destiny or not, I will always love you," Liam said softly. "Is there any chance you can love me?"

She held his hand and quoted the last stanza of their poem.

"I returned, back through the mirror,
Into my own home. I found,
I had everything I would ever want,
With the one I loved around."

Liam took Lily's hands. "I'm yours. Will you be mine?"

"Yes," Lily said, her face beaming with joy. "Yes. Yes. Yes." She paused as her expression dropped. She needed to tell him something, something that he needed to know—she would barely age in his lifetime, and he would die, leaving her alone for ages.

"Shh," Liam said as he pressed his finger against her lips. He leaned over her face and planted a soft kiss on her forehead. "I love you, no matter who you are. I love you beyond reason, for the chance of a lifetime with you entices me beyond any dissuasion."

Lily looked up into his eyes and became entranced by his loving gaze; her expression becoming one with his. "I understand as I feel the same. I love you," she said then turned her face into his and softly kissed him. His lips were warm and soft like hers. She pressed harder.

Liam kissed her back. It was a slow, longing kiss.

Suddenly, a bright aura surrounded Liam as Lily was taken aback. Liam had wings. In shock, she turned to her sister, Ema, and saw wings on her back as well. To her surprise, Mami and Papi and all the other people also had wings.

Lily now realized what God had meant when he had said to trust him. The new book of time was in a parallel universe where the people of Earth were no longer human. In this new universe, they all shared a common past but a different and even more exciting future. In this universe, humans did something totally unexpected—they evolved.

Lily smiled exuberantly, now realizing the extent of God's gift. She turned back toward Liam and exclaimed, "We are angels! We are all angels!"

Epilogue

"Four circles interfered with one another as they crossed a once still pond, creating a myriad of intersectional rings, according to some ancient plan." Ariel spoke in a loud, resonant voice, as if addressing a vast audience, though only a small group of children sat around her. Their faces shone brightly, lit by the firelight. "Harmonics rose while others faded, and as the pattern swept its entirety, no surface remained untouched—nothing left to uncertainty. For it was as certain as could be once the stones were cast."

"Who threw the stones?" a young girl asked.

"Yes, indeed," replied Ariel. "Who cast the stones? That is an interesting question."

The evening sky darkened as the second sun slipped below the horizon and the flames from the fire now provided the only light. Something within them caught Ariele's attention and she investigated them. Her stare became hard and her expression serious.

"What's wrong?" asked the girl, apprehensively.

"I sense a disturbance in the tapestry of time."

"What do you mean?"

"A stone has been cast." Ariele paused and looked into the night sky at a familiar constellation. "I must seek The Oracle, Wisest of the Wise, Keeper of the Book of Time. Something has changed. She will know what to do. I must find her."